Lost King

Other Books by Dorothy Tinker

Peace of Evon
    Book 1 of the Peace of Evon series
Gift of War
    Book 2 of the Peace of Evon series

Short Stories by Dorothy Tinker

"Infinity Hotel"
    featured in *Eclectically Cosmic*
"Dreaming of the Chaos"
    featured in *In Medias Res: Stories from the In Between*
"Swelling Tides"
    featured in *Riding the Waves*
"Embracing the Storm"
    featured in *Riding the Waves*
"Return to the Light"
    featured in *Out of Many, One*
"Master of My World"
    featured in *Eclectically Heroic*

Book 3 of the Peace of Evon series

Lost King

Dorothy Tinker

Balance of Seven

Lost King
Book 3 of the Peace of Evon series

For information, contact:

Balance of Seven
www.balanceofseven.com
dtinker@balanceofseven.com

Cover Design by Dylan Drake
www.waywordauthorservices.com
Cover Illustration by Corene "Nezumi" Werhane
corenewerhane.com
Maps by Dorothy Tinker
Copyediting by Editor Amy
Formatting by D Tinker Editing

ISBN: 978-1-947012-92-9

Library of Congress Control Number: 2018902731

24 23 22 21 20 19 18   2 3 4 5 6

To those who are lost,

either mentally or physically,

may they always find their

way back home.

Contents

Northeast Forest

Map of Evon

Fayral
Kensy
Northeast Forest
Cosley Estate
Main Highwayman Camp
The Eternal One
Cautzel
Zhulan
Tarsiu
Helloase
Schönestadt
Galay
Machtstadt
Parshen Gut
Ciudad Ocultada
Pretty Pauper
Friedlichoase
Tauresian Sea
Wildestadt
Chanser Estate
Hacienda Sageo
Central Rebel Camp
Baylin
Caypan
Lefas Estate
Pecalini Sea
Pecali
Main Highways
Ghost Trail (when not following Main Highways)

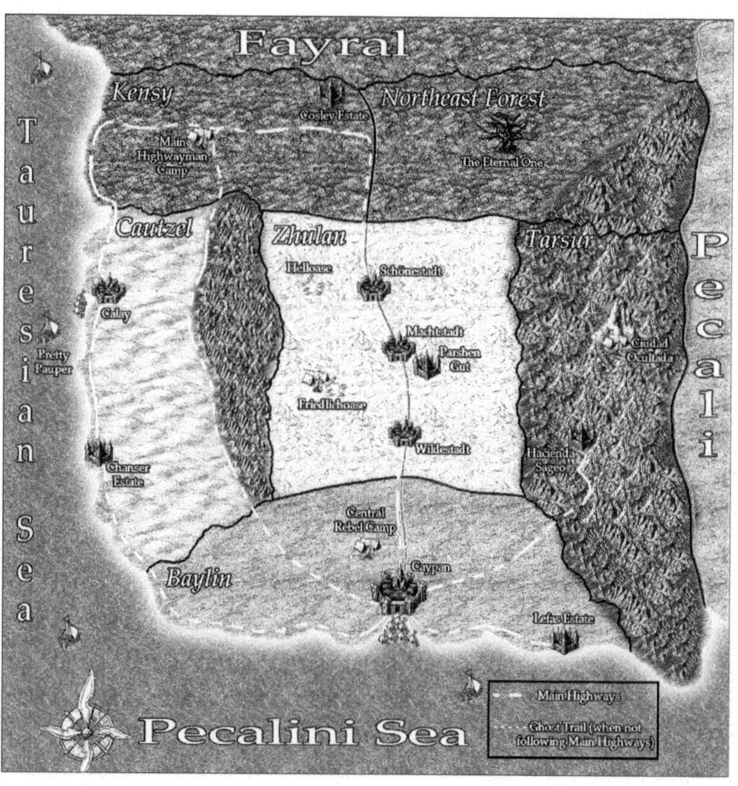

Prologue

Deep in a forest untouched by man or elf and ruled by magical creatures, a single tree towered above all others. Known to the forest's residents as The Eternal One, it had stood its vigil for so long that no other creature, plant or animal, knew its true age.

It was wide enough at its base that not even the largest dragon could encircle half its girth, and its tallest branches stretched so high, it was said they were eternally bare from both cold and wind. Its lower branches, on the other hand, drooped like a weeper and constantly caressed the ground that held it and the creatures that sought its large clearing for both peace and protection.

However, as the morning after Mid-Autumn Day dawned 224 years after the creation of the country of Evon, the habitual peace of The Eternal One's clearing was broken by a roar so loud and so daunting that most of the clearing's inhabitants fled the safety of The Eternal One's roots and branches. Only centaurs and tree nymphs refused to move, though the nymphs buried themselves deep within their respective trees and shivered from the fury behind the sound.

"You are scaring the children." The Eternal One brushed its branches against the large, glittering darkness that crouched at its base.

Teeth snapped at the branches. *"Do not chastise me, Eternal One,"* the dark dragon hissed. *"Would you prefer I keep my fury away from you where you cannot See it?"*

The tree whispered a negative. *"I only wish to know why you would react this way, Maur—"*

"Do not speak that name!" The roar that accompanied the words sent a shiver rippling through the tree's branches. *"It is Mama Dragon—nothing else."*

The Eternal One sighed. *"I forget sometimes that that is your preferred name."*

Mama Dragon snarled. *"After so many years together, one would think you could remember such a detail."*

The Eternal One swayed its branches vaguely. As old as it was, such a small detail as the preference of one name over another held little importance to the tree.

"Will you not tell me, then, what it is that upset you so?"

Mama Dragon gnashed her teeth wordlessly, and The Eternal One turned its attention away from the dragon in the hopes of deciphering an answer itself. As it so often did, The Eternal One had been showing Mama Dragon Sights from around the young country of Evon when she had released her anger.

Perusing these Sights, The Eternal One immediately dismissed the images of Cautzel, Evon's western province. That had become the young country's most peaceful province, despite the so-called pirates that roamed the seas bordering its coast. As far as The Eternal One had Seen, the pirates were not enemies of Evon.

The Sights from Evon's northern-most province, Kensy, earned a similar dismissal. The violence that had plagued the other forest for nearly two centuries had finally ended only two sevendays previously. The Eternal One knew there was little else contained within its borders that would pique Mama Dragon's interest.

Even Tarsur, the mountainous province to the east, held nothing that should have riled the dragon. There was one incident The Eternal One surveyed curiously, but it quickly discarded the Sight. It was not what the tree sought.

That only leaves Baylin to the south and the central Zhulan.

Baylin, of course, was always of interest to those who inhabited this forest, regardless of whether they had the Sight. It held the center of Evon's political power, the king's throne, which also anchored the magic preventing the magical creatures from leaving this forest's borders.

It was also true that the king had not sat upon his throne for over half a season. It was not yet long enough to break the barriers surrounding the forest, but it might be enough to raise the heads of any who watched for such things.

It is still not enough to cause Mama Dragon such grief, though.

So The Eternal One turned its attention to Zhulan. Immediately, a quiver ran through its branches.

Of course.

Here was Evon's young king, Ferez Katani, whose extended absence from the throne was a result of his travels with Mama Dragon's own daughter and her two bondmates. Here, too, was a human mage known as a Mindspeaker, who spread his magic through the minds of all four companions and interfered with the dragonbond connecting Mama Dragon's daughter to her bondmates.

Soothing its branches along the dragon's back, The

Eternal One sighed. *"You are angered by the human's interference with Flame Tongue's dragonbond."*

"How dare he?" Mama Dragon lifted her head and aimed her gold eyes at The Eternal One's trunk, though the tree knew the glare was not truly for it. *"He has no right!"*

"Calm yourself, Mama Dragon," a solemn voice interrupted.

Mama Dragon swung her head around and snapped her teeth together just shy of the centaur's face. The creature did not even twitch but simply stared at the dragon coolly.

The Eternal One sighed and twitched its branches away from the pair. It could not speak with centaurs. They did not have access to the Plant Magic that would allow such conversation. Its interference, then, would no longer be of any use.

~~*~*

Mama Dragon growled at the old centaur. *Old by their standards, maybe.* The thought was nasty, but the dragon did not care. Three centuries was of little consequence when she herself had lived for a millennium.

"He has no right to interfere in the bond, Gray Foster!"

The centaur was an elder of the forest. She thought he might understand her fury, though centaurs were so logical that she doubted he would share it.

"Who, Mama Dragon?" the centaur asked calmly. "Which bond?"

The dragon gnashed her teeth. *Honestly, a centaur's need to have all the facts before showing any emotion is annoying.*

"A human mage is interfering with young Flame Tongue's dragonbond: the dragonbond I swore to protect if anything threatened it."

"An empty promise," Gray Foster spoke with a slow

shake of his shaggy head, "when you banished the younglings from our forest with the same breath."

Mama Dragon hissed. *"I will not allow my daughter's bond to be threatened!"*

Gray Foster blinked at her slowly. "I was under the impression Flame Tongue was from another's clutch. Was I mistaken?"

Mama Dragon snapped her teeth together once more and swung her head away. He did not understand, did not know, the importance of the bond she had promised to protect.

She could easily recall the way Flame Tongue had crouched in front of her new bondmates, swearing she would allow no harm to come to them. She could still see the stubbornness in the human girl's thin, uplifted chin and narrowed purple eyes as she promised to do no less for the young red-and-purple-scaled dragon. Even the black colt had carried himself with a pride more appropriate for a fully grown magical creature, even when faced with a dragon of Mama Dragon's considerable size.

Gray Foster sighed. "You may be queen of this forest, Mama Dragon, but even your desires cannot overcome the magic that restricts us to this place. Or have you forgotten that we cannot leave of our own accord?"

The dragon snarled and swung her head back around. *"Nay, I have not forgotten, but already the king has not sat on his throne for over half a season—"*

"That signifies nothing!"

The dragon turned her head to observe the centaur with one gold eye. She rarely managed to evoke even impatience in the logical creatures.

The emotion did not last long. The centaur's face quickly smoothed, and he shook his head once more.

"I apologize."

Mama Dragon huffed and pulled her head away.

"We all have watched the throne for two centuries now, waiting and hoping that one day the kings would forget to return before a full season was finished. Even decades of war could not prevent their safe return every season. What makes you think this season should be any different?"

Mama Dragon bared her teeth, a cold amusement suddenly filling her. *"Peace may yet succeed where War failed."*

Gray Foster blinked slowly. "Already, peace has reigned in Evon for two years. We have yet to see a change."

The dragon snorted. Centaurs were often too literal for their own good. *"Two years is hardly significant when War ruled for nearly two centuries. However,"* she added with a sigh, *"you are right that I cannot yet do anything to protect young Flame Tongue's bond."*

Although I do still wish I could rip that mage limb from limb.

Gray Foster's chin dipped toward his chest. "Then you will refrain from terrifying the forest with your anger?"

Mama Dragon bared her teeth once more before burying her head under one wing. *"For now."*

Zhulan

Map of Zhulan

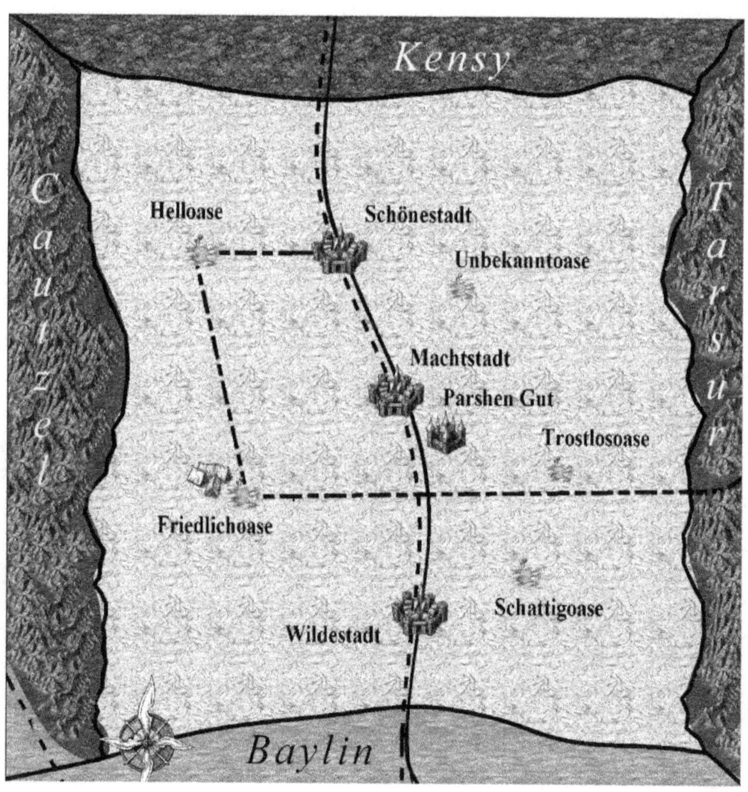

Nomad Clans

Vereinte Clans

(United under the erstehäuptling)

Katze Clan
Erstehäuptling
Hausef Kanten
(Animal Mage)
Color: Purple
Holy Animal: Desert Cat

Falke Clan
Häuptling
Meinhard Flügelschutz
Color: Blue
Holy Animal: Desert
Hawk

Pferd Clan
Häuptling
Roswalt Reiter
(Plant Mage)
Color: Green
Holy Animal: Horse

Spinne Clan
Häuptling
Genevieve Seidenstrang
(Mage Healer)
Color: Yellow
Holy Animal: Silk Spider

Wolf Clan
Häuptling Wüstenwolf Seelenesser
(Mindspeaker)
Color: Red
Holy Animal: Desert Wolf

Gift Clans

(Denying the authority of the erstehäuptling)

Schlange Clan
Häuptling Überalle
Color: Black
Holy Animal: Desert
Snake

Skorpion Clan
Häuptling Giftschwanz
(Mindspeaker)
Color: Brown
Holy Animal: Desert
Scorpion

One

Frenz Kanti woke with a groan. He hated mornings, and this one seemed to be particularly hot and bright.

Wrinkling his nose, the farmer squinted open one eye and quickly closed it when all that met his gaze was overwhelming sunlight.

Too bright for bed. I must have camped outside last night.

It wouldn't be the first time he'd decided to sleep out in the fields. With the war now two years gone, Frenz was the only person available to tend the crops. It was often simpler to spend the nights outside, especially during harvest.

Determined to enjoy a few minutes of quiet before beginning his day, Frenz sighed and let his head loll to one side.

All too soon, he realized something wasn't quite right. Despite the sunlight beating down on his body, there was a distinct lack of birdsong, a constant around his home in the forest of Kensy.

"Odd." He opened his eyes and blinked against the incessant light. Once he'd sat up and could see past the brightness, he continued to blink, taking in his current surroundings.

"Where . . . ?"

Gone were the trees he had grown up knowing. Instead, Frenz was surrounded by a flat, barren landscape, broken only by a large camp nearby that appeared to contain a modicum of greenery.

Nothing compared to Kensy's old forest.

"How in Maur's Fire did I end up in Zhulan?"

The desert province may have been no more than a two days' ride south of his farm, but Frenz had never passed Kensy's borders, not even to escape the constant violence of the war. Both he and his father had fought in the war against Fayral, his father dying to protect their land. As far as Frenz was concerned, he had no reason to leave Kensy.

So why did I?

Climbing to his feet, Frenz scanned the mostly empty horizon, noting what looked like a mountain range in the distance on the other side of the camp. He'd made a full turn before he finally realized he not only did not remember how he had come to be in Zhulan but also was completely alone.

Uttering a curse, he spun around again. "Last Chance! Last Chance!"

Please let her be nearby!

His chest tightened, his breath sped, and he dug his fingers into his palms. To wake up in a strange place with no memory of it was one thing, but to do so without his Last Chance for Hope and Freedom . . . ?

Frenz snapped his head from side to side, hoping to dislodge the thought, and shouted again.

"Last Chance!"

~~*~*

Last Chance woke to her name being screamed.

Ferez?

Immediately, she was on her hooves. If her master was in trouble, she couldn't dawdle. A soft scraping behind her made her pause, though, and she turned to see Shadow lifting his head, confusion evident in his dark eyes.

She didn't waste time explaining. *"Ferez is in trouble,"* she nickered. Then she turned and galloped in the direction from which she'd heard Ferez's cry. The stallion would follow as soon as he was awake enough to understand.

When she found Ferez, she tossed her head, seeking out the danger that had him calling for her. She stilled when she spotted nothing more than her master, who ran up to her but appeared to be safe otherwise. His blue-and-silver eyes were wide with relief, and he smiled widely.

"Thank gods." He wrapped one hand beneath her muzzle and the other behind her ears, pressing his forehead against hers. "I feared I somehow ended up here wit'out yeh."

Snorting, the mare gently pulled her head back and eyed Ferez worriedly. *"What do you mean 'somehow ended up here'?"*

Unfortunately, Ferez was no mage. He and Last Chance had known each other for years, so the king understood her cues, but he would never know her exact words.

The man smiled. "But I knew I'd ne'er leave yeh behind." He glanced around. "No matter why I decided to leave Kensy an' come out here to the middle o' nowhere." He shook his head. "Sun must've addled my mind for me to forge' that."

Last Chance huffed anxiously and dragged a hoof across the ground. *"Mindspeakers, more like."* Their magic allowed them to access the minds of other creatures and seemed to be a specialty here in Zhulan.

With a growing sense of horror, Last Chance glanced around again. The girl who pretended to be a boy was nowhere in sight. Gemini hadn't left Ferez alone since they'd begun traveling together nearly half a season ago. That she was not near him now . . .

"Shadow!" Last Chance swung her head back toward the place where she'd left him, but the black stallion hadn't followed her. The mare snorted and stomped one hoof.

"Easy," Ferez murmured, but Last Chance wouldn't be soothed. The human she considered her best friend couldn't remember their time in Zhulan. The girl to whom he'd become very close recently was missing, and Ferez didn't seem to notice. And Last Chance feared something similar might have happened to Shadow.

The mare was snapped from her worries by a thunderous roar, quickly followed by an explosion, from the center of the nearby oasis. *"Flame!"* she whinnied, certain the dragon had just become aware of her missing bondmate.

Cursing, Last Chance turned back to Ferez and nudged him hard, urging him toward the nearby camp. She had to get her oblivious friend some help, and the nomads there were currently their only hope.

~~*~*

Nightmare woke to heavy warmth. The heat was nearly unbearable, but the presence of another body beside his was comfortable enough to discourage the stallion from moving. He hadn't slept beside another horse since his weaning, so he was all too willing to enjoy the sensation while it lasted.

Too soon, the other body disappeared. Lifting his head and opening his eyes, Nightmare was quickly distracted from the pale mare by the barrenness of his surroundings. As the mare nickered a message Nightmare didn't understand and galloped away, the stallion swung his head around, attempting to find his bearings.

He must be in Zhulan. How he knew that he couldn't be certain, but perhaps Master Ekin, the Animal Mage who had raised him, had described the central province at one point. Certainly, the stallion had never left the city of Caypan, let alone Baylin, Evon's southernmost province.

Nightmare wished the mare had stayed longer so he could ask her if she knew how he'd come to be in Zhulan. As it was, the last thing he remembered was the Royal Stables in Caypan. And from what he remembered, he didn't have a master.

Strange, that. I must have a master if I've come all the way out here.

Looking around again, he snorted. *"Wherever here is."*

As he looked around, he caught sight of a large camp nearby. *Maybe someone there can tell me where I am . . . maybe even who my master is.*

Nightmare climbed to his hooves. As he stepped toward the camp, he wavered and cursed. His body felt . . . strange. He swung his head around, eyeing his black form and trying to figure out why, but he couldn't place anything specific.

I feel . . . bigger? Thicker? A shudder twitched through him. *Older?*

Tightness spread through his chest, but he stomped his hoof and shook his head. *Nay! I know I had to have traveled here somehow. That means some time has passed since I last remember. This just means it's been longer than I realized.*

The panic didn't dissipate completely, but he couldn't give in to it—not if he expected to figure out where he was and where his master was, assuming he had one. Bobbing his head sharply, Nightmare broke into a slow trot.

As he approached the camp, which had been set up within an oasis, he spotted a large herd of horses off to one side. Knowing they'd be able to point him toward an Animal Mage if they couldn't answer his questions, the stallion headed toward the herd.

Several horses lifted their heads as he came closer. One, a large chestnut, tossed his head. *"Guten täg, Shadow."*

Nightmare halted warily. It wasn't the horse's use of another language—*must be Zhulanese*—or even that Nightmare had easily understood the words—*I must've been here even longer than I thought*—that made him hesitate. Instead, the black stallion was thrown by the red horse's use of the strange name.

"I'm sorry?"

A bay mare nickered curiously. *"Are you feeling all right, Shadow? He said 'Good day.'"*

Nightmare shook his head. *"I understood him perfectly well, but my name's not Shadow."*

Silence followed his words. Several other horses lifted their heads to eye Nightmare: some with worry, others with simple curiosity.

The chestnut stallion stepped forward cautiously, dipping his head slightly. *"If that's not your name, what is?"*

"Nightmare."

The chestnut nickered softly, repeating the name. Then he swung his head toward the bay mare. *"Erdeluft?"*

The mare snorted and stepped forward. *"Do you know any of us, Nightmare?"*

"Nay. Then again, the last thing I remember is Master Ekin and the stable in Caypan, where I was raised as a warhorse, so that's not surprising."

Snorts answered his words, and several of the other horses nickered questioningly about Caypan and warhorses.

Nightmare ignored them in favor of watching the chestnut and bay trade glances.

"If you don't remember us or your current name," the chestnut finally nickered, *"do you at least remember your bondmates?"*

Nightmare stared at the other stallion blankly. *"Bondmates?"*

"Oh, nein," the bay huffed. *"If he doesn't—"*

A furious roar suddenly beat against Nightmare's ears, drowning out the rest of the mare's words. The following explosion drew the gazes of all the horses toward the middle of the camp, where smoke now billowed.

"What was that?" Nightmare whinnied.

"Flame Tongue." The bay turned worried eyes to the black stallion. *"If you don't remember your bondmates, I can only imagine what she doesn't remember."*

Nightmare hesitated, but the mare's words had piqued his curiosity. *"What does my affected memory have to do with this . . . Flame Tongue? And just what is she?"*

"She's a feuerdrache," the chestnut snorted, *"and one of your two bondmates."*

The chestnut shoved Nightmare toward the camp and the growing column of smoke.

~~*~*

Flame Tongue snapped her head back as her fire caused the structure in front of her to explode. She had not expected the curious platform to be so combustible, but she also had not expected fire to emerge with her roar.

The fire dragon hissed. *I have only lived for thirty-five years. I should not be able to spit fire for another five. What has happened?*

When Flame Tongue had awakened, it was to find herself amid the open expanse of a mostly barren desert instead of the thriving life of the Northeast Forest, the only home she had ever known. A quick glance over her body had proven unenlightening to how she had come to be there— her lithe, red-and-purple-scaled body appeared unchanged, her strong legs, whipping tail, and furled wings were unhindered by entangling vines or restrictive rope.

When the physical gave her no indication, she had turned her inspection inward. She had thought the appearance of her surroundings must be the mind trick of a djinn or perhaps a particularly mischievous gnome. Yet she had found nothing to hint at the interference of such creatures, not even a touch of magic against her sense that would cause such a realistic illusion.

What she had found instead was even more disturbing.

Foreign magic sat heavily in a portion of her mind that was solely reserved for certain mental connections— dragonbonds and lifebonds, for example. The magic formed thick layers that thoroughly blocked that section of her mind. Disbelief and anger had warred within her until she could no longer hold back the roar that had resulted in unexpected fire.

Shouts of "Flame!" suddenly drew the dragon's attention from her considerations of the blocked connections. Hissing quietly, Flame Tongue swung her head around and narrowed her eyes. Several humans ran toward her and the nearby blaze.

As she crouched, preparing to attack, she quickly observed the approaching humans. They were all dressed in pale trousers and tunics, with large cloths covering their heads and hiding all but their faces. Each one bore a long, thin cloth tied at his waist and dyed a certain color at one or both ends.

Growling, she tensed her muscles further. She had been raised with the knowledge that humans hated magical creatures and would only cause harm. These humans could be no different, not if they had stolen her memories and the creature to whom she should be connected.

Just as she prepared to pounce, one of the humans, a man with purple on his belt, raised his arms toward her and shouted, *"Flame, nein! Bitte!"*

The dragon hesitated. The man had spoken in the tongue of the animals. *And is he calling me Flame?* Thinking of the earlier cries, she crooned, confused. *Were they?*

A sudden pressure on her snout jerked her from her confusion, and she snapped her head back with a hiss. She turned her head to glare with one red eye at the man who now stood in front of her—the man with the purple-dyed belt who had spoken in the tongue of the animals.

"Who are you?" she snarled. *"Why do you address me with such familiarity?"*

The Animal Mage frowned, his black eyes flickering over her. *"Flame? It's me, Hausef Kanten."* When Flame Tongue continued to glare, he added, *"James's vater?"*

A deep growl reverberated through Flame Tongue's chest. *"Should that name mean something to me?"*

Several gasps answered her words. When magic teased at the edge of her mind—accompanied by a soft, mental *"Flame?"*—Flame Tongue turned and snapped at the source of the magic.

"Stay out, Mindspeaker! I will not fall prey to your magic again."

The Mindspeaker jerked backward, her mouth falling open as she stared at the dragon. She bore a purple-dyed belt similar to the Animal Mage's, but it was her face that marked her out from the others. Flame Tongue did not know much about humans, but she was certain their faces should have been symmetrical. This Mindspeaker appeared as though the left half of her face had been dipped in dragon fire.

The man with the purple-dyed belt and black eyes reached over and gripped the arm of the woman with the melted face. Neither of them, however, removed their gazes from the dragon.

"Es tut mir leid, Flame Tongue."

The dragon narrowed her eyes. The Animal Mage had apologized in a human tongue, one she had never heard spoken, and yet . . .

"Why do I understand your language?"

The black-eyed Animal Mage and the scarred Mindspeaker traded glances. Before either could respond, a sharp whinny drew their gazes to three horses trotting toward them. Two of the horses, a chestnut and a bay, seemed unconcerned with the presence of a dragon. Flame Tongue might have growled—*how dare such animals ignore a predator*— but her eyes were caught by the third horse, who watched her with open curiosity.

Surprised, Flame Tongue returned the regard. The third horse, a stallion, was almost pure black in color. The bright desert sunlight rippled across his coat, unhindered by the dust that surely clung to it. His hooves, which moved with certainty and precision, were nearly hidden among the feathery fringe of hair that hung down around each one. Even his mane and tail hung long and feathery—a sharp contrast, Flame Tongue realized, to the braided manes and tails of the other two.

"Erstehäuptling!" the chestnut whinnied again. As they approached, he shoved his head against the black stallion's side, causing the black horse to stumble. Flame Tongue narrowed her red eyes.

"Feuerstein." The Animal Mage nickered his greeting as he stepped toward the horses. Flame Tongue bared her teeth

when the man flicked his black eyes back toward her. *"What's wrong?"*

The chestnut snorted and scraped one hoof across the ground. Flame Tongue twisted her head to one side and eyed the animal thoughtfully. Despite her earlier thought disparaging the horses for ignoring a predator like her, she found herself more curious about their words and less about how they might sustain her.

Why do I think of them as equals?

"Shadow—"

"Nightmare," the black stallion interrupted with a snort.

The chestnut offered the black horse a single glance before turning back to the Animal Mage. *"My point,"* he nickered dryly.

Kanten nodded and stepped closer to the black stallion. *"Nightmare, my name is Hausef Kanten. Do you remember me?"*

Nightmare snorted and stomped one hoof. *"Of course not. As I told . . ."* He glanced at the chestnut. *"Feuerstein?"* He tossed his head. *"The last thing I remember is Master Ekin and Caypan, my home. I don't know how I came to be here or who my master is."*

Flame snorted. *So he doesn't belong here, either?*

"And I certainly don't remember any bondmates." The black stallion swung his head around to glare at Feuerstein. *"Whatever those are."*

Flame Tongue hissed. *"Bondmates?"*

Nightmare turned and eyed Flame Tongue once more. *"Aye, that's what Feuerstein said—that I have two bondmates and you're one of them."*

Flame Tongue snarled. *"I have two bondmates, and I don't remember either of them?"*

Worse yet was the knowledge that she might have

dragonbonded with a horse. No matter how much she might see these horses as equals, predator being bonded to prey could have damaged them both.

"Easy, Flame Tongue," soothed the black-eyed Animal Mage who kept introducing himself as Hausef Kanten. "We'll figure this out."

"You do realize that since she doesn't remember us, she has no reason to trust us, ja?"

Flame Tongue snorted. *Finally, a human who speaks sensibly.* She twisted her long neck to stare past Kanten and the scarred Mindspeaker. Behind them ranged many others dressed in the same pale clothing that left only their hands and faces visible. Only the colors decorating their cloth belts and the minute differences in their facial features gave Flame Tongue any visual indication of who might be who.

The sensible human turned out to have a much smoother face than the black-eyed Kanten, though he looked just as worn. The brown of his eyes seemed to match the brown that decorated both ends of his belt. From a quick scan of the humans gathering near her, Flame Tongue noted only one other human with brown on her belt.

"What do you know of this, Wolfrik?" asked the scarred female Mindspeaker.

"He's probably the one who caused it!"

Flame Tongue swung her head away from the humans she had been observing to find another group joining them. The man who had spoken bore a belt dyed green at both ends. The expression on his face, however, caught her more than anything else. His dark eyes were narrowed, and his mouth twisted into a sneer. She eyed him distastefully. He was certainly not encouraging her trust in these people.

The young woman beside him cuffed his shoulder. She too bore a double-green belt, and the similarity of her features to the older man's proved their relation even before she spoke.

"Vater, Wolfrik has no reason to have done this. The Drache Krieger and his companions trusted him. The Drache Krieger even owed him dankpflicht. Why do you think he would betray that trust?"

"He's a Skorpion!" The sneering man turned a hateful gaze upon the young man with the double-brown belt. "Joining the Vereinte Clans could have been a ruse to kidnap the Drache Krieger."

Kanten, the Animal Mage, sighed and shook his head. "We have no reason to believe James has been kidnapped, Roswalt."

James? Is that the name of my second bondmate? It did not feel right, but with her memories gone, Flame Tongue could not be certain.

"Do you think they'll bother explaining any of this to us?"

The soft nicker drew Flame Tongue's gaze to her side. To her surprise, Nightmare had approached her. The black stallion was watching the argument with disgust.

"Or do you think they'll simply continue fighting among themselves?"

Intrigued, Flame Tongue cooed. *"I believe they do not put enough stock in our missing memories."*

The words earned her a snort and an amused glance from the stallion. As he tilted his head toward her, his forelock shifted toward one eye, revealing a snow-white star upon the black of his forehead.

"Or perhaps too much in their own abilities to convince us?"

The dragon swiveled her head to better observe the stallion. He spoke more sense than she would have ever credited to such a prey animal. When she said so, he nickered amusedly.

"I'd say it was because I was raised by an Animal Mage," he snorted and flicked his short ears, *"but I've never been one to give humans so much credit."*

Flame Tongue crooned. Despite what she had been taught, the dragon was beginning to understand why she might have taken this horse as her bondmate. His apparent wit might have been enough to counter whatever ill effects being dragonbonded to a potential predator could have caused.

"Erstehäuptling!"

Flame Tongue and Nightmare turned their gazes toward the sharp whinny as the humans fell silent. Approaching the growing group of humans was a pale mare accompanied by another human. Unlike the humans Flame Tongue had seen so far, this one did not wear a cloth to hide his sandy-brown hair, though the rest of his clothing was the same. His eyes, which were narrowed under his furrowed brow, flashed a pale blue and silver in the desert sunlight—an intriguing color combination that Flame Tongue was certain only she could distinguish from such a distance.

"Last Chance!" Kanten stepped forward urgently as horse and man approached. *"Wha—"*

"He doesn't remember!" Flame Tongue was startled by the panic in the mare's whinny. *"He doesn't know how we came to Zhulan, I fear he doesn't remember James, and he doesn't . . ."*

She trailed off and swung her head toward, of all people, the young man with the brown eyes and double-brown belt. *"You have to help him!"*

~~*~*

Frenz was surprised by Last Chance's insistence as she pushed him toward the camp he'd noticed before. When she led him between two bodies of water, he noticed a group of people gathered in a large central area. There seemed to be some kind of argument taking place.

The group shifted, and Frenz stumbled to a halt. There, crouched warily beyond the humans, was a creature he had never expected to see. It was reptilian, with scales the color of amethysts and rubies. It stood about the height of a horse, but its body and neck were longer, its snake-like head crowned with horns. Rising from its back, a pair of half-furled leathery wings quivered.

"A dragon?"

Logically, he should fear such a creature. Yet his body remained languid. In fact, he may even have relaxed further upon seeing the creature's beautiful jewel tones.

A sudden sharp whinny startled him as Last Chance shoved him once more in the direction of the arguing people. The people, nomads if their clothing was any indication—and how did he know that?—fell silent and turned to watch him approach.

One man stepped forward, his double-purple statusgürtel declaring him a member of the reigning family of the Katze Clan. *How do I know that?* Despite Frenz's confusion, he was distracted from his questions by the man's nicker, which marked him as an Animal Mage.

Last Chance launched into a series of panicked whinnies and snorts that had Frenz running a hand down her neck in an attempt to soothe her. Instead, the motion only seemed to increase her anxiety, and she finished with a loud snort directed not at the Animal Mage who had addressed her but at the man who seemed to have been at the center of the previous argument.

The man, who wore the double brown of a noble Skorpion, shook his head. "I don't know what you're saying,

Frau Letztechance." Frenz blinked, startled by the Zhulanese translation of Last Chance's name.

"She is asking for your help, Wolfrik," the Katze noble answered. His dark eyes, however, were now on Frenz.

"I'm afraid I can't." Wolfrik's words sounded heavy with sorrow. Someone gripped the man's shoulder, while another gripped his hand.

"Then you did have something to do with this!"

The accusation was spat by a sneering man whose statusgürtel bore the double green of a noble Pferd, and it dropped the nomads back into shouting. Frenz watched the argument, bewildered. Beside him, Last Chance tossed her head and stomped her hooves. Beneath his hand, he could feel her muscles quivering. On the other side of the crowd, the dragon and the black stallion beside her watched the nomads as well. Neither looked impressed by these people.

Listening to the yelling, he thought he knew why. From what he could piece together, neither the dragon—Flame Tongue?—nor the black stallion—Shadow? Nightmare?— could remember how they had arrived here either. Nor could they remember each other or the Drache Krieger, who was supposedly at the center of the memory loss.

Frenz at least recognized the title, despite being more familiar with the rebel leader's Kensian title, the Traveler. Frenz knew enough about the man to realize the dragon and stallion must be the constant companions the Drache Krieger was rumored to have. However, how Frenz himself could possibly be connected to the other man was beyond him. Everyone knew the Drache Krieger never traveled with other humans.

"I believe he made an exception for you, mein freund."

Frenz blinked. The voice had been clear, despite the volume of the voices surrounding him.

"Es tut mir leid, freund. It seems I need to reintroduce myself."

Frenz frowned. The sorrowful tone sounded familiar. Glancing around, he noticed that out of all the surrounding nomads, only the accused man watched him, his gaze as mournful as the voice.

"Mindspeaker?"

When the accused man nodded, accompanied by a soft affirmative echoing through Frenz's mind, the farmer simply nodded in return. Despite *knowing* he had never had anyone mindspeak to him before, this man's voice was familiar and comfortable.

"My name is Wolfrik Giftschwanz, freund. I'm a Geistmagier and youngest son of the häuptling of the Skorpion Clan, one of the two clans that captured the Drache Krieger."

Frenz nodded again. Despite the apparent conflict surrounding this man, Frenz trusted his words. *And not just because Last Chance turned specifically to him for help.*

"Tha's why they accuse yeh, isn' it?" Wolfrik might be able to hear his thoughts, but Frenz himself barely could, not over the shouting. "They accepted yeh as differen' from most in yer clan, an' now they fear yeh did somethin' to make them regre' tha' decision."

Again, Wolfrik nodded. *"I promise you I had nothing to do with it. The one thing I am guilty of is failing to protect your geist."*

Frenz hummed. "Well, if it means anythin', I believe yeh." Wolfrik's eyes widened as startled curiosity echoed through Frenz's mind. "I canna imagine a man causin' such obvious damage an' stayin' to face the consequences."

Wolfrik's lips twitched, and he bowed his head. *"Danke, freund. That means more to me than you realize."*

Frenz turned his attention back to the other nomads. Although he was surrounded by nomads now, he focused on the ones whose statusgürtel were double-dyed. Those belts marked the reigning families of each clan, so their wearers would have the most influence, Frenz knew.

On the other side of Wolfrik, closer to Flame Tongue, the middle-aged Pferd who had accused Wolfrik was in the middle of a shouting match with a young woman Frenz thought might be the man's daughter. Closer at hand, the Animal Mage from the Katze Clan who had addressed Last Chance was arguing with a quiet, older woman wearing the double yellow of the Spinne Clan and a middle-aged man wearing the double blue of the Falke Clan.

"The häuptlinge?"

When Wolfrik confirmed that the three middle-aged men and the older woman were the leaders of their respective clans, the farmer cast his gaze around the group in search of the Wolf Clan's häuptling. He had already spotted two nomads, among the six surrounding Wolfrik, whom he thought must be his children.

"Wüstenwolf may be young," the Mindspeaker corrected, indicating the young man in double red at his right shoulder, *"but he's been häuptling for several jahre."*

Frenz blinked. The Wolf didn't look much older than he was. To have become häuptling at such a young age . . .

Quiet amusement filled his mind. *"Might I remind you that the Drache Krieger is still missing, freund? Now is not the time for such thoughts."*

"Right." Frenz frowned at the arguing häuptlinge. "This fighting is getting them nowhere."

A soft nudge to his arm drew Frenz's attention to Last Chance. When he met her gaze, she nodded before throwing herself up onto her hind legs and screaming. By the time the mare had dropped to all fours, startled silence reigned over the crowd of nomads. Murmuring his thanks, Frenz turned and glared at the häuptlinge.

"One o' yer own has been kidnapped, an' all yeh do is snap at each other like starved hounds." Glancing around, he was satisfied to see that even the sneering Pferd häuptling appeared to be listening. "Since Wolfrik is here an' the Drache Krieger is not, yeh should assume he is more willin' to help yeh find the Drache Krieger than to hinder yeh."

"But—"

Frenz silenced the Pferd häuptling with a glare.

"If yeh cry trap," the farmer replied, referencing one of the arguments he had heard the Pferd speak, "then I'll question the abilities o' yer warriors for yeh to think two clans can successfully execute such a ploy agains' the full force o' yer five wit'out threatenin' their own clansmen."

The Pferd went red in the face, but he didn't answer. A bark of laughter broke the quiet that followed Frenz's words. Startled, the farmer turned to find Wüstenwolf, the young Wolf häuptling who stood at Wolfrik's shoulder, watching him with a grin.

"Finally, someone other than Alys who can talk Roswalt down." The words earned the Wolf a glare from the Pferd häuptling and a smirk from the young woman standing next to him. "And Frenz has a point. Wolfrik has already provided the geisternetz with the current location of the Gift Clans. There's no reason to spend our time fighting among ourselves when we could be planning krieg against the Gift Clans."

Wüstenwolf turned and bowed to the Katze häuptling. "If you will, Erstehäuptling."

The Animal Mage grimaced. "You're right. This should be a time for kriegrat, not arguments." He glanced at the other häuptlinge. "Agreed?"

The Spinne and Falke readily agreed, but it took a nudge

and a glare from Roswalt's daughter for the Pferd to nod stiffly.

The Katze häuptling turned toward the dragon and the black stallion. When he offered them a soft nicker, Last Chance snorted and stomped one hoof, bringing the Animal Mage's attention back to her.

When Last Chance snorted again, the man blinked and nodded slowly. "If you wish, Last Chance." The mare dipped her head before nosing Frenz once and trotting over to the other two animals.

Frenz stared as his mount gently lipped the neck of the stallion. *What?* Last Chance was notorious for her dislike of stallions. *So why is she suddenly being affectionate with this one?*

A chuckle from beside him startled Frenz from his gaping, and he turned to find Wolfrik, Wüstenwolf, and the others who had stood with them. The rest of the nomads were already moving toward a cold firepit surrounded by five sturdy logs.

"Not so suddenly, mein freund." Wolfrik offered a small smile. "You joined the Drache Krieger near the beginning of the jahreszeit, and yesterday was Mitte Jahreszeit."

Mid-Season? Have I really lost that much of my memory? Frenz didn't know what season or year this was, but even six sevendays was longer than he had assumed. Yet . . .

"Half a season is still awful quick for a stallion to earn Last Chance's trust."

The Mindspeaker shrugged. "Yet you and the Drache Krieger became fairly close during that same time."

Frenz stared at the man. Wolfrik had said the Drache Krieger had made an exception for Frenz. Only now did the farmer realize he didn't even know his reason for traveling with him. "Is that—"

"Wüstenwolf! Wolfrik!" The interruption was snapped

by a woman whose face looked half-melted and who wore the double purple of a Katze noble. "Stop ignoring me. You're the ones who reminded us that time is of the essence."

"Ja, ja, Isa," Wüstenwolf called back. He grabbed the arm of the other Wolf. "Komme, Eule. We can't let them start the kriegrat without us."

Eule huffed. "Like they would dare to start without all the häuptlinge present." She glanced back at Wolfrik and offered him a sharp smile. "That includes you, Wolfrik. After this battle, you can claim your place as häuptling of the Skorpion Clan."

Frenz was amused to see Wolfrik's face color slightly. However, the Skorpion simply nodded and gripped Frenz's shoulder.

"Komme, freund. The Drache Krieger would have wanted you to witness a kriegrat, and that tactical geist of yours might provide some ideas that the rest of us can't."

With that, he steered the farmer after the Wölfe, his schwester, and the three Katzen trailing after.

~~*~*

When the erstehäuptling turned back to Flame and Shadow, Last Chance knew the Animal Mage was going to attempt to finish explaining the situation. The humans didn't have time for that, and neither dragon nor stallion looked inclined to trust any of them quite yet. Thankfully, the erstehäuptling didn't appear insulted by the mare's request to finish the explanations herself. Instead, he easily agreed and led his people toward the site of the interclan meeting they'd held only days before.

Nudging Frenz once to let him know it was safe, Last

Chance approached Shadow and Flame. She was surprised when the two accepted her easily, even more so when Shadow began to bombard her with questions. Apparently, waking up beside her had made him, and therefore the dragon, more inclined to trust her.

If that's true, the mare thought as she lipped Shadow's neck, *perhaps I could convince Flame to renew the bond between them.*

Last Chance had heard enough from the humans and the other horses to know that neither dragon nor stallion could feel each other the way they were supposed to.

And if Flame fixes their bond, maybe they'll be able to find their missing memories.

She hoped so. Maybe then the terror she had been trying to ignore would disappear.

Two

Gemini Cosley woke to a dull ache in her shoulders and a flare of pain in her left cheek. A cry ripped past her lips, and her eyes flew open.

She hardly noticed the sun hanging low over the distant, flat horizon. Instead, the sight of the unfamiliar nomade with a brown statusgürtel standing before her, along with the camp that sprawled out behind him in an unfamiliar layout, struck her cold.

Where am I?

Forcing her legs to take her weight to relieve the pain in her shoulders, she automatically reached for Flame and Shadow. Instead of finding their warm and wild presences, her geist ricocheted off a thick wall that stood in place of the dracheband. Instantly, her head began to throb, and she released a low groan.

An amused snort drew her attention to the right, where another nomade stood with arms folded. This one wore the black statusgürtel of the Schlange Clan. It was only a confirmation of what she had already known, but witnessing the two Poison Clans working together still caused a shiver to run through her body.

Her thoughts stopped as sharply as her geist had in search of her bondmates when something solid hit her in the gut, driving the air from her lungs. Her legs gave out again, wrenching her shoulders as they took her full weight again. She would have cried out, but the sudden pull on her shoulders kept her from getting any breath. She scrambled to regain her feet, the tall, rounded surface at her back digging into her spine. The moment she could breathe again, she gasped, desperate to refill her lungs.

"Welcome to Trostlosoase, ausländer," the Schlange growled.

Despite the pain, Gemi noted the insult. The Poison Clans had never accepted her as a Zhulanbürger, let alone a nomade or even Drache Krieger.

It was the name of the oase, though, that truly caught Gemi's attention.

She had spent the six months she'd lived with the Katze Clan after they first took her in learning the Zhulanese language. The name of the oase roughly translated to "Hopeless Oasis." It wasn't hard to figure out why the Schlange had told her the name: not only would the oase not be known by her vater and his allies, but the name supposedly described her own situation.

Not completely true, she thought. *Wolfrik will be able to tell Vater where the Poison Clans' camp is.*

A hard grip on her chin brought her attention back to the Schlange. For several silent moments, he simply glared at her, and she glared right back. Being tied to a post and beaten meant they were planning to keep her alive, and she wasn't going to let a little pain scare her, especially when she knew help would come.

When the Schlange released a harsh laugh, Gemi narrowed her eyes. The Schlange smirked.

"Your precious Vereinte Clans will be too busy accusing the abschaum of treachery to listen to anything he has to say." The smirk turned nasty. "And if you think we will stick to just 'a little pain,' ausländer, then you are sorely mistaken."

Gemi had barely a moment to realize what this mann must be before her vision went black and silence closed in around her. She stopped breathing as she waited for the Schlange's next move, but she didn't have long to wait.

Pain flared in her jaw as something solid connected, and her head wrenched to the side. Her breath left her in a grunt, and she bit her lip to keep from crying out again. The blow was quickly followed by another to the side of her chest.

A moment later, pain flared at her left temple, then her right side, just below the rib cage. *The Skorpion must be a boxer.* The thought was confirmed as his blows continued in a one-two pattern, first her left side flaring in pain, then her right.

The realization didn't make the pain any easier to bear. It wasn't long before her entire torso and face were sore, the pain increasing in sharp flashes with every punch. She tried to remain silent throughout it all, only whimpering and grunting when she couldn't. She refused to give the Schlange the satisfaction of hearing her cry out again.

Gemi didn't know how long the beating lasted. By the time the boxer stopped hitting her, her mouth was filled with the copper tang of blood and her cheeks were wet. She fought to keep from slumping; the pressure on her shoulders would only increase the pain and make the situation worse.

"*So,*" hissed a voice inside her head once the beating had ended, "*you do not respond to beatings.*"

Gemi physically flinched as she attempted to get away from the voice. She had never had a voice other than Flame's or Shadow's so thoroughly invade her geist, and the feeling was disturbing. The presence that accompanied the voice was slick and burning, coiling around her thoughts like animal namesake of the Schlange it belonged to.

The voice chuckled darkly. *"I did not think you would,"* the voice continued, ignoring her thoughts.

"What do you want?" she projected. The dark chuckle answered her once more.

"That is simple, Gemini Cosley."

Nein! Gemi's chest suddenly grew tight, and she struggled against her bonds. Mindspeaker or not, this Schlange couldn't know her real name! He shouldn't have known her as anything other than James Caffers!

She stilled when something long and sharp pressed against her throat. Her eyes widened, despite still seeing nothing, and her breaths burned in her lungs and past her lips.

"I want to break you."

~~*~*

Adalwolf knew the smile on his face was cruel. He could see it in the way the Skorpion he was working with took a step away from him. He felt the smile curl into a sneer at the Skorpion's obvious fear.

"Leave," he said, dismissing the Skorpion. He no longer had need of the mann's skills, and his presence would only dampen the pleasure Adalwolf would take in the torture. As the Skorpion turned and ran, Adalwolf settled his attention more firmly on the girl.

She was delectable, he had to admit. Strong-willed and defiant, as well as physically pleasing to the eye, she would make a fine frau. But she represented everything Adalwolf hated, and that was enough for him to take great pleasure in breaking her.

He twisted the blade of his scharfmond, which curled up over his knuckles, lightly against her throat. His smile deepened as her breath came even faster.

"For a fräulein so skilled with sword and scharfmonde, you are amazingly sensitive to the touch of a blade against your skin." Adalwolf didn't mention that he was enhancing her sense of touch. *"Tell me, what does the blade mean to you?"*

He chuckled as several images passed through the girl's geist. *She's almost too easy to read without the protection the drache usually provides. A disgrace, really.*

"A love for the blade itself but not the battle for which it is used?" He sneered. *"You are a fool, Gemini Cosley."*

He noted her flinch as he mindspoke her real name. While he was unwilling to share his discovery of her true gender with the rest of his clan, her fear of her own name was a weakness he would exploit quite willingly.

"And the pain the blade causes: is that, too, something you fear?"

He pressed his scharfmond harder, just enough to break the skin. Her gasp was answer enough, and he chuckled.

"You and I shall have some fun, Gemini Cosley."

~~*~*

The cuts the Schlange made in Gemi's skin *burned.*

At first, the cuts were all tiny, shallow points of pain, like that first cut. As time passed and the cuts became more numerous, they grew longer . . . deeper . . . slower. The Schlange took his time, moving his blade with a slowness that made her wonder, for the first time, if he might actually manage to drive her insane.

At one point, she felt him slice open her tunic with that

same slowness. The terror of discovery almost overwhelmed her, but the Schlange chuckled against her geist. He assured her amusedly that the bindings on her breasts were still secure and no one had reason yet to question her gender.

Before she could think on the words, his blade was on her abdomen, drawing her back down into the pain.

After what felt like hours and an infinite number of cuts later, the Schlange removed the blade. Gratitude flooded through her before something solid and gritty landed on her stomach and dragged.

A scream broke past her lips. The hand continued to rub, and she gasped and sobbed and cursed, trying to shift away from the painful touch. Even then, her body was sluggish and weak, her shoulders straining as she put more and more of her weight on them.

The hand worked, moving over her wounded stomach, then her upper chest, her neck, and even parts of her face. It disappeared several times, returning again and again to continue the harsh treatment.

Long after Gemi had subsided into pained whimpers, the hand disappeared and didn't return. Slowly, she became aware that the taunting, burning presence had disappeared from her geist as well. She remained tense, waiting for the Schlange to return, but eventually her muscles relaxed, thankful for the reprieve.

However, she still couldn't see or hear anything. The reprieve soon became daunting as the darkness pressed in on her and the silence rang in her ears.

Minutes turned to hours, or perhaps even täge. She couldn't be certain, not when she was unable to see the sun or the moons or hear the activities of the camp around her. She couldn't even be certain of her sense of touch as pain from the bruising and cuts overwhelmed everything else.

As time drew on, she began to wonder about the people around her. She wondered about their expressions as they watched her hanging there and the insults and speculations they made, which she couldn't hear. Her fingers twitched as she imagined she could feel their gazes burning into her skin, the pain of those imagined gazes mingling with the pain of her wounds.

Hours—or täge—passed. Her stomach cramped with hunger. Her throat and mouth were parched from screaming and lack of fluids.

Exhaustion. The pain of the beating and the blade had tired her, but so had the length of time she had spent standing, then hanging as her legs gave up on holding her weight. She knew, despite not being able to feel him, that the Schlange was keeping her awake.

She hung on that pole and wished for food and drink . . . rest . . . some idea of what was happening around her. She even found herself wishing for the Schlange to return, just to relieve the silence.

Then the Schlange did return, and he permeated her geist with images.

He began with visions of what she craved: Blankets laid out and covered with luscious banquets of roast pig, goat stew, corn, cactus, berries, nuts, seeds, wildflowers. Cups overflowing with water, wines, and berry juices. The water of an oasis spring bubbling as it emerged from underground. A waterfall. A bed. The soothing hands of a healer.

All these images and more passed through her geist at the Schlange's will. He lingered on each, focusing the details to the point where she knew the exact shade of each food or drink, knew every bubble of the spring's rise or the waterfall's descent, knew every contour of the bed and the healer's hands. And with each image, each detail, she felt her cravings increase, multiply.

By the time the images changed, she was sobbing, begging for relief. She could hardly hear her own voice since her hearing was silenced, but her words clawed across her parched throat and dry tongue.

The new images, however, weren't a relief. They were filled with pain, even more terrifying than the physical pain because she knew there was no escape from it.

There was fire, burning her to a crisp.

There was water, flowing over her and into her. Not in a soothing manner as she would have expected after the fire, but overpowering her and beating her and drowning her.

There was the dryness of the desert, the coarseness of the sand beneath her body, the burning heat of the sun, and overwhelming certainty that there was no water nearby.

There were insects. Not usually harmful or frightening to her, they crawled over her in such multitude that she couldn't fight the scream that tore at her throat.

The images continued to bombard her, one after the other, yet with a slowness and loving attention to detail that meant the Schlange was only playing with her.

One image flowed into another, and the image of a beautiful black desert schlange coiled before her. Like the images before it, she knew it wasn't real, but she couldn't prevent the jerk that shook her body as she attempted to avoid it.

It was useless. She was tired and hurting, and what little she could do with her body was no protection against the feind in her geist. She sobbed, and more tears slid down her cheeks as the schlange slid closer and coiled up her leg.

She had never been afraid of reptilian schlangen, at least no more than they rightly deserved. The sight of this one, though, invoked within her a deep fear that had more to do with the Geistmagier's attacks than anything she had felt before.

When the schlange was fully coiled around her leg, its head almost even with her hip, it stopped sliding against her. She closed her eyes, still sightless, unwilling to watch the schlange strike, but such an action was useless.

In her geist, she was fully aware of the schlange's head striking forward, its bared fangs digging deep into the inside of her thigh. And this image, like all those before, produced a pain that felt all too real.

She could feel its poison burning its way through her veins and slowly destroying her. The pain ripped a choked scream from her throat, which burned and stung from the screaming, the lack of water, and the blood that still spilled from her torn lip.

The image of the schlange faded slowly, but the pain, like before, remained. Unlike before, the image that took its place seemed more familiar. It was a long moment, however, before Gemi realized the scene was one from her own memories.

Nein.

Despite her earlier defiance, her denial was weak and sluggish. It was not a memory she wished to face, but her ability to fight had waned.

In the memory, she packed quickly. Not an unusual activity during her childhood, sadly, and one that wouldn't have struck her so hard if she hadn't known exactly what day the memory portrayed: the morgen of her parents' deaths.

"*Ach, ja,*" hissed the Schlange in her head. "*You were always leaving them, weren't you? So many times you left, only to return again. It was just a game for you.*"

"Nein," she whispered. She couldn't tell if the denial was only in her head.

The Schlange's dark chuckle answered her protest. *"Ja. The moment you became upset, you would pack up and leave. You never gave a single thought for how your actions affected them."*

Gemi shook her head weakly. Her body hurt too much and was too exhausted to do anything else.

"Why do you deny it?" The Schlange's voice became almost soothing. *"After all, you were a child. Everything was supposed to be a game for you.*

"But then you left on that morgen." The suddenly acidic words burned into Gemi's geist, and she shuddered. *"How did you feel when you learned that you had run away not only from your parents' murder but also from their murderer?"*

An image of Kale Caphrin, the mann her vater—her father—had introduced as her new tutor, arose in her geist.

"Ja," the Schlange hissed again. *"The Fayralese tutor—the mann you turned and ran from the moment he was introduced. How did you feel when you discovered you had met your parents' murderer?"*

Gemi knew the moment the Schlange spoke of. It had been a year later, when she was ten, that she had spied a Fayralese raiding party through some bushes and recognized Kale Caphrin among the other männer. But as she relived the memory, the hatred that had filled her was accompanied and overwhelmed by an all-consuming guilt.

"Not only were you not there when your familie needed you, but you knew your parents' murderer. And not even his death was enough to assuage those feelings, was it?"

The memory changed. Gemi stood over Caphrin's dead body. Her blade ran red with his blood and that of his companions. Instead of feeling the triumph she had expected after a jahr of seeking revenge for her parents' deaths, her guilt only swelled.

The guilt over her parents' deaths was joined by the guilt she felt over killing these männer. Human lives lost to her blade.

She sobbed.

"After that, you knew how dangerous you were." The voice had softened, as if in sympathy to her pain, but the words were relentless. *"After that, you* had *to leave."* An image of the old forest caretaker who had taken her in after her parents' deaths rose in her geist. *"You couldn't bear the thought of staying in one place."* Kephin, his black curls tousled and his green eyes red-rimmed from crying. *"You knew if you stayed too long, others would die."* Kephin's original gang, lying dead in their own camp.

"And that was only Kensy!" The Schlange's voice was a mix of incredulity and amusement. *"Even when they take you in as familie . . ."* He showed her Hausef and his familie crowded around Zuk, who lay injured. *"Maybe even especially so . . ."* There was Naldo, the King of Thieves, and her familia in Tarsur. *"You just cannot let them get too close."* Rosie of Baylin came next, her usually laughing green eyes dimmed in regret.

"You are not capable of stability." The next scene, surprisingly, was not of Captain Marlen, as Gemi had expected. Instead, Gemi sat on the wooden railing of his three-master, the *Pretty Pauper*, and stared into the dark water below. *"Even then, you knew it was better for everyone if you did not exist."*

Gemi struggled against the Schlange's venom. She didn't think that was true, but his words confused her. She couldn't remember what she had been thinking as she stared into the ocean, so close to just jumping right in. She couldn't, for the life of her, remember how her freunde and familien had been hurt if not by her.

She tried to pull up images of Flame and Shadow, who had been noticeably lacking from the images he'd shown her.

The Schlange only laughed and knocked the images of dragon and horse away.

"The only reason they have stayed with you for so long is that verdammt dracheband. Now that it is gone, they will not be coming back for you."

Her throat closed up, and the pain in her skin was suddenly nothing against the frozen tightness in her chest. She tried to fight the certainty that he was right as it formed in her geist.

Nein . . .

The thought was barely a breath.

Suddenly, an image of Ferez formed in her geist, and she clung to it. *Just last nacht we decided we could be more than just freunde.*

Dark laughter trailed the thought.

"So naïve," hissed the voice, heavy with pity. *"You honestly think your beloved king can love a boy? And even if you do tell him who you are, he will despise you for what you have done. Your relationship with the king was a failure from the start."*

Gemi couldn't breathe, and she couldn't stop crying. The cold, sharp pain in her chest had nothing to do with the beating or the blade.

Is this, she wondered with a vague detachment, *what a broken heart feels like?*

A tug at the back of her head told her the Schlange had grabbed her horsetail. *"The king could never love a female like you. This"*—he tugged hard on his handful of hair—*"is the only thing marking you as a frau."* He snorted. *"And you don't even deserve that."*

The words were all the warning she had before the sharpness of a blade touched the back of her neck, and her head suddenly jerked forward.

Something inside her broke then. Gemi wouldn't have

been able to place what, but she felt it shatter. The whine that began in the back of her throat was incessant and painful, and she couldn't have stopped it if she'd wanted to. At this point, she couldn't even care. Image after image passed through her mind, drowning her in guilt. So many hurt, so many dead: friends, family, enemies. No one survived her proximity fully intact.

It's better this way. They're all better off without me.

~~*~*

Adalwolf smiled as he pulled out of Gemini's geist. He was satisfied that she was properly broken. The guilt he had finally managed to locate, pull forward in her geist, and enhance would ensure she was no longer a threat to his clan's way of life.

Rolling his head to relieve the tension in his neck, he glanced at the Gemini moons that hung heavy and low among the stars. He shook his head. Mitternacht had come and passed. It had taken nearly nine hours to break the girl— far longer than he had expected with his mental gifts.

And he knew the torture had felt far longer for her because of all the enhancements he had made within her geist. To her, it would have seemed like täge had passed— long enough for her to feel the effects of the deprivation he was forcing upon her.

Adalwolf frowned and glanced sharply at his broken prey. He had tortured and broken strong männer in half the time he'd been forced to spend on this measly girl of only sixteen jahre.

And he had not gone easy on her. If anything, he had been harsher with her than he'd ever been with anyone, using techniques he was rarely forced to use. He'd found in her a strength to rival even the drache's, which had scared him. But he had taken that fear and used it to drive him until he could find a way to defeat her strength.

Shaking those thoughts from his head, he twitched the sides of the girl's tunic back into place. He had sliced it down the middle to use his scharfmond on the soft flesh of her belly, but he wished to keep her true identity a secret as much as she did. The more covered she was, the better.

Turning away from the broken child, Adalwolf went to find his häuptling. He had promised to let him know when his work was finished, and he had already dawdled too long by the broken girl's side.

He had taken no more than ten steps when a burst of light appeared in the sky and an eruption of flames lit the far side of the camp. Cursing, Adalwolf broke into a run.

How in Maurus's Feuer did the drache manage to find us?

Three

Flame Tongue purred. The burning tent warmed her belly
as she winged over it. It was not, however, enough to
satisfy the burning rage that lashed through her.

Her anger over her stolen memories and bondmate had
returned fully when she learned that the nomads knew the
location of their enemies. It had only grown with Last
Chance's explanations and a failed attempt to renew the
dragonbond with Nightmare.

The only thing that had prevented her from raiding
someone's mind for the enemies' location and flying off
without the humans was the soothing logic of Last Chance's
master: a human who spoke more like a war strategist than a
farmer.

Still, Frenz Kanti's reasoning could not chain her rage
completely. Not long after the nomads forded the San River,
Flame Tongue had spotted the fires of their enemies' camp.
She had had just enough sense to inform Wolfrik—the one
Mindspeaker among the nomads whom she now trusted—

before she stopped circling and sped toward the camp that held her missing bondmate.

The first fireball had been a necessity to ease the combined pressure of anger, confusion, and fear that raged through her mind and body, threatening to overwhelm her before she could find her bondmate.

She made a full pass over the camp, but any sign there might have been of her missing bondmate was obscured by the haze of red that filled her vision. Climbing higher, she glared down at the taunting mass of tents below her and breathed deeply once more. She was just opening her maw to release the fire gas when a pressure against her mind made her hesitate.

"Bitte, nein, Dame Flammezunge!" Wolfrik begged.

Flame Tongue swallowed down the combustible gas and snarled at the interruption.

"Your bondmate may not be in the tents," the Mindspeaker continued quickly, *"but my clansmänner are. Those who mean us no ill will not leave them."*

The dragon growled. With great difficulty, she recalled the Skorpion's previous request that the tents remain untouched. Still, she nearly denied his plea.

The thieves deserve to be punished!

She was distracted by the sight of armed nomads scrambling from several tents and shouting to each other. The brown and black of their statusgürtel were clearly visible to her, even in the dark of night.

"And are these free game?" She winged higher into the sky. Not waiting for Wolfrik to respond, she dived and roared, releasing the fire that would destroy her enemies faster than any of her allies' weapons could.

~~*~*

They'd traveled perhaps half an hour from the San River when Frenz heard a heavy huff from his left. Glancing to the side, he eyed the Mindspeaker who rode there.

"Wha's wrong, Wolfrik?"

The Skorpion shook his head. "Nothing is wrong, as such. Dame Flammezunge has simply lost patience and flown ahead to attack."

Frenz nodded, a sharp smile spreading his lips wide. Despite his missing memories, the farmer had heard enough from the nomads to feel a strong desire for revenge. The more he'd learned about the relationship he'd had with the kidnapped boy, the more he craved it. He couldn't fault the dragon for breaking from the strategy to which the nomads had agreed.

Leaning forward, Frenz laid a hand against Last Chance's neck. "Last Chance? Nightmare?"

His mare tilted her head, just enough to indicate she was listening. The black stallion, who ran riderless to her right, tossed his head and snorted. Frenz chuckled.

"Le's race, yeh two."

Last Chance lifted her head and whinnied loudly. The sound was echoed by the hundreds of horses that ran behind them. Swinging her head around, the mare nudged Nightmare, and both horses broke into a gallop.

A soft whoop to his left had the farmer turning to Wolfrik to find the Mindspeaker, and the häuptlinge beyond him, keeping pace. Behind them, Frenz could see in the moons-lit darkness the fierce expressions of the warriors of the häuptlinge's families. Among them were Häuptling Kanten's scarred sister and his two eldest children, the daughter of the häuptling who had accused Wolfrik, and the sister of the young Häuptling Wüstenwolf.

Behind the noble nomads, rank upon rank of mounted warriors rode, equal parts men and women. The lack of distinction had startled Frenz more than anything as they had prepared for battle, even more than the speed of their preparations. The contrast to his home province, where women were considered good for nothing more than childbirth, caring for the home, and using whatever magic they were born with, was striking.

The herd barreled across the dry land. For a while, the only sounds filling the air were the heavy hoofbeats and breathing of the horses and the occasional cries of excitement from the humans. It wasn't long before the camp became visible, the fires already dancing through it a testament to Flame Tongue's desire for revenge.

"This way!" Wolfrik called as they approached the camp.

His mount was already shifting right, directing Last Chance and Nightmare along the outskirts of the camp. At the same time, Frenz could see the häuptlinge breaking off, each one leading a portion of mounted warriors toward different parts of the camp.

Wolfrik led Frenz, as well as those among the younger nomads who regarded them as friends, toward the farthest point of the camp. While the rest of their allies would fight the Gift Clans, it had been agreed that their small group would find the Drache Krieger and get him to a place where Flame Tongue could reach him. With luck, she would renew the dragonbond.

They were approaching the small pool of water at the center of the oasis when Frenz spotted a slumped figure silhouetted against the moons-lit spring. Suddenly, his chest ached heavily, and he urged Last Chance faster, passing Wolfrik easily. The Mindspeaker might have called his name, but Frenz wouldn't be distracted from the small figure.

He swung off Last Chance's back before the mare had come to a full halt beside the post, and he stopped in front of the hanging figure. The ache in his chest rose to his throat as he finally got a good look at the boy.

Caffers—*James*, he corrected himself—was strung up by his wrists, his arms pulled taut as his body hung, unsupported by his legs. His tunic was darker than the other nomads' were and had been slit down the middle. However, instead of hanging open, the cloth clung oddly to the boy's body.

Frowning, Frenz pulled the tunic away from the boy's skin and stared, uncomprehending, at the darkness that was revealed. The farmer shifted to let the light of the moons and the fires reach the boy. His stomach cramped as he realized what he was seeing.

Blood covered the boy's entire torso. Frenz could hardly make out the bandages binding his chest or the near blackness of the rest of his bare skin. Horror chilled him, and he reached out with two shaky fingers. Praying he'd find a sign of life, he pressed them to the boy's neck.

Despite the slickness beneath his fingers, Frenz breathed out in relief. The thick coating of blood could not hide the soft flutter beneath the boy's skin.

It was steady.

Pressure against his side and back finally pulled his attention away from the boy. Last Chance and Nightmare eyed him worriedly, and Wolfrik and the others were just dismounting.

"He's alive!" Frenz called to them before turning back to the boy. He had the sudden urge to see the boy's face, which so far had been hidden behind a curtain of chin-length black hair. Reaching for the boy's chin, he hooked a finger beneath it and lifted it to the light.

He gasped and nearly sobbed. The boy's face was just as

dark and bloodied as his torso, and there was a ragged hole in his bottom lip.

But it was his eyes, dark purple and hauntingly distant, that made tears spring to Frenz's own. Those amethyst orbs were achingly familiar, despite Frenz's lack of memories, but they stared aimlessly, unseeing and hollow.

"Wha' did they do to yeh?"

Something strong gripped Frenz's shoulder, and he turned to stare at Wolfrik, who watched James worriedly. "Let's get him down, freund," the Mindspeaker whispered. "Dame Flammezunge is—"

A roar cut him off. A heavy *whumpf* shook the ground as the dragon landed nearby. Her wings were opened to their fullest, her tail scraping back and forth quickly across the ground, and her jaws spread wide. Combined with her blazing red eyes, she looked as if she would attack them as readily as she had attacked their enemies.

Nodding sharply to Wolfrik, Frenz wrapped his arms securely around James's body. He winced as a high-pitched whine became audible and pitched higher. As Wolfrik sliced the rope securing James's wrists to the post, Ferez realized that fine shivers shook the boy's body. He pursed his lips grimly.

The moment James's wrists dropped from the post, Frenz grabbed them and held them up for the Mindspeaker to cut the remainder of their bindings. Before Wolfrik could do much more than grip them as well, Flame Tongue lunged.

~~*~*

Flame Tongue growled as she swiped a hand between her bondmate and the other humans, pulling the girl against her chest. From the first whiff of her bondmate's scent, she had understood exactly why the name the nomads had provided had not felt correct. She doubted a female would have been given the name James on her Naming Day.

She continued to growl as Frenz stepped forward. He held one hand out toward her; the other hung down by his side, lightly gripping a knife.

"Easy, Flame Tongue," he murmured. "I won' hurt him." The dragon pitched her growl higher, but the farmer did not even flinch. "I jus' wanna cut the bindin's on his wrists afore they do any more damage."

Crooning in confusion, Flame Tongue tilted her head down to look at her human bondmate. She whined as she caught sight of the rope still binding her wrists and the blue tint to her hands that indicated a lack of blood flow.

When she turned her panicked gaze back to the farmer, he quickly stepped forward, caught up the girl's hands, and sawed through the coarse material. A soon as it dropped away, he backed up and sheathed the knife.

He spoke again, but Flame Tongue let her focus narrow to her human bondmate. The girl was wounded and distressed. Flame Tongue trusted this group of humans—not to mention several of the horses—well enough to guard them while she did what she needed to.

She nuzzled the right side of the girl's neck and shoulders, where she could smell her own scent most strongly. Offering a prayer to the gods that the bonding bite would work on the girl when it had not on Nightmare, the dragon opened her mouth, carefully settled her teeth across the girl's chest and upper back, and gently bit down.

~~*~*

Frenz winced as Flame Tongue bit James. He'd seen the

dragon do the same to Nightmare earlier and had known it was what she'd planned to do to the Drache Krieger. But watching the red-and-purple dragon latch her teeth across the base of the neck of a creature almost as large as she was one thing. It was a completely different beast to see her crouching over James, nearly obscuring him in her embrace, and biting down on his shoulder with a jaw as large as his torso. Protests welled up in Ferez's throat, but yelling distracted him and pulled his attention toward the enemy camp.

Several nomads ran toward them. Frenz couldn't see the color of their statusgürtel from this distance, but they didn't look friendly.

"Komme, freund!" Wolfrik unsheathed his second scharfmond. "Let's see how well the Drache Krieger's lessons took."

Frenz frowned at the Mindspeaker, though he unsheathed his sword. Before he could ask what the man meant, the enemy nomads were upon them and Frenz was forced to duck the swipe of a scharfmond.

As he straightened, stepping back to avoid another swipe, the farmer eyed his enemy. The man held his hands in front of him as though he were engaging in a fistfight.

Except fistfights don't usually involve curved blades that hover over your opponent's knuckles.

He'd seen Wolfrik's blades. He'd known that nomads fought with weapons Frenz wanted to call boxing blades. However, it hadn't occurred to him until now that he'd have to fight against them.

Frenz continued to dodge his enemy's swipes, suddenly reluctant to attack with his own blade. It wasn't so much the knowledge that he had never fought against a nomad that made him hesitate. That had never been an issue during the war, when he'd learned to fight and succeed against various techniques.

It was the cold fear seeping through him and pressing on his chest that made him reluctant. For some reason, he *knew* the consequences of attacking a nomad with his blade would be disastrous.

"Easy, freund," Wolfrik's voice whispered through Frenz's mind. *"You were injured once, ja, but the Drache Krieger trained you himself to prevent another such incident."*

The words didn't ease Frenz's fear, only substantiated it. *How long could the boy have possibly trained me?* Panic drove the thought, even as Frenz ducked another swipe of his opponent's scharfmond.

"Three täge."

Three days? That's hardly—

Frenz yelped as pain lanced through his arm and up to his shoulder. He'd become distracted and straightened too soon. He jumped back from the blade with a curse.

At least that wasn't my sword arm.

"You're thinking too hard, freund. It may have only been three days, but I can assure you, the Drache Krieger trained you until the techniques were instinctive." Amusement filled his mind. *"And when have your instincts ever failed you?"*

Frenz gritted his teeth. The Mindspeaker was right. He usually let his instincts take over when he fought.

So why am I letting fear take over instead?

"Are you going to fight me, ausländer?" his attacker suddenly sneered. "Or are you just going to dance all nacht?"

Frenz glared at the man. He was dressed in the usual garb of the nomads and fought with scharfmonde, aye. But otherwise, he was just like any other man Frenz had fought.

No reason I can't treat him like any other enemy.

The nomad snorted. "Are you mute as well as weak?"

"Nay, jus' tired o' yeh thrashin' about."

And Frenz stepped forward and attacked.

The nomad scrambled to catch Frenz's sword against his scharfmond and swiped at Frenz with the other. The farmer caught the blow against a knife he'd unsheathed at some point before twisting the smaller blade and digging the point into the man's forearm.

The nomad cried out and jumped back from Frenz. The farmer pursued him, his blade already aiming for the man's gut. Two blows later, the nomad was incapacitated, and Frenz turned to find his next opponent.

~~*~*

As soon as Flame Tongue bit her human bondmate, she feared the battle for their bond was already lost. She had hoped to break the mental barrier with the physical connection between her and the girl, but even with the bonding venom flowing into the girl's bloodstream, the barrier stood solid in her mind.

The dragon growled and threw her mental awareness against the foreign magic, but it did not even shift. She dragged mental claws across it and snapped at it, but nothing seemed to affect it.

You cannot keep me from her, she snarled at the magic. *I will not let a human, no matter how powerful, prevent me from reaching my bondmates.*

Flame Tongue continued to beat on and claw at the barrier. Surely, if she flooded the girl with enough bonding venom and applied enough pressure to the magic, something would give.

She could not say how long she had crouched there, focused on the magic, when a small pressure on her neck, just behind her horns, caught her attention. Snarling softly around her bondmate's shoulder, Flame Tongue opened one eye and glared at the human who dared to touch her.

She hesitated, though, when she spotted the human. Bearing a belt of double purple, she was one of the six who had found her bondmate. But it was her wide black eyes that caught Flame Tongue's own red one. So like Häuptling Kanten's, both in color and worry.

"What?" she demanded. Her voice growled out from around her bondmate's shoulder, but she did not fear the girl misunderstanding her. The girl's magic declared her a Mindspeaker.

"I can tell you her real name, if that would help."

The words were hardly more than a breath. Only Flame Tongue's excellent hearing allowed her to catch them.

"You know it?" Once she had realized the truth about her bondmate, Flame Tongue had wondered if any of her allies knew.

"Of course. She's my schwester." The girl paused and glanced over her shoulder. It sounded like the fighting had intensified. The girl turned back and whispered hurriedly. "Her given name is Gemini Cosley."

Flame Tongue hissed as the name echoed within her mind. Unlike the name James Caffers, this one felt utterly right, and Flame Tongue's mind rang with it.

Slowly, the ringing grew louder and deeper, reverberating through her like the voice of a siren seeking the pitch necessary to draw her in. Unlike a siren's voice, though, Flame Tongue thought this would draw her to her bondmates, not to her death.

Suddenly, a soft *crack* broke through the ringing. It was followed by several more *cracks*, each louder than the last, and the image of a black-haired, amethyst-eyed girl quickly overwhelmed her.

Unlike the human she was now biting, the one in the image—*nay, memory*—was much younger. Her hair tumbled across her shoulders and down her back in hectic disarray, and those gem-like eyes stared at Flame Tongue with confusion, fear, and not a small amount of admiration.

Gemi.

The word was a mere breath passing through her mind, but the dragon knew *that* was her bondmate's true name. *That* was the name of the girl who had stumbled across the San River with Nightmare. *That* was the name of the girl who had nearly died after tumbling from the stallion's back. *That* was the name of the girl with whom Flame Tongue had dragonbonded to prevent her death.

Holding onto that image, Flame Tongue snarled and slammed herself against the foreign magic separating her from Gemi. This time, instead of standing solidly against her blow, the magic shuddered and pieces crumbled away. Her hope restored, the dragon renewed her efforts against the barrier.

With each blow, more of the magic broke off. Soon, one portion gave way, and Flame Tongue heard a startled whinny as her sense of Nightmare—*nay, his name is Shadow!*—was restored.

"Flame?"

The stallion sounded confused, but that lasted only a few seconds before he was cursing like a drunk human. *"I swear, if that Mindspeaker . . ."*

The stallion trailed off as a heavy pressure against Flame's side alerted her to his presence. *"And Gemi?"*

Flame brushed her mind against his before turning back to the remainder of the barrier. As she had worked, her memories had slowly resurfaced. She could now remember life on Cosley Estate, the estate's destruction, and some of the years that had followed as Gemi gained her revenge and worked to unite the rebellious groups across Evon.

"Just a little longer," the dragon growled and attacked the thick magic once more.

It only took a few more blows before a shiver resonated through Flame and Shadow's minds and the barrier finally dissolved completely. With a roar of triumph, Flame pressed through the newly revealed bond.

And pulled up short when all she found was darkness and despair.

Whining, Flame stared at the mental landscape surrounding her. Where she once would have found bright, lively forests that resembled Gemi's birth province, now there were only dark, desolate mountains.

Cold swept through Flame. Even the mountainous province of Tarsur looked more alive than this.

It was not just the change in scenery that worried the dragon, either. The very air, what made up the essence of Gemi's mind, was so full of doubt, fear, and guilt that Flame could not even sense the girl's consciousness.

Snarling softly, Flame launched herself into the sky of her bondmate's mind, her gaze searching for some sign of Gemi. The dark emotions clung to her wings and body, dragging her down and making her flight slow.

She could not be certain how long she spent fighting those emotions before she discovered a sign of Gemi's awareness. What Flame had, at first, mistaken for a dark cloud hanging above one mountain's empty peak turned out to be a flock of dark flying creatures.

Once closer, Flame realized the peak was not as empty as she had assumed. At its highest point lay a small child, younger than Flame had ever known Gemi, curled into a ball and huddled in on herself. The creatures that circled her flew down one by one and besieged her.

For a moment, as Flame struggled to reach Gemi, she wondered if Gemi's memories had also been suppressed by the Mindspeaker. Only the heaviness of the emotions surrounding her and the darkness of the flying creatures convinced Flame that Gemi still remembered.

Nay, the Mindspeaker had done something much worse to Gemi than take her memories.

When Flame finally reached the peak, she snarled at the flying creatures, swiping at them with claws and lashing out with her wings and tail. Her anger quickly turned to confusion as her claws passed straight through the creatures without affecting them, and the child beneath her continued to whimper.

"Gemi?" Flame nudged the small form. A small shiver was the child's only response, accompanied by a wave of loneliness and despair that nearly knocked the dragon from the mountain peak.

Nay, Flame whined, but there was no denying the evidence.

The Mindspeaker had broken Gemi's faith in Flame and Shadow and had thrown her into a despair so deep that Flame would not be able to affect the girl's mind until she could assure her of their love and constancy.

Pulling Shadow's awareness to her own, Flame wrapped their presences around the small child. *"We are here, Gemi,"* she cooed as Shadow echoed her sentiments. *"We will always find you, no matter what."*

Four

Isa Kanten, scarred elder schwester of the erstehäuptling, ducked a scharfmond and struck with her own, finally managing to carve a deep gash in her feind's hip. She had missed the mann's stomach—her intended target—but he still faltered as he shifted his weight. His next blow glanced off her raised scharfmond as she sliced his throat with the other.

Stepping back to avoid the falling body, Isa scanned the surrounding camp. When they had first arrived, she had been shocked by the sheer number of tents the Gift Clans had set up in this tiny, stubborn oase. But as they'd begun their attack, she had been even more surprised by just how few warriors remained. They were highly trained, though, which seemed to make up the difference.

Did Flame truly manage to kill so many before we arrived?

Isa doubted it. Several times now, she had noticed movement behind tent entrance flaps, scuffles that suggested people trying to leave but held back by others. There were also the faces she had seen peering from the tents, watching with wide eyes as the Vereinte Clans took their revenge.

"Isana!"

Isa twitched her head to one side. The mental voice had disrupted her observation, and she reached her magie through the geisternetz to find the source.

Most of the geisternetz was distracted by the physical conflict, but there was a portion of it that appeared to be locked in mental battle. Brushing against one of the geister involved, she quickly discovered that Wüstenwolf had been engaged by Häuptling Giftschwanz and what appeared to be his three eldest sons, all of whom were Geistmagier. The Wolf häuptling had enlisted others to lend their magie against the Skorpione.

"Isana!"

The cry cut through Isa's geist again, even as she considered joining the battle against the Skorpione. Realizing the cry wasn't coming from the battle-locked group, she turned away in search of its source once more.

Searching the geisternetz, Isa quickly found the two other Geistmagier who weren't distracted by the physical: her niece, Ulla, and their newest ally, Häuptling Giftschwanz's youngest son.

"Wolfrik?"

"Isana, we've found the Drache Krieger. He's alive, but . . ."

A chill ran down her spine. *"But? But what?"*

"He looks broken, Isana."

The words were quiet and despairing, and the chill settled into Isa's stomach. Most might know the Drache Krieger as a boy, a young warrior who helped Isa's bruder unite the clans after centuries of disparity. But to Isa, Gemi was just another member of her bruder's familie, her niece.

If they managed to break Gemi . . .

"*He reeks of Geistmagie, too,*" Wolfrik continued, "*magie I recognize.*"

The cold in Isa's stomach suddenly wrenched into boil, and she clenched her fingers more tightly around the hilts of her scharfmonde. Her entire vision narrowed to a point, and she snapped her head around to stare toward her sense of Wolfrik.

"*Show me!*"

Wolfrik's mental presence tensed beneath the lash of her demand, but he offered a name and the image of a Schlange several jahre older than him. Isa wasn't interested in either. Instead, she latched onto the impression of magie that accompanied them, breathing it in as a hunting hound would the scent of its prey.

"*Danke!*"

Wolfrik murmured a reply, but Isa was already turning her attention back to the camp. Spreading her awareness, she sought the magie of the mann Wolfrik had named—this Adalwolf. As she did, she collected her clansmänner to her, calling on them for assistance.

If the Schlange had hurt her niece, he would not survive the battle.

She had gathered the power of nearly every Geistmagier not helping Wüstenwolf by the time she found an area flooded with the magie she sought. While most of the fighting dwindled as the Vereinte Clans overwhelmed the Gift Clans, the battle here still continued strong. It took nearly a full minute of staring for Isa to understand why.

Her gut twisted. Of the ten nomaden fighting, only one actually bore the brown or black statusgürtel of one of the Gift Clans. Yet even he appeared to be more of a bystander than a participant. The rest, their statusgürtel marked with purple, red, yellow, blue, or green, fought among themselves, turning their scharfmonde on each other and aiming to kill.

As she watched, something flickered within her geist, and several of the fighting nomaden suddenly wore black and brown where she knew she had seen more colorful statusgürtel only a moment before.

Growling, Isa slashed her magie across the first layer of her geist, slicing through the foreign tendrils seeping through her defenses. A hiss filled her geist as her allies' statusgürtel returned to their correct colors.

"Let them go, Adalwolf!"

The Schlange's only answer was silent laughter against her geist. Her fighting allies paused in their attacks and glanced at each other in obvious confusion.

"She caused this!" The gruff accusation rose from within the crowd—Adalwolf! "She's the one who turned us against each other."

Isa cursed. The other nomaden, her allies, turned on her as one. Just beyond them, she spied the Schlange offering her a cruel smirk.

"Can you fight your own people, Isana Kanten?"

Isa snarled and ducked one of her allies' blades. She wasn't surprised that the Schlange knew who she was; her scarred face had been well known throughout the clans even before unification.

His complete disregard for the geister of others—it made her blood boil even more furiously. Even if he wasn't the force behind Gemi's pain, that would have been enough to condemn him.

Dodging attacks, she directed the power she'd gained from the geisternetz toward her attacking allies' geister. She didn't have the skill of concentration to remove the

Schlange's influence from them completely, but she could at least confuse them until she'd disposed of him.

~~*~*

Adalwolf smirked as Kanten ducked and danced away from the blows of her freunde. Despite the fierce appearance of her half-melted face, he knew she would be unwilling to risk their lives the way a Schlange would. It wouldn't take long before one of them caught her with his blade. She was doomed.

Not that he feared confronting her himself. Despite rumors that she was the strongest Geistmagier among the Vereinte Clans, Adalwolf doubted the frau could best him in a contest of the geist. But if he could destroy her without spending much effort, he was unwilling to pass up the opportunity.

Unfortunately, the hexe wasn't cooperating. Somehow, she managed to stall her clansmänner's attacks. As soon as they faltered, she twisted past them and strode straight for Adalwolf.

Adalwolf snarled, a sound born of anticipation as much as hatred. If Isana Kanten could hinder nine nomaden and yet still focus so intently on Adalwolf, she was more powerful than he'd expected. The Schlange thrilled at the chance to prove his magie against such a person.

He met her, scharfmond to scharfmond, geist to geist. They pressed forward with blade and magie, each attempting to find an opening in the other's defenses.

Adalwolf hissed triumphantly as he pushed past her defenses first, slipping his magie into her geist. He had a quick glimpse of bright water and tangled greenery before the bite of a blade against his wrist forced him back. He snarled.

Kanten simply bared her teeth in response. *Such a fitting expression,* he considered, admiring how the expression complemented her scarred features.

Unfortunately, the thought cost him.

Kanten quickly locked blades with him and shoved through his mental defenses, faster than should have been possible. He scrambled to rectify the situation and throw her back out, but she had already dived further into his geist than he had first recognized.

Already, she had begun to tear at his geist.

Snarling, Adalwolf slammed down walls around her presence. If he couldn't remove her, then he would imprison her.

A dark, violent chuckle reached Adalwolf's ears then. He recognized it well, having heard it time and again over the past few siebentäge. It belonged to the disembodied voice that had given Adalwolf the information he'd needed to lead his clan and their allies against the Vereinte Clans. That it would come to him now though, when he hadn't heard it since they'd captured Gemini Cosley, was distracting.

"Now is not the time!" Adalwolf snapped mentally. He couldn't allow his focus to be diverted from the magie threatening to overwhelm his geist.

"Now is exactly the time, Geistmagier."

Adalwolf gasped. He could no longer see the tents and nomaden surrounding him. Neither was he seeing the maze of tents of his own geist. Instead, his vision was filled with a view he could hardly process.

Lights dotted a strangely familiar scene. It appeared strangely distant yet, at the same time, painfully exact in its detail. As Kanten broke free of her impromptu mental prison, the vision shifted and Adalwolf finally realized what he was seeing. It was an aerial view of an oase camp, reminiscent of memories he'd seen when he had invaded the drache's geist.

The realization was followed by the sharp understanding that it was a view of Trostlosoase during the current battle. Whether it actually showed what was currently happening, Adalwolf couldn't be certain.

Pain ripped through Adalwolf's geist, a sure sign that Kanten was wreaking havoc while he was distracted.

"Why do you show me this?" He reached for the voice that had advised him these last few siebentäge. The presence he found was thicker than he remembered, as if the voice had gained substance since he had last felt it.

"To show you what your arrogance has wrought."

Confusion mingled with pain. Adalwolf had the vague impression of falling to his knees. He could no longer control his physical body. The mental battle and distraction had made certain of that.

"Yet you still don't understand, do you?" The dark sneer no longer held the humor to which the Schlange had become accustomed. *"Shall I show you, Adalwolf?"*

Adalwolf's attention was forcibly directed to the oase's spring. Beside it crouched the drache, her teeth firmly entrenched in the body of Gemini Cosley. The black stallion leaned against her side. Despite Adalwolf's desire to focus on that and fume, he was directed to the battle occurring only body lengths away.

Six nomaden fought fiercely to protect the drache and her bondmates. Despite the pain spreading through his geist, Adalwolf could see just why the voice was showing him this.

"They trust Wolfrik enough to let him fight by their sides?"

The question didn't hold nearly enough incredulity for Adalwolf's liking, but he blamed that on the pain.

"And enough to follow him here to the camp of your clans."

Adalwolf hissed. *"How? They should have turned against him and torn him apart."*

"They might have if you had not left alive the one mann capable of talking them out of it."

Adalwolf recalled the voice's words from when he'd learned that Gemini Cosley's human companion was the king of Evon: he would lead an army to hunt Adalwolf down if he was left alive.

"Making him forget should have been enough."

The words were weak now, buried in pain. For the first time, Adalwolf feared there was something that could defeat him despite his Geistmagie and it would tear him apart until he was nothing but an empty shell.

"Yet it obviously was not!" the voice snarled. *"And even if it had been, who are you to defy me, mortal?"*

Cold washed through Adalwolf, numbing him to the pain for several long seconds. *Mortal?* A disembodied geist had no reason to refer to Adalwolf as such, unless . . .

Who are you?

The thought was nearly lost among the pain. Adalwolf forced himself to focus, needing to know the truth.

"What are you?"

The violent chuckle returned, digging deeper into Adalwolf's geist than he had ever heard it before.

"I have been speaking to you for nearly a month, and only now you wish to know who I am?"

The violent presence settled deeper, filling him more than Kanten ever could.

"Very well, then." Violence ripped through Adalwolf, so pure he would have screamed if he still could. *"I am Krieg."*

I am War.

~~*~*

Unknown to the mortals, a humanoid figure of black and red sneered as the Schlange collapsed. The human's mind was gone, destroyed by the Kanten Mindspeaker. The body would soon follow.

Such a waste.

Black and red swirled murkily beneath translucent skin as the demigod paced angrily alongside the body. War had spent the last four sevendays guiding the human against his enemies, leading him to capture the one person the Gift Clans saw as a threat above all others.

The one "mortal" War even cared about right now: his physically incarnated twin.

Pea—

War stopped still and hissed, clamping his hands around his temples. For two hundred years after she'd disappeared into the Cycle of Incarnation, he'd mourned her loss and dealt with the pain of her absence. But now that she had returned to the Mortal Realm, he couldn't even think her name without such pain rising up within him that it threatened to tear him apart.

War risked a glance at the still creature clutched within the dragon's arms. Her purple soul moved darkly and sluggishly within the mortal form. He nodded. That was at least one thing he could take pleasure in since Adalwolf's disobedience. The amnesiac king might have been able to redirect War's influence on the clans from the Skorpion siblings to the Poison Clans, but he hadn't been able to do it fast enough to save *her* from some understanding of the pain War had been through since her "death."

Now if only Adalwolf had broken her enough to make her remember who she truly is, I might not have interfered.

War sneered down at the worthless body at his feet before turning his attention to the surrounding camp. The few Poison Clan nomads who still fought would soon be defeated, he was certain. There was no reason for him to remain here now that his link to the clans had been destroyed.

"To Tarsur, then," he muttered. "Surely I can find something there to remind her of the truth." Closing his eyes, he Transported himself away from the dwindling battle.

~~*~*

Isa shivered as she stared down at the Schlange's body. She should have felt satisfaction from destroying the mann, especially after seeing his memories of torturing Gemi. Yet the chill she had felt when Wolfrik first caught her attention had returned.

Adalwolf had been a formidable opponent. His magie had rivaled her own in strength. Even with the assistance of the others to distract the nomaden he had influenced, she had feared she would not be able to defeat him.

But the tides had shifted in her favor when that strange voice began to speak to him. Isa had been all too willing to take advantage of the Schlange's distraction, but she had seen the vision the presence had shown him and heard its words. Both had shaken her, though not enough to keep her from her vengeance.

Now Isa turned her eyes toward the spot where she'd last heard the voice. Its words still rang through her geist, tightening her chest and threatening her breath in a way she refused to acknowledge. It had called itself Krieg and spoken of Tarsur and of making "her" remember. Isa feared it was the disembodied enemy Gemi and Frenz had mentioned.

Then there's the matter of the king.

Bitterness filled Isa's throat. It didn't come so much from the knowledge that Ferez Katani had hidden among them as from the realization that they might have lost Evon its king while he was under their care.

Isa's worries were cut short as fear suddenly rang through a geist to which she was always connected. Cursing, Isa turned back to where she knew her younger bruder still fought.

"Hausef!"

~~*~*

The black-eyed erstehäuptling hit the ground hard. Pain ripped through his back and right arm, and darkness threatened his vision.

"You will pay for killing my son, Kanten!"

Hausef, who had yet to see his attacker, froze in his attempt to turn over. That overpowering voice was familiar, and the reference to him killing a son . . .

Hausef's last opponent had worn the double black of a Schlange adliger.

"Überalle."

The Schlange häuptling snarled and snatched Hausef up and around by his wounded shoulder. Thick fingers dug into torn flesh and strained muscles, stealing what little strength Hausef still had. He blinked back flashes of darkness and focused on steadying his breath. He barely managed to meet the massive Schlange's angry glare.

"You think you are better than the rest of us," Überalle snapped. "You call yourself erstehäuptling and demand we follow you, but I won't have it!"

He shook Hausef, who gasped and squeezed his eyes shut. The pain in his back was spreading lower.

"I will kill you, Kanten, and Protect what is mine. Do you understand me?"

"Bruder, nein!"

At first, Hausef thought the words were Isa's, and he opened both his eyes and his mouth to warn her away. But his words died before they could leave his tongue. The frau approaching from behind Häuptling Überalle not only was missing his schwester's scars but also wore a strap across her eyes, marking her as blind.

"Stay out of this, Madelhari!"

"Nein, I won't!" Despite her blindness, the frau's steps were unhesitating, her stride confident. "I won't let you destroy our clan more than you already have."

Überalle's fingers dug deeper into Hausef's shoulder, drawing another pained gasp from him. The Schlange häuptling swung around to glare at the frau as she came to a stop only feet from them.

"How dare you!"

"I dare because no one else will, bruder. When you became häuptling, you promised me you would right our ancestors' wrongs and return our familie to its true purpose. Instead, you corrupted the name Überalle even more than our vater did."

"I gave our clan purpose," the Schlange häuptling snapped. "I Protected the ways of our people."

"And destroyed our clan in the process!" Desperation colored the words. "Look around, bruder! Our people are dying. It's not our clan you Protect, but your verdammte values. They aren't even the ancient ways!"

"Enough!" Überalle snarled. "I will not stand here and

listen to such drivel from you, Madelhari. Yours is not to question me."

He turned back to Hausef and raised his scharfmond to the erstehäuptling's throat. "I must Protect what is mine!"

Hausef tried to pull away from Überalle's one-handed grip, but his fingers might as well have been stone. The pain in Hausef's back was spreading toward his hips. His legs felt as though they were made of cloth for all the strength that was left in them. As it was, it was only Überalle's hold that was keeping Hausef upright.

The one thing he managed in his struggles was to catch sight of a young face peering around Madelhari's shoulder. The child stared at him with wide eyes, her bottom lip caught between her teeth. There was such pain and determination in her gaze that Hausef closed his eyes and let his body go limp.

I've failed, he thought as cold steel pressed against his throat. *I've failed my people . . . my familie . . .*

Überalle's blade burned as it broke the skin.

Gemi . . .

Regret and resignation filled him until he didn't even dare to fight against the pain. Even the screams ringing through the air couldn't make him fight.

My people looked to me for peace, and this is where I've brought them: krieg and the attempted destruction of an entire clan.

A sudden jerk ripped through Hausef's body, and the burning pain abruptly slipped around the side of his neck. Just as quickly, the fingers on his shoulder disappeared, and Hausef collapsed to the ground with a pained grunt. Snapping open his eyes, he stared uncomprehendingly up at Überalle, who knelt beside him, mouth half open and unarmed hand half raised toward his shoulder.

"Nei—"

Überalle choked, his face sagged, and he dropped forward, unmoving. Hausef stared at the scharfmond embedded in the mann's upper back and neck.

Fatal . . .

The disconnected thought filled Hausef's geist, leaving awareness for little more than someone's choked sob and Isa's voice calling his name. Hausef didn't know how long he'd been staring at the buried blade when a hand appeared and wrapped around its handle. Snapping his gaze up to the hand's owner, he had to close his eyes a moment later as his vision spun and his geist wavered.

"Steady, Erstehäuptling. I didn't stop my bruder only for you to die because you worsened your own wounds."

Hausef was vaguely aware of both Isa and a Heilemagier she had summoned speaking as well, but it was the blind frau's words that pulled him from his dizziness.

"You saved my life."

Madelhari Überalle tilted her head as she wiped the blade of her scharfmond clean, and the lines around her lips softened. Hausef had the disconcerting feeling that she was staring right at him despite the strap covering her blind eyes.

"You are the erstehäuptling, Hausef Kanten, no matter what my bruder wished to believe. I have Seen the chaos that would have followed your death, and even my bruder could not have Protected against it."

Beside him, Isa stiffened. "You have the Heiligesicht?"

The words were hardly more than a whisper, but Hausef's breath hitched. Out of all the magie at the clans' disposal, the Heiligesicht was so rare that the Zhulanese didn't even have a word for those born with the gift.

"A Seer," he breathed in awe, though his next thought quickly chilled him. *That explains her unerring aim.*

Madelhari offered a wan smile and a shallow nod. "A

Seer, ja. It is the reason for my physical blindness." She brushed her fingers against the strap over her eyes. "That I might See better."

Hausef grimaced. He had never agreed with the belief that blinding a child born with the Heiligesicht increased the gift. He'd always considered it a weak excuse to cover a painful test of the child's claim.

"You're a Seer, yet you killed your own bruder?"

Hausef glanced at his schwester curiously. She wasn't normally one to regret the death of a feind, especially one who had threatened her familie, but she stared at the Seer, pale-faced and wide-eyed.

"Yet?" Madelhari mused. "I think you confuse the Heiligesicht with the ability to convince others of what I See, Isana Kanten."

The Schlange shook her head. "The first vision I ever Saw was of my bruder dying by my hand. I could not fathom then why I might do such a thing, but my bruder has broken so many promises since he became häuptling. Even if I hadn't known he would die by my hand, I couldn't let him continue as he was. His very magie was destroying our clan. I had to end it."

His magie? Hausef frowned, distracted by her use of the phrase. *Überalle didn't have magie. I've known that since—*

"As did I."

Hausef started and stared. That was the child he had noticed before. Her words were strong despite the wetness on her cheeks, and her gaze was direct. Hausef blinked. She was older than he had first thought. *Perhaps Gemi's age?*

Madelhari laid a hand on the girl's shoulder. "Erstehäuptling, may I present Rosa Überalle, my bruder's eldest remaining child."

Hausef nodded, trying to ignore the heaviness that took

up residence in his heart. Rosa was eldest now because he had killed her older bruder.

He was trying to kill me, he argued silently.

The guilt only grew heavier.

"Es tut mir leid for your loss, Fräulein Rosa."

The girl shook her head. "I don't blame you, Erstehäuptling. My vater Protected his values even as our clan was dying around him. It is not your fault Klaus did the same."

"I—"

"Hausef!"

"Erstehäuptling!"

The cries interrupted Hausef, and he glanced around to find the other häuptlinge converging on them. Roswalt of the Pferde and Meinhard of the Falken still had their scharfmonde in hand, while Genevieve of the Spinnen was half carrying a limping and bloody Wüstenwolf.

Hausef was so distracted by the sight of the wounded Wolf that he didn't realize Roswalt had turned to the Schlangen with raised blades until Rosa cried out. "Bitte, we mean no harm!"

"Roswalt, stand down!" Hausef followed the command with a groan as the pain in his torso flared.

"Honestly, Erstehäuptling." The Heilemagier huffed and coaxed him into a more comfortable position. "You must rest."

Hausef grimaced but let the Heilemagier do her work. He just hoped someone stopped Roswalt before he did something regrettable.

~~*~*

Meinhard grabbed the Pferd by the arms before he could

attack. "You heard the erstehäuptling, Roswalt." Tugging him away from the Schlangen females, he added lowly, "They aren't a threat to any of us."

"But—"

"Nein, Roswalt!" Suddenly, the Falke wished Alys were nearby. Out of all the clans, she was the only one who could reliably control her vater's temper. "The battle is over. I'm sure Hausef has already begun to talk peace with these Schlangen."

Roswalt sneered and broke away from Meinhard's grasp, but he didn't approach the Schlangen again. Nodding, the Falke turned back to the females.

The blind frau turned to face him as well, and Meinhard glanced away quickly. He didn't need to be told to know she had the Heiligesicht. It was the only reason his magie would react to her nonexistent gaze as if he were being hunted.

Like any Schutzmagier, his magie was subtle, preferring to act without acknowledgment or discovery. After all, it was so much easier to Protect something when others didn't realize you had magie to actively do so.

It was the reason his familie had spent generations encouraging the belief that Schutzmagie had been lost along with the six other magie that had disappeared about a millennium before. It was sometimes difficult to explain why their line bore other kinds of magier when most of them were supposedly nonmagical, but the anonymity of their Schutzmagie was worth it.

As he turned from the Seer, his gaze landed on the girl beside her, whose gaze was fixed on Hausef. He blinked. She radiated Schutzmagie.

Another line of Schutzmagier?

Meinhard had never had to deal with Häuptling Überalle himself, but he did recall the rumors that the Überalle familie was a häuptling line that depended on physical strength rather than the magical that most of the others did.

I suppose that explains the conflicting Protections I sensed earlier.

Meinhard grimaced. If he was correct, this girl had used her magie to cancel her vater's so the mann could be killed. It was the only way he knew to kill a Schutzmagier who was actively focused on his Protections.

"Unfortunately," the Seer spoke, pulling Meinhard's attention reluctantly back to her, "while the physical battle might have ended, I fear the worst is not yet over."

"What do you mean?" Roswalt snapped before anyone else could ask.

The Seer bowed her head, but it was Isa who answered, her voice rougher than Meinhard had ever heard it.

"James."

Five

As Madelhari had known it would, the fighting ended with her bruder's death. Now, healers and Heilemagier swarmed the camp, healing wounds and doing what they could to save the lives of those who had fought.

She wasn't really concerned about the lives of the Schlangen who had fought. Those warriors never would have accepted life among the Vereinte Clans, which was inevitable, or Rosa as their next häuptling, despite the ancient tradition that said frauen made just as strong leaders as männer.

Even the Skorpione who had fought had been restricted to those with similar beliefs. While Madelhari had spread news of the coming attack among the more accepting of her clansmänner, she had heard murmurs from several Skorpion Geistmagier concerning Wolfrik Giftschwanz and his own warnings. Together, they had saved the majority of their clans from a retribution that could have easily destroyed them all.

What did concern Madelhari was the Drache Krieger. The child had spent the entire nacht under the full power of Adalwolf, unacknowledged son of Madelhari's bruder and—

the Seer grimaced—her eldest nephew. Not for the first time, Madelhari silently cursed her bruder for taking up with the clan schlampe all those jahre ago.

Not that she believed it would have made a difference if Adalwolf had never been born. She had Seen the being that had whispered in her nephew's ear since this entire mess began. No doubt the being would have found another Geistmagier to influence instead if Adalwolf hadn't been available.

Madelhari sighed and turned her head to observe the camp. Nearby, the häuptlinge of the Vereinte Clans had fallen into a solemn discussion of the battle's consequences. The mingling colors of their souls flared and dulled as their passions rose and fell.

Beyond and within the nearby tents—which Madelhari couldn't even See with the Heiligesicht—hundreds of multicolored souls moved throughout the camp. Despite the apparent chaos, her attention was drawn to one particular set: a group of human- and pferd-shaped souls surrounding a large, colorful soul in the shape of a crouching drache.

The drache remained utterly still, the usually bright colors of her soul subdued. Against her side leaned a similarly subdued pferd.

It was the soul in the drache's arms, however, that caught Madelhari's wandering Heiligesicht. Unlike the surrounding humans—or any other mortal creature the Seer had ever met—the soul of the Drache Krieger contained only a single color: a purple so dark as to be nearly black.

The darkness was a sign of the damage Adalwolf had caused, but the single color represented a purity Madelhari had only ever Seen in one type of being: the halbgötter, the demigods. According to the old religion, the halbgötter were immortal beings born to influence certain aspects of mortal life.

Speaking of . . .

Madelhari frowned as she noticed a silver being standing among the humans surrounding the drache. Unlike normal souls, which looked more like colored air taking the rough shape of their mortal shells, this silver being looked physically defined to Madelhari's Heiligesicht.

The being was humanoid in shape, its features perfectly visible to the Seer, even at this distance. Even so, its entire form shone pure silver, a color Madelhari vaguely remembered seeing in some of her mütter's most precious jewelry before her Heiligesicht was discovered and her eyes were taken from her.

Ignoring the bitterness that answered the memory, Madelhari watched as the silver effeminate creature moved through the small crowd, fluttering her hands over the humans without touching them. Remembering the red-and-black being who had influenced Adalwolf these last few seibentäge, Madelhari turned sharply, seeking more of the pure-colored beings with her Heiligesicht. She quickly spotted two more.

Some distance away, a white one, duller than she would have expected, knelt between two dim souls. The Seer frowned when she spotted them. They were obviously gravely wounded, but neither soul belonged to a warrior who had fought in the battle.

After a long moment, Madelhari bowed her head and gritted her teeth. She thought the two must be laid out near the tent that had been caught in the drache's fire.

If they die . . .

She shook her head and turned her attention to the other

halbgott she had Seen. She was surprised she hadn't noticed it earlier. The being—another female—was a pure pink, brighter than the desert roses she remembered from her childhood. However, it wasn't the color that had Madelhari chastising herself for overlooking it, but the fact that it stood right next to Rosa.

The pink female's gaze moved frequently between the häuptlinge and the Schlangen. As Madelhari watched, the halbgott turned back to her and caught her staring. The Seer didn't look away; she was too curious to find out what the pink immortal would do when she realized she had been discovered.

To her surprise, the pink female smiled widely and offered Madelhari a small bow before waving the Seer toward the häuptlinge.

Join the discussion, the being seemed to say. *Make freunde.*

Madelhari snorted. The idea that she could understand the being was ridiculous; the Heiligesicht only offered Sights, not sounds.

Still, the thought was practical. Madelhari turned back to the häuptlinge and stepped forward to offer her own thoughts on how the clans should proceed.

~~*~*

The pink Liebe huffed as the Seer finally joined the häuptlinge's discussion, pulling her niece with her. It was disconcerting that the frau knew she was there, but she wasn't unwilling to influence her so directly, not with the täg they'd all been having.

"Verdammt Krieg," the pink halbgott muttered, cursing her youngest bruder. The red-and-black halbgott had already disappeared too, leaving Liebe and the rest of their schwestern to clean up his mess. "This entire situation is getting out of hand."

Movement caught her attention, and Liebe lifted her gaze to the häuptlinge. Isana Kanten was staring toward her intently, though Liebe *knew* she couldn't see her.

The pink halbgott groaned. *First the Seer, now the Kanten Geistmagier?* She hadn't even realized the scarred frau was powerful enough to hear immortals.

And unlike the Seer, I don't want the Geistmagier knowing I'm here.

Seers were supposed to know things others didn't. It was a consequence of their connection to the Schicksale. At the very least, they knew how to be discreet.

Liebe wasn't sure Kanten would be.

Unwilling to risk the Geistmagier overhearing more from her and satisfied that she had at least started the relationships between these people, Liebe moved away from the group and sought out her schwestern.

White Leben leaned over two bodies near the burned remains of a tent. Her expression was tight, her eyes narrowed, and Liebe knew her own presence wouldn't be welcome.

Silver Hoffnung, on the other hand, flitted anxiously among the small group that had accompanied the king to find their physically incarnated schwester, Frieda. The obvious restlessness worried Liebe, and she hurried over.

Once closer, Liebe whispered her schwester's name. Hoffnung started and spun around, her silver eyes wide and her lips parted in a gasp.

"Oh, Liebe, it's you. I—"

She stiffened and spun back toward the drache, but Liebe couldn't see why. Nothing had changed in that moment. The drache and her bondmates remained unmoving; the humans stood nearby and watched them worriedly.

"I can't—why?" Hoffnung glanced over her shoulder, and Liebe started. Fear filled Hoffnung's wide silver eyes.

"Why did he have to do this, Liebe? No one . . ."

She stepped toward the drache, then seemed to think better of it and turned to one of the humans—the amnesiac king, Liebe noted idly.

"He still feels hope. Why does he still feel it when . . . ?"

Liebe breathed in sharply. Gripping her silver schwester's arm, she pulled the silver halbgott around to face her.

"Hoffnung, what's wrong?" Glancing past her, Liebe added, "Have you been trying to influence Frieda?"

"What—I—nein!" Hoffnung shook her head emphatically. "Frieda's lost. Frieda . . ." She made a sound that reminded Liebe of a human sob. "He hurt her, so badly, and now . . ."

Liebe stared as her younger, silver schwester fell into incoherent mutterings. *This isn't right. There's no reason she should be . . .*

She stiffened, remembering the flare of emotion she'd been feeling when the Geistmagier had overheard her. *If I'm feeling anger and Hoffnung's feeling lost . . .*

The situation was worse than she'd thought. This wasn't just a matter of Hoffnung attempting to influence Frieda. That would have simply exhausted the silver halbgott.

Nein, it's not that simple.

Liebe focused on Frieda's nearly black soul and winced. The physically incarnated halbgott was radiating fear, guilt, and loneliness: all negative emotions.

Liebe closed her eyes and reigned in her influence, uncertain how it might be affecting the mortals.

With her power under control, Love gripped her sister's arms and forced her to look at her.

"Hope! Drop your influence and go find Fear."

Silver eyes darted away from her gaze.

"Can't," Hope muttered. "Have to . . ."

Love clamped her lips together to hold in a growl. The negative emotions were definitely affecting them both.

"We have to get away from Peace." Love spoke slowly, reaching for the love and happiness that were her usual mood. She couldn't find them.

"But—"

"Neither of us can affect her, Hope." Not completely true, but Love didn't think she could invoke much love in her youngest sister now, not when the girl was feeling so alone. "But she's affecting us, and we'll only cause more damage if we stay here."

Hope whined and glanced back at Peace. After a moment more of staring, the silver demigoddess nodded, closed her eyes, and Transported herself away.

Love sighed, hoping her sister found Fear quickly enough. She would need her twin to balance the Chaos threatening to overwhelm her.

To overwhelm us both.

After another long look at Peace's dark form, Love turned away and sought out Life. The eldest demigoddess still knelt between two dying humans; the color shining through her skin was grayer than it should have been.

Determined to send Life to her twin before finding her own, Love approached her elder sister and knelt in front of her.

"Life."

A slight wrinkling of her forehead was the only acknowledgment Life gave that she heard. Her eyes were closed, her hands hovering over the two mortals. Her entire body, Love realized, was shivering.

"Life, we need to leave."

Life mumbled softly, and Love stared. The elder demigoddess had spoken solely in Zhulanese. Not even Zhulanbürger spoke only Zhulanese anymore, opting instead for a mixture of Zhulanese and Fayralese that had served them for centuries.

"Life, you need to go find Death, now. This is hurting you." *Killing you,* Love wanted to say, but she didn't know if that was even possible.

"Nein," Life breathed. "Ich will keinen tod."

Love groaned. If Life refused to leave, Love didn't have much chance of moving her. *Not before she's far too exhausted to fight me, at least.*

Trying to find some way to convince Life to leave immediately, Love glanced at the two mortals she was attempting to save and blinked. She recognized them. They were a couple she'd fought over with Hate for years to bring together. She'd finally succeeded two seasons before, and now . . .

Pressure built in her throat. The sensation was strange and uncomfortable. Even when Peace had disappeared into the Cycle of Incarnation, Love hadn't felt the urge to cry like a human.

"Nay." She shook her head hard. She was letting Peace get to her.

Gripping Life's shoulders, Love leaned forward. "I know it's difficult, Life, but we have to leave. You have to . . ."

She glanced at the two men, took a deep breath, and forced out the words. "You have to let them die."

"Aber—"

"Nein!" Love grimaced. "Nay," she corrected. "You have to let them go, Life. You're not doing them any good."

Life finally opened her eyes, and Love sucked in a sharp breath. Life's eyes were *gray*, darker than the dull color shining through her skin.

"Life, please!"

Life stared at her for far longer than Love was comfortable with before finally nodding slowly. She pulled her hands back from the two men.

"Go find Death." Love wasn't certain her sister had understood the words earlier.

"Tod," Life whispered. Slowly, she closed her eyes again and disappeared.

Love swallowed. *Now to find Hate before Peace's emotions affect me permanently.*

Before Transporting herself, Love glanced back at her youngest sister one last time. *At least there's one reason not to despair.*

Even from this distance, she could feel affection and the possibility of love radiating from Ferez Katani toward Peace. His missing memories didn't seem to matter.

I just hope that'll be enough.

Closing her eyes, the pink demigoddess Transported herself away in search of Hate.

~~*~*

Ever since the fighting stopped, Frenz had crept steadily closer to Flame Tongue and her bondmates. He knew the dragon needed to reestablish the bond, but the urge to comfort and protect the purple-eyed boy had become nearly overwhelming once he wasn't distracted by attacking nomads.

Now he stood right next to Flame Tongue's head, and neither she nor the black stallion lying against her side showed any sign of noticing him. Worried, Frenz knelt and carefully slid a hand up the side of the dragon's jaw. She didn't even twitch.

A quiet nicker drew his gaze up, and Last Chance nudged Nightmare's neck anxiously.

"Last Chance." When she met his eyes with a worried one, he smiled slightly and brushed her muzzle with his free hand. "We'll get them back."

The pale mare dipped her head. Lowering herself to the ground beside Nightmare, she crossed her neck over the stallion's and settled her muzzle against the dragon's neck.

Dropping his gaze back down, Frenz let his fingers brush down Flame Tongue's jaw until they reached James's shoulder. Hesitating only a moment, he gently pushed aside black hair so he could see the boy's face.

Already, the dark skin had lightened, and the hole in his bottom lip didn't look quite so large. Many of the cuts had even closed well enough that Frenz wondered if the boy would have any scars from the encounter.

Perhaps the thought should have comforted Frenz. Instead, an emptiness opened up within his chest, and his breathing grew shallow. His hand trembled as he slid his fingers through the gritty slick coating the boy's cheek.

"I'm sorry," he whispered. "I couldn' protec' yeh from this."

A light touch on Frenz's shoulder drew his gaze upward. Wolfrik stood beside him, holding out a small object with one hand. When Frenz only stared at it without recognizing it, Wolfrik crouched beside him and pressed it into Frenz's hand. The farmer winced. Cool liquid slid down his wrist, quickly dampening the sleeve of his tunic.

"Wha—"

"Heilemagie is thorough, freund, but it cannot remove what coats the skin."

Frenz inhaled deeply, if a bit unsteadily. Nodding, he turned his focus back to the boy. Mindful that James was probably still in pain, he gently ran the cloth over his face. Down one side and under his chin. Across his forehead and down the other side. Down his nose and across his cheeks.

As he worked, Frenz spoke softly. He told James he was safe, that no one would hurt him anymore. He pleaded with him to be all right, to wake up. He confessed his own desire to know him, to relearn what he had forgotten.

Frenz didn't know how long he'd knelt there, gently cleaning the boy's bloody, gritty skin and quietly rambling. He was just wondering aloud why the Traveler had accepted him, a mere farmer, as a companion when pressure on his shoulder stopped him short.

Falling silent, Frenz glanced over his shoulder to find not Wolfrik as he had expected but Hausef Kanten staring worriedly past Frenz. The erstehäuptling's neck, chest, and arm were covered in bandages, and he leaned heavily on his scarred sister.

"How is he?" the older man whispered.

Frenz shook his head. "He—" He swallowed. "He isn' wakin' up. An' Flame Tongue an' Nightmare aren' respondin', either."

"They're lost in the dracheband, Erstehäuptling," Wolfrik added. "And with Dame Flammezunge's mental defenses . . ."

"There's no going in after them," murmured Isa.

Frenz shifted into a more comfortable seated position. "So we jus' wait for them to wake on their own, then?"

"I don't know," Isa muttered. "We hardly know how long that will take."

"What would you suggest we do, schwester?" Hausef asked tiredly. "We can't exactly carry Flame all the way back to Friedlichoase."

The scarred woman didn't answer.

Beyond her, Wolfrik shook his head. "A portion of the clans could always stay here until they wake, Erstehäuptling." The Skorpion glanced at an older woman who wore a band across her eyes. Frenz didn't know how she could have seen the look, but she nodded.

"My bruder had planned for our two clans to remain here for two more siebentäge." Frenz glanced around, wondering how that was possible with such sparse water and vegetation. "Since there are now fewer of us, there's no reason young Wolfrik's idea could not work."

Hausef grimaced and nodded. "Very well. Those who can travel will return to Friedlichoase with news. At least this will give the healers and Heilemagier more time to care for the injured."

"And we can get Wolfrik settled as häuptling," spoke up Eule, Häuptling Wüstenwolf's sister. She flashed a sharp smile at Wolfrik, whose face darkened in turn.

The blind woman laid a hand on the shoulder of a girl Frenz hadn't noticed earlier. "And Rosa, as well."

As the others began to discuss sleeping arrangements and temporary shelter for the Drache Krieger, Frenz tuned them out and turned back to James. His face was clean now, the bruises faded to a dark yellow, and there was almost no sign of the cuts that had left the boy so bloody.

Frenz smoothed a hand down James's cheek once more. "We'll take care o' yeh, James."

He frowned. The words weren't quite right.

"*I'll* take care o' yeh."

Better.

~~*~*

Even as they fell into the mundane discussion, Hausef kept an eye on Frenz and didn't miss the farmer's gentle touch or even his soft words. A sad smile tugged at his lips.

Gemi's been through so much. She deserves happiness.

Last nacht—*was Adlerfest only then?*—Hausef had thought she'd found it, too. The entire camp had rung with the news that the Drache Krieger had finally found someone he was interested in. At one point, Hausef had even seen just how happy Gemi and Frenz looked together.

With the battle over, Adlerfest seemed like a dream. Gemi had been beaten and tortured and refused to wake up. Flame and Shadow were unresponsive. Even the mann who had made Gemi so happy couldn't remember meeting her, let alone their brief courting.

So why doesn't it seem to matter?

Hausef would have expected the farmer to be wary of any hints they dropped about a possible relationship between him and the Drache Krieger. Instead, he had watched the farmer become more curious, more interested, and most of all, more worried about his missing companion.

Now Frenz touched and spoke to Gemi as if he hadn't just found her hanging here—as if he felt something for her that wasn't based on the words of others.

"Even we Geistmagier don't fully understand a mann's geist, bruder." Isa's words whispered through his geist. *"But the reasons behind his emotions aren't what you should be worrying over."*

Hausef glanced curiously at his schwester. She still focused on the conversation with the others, but he could feel the anxiety in her mental presence.

What worries you, Isa?

She finally glanced at him, and he was surprised to see fear in her eyes. *"I'm more worried that he doesn't remember who he really is."*

Hausef frowned. He remembered the impression he'd had during the Gleichrat several täge ago that Frenz Kanti was much more than he claimed to be.

He's not just a farmer, then. A soft agreement whispered through his geist. *Do you know who he really is?*

Isa turned back to the others surrounding them, apparently returning her attention to the conversation. He nodded. *Not now.* There was too high a chance that someone would overhear if she mindspoke what she knew. *Better to wait until we're alone.*

Hausef might have questioned his schwester's decision to keep the information between the two of them. Only his suspicion that Gemi also knew the truth about her newest traveling companion stilled him. *She would have had a reason for keeping it a secret.*

"A very good reason," Isa confirmed before pulling back from his geist.

Hausef sighed. Knowing he would learn nothing more right now, he rejoined the conversation as well.

Six

Despite his desire to stay by James's side, Frenz was enlisted to help with cleanup as soon as a temporary shelter had been set up for the boy. Frenz didn't argue. He still remembered the war and how much effort the post-battle activities required.

He spent the next few hours helping to sort through the dead and the injured: attempting to make the injured comfortable until a healer could reach them and preparing the dead for Einäscherung, the nomads' ceremony of burning the dead.

By the time Frenz could seek a bed, the sun had already hung above the distant Tarsurian mountain range for several hours. The heat and the heightened emotions of the last twenty-four hours combined to make his body heavy, and his eyes drooped as he ambled toward James's small tent.

To his surprise, he was intercepted by the Katze Clan's Mage Healer, Mandel. The Healer gripped his arm and propelled him away from the small tent, out of which Flame

Tongue's body protruded. Against her side, Last Chance and Nightmare still lay together.

"They don't need any distractions, Herr Kanti." Mandel's voice sounded tight. "I suggest you find a bed elsewhere."

"But—"

The Healer returned to James's tent, obviously not listening.

Frenz stared after him. *Flame Tongue and Nightmare weren't even reacting when I left. How could my presence distract them?*

Anger flushed through him, but Frenz didn't have the energy to pick a fight with the Healer. Obediently, he turned back to the main part of camp and went to inquire about another bed.

He hadn't gone far before Wolfrik found him. The Skorpion offered him a grim smile and squeezed his shoulder.

"Es tut mir leid, freund. I hadn't expected them to keep you from the Drache Krieger."

Frenz shrugged one shoulder. "Maybe they're righ' to. They've known him longer than I have."

Or rather, they actually know him.

Wolfrik's lips tightened, and his eyes narrowed. For a moment, Frenz thought the other man would argue, but he must have realized how tired Frenz was. Wolfrik soon shook his head and patted Frenz's shoulder.

"Komme, freund. There are extra beds in my familie tent."

Frenz nodded and followed Wolfrik through the camp. It wasn't until the Skorpion pulled open the tent's entrance flap and waved Frenz through that the farmer realized Wolfrik's family tent had previously been home to four men, all now dead.

Frenz paused in the entrance. "Yeh sure this is all right?"

Wolfrik chuckled quietly. He sounded as tired as Frenz felt.

"Käfe and I are the last of the Giftschwanz line. As this is the Giftschwanz tent, we are the only ones with the recht to invite guests here. No one can tell us nein."

Frenz shook his head but stepped farther into the tent. "Tha's not exactly—"

He fell silent. On the far side of the tent, Käfe was already curled up in some bedding. Behind her lay the erstehäuptling's eldest son, Zuk, one arm clutching her protectively against his chest. Frenz bit his lip and glanced away.

Wolfrik chuckled again and patted Frenz on the shoulder. "Like I said, freund, for the first time in our lives, there is no one who can deny us the simple pleasure of a guest of our choosing. Now get some sleep."

Frenz nodded and stumbled toward an unoccupied bed. Glancing over his shoulder only to make sure he hadn't chosen Wolfrik's, the farmer collapsed into it and quickly fell asleep.

~~*~*

Darkness closed in around him. It pressed against his eyes and ears and created an aching silence that had him breathing more harshly just to try to break it.

That darkness pressed in on his body, as well. It felt like ice against his skin, chilling him enough to make him shiver. The pressure built against his chest and his throat, and it only spread from there.

He gasped for breath and flailed at the darkness, but his hands met nothing and breathing became more difficult. Frustration and fear clawed at his throat, but the pressure there prevented the scream that wanted to break free.

Why? *he gasped, but the sound didn't reach his ears. Cold trailed slowly down his cheeks.* **Why?**

~*~*~

"Frenz!"

His eyes flew open. His hand reached for his boot before he turned on his attacker and swung.

A sharp curse preceded a soft *whumpf,* and Frenz hesitated, blinking. Wolfrik reclined on the ground near him, the wide, shimmering cloth that normally covered his head tilted and torn, and his eyes wide. In Frenz's hand was one of the knives he kept in his boots.

"Frenz?" Wolfrik whispered after they'd sat there for nearly a minute. "You're safe here, remember?"

Frenz shivered and closed his eyes. He felt cold and his breath came harshly. "Sorry." The word came out ragged, and he inhaled deeply, attempting to calm his heavy breaths.

Slowly, a hand wrapped around his wrist. Frenz squeezed his eyes shut more tightly, keeping himself as still as possible as Wolfrik twisted the blade from his hand. A soft *thunk* let him know Wolfrik had dropped it to the ground.

"Komme." Wolfrik gripped Frenz's shoulder firmly. "Let's get you some food, freund. Perhaps you'll feel better then."

Frenz swallowed and allowed Wolfrik to lead him from the tent. The instinct to fight still thrummed through his body, and it scared him. He hadn't felt this way since the war.

It was supposed to be over.

Once he was seated with a platter of food, Wolfrik informed him that Flame Tongue and Nightmare—or Flame and Shadow, as they were apparently insisting they be called now—were awake.

"An' James?"

Wolfrik shook his head. Frenz closed his eyes and swallowed. The cold with which he'd awoken was settling in his chest.

"Did they a' leas' renew the bond?"

"Ja, and they even convinced his body to eat. But the Drache Krieger is no more responsive now than he was when we cut him down from the post."

Frenz took a deep breath to fight the pressure rising in his throat. "Can I see him?" he asked gruffly when he realized it was futile.

Wolfrik squeezed his shoulder once more. "Finish eating and I'll take you to him. You don't want to give Heilemagier Mandel any more reasons to turn you away."

Frenz nodded and hurried to finish his meal.

The sun was just disappearing behind the western horizon when Wolfrik led Frenz toward James's tent. The structure had been better fortified while he slept and now looked like a proper, if smaller, nomad tent.

Despite the relatively small size, the tent was filled with people when they arrived. Those of the Kanten family who had come to Trostlosoase sat or stood around James while the Healer knelt right next to him. Even Käfe was there, leaning against Zuk's side and staring sadly at the boy.

As soon as Frenz stepped into the tent, Käfe glanced at him and quickly tugged Zuk toward the entrance. Zuk squeezed Frenz's shoulder as he passed and offered a wan smile.

The pair was soon followed by the erstehäuptling's eldest daughter, Ulla, and her courter, Raymond. While Raymond nodded to Frenz and ducked through the entrance, Ulla lingered and frowned up at Frenz.

"What does my bruder mean to you, farmer?" she muttered after a minute of silence. He blinked at her, startled by the sudden interrogation. "You don't even remember him, and we can't retrieve your memories the same way Flame and Shadow regained theirs."

Frenz inhaled sharply and clenched his fists tightly against his thighs. It was the first time anyone had suggested that regaining his lost memories might be impossible, and the sudden urge to punch the young woman caught him off guard.

Wolfrik wrapped a hand around his arm. "Easy, freund."

"Ulla, that's enough," Hausef ordered softly. "There's no need to say such things."

Ulla turned and opened her mouth. Just as quickly, she snapped it shut again and pushed past Frenz and Wolfrik.

"Es tut mir leid, Frenz." Hausef's words filled the tent as soon as its entrance flap had fallen still. "I'm afraid Ulla doubts your emotions could have survived the suppression of your memories."

Frenz eyed the erstehäuptling warily. "But yeh don't?"

Hausef shook his head slowly and sighed. "I saw the care you took with James last nacht. Despite your lack of memories, you do feel something for him."

Frenz dropped his gaze, uncertain what to say. The affection and protectiveness felt right, but Ulla had a point. *How can I feel something for him when I can't remember anything about him?*

"As I said last nacht, freund," Wolfrik murmured through his mind, *"when have your instincts ever failed you?"*

Frenz bit his lip to restrain a humorless laugh. *Less than an hour ago when I took a swipe at you with my blade.*

"That was different. That was the remains of a terrible dream, not your response to the real world."

And what can I consider real when I don't even remember the last half season?

"There's also a chance Ulla might be wrong about retrieving your memories," Isa added before Wolfrik could respond. "Unlike Flame, you don't have an aversion to Geistmagier accessing your thoughts. I believe, between my power and Wolfrik's knowledge of your memories, we might be able to recover what you're missing."

"I don't—"

A sharp glance from Isa quieted Wolfrik. When they both remained quiet, Frenz knew the discussion had become mental. After a couple minutes of intense staring, Wolfrik sighed and glanced away, nodding slowly.

"Perhaps."

Frenz glanced between the two Mindspeakers, his body thrumming with energy once more. If he could remember the last few sevendays . . . if he could remember his time with James . . .

He looked down at the boy. James looked as though he were simply sleeping. His chest rose and fell steadily, and his skin was unblemished. There were no scars to show for the wounds he'd been subjected to only a day ago.

But he won't wake up. The knowledge brought back the pressure in his throat. *I can't leave him when he's like this. Who knows what he had to deal with at the hands of that Schlange.*

A light pressure on his arm made Frenz jump. He was halfway into a defensive crouch when he realized Hausef now stood beside him. The man offered him a soothing smile, but the worry in his eyes had Frenz swallowing and dropping his gaze.

This man, erstehäuptling of his people, had accepted Frenz into his camp, into his clan, and—if Frenz understood him as well as he thought he might—into his family. He had accepted Frenz's emotions for his adopted son despite Frenz's current lack of memories and Frenz's status as an outsider. It was humbling.

"Why don't you sit with James while Isa and Wolfrik work?" Hausef murmured. "I'm sure you've been anxious to return to his side."

Frenz flashed Hausef a grateful smile and quickly took the man's previous place at James's side. He picked up the boy's hand and squeezed, ignoring the twist in his gut when the hand lay limp in his own. The chill of his skin, though, only made the feeling worse.

Leaning over James, he brushed a few short strands of hair out of the boy's face and stared. His face looked soft in sleep, his cheeks and chin round, his nose small. Frenz was suddenly struck by just how feminine and vulnerable James looked.

So much in need of protection.

"Frenz?"

The whisper drew his attention reluctantly away from James, and he looked across the boy at Isa and blinked. Her face was softer than he'd expected, the unscarred side of her face smooth as she watched him. Her eyes were gentle as he met her gaze.

"Are you ready?"

Frenz hadn't expected such a question from the brusque woman he'd met yesterday. However, he nodded and turned back to James, unwilling to focus on anything else if he had the choice.

A soft touch at his temple and one to the back of his neck were the only warning he had before his mind thrummed in much the same way his body had only moments before. He gasped and closed his eyes, his grip tightening on James's hand.

As he'd only been aware of Wolfrik's presence in his mind when the Skorpion addressed him, Frenz hadn't expected to feel the Mindspeakers' combined magic. But the power only seemed to increase, the thrum steadily growing until Frenz swore his head vibrated with it.

Then the vibrations narrowed, and Frenz groaned as the Mindspeakers focused on a specific area. Frenz didn't know what it was, but he hoped it was his missing memories. He wasn't sure how long he could stand the strange vibrations.

Suddenly, the vibrations became insignificant as panic tightened his chest and pressed up his throat, making it hard to breathe.

"Nay!" he gasped.

I can't lose James! Whatever they're doing, I can't—

A grunt filled his ears. Someone grabbed his arm. "Nay!" he gasped again and twisted, reaching for his boot.

He snarled when his fingers didn't find the blade that should have been there. *How could I leave my knife behind?*

The missing blade distracted him, and whoever had grabbed him strengthened his grip. Frenz snarled again.

"Frenz, bitte, you're among freunde!"

He stilled as the words cut through his panic. He was breathing rapidly, his head spun, and the knuckles of his right hand ached. *Twice in one day? In one hour?* The cold from before filled his body again.

"Wha's wrong wit' me?"

"Perhaps Adalwolf built that reaction into the barrier hiding your memories."

Frenz lifted his gaze to Isa. Her voice had sounded rougher than usual, and she rubbed at her shoulder. He blinked and flushed as he realized he had hit her in his panic.

"Whatever the reason, perhaps we shouldn't try that again," Hausef replied.

Frenz shook his head before he even thought about it. "Please, nay."

"It's all right, Frenz." Wolfrik loosened his grip on Frenz's arms. "We won't force you through this if you don't want it."

Frenz lowered his head and shook it again. He wanted his memories back, but not if it cost him James. He couldn't remember why, but he wouldn't be able to live with that.

Wolfrik said something else, but Frenz stopped listening. His attention had returned to the boy, and he refused to let it wander again. Soon, Wolfrik, Hausef, and Isa left the tent. Only Mandel remained, but he stayed silent, allowing Frenz an illusion of privacy with James.

~~*~*

"What was that?" Isa hissed as soon as the entrance to Gemi's tent closed behind them.

"Isa." Hausef laid a hand on her arm, but she shook him off. He hadn't been in the king's geist when the mann panicked.

"That wasn't Geistmagie reacting to us!"

Out of the corner of her eye, Isa saw her bruder frown, but her glare was for Wolfrik alone. He was the one who knew the king's geist.

"Yet you claimed it as a possibility," Wolfrik answered softly.

Isa snorted. "Ja, because I could see he was panicking enough as it was." She jabbed a finger into Wolfrik's chest. "But you know what it really was, don't you?"

The Skorpion glanced around. "Shall we take this to my tent?"

Isa pursed her lips, suddenly remembering they were still

out in the open. Several people eyed them curiously as they passed.

"This does seem to be a conversation we might prefer to save for a more private setting," Hausef added.

Isa nodded sharply and stalked off toward the Giftschwanz familie tent. Thankfully, the tent was empty. *I would hate to have to kick out Käfe and Zuk because they thought to come here too.*

Once the three of them were secured in the tent, Isa pressed Wolfrik for an answer. The Skorpion frowned.

"You said you knew who he was, that he was . . ." He hesitated and glanced toward the entrance.

"The king of Evon, ja," Isa answered softly. Hausef nodded.

Wolfrik sighed. "Then I'm sure you can understand why he was struggling with doubts before he began courting the Drache Krieger."

Isa groaned softly and closed her eyes. *Because his throne requires him to find a noble lebenfrau, and he still doesn't know Gemi's true heritage.* She might have found the situation amusing if it hadn't concerned her niece and the king.

"And you believe some part of him still remembers those doubts," Hausef murmured, "even if he doesn't realize it?"

Isa opened her eyes in time to see Wolfrik nod. "And telling him the truth of who he is won't help, either. He only trusts us as much as he does because he has an obvious hole in his memory. He won't easily believe that the rest of his memories aren't true."

Hausef rubbed his temple. "We can't just let the king continue believing he's only a farmer. That's hardly an option when the clans pledged loyalty to the throne."

"We can only wait until James wakes and hope the king trusts him enough to believe the truth from his lips, bruder."

Hausef sighed and shook his head. "Very well." Isa felt his geist work over the situation. "I'll have to send a message to Naldo soon."

"Naldo?" Wolfrik inquired.

"Naldo Ramírez, king of the Tarsurian diebe," Isa answered. "He'll be expecting James in a few täge."

"And even if James wakes by tomorrow nacht," Hausef added, "he'll be in no condition to travel to Tarsur."

Isa pursed her lips and nodded. The violent voice she'd heard during her confrontation with Adalwolf had spoken of moving on to Tarsur.

I don't know what you have planned for my niece, Krieg, but we won't send her into your grasp when she has no way to protect herself.

~~*~*

Freiflügel, the falke Hausef chose to carry a message to Naldo, was a favorite of the Kanten männer. Of course, Freiflügel's entire familie was favored by the two Tieremagier, but Freiflügel was the bird they called on most, especially when they had messages for the other clans or their counterparts in the other provinces.

For this reason, Freiflügel knew the location of each of the drache's groups and whom to approach in each. In Kensy, the Tieremagier fledgling was just as willing to pass on messages as the one who favored snakes. In Baylin, Freiflügel always approached the Magier who preferred the bounding lopes of the plains to Freiflügel's winged brethren. In Cautzel—or, more often, at sea—the rat Tieremagier of the *Pretty Pauper* was Freiflügel's contact.

However, compared to all of them, the Tarsurian diebe

had strange customs. Ever since Freiflügel's first flight to the stadt that lay nestled in the mountainside, the diebe had always presented him with the most complicated process for delivering messages.

First, the Tieremagie that infused the surrounding valley would force him to circle and wait until the Tieremagier called for him. Then, once the magier had reached for him, Freiflügel would be drawn to a small aperture in the stadt's sheer façade, a hole hardly big enough for a bird larger than Freiflügel to land. It certainly wasn't big enough for anything larger than a sparrow to fly through, which meant Freiflügel always had to awkwardly maneuver down the short tunnel between the aperture and the room where the Tieremagier would be waiting.

The worst part was that once the magier had read whatever message Freiflügel carried, he would tie it back to the falke's leg and send him back through the too-small tunnel in search of the king of the Tarsurian diebe.

There are some humans I will never understand.

He had once considered mentioning the odd process to Hausef. However, he had never heard even the drache mention it as being unusual—and surely she would have—so Freiflügel had long ago decided it must just be the way of the diebe . . . no matter how inconvenient it might be for him.

Now, Freiflügel flew fast. Hausef had insisted this message was urgent, and with the Gift Clans' camp so much closer to the Tarsurian mountain range, it didn't take him long to reach his destination. In fact, the sun was still several hours from rising when he began to circle the hidden valley.

To his surprise, the Tieremagie reached for him as soon as he felt it. Dropping toward the cliff face, Freiflügel landed on a small ledge with a soft screech. He knew he'd found the right entrance into the stadt, but only because he could feel the pull of the magie. In the darkness of the nacht, he could hardly see well enough to tell the rock from the holes that littered it.

Snapping his beak fretfully, Freiflügel steeled himself and began the awkward shuffle through the tiny tunnel that was his only option.

Long minutes later, Freiflügel finally saw the flickering light of fire and knew he had nearly reached the Tieremagier's room. He also knew, by the cries that echoed down the tunnel, that he was not the only bird to be carrying a message tonight.

"*¡Necesito advertir a los Ocultados!*"

The words echoed down the tunnel to Freiflügel before he even reached the magier's room. By the time he had hopped out of the tunnel and onto a small table beneath its exit, the other bird, a large eagle with golden wings and a slash of white across its head, had repeated the message five times with no response.

Freiflügel had traveled enough to understand the eagle's words, and they made him curious. However, the eagle had yet to explain why it needed to warn the Ocultados—that was what the Tarsurian diebe called themselves—and it didn't sound like it would . . . at least not in a way Freiflügel could understand.

"*Cállate, Valto!*" The Tieremagier finally cupped a gentle hand around the back of the eagle's head. Unfortunately, the larger bird—Valto—didn't appear willing to calm down, and it snapped at the Tieremagier's hand before repeating his message.

The Tieremagier rolled his eyes and huffed. "*I heard you the first time. Will you quiet down if I promise to deliver the mensaje immediately?*"

Valto turned his head, eyeing the Tieremagier warily. Freiflügel clacked his beak and ruffled his feathers. He didn't understand why the eagle was having such a hard time trusting the Tieremagier. He'd never done anything wrong, as far as Freiflügel knew.

Unless you consider his inconvenient delivery process. However, Freiflügel didn't think that would warrant such a look.

Finally, Valto ruffled his own feathers and gave a final chirrup of his message before launching himself at the ledge above the table on which Freiflügel now stood. Freiflügel squawked as a dusting of feathers drifted down on him as the eagle shuffled into the small tunnel.

"Return to your maestra, Valto!" the Tieremagier called after him. *"I won't be happy if I learn you tried to pester the rey with a mensaje he can't understand."*

Valto squawked an unhappy agreement as his tail feathers disappeared from sight.

Freiflügel chirruped and turned to preening as the Tieremagier grumbled and began pulling out parchment, a feather, and a bottle of writing liquid. He could sense, from the magie around him, that the magier wasn't quite ready to speak with him yet.

Several minutes later, a bird smaller than Freiflügel appeared on the ledge of the tunnel. It had plain black-and-brown feathers, a long, pointed beak, and beady eyes. Its movements in the tunnel weren't nearly as awkward as Freiflügel's or Valto's had been. Freiflügel thought it and its familie must be more accustomed to such small spaces.

"¡Ven, Piegro!" The Tieremagier didn't even look up from the message he was writing. *"I need you to carry a mensaje to Deligero. He needs to know what treachery he faces."*

Freiflügel stilled and tilted his head so he could peer at

the magier from under one wing. He didn't recognize the name the Tieremagier had mentioned, but he knew it didn't belong to the king of the Tarsurian diebe.

Perhaps one of his advisors?

That didn't seem right, either, since Freiflügel had seen this magier address the king and his advisors on several occasions. What reason would he have to send a message when he could simply speak to the others himself?

Then who is this Deligero? And why would the Tieremagier need to warn him of treachery?

Freiflügel shook himself a moment later. *Well, whatever it is, it has nothing to do with me and mine. Especially if the drache stays with the clans for a while.*

Putting his curiosity from his geist, Freiflügel returned to preening until the Tieremagier had tied the roll of parchment to Piegro's leg.

"Remember," the Tieremagier added as Piegro flapped up to the tunnel's ledge, *"take that straight to Deligero. If Aquilina gets her hands on it, the treachery Deligero faces will surely double."*

Piegro cawed in agreement and quickly disappeared into the tunnel.

"Now," the Tieremagier continued sharply as he turned to Freiflügel, *"what does Hausef want?"*

Freiflügel lifted his head and squawked indignantly. He understood the Tieremagier was a busy mann, but he didn't have to take such an insulting tone when speaking about one of Freiflügel's humans.

The Tieremagier sighed and nodded. *"Lo siento. Lo siento,"* he apologized. *"You're right. I'm just feeling un poco heckled, is all."*

Freiflügel eyed him. Finally, he hopped forward and offered the leg that held Hausef's note.

The Tieremagier spent a long time reading the note. By the time he laid it down, the falke was certain he'd read it several times. The soft chuckle he released a moment later surprised Freiflügel.

"So Nadie will no be returning this estación." Freiflügel eyed the Tieremagier, curious why he was now speaking in the tongue of the humans. "Naldo will no be happy to hear it, but perhaps es for the best. Nadie would simply interfere en our plans—plans that no concern him."

Grabbing the note, he rolled it up and tied it back to Freiflügel's leg. Switching back to the tongue of the animals, he muttered, *"Carry it to Naldo. If he's not still in bed, he'll be in his study."* With that, he waved Freiflügel away and turned back to his desk.

Clacking his beak, Freiflügel leaped up to the ledge and twisted his head around to eye the Tieremagier. *What an odd mann.* He turned back around and began the awkward shuffle back out to the stadt's outer wall. *He says some of the strangest things sometimes.*

They weren't strange enough for Freiflügel to mention them to anyone else, but they were still odd.

Seven

19 Mid Autumn
224th year of Evon

Not far from the Mortal Realm, black-spirited Death and white-souled Life lay together in the spiritual pocket realm they had created as their sanctuary several millennia ago. It was a small sphere, no larger than many of the structures humans built for homes. It held nothing to hint at life, only granules of spiritual energy that resembled blue and purple sand filling its bottom. Its "sky" was a swirl of black and white, scattered with flecks of color that were sometimes reminiscent of the stars of the Mortal Realms.

And occasionally, like now, they would coalesce into two miniature balls representing the Gemini moons.

Death closed his eyes as pain lanced through his chest. The moons used to be a pleasant reminder of the dual nature of the world. Now, ever since Peace had been incarnated and named for them, the sight of the moons invoked in Death a disconcerting helplessness.

A whimper drew his attention down to Life, who slept fitfully against his side, one fist clenched tightly against his chest. Tightening his grip around her shoulders, he caressed the side of her face and wished, not for the first time, that he could ease the nightmares that had plagued her rest since they had sequestered themselves away.

Nightmares. The black demigod shivered. The pair of them had lived for numerous millennia, and this was the first time one of their mutual slumbers had been fraught with strain that neither of them could dismiss.

"What happened in Zhulan, sister?" Death murmured, though softly enough not to wake her. Since the beginning of the season, he had done his best to remain as far from their youngest sister as possible. While Life and their other two sisters had gone to Trostlosoase to do what they could for Peace and her allies, Death had been in Fayral, overseeing a duel to the death.

When Life had arrived, gray and muttering in Zhulanese, Death had immediately dropped his influence, hugged her to his chest, and Transported them to their sanctuary. Just before they disappeared, he had observed the two duelists, both of whom were wounded, staggering to the ground.

Death caressed Life's face idly.

If he had not removed her as quickly as he had, Death knew the two duelists would have become lifeless. Not dead—Life could not cause death, no matter what state she was in—but they would have had their energy drained and been left in a comatose state from which no healer, magical or otherwise, could rouse them.

It had been millennia since Death had seen it happen, and never at Life's hands, but he easily recognized the signs. It was the Chaos that Life and Death had been born to fight, a Chaos against which they had struggled for their first millennium before it finally succumbed to their influence.

That it had returned now only increased Death's uneasiness about the season.

A soft trill broke Death from his contemplations, and he turned to find a large head poking through the side of their pocket realm. The head resembled that of a large bird of prey. The feathers covering it each shone a different color, its beak gleamed a bright yellow, and its piercing eyes glowed a violet much deeper and older than Peace's could ever be.

"Aquila," Death murmured.

He knew better than to ignore the Royal Eagle, especially when she had made the effort to seek them out in their personal sanctuary. It was not easy, he knew, to break through the barriers created by other immortals.

"The Ladies wish to see you, Death," Aquila trilled musically.

Death turned his gaze back to Life. She had not woken since their arrival, but her soul was no longer tinged gray as it had been. Despite the nightmares, their rest had helped filter out whatever negative influences had caused the Chaos.

Still . . .

"I do not wish to leave Life."

A soft clacking drew his gaze back to Aquila, who quietly snapped her beak. *"I did not say you should, child."*

Death winced and dropped his eyes. The softness of her tone was tempered by a disdain in her eyes that he recognized all too well.

Despite being the eldest of the demigods, he and Life were still much younger than the other deities. Their parents, the Fates, and the Guardians of the Cycle of Incarnation were all children of Magmater, the Great Mother herself. They had never questioned their roles in this world—their duties.

Life and Death, on the other hand, were much closer to

the mortals. The eternal struggle against the Chaos and the endless cycle of mortal lives had threatened to destroy their sanity before they created The Game. With its rules, it became a buffer between them and the mortal lives they affected.

With the birth of each new pair of demigods, Life and Death had altered The Game to include them. It had served them well, and none of their siblings had shown signs of succumbing to the Chaos the way Death and Life had once feared they would.

Until Peace threw herself into the Cycle and changed everything. Even after two centuries, Death still did not understand Peace's reasons for that.

A soft screech brought Death sharply back to the present. "I am sorry, Aquila. You were saying?"

The Royal Eagle glared at him. *"The Ladies requested you both, and they will not take nay for an answer!"*

With a sharp snap of her beak, Aquila removed her head from the pocket realm, leaving the "sky" to quiver in the wake of her sudden retreat.

Death winced. *It must be serious if the Ladies sent her with a message like that.* The Fates usually did not bother using Aquila since they had their own way of contacting the demigods. However, if they thought Death and Life had been ignoring them . . .

Turning back to his sister, Death gently shook her shoulder. "Life, it is time to wake."

The white demigoddess whined and tucked herself more tightly against Death's side. Caressing her face again, Death leaned down and pressed black lips to her white temple. "The Ladies are looking for us, Life. We cannot leave them waiting."

She groaned and rolled over. When she opened her eyes,

Death was glad to see he had managed to leech the darkness from them. They might not have been as bright as he would have liked, but he feared that would not be possible until the season had passed.

"Nay, we must not," Life whispered.

With care, Death helped her to her feet. Once certain he had a firm hold on her, he Transported them both to the Tapestry Room, the realm of the Fates.

As he always did upon arriving in the Tapestry Room, Death took a moment to admire the work of the Fates. The realm was cavernous and quite easily larger than any human city he had ever seen. Scattered throughout it were pillars as wide as buildings, which stretched from floor to ceiling. Many were swathed in the Tapestry of Mortal Life.

Unlike tapestries that humans made, the Tapestry of Mortal Life did not appear to have any rhyme or reason. In fact, Death was certain only the Fates themselves could interpret the Tapestry, since to him it was just a conglomeration of color.

"Are you just going to stand there gawking, or are you actually going to come speak with us?"

Death grimaced and turned to face the aggravated voice. He could admit, to himself at least, that he had been hoping to delay a confrontation with the Fates.

Not practical, perhaps, but the Ladies can be intimidating enough without being angry.

Despite the expanse of the Tapestry Room, Death's Transportation had positioned them fairly close to the large loom that was the center of the Fates' work. Ranged around it were three multicolored females: a pale youth of smooth skin, fine hair, and gentle expression, a richly colored mature female whose thick hair fell in waves around her calm, warm features, and a dark ancient whose craggy features always stood in stark relief against her wrinkles.

Neris the Maid, who spun soul material into strands for the Tapestry of Mortal Life. Tapeta the Matron, who worked the loom to weave the Tapestry. And Findi the Crone, who fingered individual strands of the Tapestry and ultimately removed them with her double-edged blade.

Findi, whose raspy words had greeted them, glared at them, her heavy brow thick above her sharp eyes. Her expression softened, though, when Life stumbled in their approach.

"You should not have pushed yourself so hard, Life," the Crone admonished. "You had to have known you were doing the humans no good."

Life shook her head wearily. "I hardly remember what happened after Peace broke."

Death stiffened. "What?"

Findi huffed. "Young War has fallen to the Chaos and now pulls his twin down with him."

"What exactly happened?" Death demanded. He hoped one of Findi's sisters would answer. The Crone was never very forthcoming with details.

"War had a Mindspeaker torture Peace," Tapeta answered firmly, her eyes never leaving her work. "Chaos now taints her soul and leeches out to infect others."

"By Carith . . ." Death squeezed his eyes shut. Beside him, Life wavered, and he clamped his arms around her to hold her upright. "Is there anything we can do?"

"You cannot interfere," Neris commanded in her breathy tones. "War and Peace must counter the Chaos themselves. Anything you attempt will only expose you to its influence."

Death shook his head. *What have you done, brother?*

"If we cannot help them, why did you call for us?" Life murmured.

"You cannot deal with War or Peace directly," the Crone corrected, "but you can prevent War's actions from causing too much damage."

"You would have us continue what we began in Machtstadt?" Death glanced at Life. Machtstadt had exhausted her, even if it had not reached the level from which she was now recovering.

"Tarsur should not be as troublesome as Machtstadt," Tapeta stated. "That being said, this season has been extremely difficult to predict with both Peace and War influencing the actions of so many others. You will have to depend heavily on your instincts to know when to act."

This time, when Death looked at Life, she met his gaze with worried eyes. They had not had to depend on their instincts more than the Fates since the time of the First Chaos.

"Where would you have us go?" Life whispered.

The Ladies remained silent as Findi and Neris turned to watch Tapeta consult the Tapestry.

"Wild Eagle Pass," the Matron finally replied. "And do hurry. War has already begun to spread the Chaos in Tarsur."

~~*~*

21 Mid Autumn, 224
Trostlosoase, Zhulan

"The nightmares are getting worse!"

The entrance of the Giftschwanz tent had just dropped behind the last of the häuptlinge and their closest familie advisors. Hausef grunted as he settled onto the bedding he'd been using for the past few täge. Blinking wearily, he watched as the others settled throughout the tent.

"You speak like that's not the very topic we're here to discuss, Roswalt," Meinhard snapped in return.

"Easy," Genevieve soothed, her voice scratchier than usual. "Anger will get us nowhere."

"Neither will stalling." Isa shook her head. "More of our people are complaining about the nightmares every täg. Those of us who've been able to fight their effects are now falling to them more frequently."

Hausef sighed and rubbed his temples, allowing his eyes to fall shut briefly. Isa was referring to the Geistmagier. At first, most had been able to protect their geister from whatever had been causing the nightmares that had plagued their people since the Battle of Trostlosoase. Now, after four täge, the nightmares seemed to be plaguing the magier—all of them—more heavily than anyone else.

When ominous shadows began to creep across the back of Hausef's eyelids, he shook himself and peeled his eyes open. Like everyone else, his desire to sleep was countered by the fear of what would greet him when he closed his eyes. The few hours he had managed in the last few täge seemed to have left him more exhausted than before he'd slept.

"The animals are being affected, too," Käfe murmured. Her head lay on her bruder's shoulder, and her eyes drifted slowly shut, only to jerk open in the next second.

"Käfe's right," Hausef muttered. "Most of the food animals refuse to eat, many of the pferde spend most of their time snatching what sleep they can—"

"And our spinnen have stopped spinning the silk we need for our clothes and tents," interrupted Kulbert,

Genevieve's eldest son. He sat slumped beside his mütter, his head on one hand and his elbows planted on his knees.

"While our skorpione now threaten their masters, and the birds and insects have fled the oase," Käfe finished mournfully. "Even my beetles have disappeared."

"And mine and Zuk's falken." Hausef sighed. "I don't know what is causing these nightmares, but they have the animals terrified."

Silence answered his words, and he watched the others struggle against the exhaustion that haunted them. It looked like Käfe and young Rosa were just succumbing to the impending sleep when Wüstenwolf cleared his throat harshly, startling everyone awake.

"I hate to be the one to say this, but many of the warriors think Flame is taking revenge for James's treatment."

"Of course they do!" snapped Isa. "They need a scapegoat, and these nightmares are too powerful to be caused by humans."

"And she has access to Geistmagie beyond any human's," Eule pointed out.

Isa attempted to glare at the Wolf, but the expression looked more weary than angry.

"Flame's never been able to touch the geister of a non-magier. She's too young to do anything like this."

"Perhaps not consciously." Wolfrik shook his head. "I don't think Wüstenwolf and Eule are actually arguing that Flame is behind these nightmares, simply that our people believe so."

"And we cannot deny the charge without providing a satisfactory explanation," Alys added before breaking into a yawn.

"Unfortunately, the truth would hardly help matters."

Everyone turned to stare at Madelhari. The Seer had

remained silent since they'd entered the tents, but even those words had sounded like a struggle for her. She sat slumped against Rosa, and Hausef realized suddenly that she was using the girl for support as much as she was providing it.

"You know the truth?" Roswalt asked incredulously. "Why haven't you said anything?"

Madelhari remained silent for so long that Hausef wondered if she had fallen asleep. The nightmares had taken a heavier toll on her than on anyone else, which no doubt had as much to do with her physical blindness as it did with the power of her Heiligesicht. Unlike the rest of them, she had no way to escape the shadows that haunted the darkness behind closed lids.

"Tante." Rosa shook the Seer's arm. Madelhari sighed and shook her head slowly.

"No matter how desperate for rest I might be, I had no wish to force the erstehäuptling to choose between the clans and his familie."

"What's that supposed to mean?" Roswalt snapped, but Hausef's breath froze in his chest.

She can't possibly mean . . .

"James?" Isa gasped. When Madelhari nodded, Isa shook her head. "But how? James isn't a magier. He doesn't have the power to cause this."

"This isn't about magie, Isana. The damage Adalwolf wrought . . ." Madelhari shook her head. "The Drache Krieger's soul is nearly black, and that darkness has been leaking out and affecting the rest of us since the battle began."

"Damage to the soul?" Genevieve muttered. "I don't know any Heilemagier who can Heal on that level."

The Seer offered the Spinne a tight-lipped smile. "Which is why I was keeping the information to myself. I believe only the Drache Krieger's bondmates can heal the damage, but it is taking longer than I had hoped it would."

"Meanwhile," Roswalt griped, "the rest of us suffer through haunted dreams on the off chance James will recover before we lose our sanity."

"Or our lives," muttered Valborga, previous häuptling of the Falke Clan.

"Mütter," Meinhard cautioned wearily.

"We can't expect the erstehäuptling to make this kind of decision," Genevieve murmured.

"Perhaps not," Valborga answered, "but we all know the Drache Krieger would not wish to cause such pain either, yet he does."

Hausef closed his eyes and clutched his head between his hands. *What am I supposed to do? Send Gemi away when Flame and Shadow can't even convince her to wake?*

"I can't believe—"

A reverberating roar cut through Isa's disbelief. Before Hausef's ears had even stopped ringing, he staggered to his feet and joined the others at the tent's entrance.

~~*~*

Frenz winced in pain and clutched at his left cheek and right ear. He'd woken to human screams, curious croons, and odd soft *thunks* and *whumpfs*. Worry had driven him from James's tent, where he'd spent most of his time since the failed attempt to retrieve his memories.

As soon as he'd shoved past the entrance flap, he'd been struck in the face by something small. Disoriented, he was certain only Flame's sudden and loud presence in front of him had prevented further assaults.

By the time he'd blinked past the pain, Flame had fallen

into snarls. Her bright red and purple wings were raised, blocking his view of his attackers. He reached out and tugged on the edge of one wing, hoping to get her to drop them.

The movement failed to even gain him a glance from the furious dragon, who seemed to be quarreling with someone or something. Frenz couldn't see if it was an animal or Animal Mage, but the variety of sounds argued for mage.

Suddenly, something nudged urgently at his shoulder. Spinning back toward James's tent, he found Shadow and Last Chance standing between the tent and Flame's hindquarters. Despite using the stallion for support, the weary mare nudged Frenz again before swinging her muzzle up toward her back.

It was then, as he stared incredulously at his mount—*surely, she can't be suggesting we leave*—that human voices joined the tumult. While most spoke in Zhulanese, the little Fayralese he heard—". . . nightmares . . . ," ". . . your revenge . . . ," ". . . can't take it . . ."—convinced Frenz that leaving wasn't so much a choice as a requirement.

Rubbing Last Chance's nose, he ducked back into the tent, where the nomads had stashed their tack and saddlebags.

He was just tightening the last of the straps on Last Chance's tack when someone gripped his shoulder and pulled him away from her. He nearly swung, thinking it must be an attacker, but the person pressed several objects into his arms.

"Es tut mir leid, freund." Wolfrik spoke quickly as Frenz shoved the full water flagons into his saddlebags. "Bitte, understand, this was not our idea."

Not our idea. That could encompass so many people, or so few. However, Frenz suspected Wolfrik meant those among the nomads whom Frenz had come to trust: Hausef

and his family, Wolfrik and Käfe, and most of the other
häuptlinge.

This was only confirmed to him as Isa, Käfe, and Eule
appeared out of James's tent, carrying the unconscious boy.
All three looked exhausted—*is that because of the nightmares
someone mentioned?*—but they were gentle as they lifted the boy
onto Shadow's back.

"Es tut mir leid, James." Isa squeezed the slumped boy's
knee as Eule and Käfe tied him into the saddle. "My bruder
would have stopped this if he could, but—"

"But the häuptlinge can barely keep people from
attacking *them*, let alone Flame!" Eule gave one final jerk to
the rope. Shadow swung his head around and nipped at her,
but the Animal Mage growled and bared her teeth right back.
"Leave off, Shadow! You haven't seen the darkness that
threatens our sleep. You're lucky our familien are as devoted
to the Drache Krieger as we are, or—"

"Eule, enough!" Isa snapped.

The Wolf glared at the scarred woman before spinning
away with a huff. Wolfrik reached for Eule's hand as she
stomped by, but she growled and slipped past him.

"Let her be, Wolfrik," Isa ordered when it looked like
the Skorpion might follow. "The exhaustion has her—has all
of us—on the edge of violence." She shook her head. "And
she's right. If we didn't care so much for James, Shadow, and
Flame, we'd probably be leading the mob instead of resisting
it."

Frenz opened his mouth to ask more about the
nightmares—and why they hadn't affected him—but Last
Chance chose that moment to shove her snout into his side
and urge him to mount. Nodding, he reached for her saddle,
but Käfe caught his arm and shook her head.

"You'd best ride Shadow," the quiet Animal Mage

insisted. "Last Chance has been suffering from the nightmares, same as the rest of us. She won't get far with you on her back."

Frenz turned to look at Last Chance. Despite her attempt to meet his gaze levelly, her head hung lower than it should, her ears drooped, and she blinked too often for Frenz's comfort.

"Right." He stepped toward Shadow, who urged him up with a heavy press of his snout.

Isa gripped Frenz's knee once he was seated behind James. "Trust Flame and Shadow to guide you. Flame knows the eastern oasen better than the clans do. She'll keep you safe."

Frenz nodded. "Thank yeh."

"Nein," Isa countered. "It is we who should be thanking you, Frenz. You'll be taking care of James."

Uncomfortable with the sharp solemnity in the scarred woman's eyes, Frenz nodded again, wrapped his arms around James's limp form, and picked up Shadow's reins. A quick nudge to the stallion's sides urged both horses into a trot.

As they left the light of the camp's fires behind, Frenz heard Isa shout. "Go, Flame! Bitte, go!"

A deep roar vibrated through Frenz's bones. He glanced over his shoulder and watched worriedly as the dragon swiped at the large crowd—*Did half the camp want us gone?*— before she launched herself into the air and flew toward the darkened horizon.

~~*~*

Freiflügel ruffled his feathers and glowered at Hausef. Unfortunately, his human appeared too tired to even notice as he slowly scratched a feather across parchment.

127

Occasionally, his eyes would drift shut and the feather would stop moving. When that happened, Freiflügel would chirrup, jerking the Tieremagier awake and setting him to writing again.

Freiflügel continued to glower, despite his human's obvious oblivion. He didn't want to be here. Up until the drache's sudden departure, darkness had radiated through the Gift Clan camp and threatened every living creature in the area. Everything that could flee had, including Freiflügel and his familie.

Now Hausef had called Freiflügel back, claiming he had another message for Naldo of the Tarsurian diebe. Freiflügel had only returned because of the power behind Hausef's call. The remnants of darkness still lingering throughout the camp worried Freiflügel, and he refused to remain longer than necessary.

If only Hausef would hurry up and give me his note.

Freiflügel screeched, letting Hausef know exactly what he thought of the human's lack of urgency. The Tieremagier only shook his head slowly and sighed.

"I understand, Freiflügel." His voice was barely a whisper, and Freiflügel was certain he only heard him because the words were directed by the mann's magie. *"But I'm so tired."*

"Then find your tent and send the note later." Freiflügel thought it an obvious solution. Hausef could get the rest he obviously needed, and Freiflügel wouldn't have to risk the strands of darkness that still lingered.

Hausef shook his head and wrote some more. *"Naldo needs to know to expect James."* After a moment of scratching, he added, *"I'm afraid for my son, Freiflügel."*

Freiflügel tilted his head and let his feathers smooth down. *"Why?"* he chirruped curiously. *"The drache's human is the most resilient of all your fledglings."* He shook himself and screeched. *"I mean, he's been leaving the nest since before you found him."*

Freiflügel had meant the words as a reassurance, but Hausef's expression only became grimmer. *"Which is why his current state is so worrisome. What could Adalwolf have done that would damage James's soul? Adalwolf was a Geistmagier, not . . ."*

Freiflügel huffed. *"Well, I don't know anything about souls, but I can seek out the drache on my return from Tarsur and bring you news of your fledgling, if it'll reassure you."*

The pulse of warmth with which Hausef answered the offer had Freiflügel turning to preen, while his human returned to his note with increased vigor.

It wasn't until Freiflügel was winging away from the oase that he realized he'd completely forgotten about the lingering darkness.

Eight

Eastern Zhulan, Evon

Flame growled and gnashed her teeth. Even four hours after leaving Trostlosoase, red heat still simmered through her mind and boiled within her chest.

How dare they accuse me of causing their nightmares? Of taking revenge on people I have considered family for six years?

Even Isa and Wolfrik's attempted explanation of the "truth" had not helped. *Even if Gemi somehow caused their nightmares, how can they simply send her away when she cannot even move on her own?*

"It's not like this is the first time we've been sent off to fend for ourselves," Shadow snorted.

Flame snarled when she realized the stallion was referring to their exile from the Northeast Forest.

"That was different! James considers the Katze Clan to be family, yet they abandoned him when he needed them." Even in her anger, Flame refused to risk Gemi's true identity by mindspeaking her true name, even so far from known civilization.

"And you didn't consider Mama Dragon to be family?"

Flame bared her teeth, but the soft words were enough to deflate her anger.

Aye, Mama Dragon had been the closest thing Flame had had to family before she bonded with Gemi and Shadow. She had saved Flame from the creature that had killed her clutch mother and siblings only sevendays after they had hatched. The dragon elder had raised Flame as though she were her own, despite being past her breeding years.

"And yet she still exiled you."

Flame crooned a reluctant agreement. She wanted to argue that the punishment for their crimes against the laws of the forest—Gemi's trespassing and Flame's dragonbond—would have been death if they had been caught by anyone else. However, she understood the stallion's point. A leader's responsibility was to his or her people. Like Mama Dragon, Hausef could not hold even the life of one he considered to be his child above those of his people.

"At least the nomads didn't exile us," Shadow muttered. *"We can always return . . . once James is feeling better."*

Flame snapped her jaw open and closed hard enough to produce an audible click. She refused to acknowledge the possibility of Isa and Wolfrik's "truth." It was as ridiculous as the idea that Flame was the source of the nightmares.

She flew in silence for several minutes longer before she became aware of agitation in the bond.

"Shadow?"

"Flame, is there an oasis nearby?"

The dragon snorted and scanned the ground. *"You passed one maybe fifteen minutes back. Why? The sun will not rise for several hours yet."*

The agitation became full-blown worry and fear. *"I don't think Last Chance will make it that long."*

With a hiss, Flame snapped her gaze down to the others. Shadow had slowed to a walk, and Last Chance was stumbling along beside him. Ferez had leaned over, one arm still hooked around Gemi's waist, the other hand buried in Last Chance's mane.

"Why did you not say something sooner?"

"You were too angry, and she—"

Shadow's attention was suddenly diverted. *"But you need to rest!"*

Even from this height, Flame could see Last Chance toss her head, though the motion was not as dramatic as she probably meant it to be. Through the bond, Flame heard her nicker wearily about night terrors.

The dragon growled and snapped her teeth again, though this time it was meant as a chastisement for herself. She had been so intent on defending herself and her helpless bondmate from the nomads' accusations, she had not considered what damage the Mindspeakers' "truth" could be causing her other friends.

Whistling a quick warning to Shadow, Flame dropped into a dive and landed heavily a few feet in front of the horses. Nudging the mare, she repeated Shadow's insistence that she needed sleep.

"Can't . . . too dark . . ."

Curiosity welled up in Flame, and she contemplated inquiring just what the nightmares entailed. Only Shadow's glare and his emphatic *"Don't!"* kept her from asking.

Instead, she crooned and nudged Last Chance's chin with her own snout. *"What if the source of the night terrors was no longer nearby?"*

Last Chance stared at her blankly, but Shadow snorted a protest.

"We can't just split up! Besides, we don't know that Isa and Wolfrik are right about James causing the nightmares."

Flame growled. *"I do not like the idea any more than you do, but we will not make it out of Zhulan if Last Chance cannot sleep."*

"I hope this argumen' is o'er where to stop for rest. Last Chance canna travel much farther."

All three animals snorted. Flame lifted her gaze to the amnesiac king, who watched her expectantly. For the first time Flame could remember, she wished she had magic beyond her years. She had lived among humans for years and had always communicated well enough using Gemi, Animal Mages, and Mindspeakers as translators.

Now, with Gemi still unconscious and no mages in sight, Flame wished her mindspeech were powerful enough to reach nonmagical minds. Perhaps then, they could have explained their knowledge of the situation to Ferez and he could have thought of a solution they had not. It would not have been the first time his unique experiences proved useful.

Unfortunately, Flame had no way to communicate the necessary information to the king in more than general terms. She would have to hope he understood her actions well enough.

She reached for the ropes securing Gemi to Shadow's back. *"There is an oasis about fifteen minutes' walk back to the west and a few minutes to the north. I will take James to an oasis farther east. That distance—"*

She fell silent and still as Ferez's hands joined her own on the ropes. Lifting her snout, she stared at the king, who merely glanced at her and nodded before returning his attention to the ropes.

~~*~*

When Frenz had mounted Shadow to leave Trostlosoase, he hadn't realized just how difficult the ride would be when he couldn't understand even one of his companions. Yet Isa had insisted he trust Flame and Shadow to guide him. So when Flame began untying James with no oasis in sight, Frenz didn't understand why, but he trusted the dragon knew what she was doing.

Of course, he had his suspicions. He had heard enough of the nomads' accusations to know there just might be a connection between Last Chance's exhaustion and James's unconsciousness. He didn't know what exactly the connection was. But if Flame was convinced enough to think James should be separated from the horses, then that was good enough for him.

Once the ropes had been removed, Flame carefully wrapped her arms around James's limp body and began to pull him from Shadow's back. Suddenly aware that the dragon might fly off with the boy and leave him behind, Frenz grabbed one of her forearms and met her eye when she stilled and turned to stare at him once more.

"If yeh're takin' James elsewhere, I'm comin' with."

Flame snorted, her red eye narrowing. Last Chance nickered softly while Shadow reached around and nudged the dragon, snorting in turn.

Apparently, that was all the convincing Flame needed. She nodded and nudged Frenz's hand where it still held her arm. Murmuring his thanks, he let go and watched the dragon gently pull James from the saddle and gather him against her chest.

Once settled, she turned her gaze back to him and motioned her snout up toward her back, rustling her wings as she did so. Accepting the silent instructions, Frenz dismounted from Shadow and, grabbing the saddlebags from Last Chance, climbed up onto Flame's back.

As he situated himself between her neck and her wings, Frenz knew he must have seen James ride the dragon just as he knew he had never ridden her himself. Though he couldn't remember how, he knew where to sit to keep from falling off, yet despite years of riding horses, the overly wide back between his thighs felt completely foreign.

Once he was comfortable, Flame snorted, nudged his leg once with her snout, and with no other warning, launched herself up into the air.

The sensation of being crushed against Flame's back was nothing compared to the feeling of the wind tugging at his hair and pressing against his eyes and cheeks. Despite the clenching in his belly and the sudden racing of his heart, Frenz grinned and whooped breathlessly, though he kept his hands tightly clenched around the small horns that decorated the crest of her neck.

The wind and pressure eased once Flame had leveled off. Frenz breathed deeply, reveling in the smooth gliding motion of hard muscles working steadily beneath his legs. The sensation brought a thrill and ache to his throat as he remembered the days when he could still ride horses bareback, before he was forced to join the war and take on a more civilized riding style.

A soft croon caressed his ears, interrupting his reminiscence, and he opened his eyes. He didn't have a good view of Flame's head from where he sat, but the bobbing motion he could see convinced him she was enjoying the flight as much as he was.

Grinning more widely, Frenz risked releasing the horns with one hand and leaned over to rub the dragon's shoulder.

As he did so, he caught sight of the land speeding past below them, and gasped.

He had ridden hard before, pushing his mounts as fast he could when needed, but never had the ground disappeared so quickly beneath him. Nor had it ever seemed so far away.

It occurred to him, briefly, that humans were not made to be so high and that if he were to fall, he wouldn't survive the drop. But his grin only widened, and he laughed, scanning the ground as well as he could in the moons-lit night.

The desert ground was not as uniform as he might have expected. Here and there, Frenz noticed strange rock formations rising from the dry ground. The occasional movement and glimpse of odd vegetation also proved that the desert was not as barren as one might think.

Frenz was contemplating an arch-like rock formation to the north when Flame suddenly slowed and began to circle. Glancing down, he discovered a small splash of lushness amid the dryness he had seen so far. The oasis was too small to support one of the clans for any length of time, but Frenz suspected it was large enough to support the three of them for several days.

Hopefully, we won't need to stay that long. Frenz worried his lip with his teeth, thinking of the unconscious boy in Flame's arms and Frenz's exhausted mount. *Maybe just long enough for Last Chance to recover. Who knows how long we'll be safe out here.*

~~*~*

Flame observed Ferez as he tucked Gemi into her bedroll and settled into his own beside her. As soon as they had landed, the king had begun to set up camp, allowing Flame time to take care of Gemi's physical needs. Flame even suspected he had taken his time on purpose. He seemed to have well accepted Flame's fierce protectiveness of her bondmate's modesty, though he could not understand the true reason. When she had returned to the camp and laid Gemi on her bedroll, he had simply nodded and begun to settle them both for sleep.

However, it was not his trusting acceptance that made her pensive as she watched him. Nor was it even worry for Last Chance and Shadow. Before landing, she had received news that the two had reached the oasis to which she had sent them. Already, Last Chance slept, her steady breathing and stillness indicating a lack of nightmares that had been missing the last few days.

Nay, it was only her own reactions that filled her with wonder. Before tonight, she had never carried anyone other than Gemi upon her back (unconscious family members aside). And until she had been in the air, with Ferez laughing and clinging to her horns, it had never occurred to her there might be someone other than her bondmate whom she would enjoy carrying.

"Don't know why you're so surprised," Shadow muttered quietly. *"I thought we already knew we cared for them."*

Flame snorted. *"We care for many, but I have never allowed anyone to mount me like James does. Not even Maxwell."* The young Kensian Animal Mage whose magic Flame had nurtured these last seven years was perhaps the one human to whom Flame herself was closest outside of her bondmates. Even he, though, had never been allowed to climb upon her.

Shadow huffed. *"Well, this was necessary. We all know Frenz never would have let you take James and leave him with Last Chance and me."*

Flame growled. *"You do not understand."*

"You're right. I don't."

Flame's growl deepened. *"I am not a horse to be ridden by anyone who pleases. I—"*

Confusion swept through the bond. Flame huffed. She did not know how to explain the oddness of her emotions to Shadow. A magical creature would understand her indignation that most humans would ride her like a simple beast of burden. That she had enjoyed flying with Ferez— that he seemed to have appreciated the flight . . .

"It is not . . ." she began, searching for words that Shadow might comprehend, *"a pleasure I would have expected to experience with someone . . . outside of the bond."*

Surprise rang through the bond, followed by a sudden softness Flame rarely felt from the stallion.

"I didn't realize it meant that much to you. Do you . . . ?"

Shadow's thoughts churned. Flame snapped her teeth together as she recognized the suggestion in his thoughts.

"It was the best way I could think to explain. I did not mean . . . James would not . . ."

Flame fell silent, flustered heat rising in her throat. She could not believe Shadow would actually think . . .

"Would it be such a bad thing to bond with him . . . ?"

Or her? Flame caught as the stallion trailed off. Flame nearly snorted but refrained. She was not the only one struggling over new emotions.

"James would never agree to include Frenz in the dragonbond."

Shadow rolled his shoulders. *"I don't see why not. Frenz may not know the truth yet, but James is closer to him than anyone else we've ever met."*

Flame growled softly. *"Perhaps, but that was before he was kidnapped and tortured. You have seen the darkness in his mind as surely as I have."*

"And we'll pull him back from that," Shadow nickered softly. *"We have to."*

Flame huffed but did not reply. There was nothing to say. They had been trying to reach Gemi since they found her, but she still refused to acknowledge that they were even real. They might have convinced her body to eat and relieve itself, but Gemi's consciousness was still huddled on that barren mountaintop, besieged by dark creatures tied to her own doubts and fears.

Flame did not know how to fight that.

~~*~*

22 Mid Autumn, 224
Valle Ocultado, Tarsur, Evon

This time, when Freiflügel arrived at the hidden valley, the sun had already begun to drop its rays over the valley's fields. As Freiflügel circled idly per the Tieremagie's silent commands, he observed the humans who already ranged across the valley. Some watched over sheep and goats, while others simply turned their attention to their food plants.

Freiflügel was just beginning to contemplate a small, skittering rodent when he felt the beckoning pull of the magie. Huffing softly, the falke glared down at the mouse— *Isn't this your lucky täg?*—before gliding back toward the sheer cliff face that made up the hidden stadt's façade.

When he reached the Tieremagier's room, the mann was standing on the other side of the table at the tunnel's entrance. Freiflügel paused on the tunnel's ledge, his sharp gaze honing in on the mann's hands. They were cupped together loosely enough for him to see movement between them.

"Lo siento, Freiflügel. It seems I pulled you away from your breakfast." The Tieremagier lifted his hands, and Freiflügel

bobbed his head as he caught sight of a small snout pressing between the mann's fingers. *"I only hope this will make up for it."*

Before Freiflügel could agree that the Tieremagier's offering may very well make up for not being able to chase the mouse he'd been eyeing earlier, the Tieremagier lowered his hands and dropped his captive onto the table.

The rodent, which looked more like a small rat than a mouse, wasted no time in darting for the edge of the table. Unfortunately for it, Freiflügel had the instincts of a hunter. As soon as the Tieremagier opened his hands, the Falke dropped to the tabletop, catching the rat with his talons and closing his beak on its neck.

Minutes later, a soft curse dragged Freiflügel from his meal. He twisted his neck to stare at the Tieremagier. To his surprise, the mann was holding Hausef's letter, which he must have grabbed while Freiflügel was distracted.

Chirruping curiously, Freiflügel inquired about the Tieremagier's sudden distress, but the mann waved a hand dismissively. "Es nada." Freiflügel tilted his head, wondering if the Tieremagier even knew he'd spoken in a human tongue.

Like last time, the Tieremagier seemed to read the note several times before he finished with it. However, instead of rolling it back up and retying it to Freiflügel's leg, he simply slipped it into his pocket. When Freiflügel ruffled his feathers and screeched a protest, the Tieremagier shook his head.

"Naldo's too distracted right now to learn of this from a note, amigo. This is something he'd be better off hearing straight from me." Freiflügel continued to glower, and the mann shook his head. *"Do not fear, amigo. Naldo will receive this news. You have my word."*

Freiflügel eyed the Tieremagier for a moment longer before shaking himself and returning to his meal. Once finished, he turned back to the mann, who only waved him toward the tunnel entrance.

"Return to Zhulan, amigo. I'll carry your news the rest of the way."

Freiflügel screeched again. For some reason, he felt like he should be protesting more, but he couldn't place why. Instead, he leaped up to the tunnel entrance and began the uncomfortable shuffle toward the outside.

He paused on the outer ledge, stretching his wings and otherwise enjoying the freedom of the outside world after the stifling closeness of the tunnel. He was pondering his trip home—he still had to find the drache before he could return to Hausef—when a soft caw had him jerking his head around.

Above him, clinging upside down to the rock of the cliff face, hung the black and brown bird he'd seen on his last visit. *"Piegro?"* He thought that was what the Tieremagier had called him.

Piegro twisted his head. His only response, though, was another soft caw, repeating his earlier request for Freiflügel to move so he could *"return to Maestro."*

How rude, Freiflügel thought as he shook himself and launched into the air. *I'm glad I live in Zhulan and not in Tarsur. With the strangeness of the männer and the rudeness of the birds, I don't think I would enjoy it much here.*

~~*~*

Eastern Zhulan, Evon

"Why are we here, Love?" Hate whined as he tugged at the hand his twin gripped tightly. "There's only Chaos here."

The scathing glare Love tossed over her shoulder made him wince. He would have flushed, too, if his soul didn't already shine red.

"If you want to leave, fine, you can. But I want to check on Peace."

Hate grimaced, but he didn't try to tug his hand free again. As much as he did not want to be here, he wasn't about to leave Love alone amid the Chaos, either.

"As long as you understand I'm here under protest."

Love flashed him a grin as bright as her previous glare had been dark. Hate swallowed against the answering warmth that filled his chest but obediently followed as she quickened her pace.

Despite the constant contact they'd kept since Love's flight from Trostlosoase, neither of them had been completely stable since Mid-Season. Hate suspected he knew why, too. While Love had been present when their youngest sister was broken and tainted, Hate had been in Tarsur observing the rogue thieves when War arrived to begin spreading the Chaos there.

Hate shivered as he remembered the sudden imbalance of hatred and affection he'd felt within himself even before spotting his youngest brother. Even so, no matter how much he *hated* the Chaos he'd felt then, it was nothing to the fear he'd felt when he finally gained a glimpse of War.

He nearly hadn't recognized the violent demigod. His soul, normally a bright swirl of distinct red and black, had glowed a dark, murky maroon that churned sluggishly beneath his transparent skin. He had grinned maniacally, and the wild darkness in his eyes had caused Hate to flee before he could even consider what War's state meant.

Certainly nothing good, he thought as he turned his attention to their current surroundings.

Love had Transported them to the Zhulan desert, near the oasis where Peace's stallion and his mare companion currently rested. To Hate's surprise, the mare had been free of the taint the Ladies had claimed would plague any who came close to the broken Peace.

Now Love dragged him across the desert toward the presence that shimmered in the midday sun and called to them like a beacon of ill omen. Hate knew she didn't dare Transport them closer. The Chaos could make magic unpredictable, even for immortals.

They were just approaching an oasis nearly hidden by the form of Peace's dragon when Love stumbled to a halt.

"Love?"

"Do you see that?" she gasped.

Frowning, Hate stared at the oasis. The dragon lay curled around half of the small oasis, her wings unfurled and hovering over the few small trees and the small pond it contained. He assumed she was sheltering Peace and the king, but he couldn't see them from this angle.

"I don't—"

Love tugged on his hand, pulling him to the left. He shuddered.

Just beyond the dragon, whose soul glimmered just as brightly as Hate had become accustomed to seeing in his sister's bondmates, Peace lay still, her dark soul throbbing menacingly. The sight nearly had Hate fleeing despite his conviction to remain by Love's side. As it was, he tightened his grip on her hand and shook his head.

"She's as tainted by Chaos as the Ladies said she was."

"Not Peace!" Love hissed, nudging her twin sharply. "The king!"

Hate blinked at her before turning back to the oasis. The king slept beside Peace, one hand cupping her shoulder and his body curled protectively around hers.

For a moment, Hate couldn't understand why his twin was so concerned with the king. His soul, a clear, distinct blue and silver that Hate knew matched his physical eye color, looked the same as it always had. Not even—

Hate breathed in sharply. "He's not tainted!"

But that wasn't the whole of it. After all, considering the connection his soul had with Peace, Hate should've expected the king's soul to be free from the taint of Chaos. While their siblings most likely couldn't recognize the Soul Bond for what it was, Love and Hate had been arguing over its formation for centuries now.

What disturbed Hate was the way the king's soul *interacted* with the Chaos leaking from Peace's soul.

Hate would have expected his soul to be shielded from the Chaos, just as the dragon's was. It was the way such bonds reacted to Chaos in the bond, as Love and Hate had observed during the centuries they fought the Chaos they'd been born to balance. Instead, the king's soul seemed to gather the Chaos into itself and transform it. There was no other way Hate could think to describe what he was seeing. He might have also said the man's soul was forcibly drawing the Chaos out of Peace, but . . .

"That is not how Soul Bonds work."

"Not a normal bond, nay." Love gave a slow shake of her head. "But neither Peace nor the king is a normal soul, right? Perhaps this is how theirs works?"

Hate nearly laughed at his twin's confusion. Only her reference to the unusualness of the king's soul tempered his amusement and earned her a glare instead.

They rarely discussed the odd color of the king's soul. Most mortal souls consisted of so many colors representing so many things that only those who constantly dealt with them could interpret what they all meant. But this particular soul consisted of only two colors: far too reminiscent of a demigod's soul for Hate's comfort.

And there isn't even a second such soul to balance it.

He shuddered again.

"Oh, for . . ." Love rolled her eyes. "We've been dealing with this soul for generations, Hate. He's never caused us any harm."

"Until Peace followed him into the Cycle," he muttered. "I hardly consider that harmless."

"Neither of them had control over that. You know that as well as I do."

Hate clenched his jaw. It was the same argument, time and again, over a situation neither of them could change. The Soul Bond had been strong enough by the end of the king's last incarnation two hundred years ago to force Peace to follow his soul when it returned to the Cycle. It had only grown firmer since the beginning of the season, when the king met Peace for the first time.

Before Hate could think of anything else to say, he heard a distant *thrum*, like a taut thread being plucked. At the same time, a soft jolt traveled through the center of his being.

"Damn it," he muttered, rubbing at his chest. "Love."

"The Ladies are calling." She sighed and rubbed her own chest. "Do you think we can risk Transporting ourselves from here?"

"I think we'll have to. You know the Ladies don't like to be ignored." He eyed Peace's dark soul warily. "At least the Chaos seems to be under control?"

Certainly, none appeared to leak past the king and dragon.

Love nodded and stepped closer, pressing herself against his chest. Wrapping his arms around her, Hate buried his nose in her pink hair and let the Mortal Realm fade away.

~~*~*

So dark . . . so cold . . . so lonely.

It felt like she'd been there forever, hiding, protecting herself from the dark creatures that screamed at her and tried to hurt her. But she'd cut herself off, hidden herself away, and their sharp talons and beaks and teeth might claw at and catch her flesh, but they wouldn't hurt her the way they wanted to.

I won't let them.

So lonely.

Doesn't matter.

She'd been hurt. She couldn't remember how—remembering would bring back the pain—but she wasn't going to let it happen again.

The dark creatures were tricky, though. Not only did they scream at her about things she didn't want to hear, but they also spoke to her in soft voices that made her think of love and happiness. Those comforting voices had brought her closer to remembering than the screams had, but the shock of returning pain had been enough to convince her that the soft voices meant her as much harm as the screams did.

So lonely. Why must I be alone?

Because others bring pain.

Do I bring pain?

Thoughts flitted, memories brushed against her, painful pressure rose within her. She shoved them away.

Best not to think about it.

The questions and complaints quieted. Sometimes, she wondered if those, too, belonged to the dark creatures. But they were spoken in a young voice she recognized as her own. A child, lost, in need of protection.

Protection I can provide.

"Gemi."

She stirred. The soft voices had returned. Familiar, as always. She couldn't remember who would speak to her like that, but the memories would only cause pain, so it was best to forget.

"Please wake up."

She lifted her head. The voice sounded louder than it had before.

Are they real?

Nay, they can't be.

But as she looked around, she realized the screams that had been her constant companions for so long had lessened. The dark creatures seemed fewer, too, but she couldn't be sure; she had never taken the time to count them.

"Please, Gemi. You must wake."

They sound concerned.

Memories rose in her mind as she tried to put the voices to faces, to people. Pain accompanied them. She whined and shoved the memories back down.

Too much pain.

She couldn't let the soft voices distract from that. Even if they were real, they couldn't protect her from the pain. No one could.

Only I can.

She dropped her head again and buried it beneath her hands. She curled tighter in on herself. She would ignore the screams and the voices and everything else.

Only I can protect myself.

Tarsur

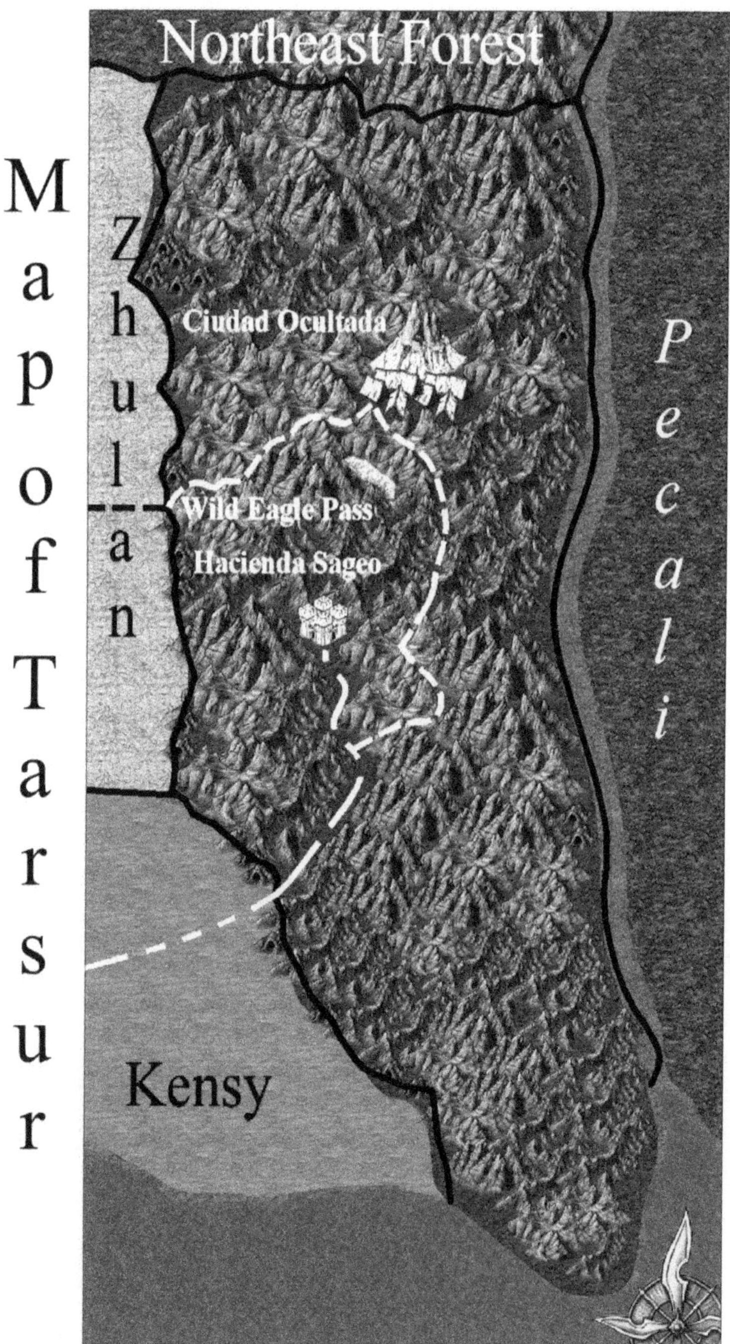

Map of Tarsur
Northeast Forest
Zhulan
Pecali
Ciudad Ocultada
Wild Eagle Pass
Hacienda Sageo
Kensy

Nine

Two days later
24 Mid Autumn, 224
Ladrasid, Tarsur, Evon

Pastora Ovillana laid down her mending and stared out across the fields of Valle Ocultado. Naldo had warned her not to expect Gemi on her usual *día*, but she couldn't prevent worry from filling her as the sol began to disappear over the lip of the valle.

I wish mijo had at least taken the time to explain why Gemi might be tarde.

For the last four años, Gemi had arrived in Ladrasid on the twenty-fourth of every Mid Spring, Mid Summer, and Mid Autumn, riding through the farmland and grazing fields that spread from the pueblo to the narrow paso that was the only entrance to the valle. Only Winter had ever seen her absence due to the heavy snow, which made the quick travel Gemi preferred impossible.

Pastora sighed. *Naldo and I will have to talk about letting his duties as rey distract him from his familia.*

There had been a time, after Naldo became Rey of the Ocultados, when her hijo would have visited Pastora and her rebaño every siétedia. Over time, the regular visits had dwindled, but he had never been too ocupado to visit her for such an important discussion. The one-line note he'd sent her several días before had been an unpleasant surprise.

"Seño—um, lo siento. ¿Mamá?"

Pastora blinked and turned to find little Mora, the latest addition to her rebaño, staring at her from behind the door of the casa. Her large brown eyes were red-rimmed, a testament to the freshness of her grief for her lost padres.

"¿Sí, chiquita?"

Mora dipped her chin and peered up at Pastora through her black bangs. "You were lookin' sad, M-Mamá. Why're you sad?"

Pastora smiled slightly. "I thought I was expecting someone, chiquita. That's all."

Mora sucked her bottom lip in between her teeth. After a moment of worrying it, she crossed to the edge of the veranda and leaned out, frowning at the nearby field.

"They no comin', then?"

Pastora drew in a deep breath, hoping to banish the sudden tightness in her chest. "No, no just yet."

I hope. She couldn't ignore the doubt now niggling at her mente.

Mora continued to watch the fields. With a soft sigh, Pastora picked up the cloth she'd put aside earlier and resumed her needlework.

"¿Mamá?" Mora chirruped a few minutes later.

Pastora hummed idly. She was focused on a particular rip

that felt wider than it looked. *Maybe I should light the lamps. That might help.*

"Es that who you're waitin' for?"

Pastora lifted her head and frowned at Mora. The chica was pointing out toward the fields, her wide eyes staring back at Pastora earnestly.

"What're you talking about, chiquita? Es too dark to see who's coming en from the fields."

"But, Mamá, there be luz en the paso."

Pastora jerked her head up and peered out across the fields. Sure enough, a warm glow had appeared, too distant to be lamps the farmers or shepherds might have lit to fight off the encroaching darkness.

Who . . . ?

Setting aside her mending once more, she rose to her feet and crossed to the edge of the veranda, hoping for a better view. It couldn't be Gemi. With a dragona as her bondmate, she had no need for torches or lamps to light her way during the noche.

A deep lowing sound reached her ears then, and she stilled, ice gripping her chest.

"Why're they blowin' huntin' horns, Mamá?"

Pastora shook her head. *¡No! Why would . . . ?*

The horn sounded again, louder, and she knew there was no denying its meaning. Ignoring Mora's insistent questions, Pastora dashed across the veranda and grabbed the bell used to call in the gente from the fields . . . or warn of an attack.

She nearly missed the first screams as the bell's clangs rang out. The warm glow that had been in the mouth of the paso began to spread. Specks of luz leaped into the sky, only to fall toward the open fields.

"¡No!" Pastora yelled, her hand faltering. She had two chicos out in those fields.

"¡Mamá!" Mora cried. Pastora was suddenly aware of hands tightly clutching her skirt. "The bell, Mamá! No stop!"

Pastora pressed her lips together and tightened her hold on the bell. She could do nada for her chicos but warn the valle of the attack and pray to the dioses that they would be safe.

~~*~*

As a resident of Ladrasid, Cabro had been witness to several guerras among the ladrones as they fought over who controlled Ciudad Ocultada, which lay nestled at the back of Valle Ocultado.

However, the guerras of the ladrones were sneaky and quiet. When the horns of guerra sounded and flaming arrows lit the sky, Cabro knew the valle's attackers were no mere ladrones.

"To the ciudad!" he shouted as flames bloomed in the fields around him. He bleated the same a moment later, grabbing the nearest goat by its horn and reaching for the rest of his herd with his magia. Around him, others whistled and shouted, calling for their perros to round up the flocks and herds.

Cabro had barely made it five steps when a scream sounded to his left, followed by rapid barking. Spinning toward the sounds, he cursed. There, among growing flames, a small figure collapsed.

"Guido!" He cursed himself for momentarily forgetting his apprentice. Shoving the goat he was leading toward the ciudad, Cabro repeated the command and strode toward the flames.

A moment later, he gasped and bit his tongue. Something had clamped down hard on his trailing hand.

Hissing, he turned to find one of his goats, a large, old male with long, twisting horns, staring flatly at him, his hand in its mouth.

"*¡Bocamet!*" he growled between clenched teeth. "*What in the Fuego de Mauro are you doing?*"

"*To the ciudad.*" Bocamet's words were as flat as his eyes.

"*¡Sí!*" Cabro curved his free hand beneath the goat's chin in hopes of breaking its hold. "*You need to head for the ciudad. I'll join you once I've got Guido.*"

"*No,*" Bocamet bleated. "*To the ciudad.*"

Cabro hissed. Sometimes he wondered why his Animal Poder had to be goats. They were stubborn beasts, and possessive to boot. Too often, they believed the orders given to them pertained as much to their herders as to themselves.

"*Bocamet,*" he growled. "*Return—*"

A loud bark suddenly interrupted him. Fiela, a shaggy perra, bounded toward them. In the luz of the surrounding fires, he could see that her spotted gray coat had been singed away in several places.

"*Cabro, help!*" she yipped. "*Guido's hurt!*"

Nodding grimly, Cabro turned back to Bocamet and used his magia to force the goat to release his hand. Bocamet did so with a grunt but still refused to leave with the others.

"*Fine!*" Cabro snapped. He spun around to follow Fiela toward the dancing flames. "*Then follow, if you must!*"

Bocamet followed without further complaint.

~~*~*

"No es that simple, Majestad."

Naldo Ramírez sighed and rubbed his forehead. Pablo might have been one of his padre's best amigos, but the small, wiry hombre could be annoyingly dense at times.

"We've heard his nombre numerous times en conexión to recent ataques. What about that es no simple?"

Pablo's sharp features settled into a glower, and he crossed his arms. "You declared Deligero dead nearly five años ago. You canno' expect us to accept he might be alive because of a few rumors."

Naldo clenched his fists and dug his nails into his palms. *I can't punch him just because he doesn't trust my instintos.* He ignored the whisper of thought that his padre had always praised those instincts. *He never would have condoned violencia in response to a mere disagreement.*

"We canno' take the chance he might be alive," Naldo snapped when he thought he could control his hands.

"And if he es no alive, Naldo?"

That was Raeka. Naldo relaxed as he turned to face her. If he considered Pablo a disapproving tío, Raeka would be Naldo's elder hermana, always supportive and always there. Time and again, his padre had set her to watch Naldo, and she had always used that time to train him in the ways of the ladrones.

"Even if he es no, we canno' just ignore the increased ataques. We've promised the pueblos protección against the ladrones these last four años. I will no back down from that now."

That earned him nods from most of his pandilla, those he trusted most among the Ocultados. Raeka offered him a small smile, which he returned. Only Pablo still looked disagreeable.

"¡Majestad! ¡Majestad!"

The door of his study flew open, and a young hombre stopped in the doorway, gasping for breath. He looked an año or two shy of Coming of Age, but the small eagle embroidered on the left shoulder of his tunic marked him as one of Ciudad Ocultada's mensajeros.

"What es it?" Naldo asked when the chico remained silent except for his heaving breaths.

The mensajero gulped down one more breath of air and wheezed. "Ladrasid . . . es under ataque, Majestad!"

Naldo grimaced. "Raeka, gather your banda and go down to the pueblo. We canno' allow the ladrones to gain—"

"No es ladrones, Majestad!" The mensajero grabbed Raeka's arm as she tried to slip past him. He didn't appear to notice the cold look she offered him. "They attack wit' arrows and fire, and the villagers are already retreating back to the ciudad."

Naldo cursed and dragged a hand through his hair. Ciudad Ocultada was built into the side of the montaña and could withstand such direct assaults. The valle, however, was open and, despite the single obvious entrance, much more vulnerable to such violence.

"Es there any indicación of who our enemigos are?"

The mensajero hesitated. "I am no sure if it es connected, but I thought I heard hunting horns just afore the ataque began."

Cold flooded Naldo's chest. Horns of guerra could only mean nobles. No one else would consider such notice necessary.

"¡Naldo!" Raeka hissed. He nodded.

"Take the mountain paths to the paso. If they brought an army large enough for this kind of assault, they'll still be bottled up there. I wanna know which noble has discovered the valle."

She nodded sharply, ripped her arm from the mensajero's grasp, and disappeared through the doorway.

Naldo turned to the rest of his pandilla. "Teodoro, take an inventario of the supply chambers. We need to know how long we can safely wait out the assault."

"Claro que sí, Majestad."

"For that matter, we'll need an updated census of the ciudad and the pueblo. ¿Mateo?"

"I'll have mi banda begin the count immediately."

The two hombres, twins with whom Naldo had grown up, followed Raeka out of the room.

"Pedro, take your hombres up to the battlements. If our enemigos get too close, do no hesitate to fire upon them. Oh, and make sure someone es set to ringing the alarm bells. I do no like that I have no heard them yet."

The large, silent Ocultado, another contemporary of Naldo's padre, gave only a quick nod before striding out of the room to execute his orders.

"You certain that es wise, Majestad?" questioned Pablo, the only member of his pandilla still remaining. "I doubt Nadie would agree wit' such violencia against the hombres of the rey."

Naldo frowned at the small hombre. He had never been one to use Gemi's possible thoughts against Naldo, and Naldo couldn't understand why he would start now.

"Nadie would no allow our fidelidad to the rey of Evon to threaten our gente, and neither will I. Understood?"

Pablo met his gaze calmly. "Very well. Did you have orders for me?"

Naldo watched Pablo silently for a moment before nodding. "Take your banda to the entrances of the pasajes secretos. We canno' risk the ladrones taking advantage of the attack to find their way ento the ciudad."

Pablo gave a small, curt bow, something he only ever did

when he was feeling particularly contrary, and left the study. Naldo stared after him, confused.

He can't still be upset about my concerns over Deligero, can he? Not with this attack interrupting any plans I might have made to find him.

He was dragged from his thoughts by a soft "Er . . . ¿Majestad?" Blinking, he realized the mensajero still hovered in the doorway.

"I spotted Señora Pastora afore I came up here, and Nadie was no wit' her. Do you think he'll make it ento the ciudad all right?"

Naldo closed his eyes and sighed. *And perhaps that's why Pablo mentioned Gemi.* He hadn't explained, even to his pandilla, why they couldn't expect the chica on her usual día.

How do I explain that mi hermana, the only persona they see as my equal, was tortured and overcome by a rogue in Zhulan?

"¿Majestad?"

Naldo shook his head. "I am no expecting him for several días yet." *If then.* He hadn't heard from Hausef since the nomad informed him of Gemi's unconsciousness. "Hopefully, we can nullify the threat afore he arrives, ¿sí?"

The chico still looked worried, but Naldo knew how to distract him. "Now, you mentioned Señora Pastora. Could you help me find her?"

The mensajero nodded slowly, but he was quick enough to lead Naldo away from the study that the rey didn't have reason to complain.

~~*~*

Pastora scanned Plaza Central, hoping to find the remainder of her rebaño. At her side, Mora clung tearfully to her skirt while Nita, Pastora's eldest, attempted to calm her. Only her two youngest hijos were still missing.

Both had been out in the fields with their mentors.

"¡Fabio!" she called. "¡Guido!"

Nita finally managed to detach Mora from Pastora's skirt and swing her up onto her hip. Mora buried her face into Nita's shoulder, winding her arms around the young mujer's neck.

"They will no be able to hear you, Madre."

Pastora pursed her lips grimly and idly patted Mora's back. Nita was right. Plaza Central was crowded with villagers, all searching for their loved ones. The volume of the yelled nombres was only surpassed by the joyful cries as familias were slowly reunited. Even the alarm bells ringing from the depths of Ciudad Ocultada could barely be heard.

"I'm worried, Nita."

"I know, Madre."

Nita squeezed Pastora's arm, but Pastora had already turned back to searching the crowd. She didn't know how long she had been at it when a deep voz caught her attention.

"Do no mistake mi quietud for acceptance, chiquito."

"But the plantas are cryin', Abeto!" answered a familiar young voz. "We canno' just let them get away wit' it!"

Pastora jerked around. "¡Fabio!"

The deep voz, which had begun to respond, faltered. "Perdone, por favor," it rumbled. A moment later, a tall, thick hombre pushed through the crowd, a shorter, willowy chico following close behind him.

"Oh, Fabio!" Pastora pulled the chico into her arms. "Are you all right?"

Fabio tapped her arms furiously. "I'd be better if you'd lemme go, Madre."

Pastora pulled back and gripped his shoulders, scanning his body for injuries. When she found none, she studied his rolling blue eyes and the taut lines of his face.

"Have you seen Guido?"

Those blue eyes widened, and Fabio's face slackened. "No es wit' you?" Pastora shook her head, and Fabio ducked out of her grasp to begin scanning the crowd as well.

Pastora's lips twitched. Fabio and Guido were the only ones among her rebaño to be actual hermanos. No matter how often Fabio complained about his younger hermano, he had always been fiercely protective of him.

"We were en two completely different parts of the fields, and I have no seen him since we came to the ciudad." He glanced back at Pastora, his wide eyes making him look younger than his fourteen años. "You think he es all right?"

Abeto patted Fabio on the shoulder. "I'm sure Cabro es keeping—"

"¡Curanderos!" someone shouted. "We need curanderos!"

Pastora spun toward the ciudad's outer gate even as Abeto cursed. At first, she couldn't see anything beyond the personas around them. Then the crowds shifted, and she gasped.

Cabro limped through the gate, a nearly unconscious hombre half slung over his shoulders. Behind him, more hombres staggered in, some of their own volition, others half carried. All of them bore burns of some kind, while a few had obviously been struck by the falling arrows.

"¡Cabro!" Pastora shoved her way through the crowd. Abeto and Fabio's voces drifted after her, but she ignored the Magos Botánicos.

By the time she reached Cabro, the stocky hombre was

handing off his wounded companion to a couple of waiting mujeres. He turned to her with a grimace as she questioned him about Guido.

"We have him," he answered grimly before bleating sharply. A moment later, a large goat pressed past two hombres. A small body was slung over its back, and a familiar spotted gray perra followed right behind it.

"¡Guido!" Pastora rushed toward the goat. She was pulled up short by a solid hand on her shoulder. A moment later, the goat snapped its teeth together where her own hand might have been.

"I would no rush at Bocamet like that," Cabro muttered. He lifted his free hand, and Pastora stared at the teeth marks imprinted upon his flesh. "He's taken his assignment to protect Guido very seriously."

Pastora's eyes widened as they turned back to the goat. "Es he . . . ?" Pastora pursed her lips, unable to finish the thought.

Cabro huffed. "He es alive, but his injuries are bad. I had to put out the fires afore I could reach him, and he took an arrow to one leg."

Pastora pressed her hands to her lips and choked back a cry.

"¿Guido?"

Pastora turned. Fabio stood behind her, his eyes wide as he stared at his injured hermano. "Oh, Fabio." She opened her arms and beckoned him toward her. "Ven, mijo. Let's see if we canno' find un curandero for your hermano."

"No need to go looking, Pastora."

Corteza, a tall, stocky mujer, pressed past Fabio, directing him gently into Pastora's arms. She glanced sharply at Cabro and motioned toward the goat.

"You'll have to remove the chico from his back, sí,

Cabro? I do no fancy Healing mi own wounds on top of all of yours."

Cabro grunted.

A shouted "¡Madre!" tore Pastora's attention from the magos. The voz was deep and familiar, and she was sharply reminded of her earlier thoughts about her eldest hijo's inconsideration. By the time Naldo appeared through the crowd, Pastora had her arms crossed, frowning.

"Where have you been, Naldo?"

Naldo snapped his jaw shut and blinked at her for a moment. "Er . . . I just learned of the ataque, Madre. I came down as soon as I could."

She huffed and waved a hand dismissively. "No now, mijo. These past few días."

Naldo grimaced. "Lo siento, Madre. I've been dealing wit' an increase in ladrón ataques for siétedias." He dragged a hand through his hair. "And now this ataque and Nadie's tardiness en top of it all."

"And just what do you know about Nadie? Your note was no very informativo."

Naldo frowned at Pastora before glancing sharply at the personas surrounding them. Pastora's breath caught in her chest. If Naldo didn't want to talk about Gemi with so many personas around, she could only imagine the kind of trouble her hija must be facing.

"Graucen, stop estalling!" Corteza's sharp voz pulled Pastora from her contemplations. "These personas need healing, no excusas."

"I'm just saying I'd be of more use if you'd let me make them some pociones. You know mi hands-on magia es of little use."

Pastora frowned. She recognized the nombre Corteza had used, if not the voz of its owner. Turning, she was just in time to see Corteza slap the thin hombre beside her and then shove a bag into his hands.

"If I hear you've been making pociones again, I will no hesitate to turn you over to the rey. You're lucky to be allowed the use of your magia at all after what you did."

"Sí, Corteza," Graucen grumbled. He dropped into a quick bow before striding toward a large group of injured personas.

As soon as he was out of earshot, Pastora stepped up to Corteza. "You will keep him away from Guido, sí?"

It had been nearly five años since Graucen had last touched potions. Even that was not long enough, as far as Pastora was concerned. After the part he had played in hurting Gemi and her bondmates when they had first arrived in Tarsur, she couldn't trust the Curandero Mágico with any of her rebaño, even with his limited magia.

"Claro que sí," Corteza answered easily before crouching down and laying her hands over Guido's wounds.

~~*~*

Much later, Naldo sat in his study, feeling drained.

It had taken several hours for Ciudad Ocultada to settle into a calm and quietness that belied the fires still raging both in the valle and in the hearts of his gente. They'd lost five of the injured hombres who had come in from the fields, at least eleven more were missing, the fires were destroying what should have been their winter food supply . . .

And Guido's still in critical condition. Naldo buried his head in his hands. *How can I protect mi gente when I can't even protect mi familia?*

A soft knock at the door of his study barely pulled him from his thoughts. He called his visitor in with a soft "Ven."

When nada more than the opening and closing of the door answered his call, Naldo finally looked up and blinked.

"Raeka?"

The normally stolid mujer was slumped against the door, her eyes wide and face pale. Naldo felt his chest tighten. What could she have possibly seen in the paso that would make her look like this?

"Did you see who our enemigo es?"

She nodded slowly. He had to repeat her nombre twice more, though, before she answered.

"The duque." She finally met Naldo's gaze with wide eyes. "Our enemigo es the duque, Lord Peln Sageo."

~~*~*

War grinned. A red glow lit the entirety of the Hidden Valley. It hardly mattered that the duke's men had ceased their attack and had set up camp for the night. It didn't matter that most of them cringed away from the damage they'd caused.

What matters is that Pea—

The thought became a scream as pain erupted within him. He struck out with one hand and clutched at his head with the other. *Why . . . ? I can't . . . !*

He snarled and forced back the pain and the accompanying thoughts. "She will pay!" He glared at the pacing form of the man he had stolen from *her* influence. "She will lose every influence she's gained, one way or another, until she has no choice but to remember who she is if she hopes to survive!"

Grinning savagely, he stepped closer to the pacing man and reached out a hand to pluck at the air. The man stilled, his breath heavy as he stared out over the burning fields.

"What do you say, Peln?" War drawled. "*She* betrayed you, didn't she? Lied to you? Now it's time for *her* to pay."

The duke didn't respond. War didn't expect him to. His words were for the man's soul, not his ears.

And his soul was drinking them in, darkening as War's influence grew stronger. His influence would only continue to grow as the duke's desire for vengeance remained unquenched.

"Aye!" War leaned closer. "You shall have your vengeance, Peln. The death of your son demands no less."

And then war will reign once more.

Ten

Three days later
27 Mid Autumn, 224
Somewhere in the Tarsurian Mountains

I am really beginning to hate Tarsur!"

Shadow kicked out with his hind legs. A heavy *crunch* accompanied the solidity of a body beneath his hooves. His grim satisfaction was short-lived as his opponent was replaced by several others, each scrabbling to find a handhold on what little remained of his tack.

Last Chance's front hooves connected with the skull of one thief who had managed to wrap his fingers in Shadow's mane. *"Now is hardly the time to be complaining about the province."*

"Why not?" He reared up onto his hind legs. *"Never once, since James, Flame, and I started traveling the Ghost Trail, have thieves attacked us. And now . . ."*

Screams rose around Shadow as he dropped to all fours, but a flash of metal distracted him. On the other side of the growing band of thieves, Ferez tightly gripped his lone remaining dagger in one hand and traded blows with several men, all the while valiantly trying to keep them from reaching Gemi.

"*Flame!*" Shadow shouted through the dragonbond.

"*I am flying as quickly as I am able, Shadow.*"

"Through *the mountains?*" Incredulity joined the irritation churning within Shadow as Flame turned sharply around a particularly thick peak.

"*Your understanding of Tarsur's elevation is severely lacking!*" A stinging touch accompanied the dragon's words.

Shadow snorted and tossed his head. He knew he wasn't the source of Flame's anger; that was the thieves, whose timing was impeccable as they had attacked while the dragon was gone in search of food and water. But being the dragon's only outlet for her anger still wasn't pleasant.

"*Now is not the time for pleasantries,*" Flame growled. "*And if those thieves lay even a single hand on James, they will not live long enough to regret it.*"

Even as she said it, two men circled past Ferez and began pawing through the half-empty saddlebag lying next to Gemi. One man was just reaching for Gemi when Ferez finally noticed.

The thief soon collapsed, a dagger protruding from his chest.

A minute later, Ferez's hands were bound in rope, the dagger had been pulled from the dead body, and Shadow and Last Chance were doing everything they could to avoid the lassos being wielded by several thieves. Gemi, to Shadow's dismay, was lost beneath a flurry of greedy hands.

Two ropes had just slipped over Shadow's head when a roar shook the rock beneath his hooves. Cursing, the stallion dropped his head and leaped toward the nearest wall of rock, praying to the gods that Flame had the sense to avoid a fire attack.

"I am not so far gone in my anger as to risk injury to my bondmates." The growl reverberated through his mind just before the ground quaked and Shadow collapsed to his knees.

Screams rose around him, only to be drowned out by another roar. Shadow kept his eyes shut and his body pressed close to the rock wall, unwilling to climb to his hooves and risk approaching Flame, even to ascertain whether Last Chance and Ferez had made it to safety.

The cacophony of screams and roars lasted for several long minutes before Shadow heard a series of loud crunches and silence suddenly rang in his ears. Even then, he remained still, uncertain he wanted to see what damage Flame had wrought.

"No worse than we have seen and done before," the dragon crooned softly. Thankfully, she refrained from sending an image through the dragonbond, though Shadow could feel her desire to prove the statement.

"Shadow? Frenz?" Last Chance whinnied.

Shadow snorted and finally lifted his head, nickering a soft *"I'm all right"* to reassure the mare. He did his best to ignore the bloody and broken bodies strewn across the ground.

"Everyone all right?" Ferez called out.

Flame's answering croon broke off suddenly as worry shot through the bond. A moment later, Shadow was on his feet and trotting around Flame to where Gemi had been lying.

When Shadow reached them, Ferez was kneeling over Gemi, shaking off the remnants of his rope bindings. *Flame must have cut them,* Shadow realized idly. After checking Gemi over, the amnesiac king glanced up with a grim smile.

"He's no worse for wear, bu' they stole the rest of our weapons." He shook his head. "They e'en though' to grab James's throwin' knives an' scharfmonde."

Flame growled. *"And they attacked before I could find a decent source of water."* Images of barren rock, all too reminiscent of the scene in Gemi's mind, flashed through the bond.

"What about greenery?" Last Chance nickered. *"Food animals for Frenz?"*

"Or for yourself?" Shadow eyed the dragon worriedly. The emergency provisions Gemi usually kept had been stolen by thieves only the day before, and Shadow and Last Chance had managed to find some scrubby vegetation around midday yesterday. However, Flame hadn't found anything for herself since before they'd entered the mountains three days before.

Flame huffed. *"I spotted a few rodents, but water was my main concern."* Growling, she shook her head vigorously. *"If I had led you to the correct path when we first entered Tarsur, we would not be facing these obstacles."*

"You can hardly blame yourself for that, Flame," Shadow nickered. *"We've all been distracted since Mid-Season. You could hardly have been expected to remember that the oasis we were traveling from was so much farther north than we're used to."*

"I should have kept it in mind."

"Easy, yeh three," Ferez muttered idly. "Arguin' won' get us anywhere." He brushed several limp strands of black hair out of Gemi's face. Shadow shifted uncomfortably. It was still odd seeing Gemi with short hair.

"Frenz is right," Last Chance nickered. *"We'll just have to press on and hope we find food or water as we go."*

The mare nudged Ferez. When the king glanced up at her, she tossed her snout toward Shadow. Nodding, Ferez picked up the now empty saddlebag and tossed it onto the stallion's bare back. Shadow and Last Chance had been alternating carrying their two humans, and today was Shadow's day.

With care, Flame lifted Gemi onto Shadow's back and held her there while Ferez used the rope still dangling around Shadow's neck to tie her in place. No doubt the rope they'd had was lost with the rest of their gear.

Flame was about to help Ferez up onto Shadow's back as well when Ferez called for her to wait. "Hold on. This looks . . ." He slipped his fingers along the edge of Gemi's cloth belt. Shadow snorted as the man turned the edge of the belt down and something fell from it.

"Better," Ferez added as he straightened her belt. "Tha' looked uncomfortable."

Shadow snorted as Ferez asked Flame to help him mount and lowered his snout toward what had fallen from Gemi's belt. A couple of sniffs only provided the scent of rock, but a twist of Shadow's head produced a glint of orange among the gray beneath him.

"Flame?"

"I see it," she answered. Instead of helping Ferez up, she reached past him with one delicately clawed hand and picked up the source of the flash.

"It's just a piece o' stone tha' go' caught in James's belt," Ferez assured as the dragon lifted the small, jagged stone from the ground. "Tha's all."

Shadow snorted and tossed his head. *"Not quite."*

Flame hummed her agreement. *"It seems the thieves didn't quite get everything."*

Ferez stilled and glanced between dragon and stallion. "It is important, then?"

Shadow snorted and eyed the man curiously. He knew Ferez had no way to actually understand animals, and yet . . .

"Yet he can read our cues remarkably well." Flame hummed

again and pressed the stone into the palm of Ferez's hand. A gentle croon, a nudge to his shoulder and then to his hand, and Ferez was frowning thoughtfully down at the jagged gray stone.

"I'm no' sure I—"

He fell quiet as the stone began to radiate a soft orange glow. The light didn't last long—its sudden appearance had no doubt interrupted Ferez's concentration—but it was enough to confirm Shadow's suspicions.

"Wha' was that?" Ferez asked.

All three animals huffed. As much of their cues as Ferez could understand, they wouldn't have been able to explain to him the stone. *"Just keep it on you,"* Flame insisted, closing his fingers around the stone with her own. Ferez nodded and pocketed it and then mounted with Flame's help.

~~*~*

"I still can't believe we've been attacked by four different bands of thieves in four days," Shadow muttered for perhaps the twentieth time since they'd left their bloody camp.

"It's seventeen, if you include the complaint you made during this morning's battle," Flame grumbled. *"As that is at least sixteen times too many, I would ask you again to refrain from repeating it."*

"Please, Shadow," Last Chance nickered tiredly, *"enough of the complaining. Please!"*

The stallion huffed. *"I just find it odd, is all. Why, after all the quiet years of traveling the Ghost Trail, are we are only now encountering these bands of thieves?"*

Last Chance swung her head from side to side. *"Perhaps it's the new path we're following? Flame did say this was not the Ghost Trail you're accustomed to."*

"Perhaps, but the rogues have never been so bold here in Tarsur."

"Not since Deligero died, at least," Flame corrected.

Shadow snorted. *"Are you suggesting the rogues might have gained a leader here in Tarsur like they did in Kensy, Flame? I think the person would have to be as vicious as Deligero was to succeed in that."*

"Who was Deligero?" Last Chance asked.

"The most bloodthirsty thief we've ever met," Shadow answered. *"He fancied himself the king of thieves and even killed Naldo's father, the previous king of thieves, to make it so."*

"But Naldo is the current king of the thieves, aye?" Shadow nickered in agreement. *"Then did Naldo kill Deligero?"*

Shadow hesitated. *"Not exac—"*

"Ah-ha!"

Shadow's head shot up so quickly, he nearly lost his balance. *"Flame?"*

At first, silence answered his query, and he reached for the dragon through the bond. Images of rock rushing past and a small animal fleeing ahead had him jerking his head to the side and pulling away from the bond. He really did not want to see what Flame had in mind for the small creature.

When a hissed curse shot through the bond, Shadow ignored it. He thought Flame must have lost her quarry, and he didn't want to face the ire of a hungry dragon. However, when distant shouts and screams reached his ears, he turned back to the bond.

Before he even had a chance to ask what had happened, images of uniformed men raising bows and swords tumbled through the bond. The sensation of too many restricted limbs pressed on his mind, along with a sense of growing warmth in his chest that alarmed him.

"No fire, Flame! Look at their uniforms!"

Each and every man was dressed in gray, the color of Tarsur.

More specifically, the color of the province's duke.

Flame swallowed down the warmth in her chest and growled. *"We should not be anywhere near Hacienda Sageo. Why are so many of the duke's men out here?"*

"Show me where you are, Flame, and we'll—"

Pain suddenly echoed though the bond, and an angry roar filled Shadow's mind. He was still struggling with the tumult of images and sensations when pressure on his sides and neck pulled him back to himself.

Last Chance whinnied sharply. *"Shadow, what's wrong?"* The stallion was idly aware of Ferez asking the same thing.

"Flame." He tossed his head and tried to figure out the best way to reach the source of the roar he could still hear echoing off the surrounding rock walls. *"She's been captured and injured and . . ."*

He snorted and leaped into a trot, hoping their original path would lead him to Flame. He might be accustomed to pain through the bond, but not knowing the location of his bondmate was wholly unacceptable.

~~*~*

Flame roared and snapped at the soldier who had sliced his sword across her chest. She did not care that the blade had barely slipped deeper than her scales. Hunger and thirst gnawed at her belly. Pain lanced through her wings and legs as she struggled to escape the entangling cloth of the tent she had been unable to avoid flying into. On top of those, the soldier's attack could not be allowed to go unanswered.

"Idiotic humans!" The soldier had danced out of reach and several of his fellows were nocking arrows to their bows. *"Release me, and we will see just how willing you are to attack me."*

Several of the soldiers loosed their arrows, and Flame

roared again as one embedded itself in her left shoulder and another lodged itself in the right side of her chest. The rest bounced off her scales, clattering to the ground around her.

"What in the nombre de Carito is happening?"

With a hiss, Flame opened her eyes and peered toward the sharp voice. A man dressed in the distinctly colored armor of a knight strode quickly toward the group of soldiers attacking her.

"We're under ataque, Sir Gervasio!" shouted one of the soldiers.

"*I will show you 'under attack,' human!*" Flame snarled, struggling against the cloth restricting her movements.

"*Cálmate, amigo. You'll only hurt yourself if you keep struggling like that.*"

Flame stilled and snapped her head around to find the source of the growled words. Behind the knight trailed several other men. Among them, a large, burly man wore Animal Magic like a coating of fur.

"*You call me 'friend,' when your own people have attacked me?*" she hissed.

"Turi?" questioned the knight, but the Animal Mage shook his head and waved a dismissive hand.

"I do no think it . . ." He paused and contemplated Flame quietly before continuing. "I do no believe she meant to attack us." Switching to the language of the animals, he added, "*Did you mean to attack us?*"

Flame snorted and shifted. She stopped and hissed in pain when she felt her wings bend unnaturally. "*I can understand your human tongues perfectly well, mage. And nay, I was not intending an attack on you.*" Glancing around curiously, she added, "*Merely a mountain hare, which has now eluded me.*"

The mage, Turi, chuckled and patted the knight on the shoulder. "She es only hungry, Gervasio. And no for human flesh," he added quickly when several of the soldiers gave cries of alarm.

Flame eyed the soldiers speculatively. *"I do not know. I might be willing to make an exception, as hungry as I am."*

Turi only laughed harder. "Do you think we can spare some meat for the pobre, Gervasio? It sounds like she es starving."

Flame did not know if she should be offended that the mage was calling her "poor one" or if she should ignore her pride and beg for food.

"What is going on, Flame?" Shadow suddenly pressed against her mind.

Flame let the thought *I do not know* flow back through the bond, never removing her eyes from the men in front of her. *But keep out of sight for now. I do not want to risk James and Frenz falling into the hands of these men.*

"I would rather you hadn't either," Shadow nickered but remained silent otherwise.

"I don't rightly care if it has hunger or not," Sir Gervasio snapped. "I would like to know what a dragón is doing within Evon's borders."

Turi sobered and glanced curiously at Flame. "That es a good point, amigo. Criaturas mágicas have no roamed Evon for two hundred años. Where did you come from? Are you lost?"

"Well, we are certainly lost," Shadow nickered.

Flame refrained from sending a sting through the bond but only because she had to decide how to answer without giving away her companions. Unfortunately, someone else spoke first.

"How she came to be in Evon is not what you should be asking, Gervasio." Flame hissed as Lord Sageo strode up to the knight. "The question is, where is her bondmate, Caffers?"

~~*~*

Peln Sageo didn't know if he was happy or angry that the dragona had appeared. Certainly, he could only assume her presence meant the ladrones Caffers had praised so highly at the beginning of the estación were the very ladrones who had killed Alano.

Grief threatened to overwhelm Peln, but he shoved it aside. He couldn't afford to let the emotion cripple him, not when there was still so much to do to avenge the death of his hijo.

"Caffers?" Gervasio muttered. "You mean Nadie?"

Peln nodded. As his Capitán de Caballeros and his best amigo since childhood, Gervasio was one of Peln's closest advisors. He was one of the few hombres privy to the information Peln had learned earlier in the estación. The only thing he had refrained from sharing was Nadie's dragona and the vínculo de dragón that connected them.

Conexión mágico or no, the presence of a dragón in Evon is still an ill omen.

"But, Milord," his Mago Botánico, Arlo, muttered from nearby, "I thought you said Nadie's ladrones sought paz. If Nadie es here . . ."

The dragona growled, gaining Turi's attention. The Mago Animal frowned thoughtfully at the criatura before replying.

"We are at the mouth of Valle Ocultado."

"Turi!" Gervasio snapped, but Peln gripped his arm and shook his head when the caballero met his gaze. Peln wanted to know the dragona's response. If she hadn't even known where they were, perhaps there was still some verdad to Nadie's words of paz and unity.

~~*~*

Flame hissed, and not just because of the sharp pain in her chest or the throbbing ache that had settled in her wings. She had managed to find the Hidden Valley without realizing it, but the duke of Tarsur had set up camp with his men right at the valley's main entrance.

"Why?"

For the first time since he had begun speaking to Flame, the Animal Mage looked uncertain. He glanced at the duke. "I do no know if I should tell you why."

"No razón not to." Lord Sageo's words were amicable enough, but there was a dislike in his gaze that Flame did not remember seeing through Gemi's eyes.

"The ladrones that call this valle home killed my eldest hijo and sent his bloody ring to me as proof. We are here to punish them. That is why."

Flame jerked her head back, too shocked to worry about the position of her limbs. Her shock was echoed by Shadow's own as he registered what she had heard.

"He can't be serious."

Unfortunately, the tightness of the duke's expression and the dislike in his eyes argued otherwise. *He believes this to be true.*

"But it can't be true," Shadow argued. *"Naldo wouldn't do such a thing."*

Flame closed her eyes and lowered her head to the ground. *Perhaps not,* she sent through the bond, *but this would not be the first province we've encountered this season to have fallen to chaos.* Images of a harbor full of pirate ships surrounded by the king's men, Kensian rogues in uniform, and Zhulanese guards out in force in the city streets filled her mind.

"Markos, then?" Shadow flashed an image of Mama Caler, the Kensian Seer, through the bond. She was the one who had first warned of the powerful enemy who used the name Markos.

Flame stiffened as the image recalled another to mind, one she had ignored in her anger at being chased off by the nomads. Isa's final touch to her mind had not been the proposition that Gemi was the source of the nightmares.

Instead, it had held an impression of violence and a warning that *"Markos may yet be waiting for James in Tarsur."*

Flame's wings trembled. *I do not know.*

"Well, dragona," Lord Sageo snapped, "what do you say to that?"

Without lifting her head from the ground, Flame opened her eyes and met the duke's gaze. *"My condolences, Lord Sageo. The death of family is never easy to bear. I can only imagine the loss of one's child is the most difficult of all."*

For a long moment, the Animal Mage simply stared at her. It took a nudge from the Plant Mage beside him and someone's hissed "Turi!" for the man to translate what she had said.

Unfortunately, the words did not seem to be what the duke wanted to hear. As Turi spoke, Lord Sageo's face gradually grew redder, until Flame began to fear for his health.

"And you have nada to say to the accusations we bring against these ladrones?"

Flame jerked her head up from the ground. *"And why should I?"*

"Flame," Shadow cautioned.

"Nay!" she growled, suddenly too angry to keep her

thoughts to the stallion silent. *"He has no right to demand explanations from us, not when we have wandered, lost, for nearly four days and only just arrived."* Lifting her head as high as she could with her body still tangled in the tent, Flame glared down at the duke. *"Not when the only kindness he has ever shown us is in calming Lord Lefas when he would have spoken against us."*

Shadow released a long huff. *"And if you keep talking like that, he won't show us kindness at all, Flame. They must have food and water. If we could—"*

"Very well." Flame snapped her attention back from the bond and focused on Lord Sageo, who spoke lowly. "If you will not cooperate, then you can remain here, bound, until Caffers arrives. Perhaps I can get answers from him."

"But, Milord," the Animal Mage protested, "I have not told you what she said."

Lord Sageo shook his head. "As violent as her response was, I cannot imagine I want to hear it."

He turned to the knight. "Have your hombres untangle her enough to prevent her from injuring herself, but do not release her. I want Caffers to understand he has no choice but to come speak with me. I want to hear from his lips how the death of my hijo works into his 'quest for paz.'"

~~*~*

Shadow cursed. Lord Sageo wanted answers from the one person incapable of giving them. Glancing back at his passengers, he snorted. Gemi was still as insentient as ever, and Ferez . . .

At least he's awake.

Unfortunately, his consciousness could hardly balance his lack of memory and his ignorance of his throne. Even worse . . .

Shadow shuddered. *Even worse is that Lord Sageo will meet him like this. No matter how he might dislike us now, the duke will hate us when he realizes Ferez doesn't remember his true self.*

An issue we might be able to avoid if the duke never sees Frenz. Flame's thought was quickly followed by a snarled *"Be careful!"* aimed at one of the soldiers attempting to untangle her.

"How—"

Shadow snorted as he realized what the dragon was thinking. *"But the secret passages haven't been used since Naldo claimed the title of king."*

That does not mean they are no longer there, Flame silently pressed through the bond. She continued to growl and snarl at the humans, but she refrained from hurting them. Already, she was regretting her earlier outburst and contemplating the likelihood of convincing the Animal Mage to find her some food and water.

"Even if they are still there, you can hardly expect me to go looking for them while you're being held captive."

Flame turned her growl on Shadow. *And you cannot come here when James is as vulnerable as he is. Lord Sageo has too many men for us to protect him from them if they wish him harm.*

Besides, she thought, watching as one human warily reached for one of the arrows stuck in her scales, *it is not as if I am completely defenseless here.* She snapped lightly at the man just to watch him jump away with a small scream.

"Shadow?" Last Chance's nicker pulled the stallion's attention back to his physical surroundings. They had slowed to a walk as the trouble around Flame had progressed, and the mare now kept pace beside him. *"What's happening?"*

Shadow huffed and explained his understanding of the situation.

Once he finished, the mare snorted. *"This isn't good. Peln has always been quick to jump to conclusions, and he can be stubborn when he thinks he knows the truth. Even if your friends aren't behind his son's death, it'll be extremely difficult to convince him otherwise."*

All the more reason for you to aim for the Hidden City, Flame pressed. *We need to know what has happened, and we will not find answers if we give in to the duke's demands.*

Shadow huffed and eyed his passengers once more. Ferez watched Shadow and Last Chance curiously, but his arms were tight around Gemi's torso, holding her in place. Although the amnesiac king knew nothing about the situation, Shadow had no doubt what his choice would be.

"Very well," he nickered. *"We'll head to the Hidden City."* He glanced around at the surrounding rock. *"But you have to help me figure out where the entrance to the secret passages is. I'm still lost."*

Both females snorted. Flame dove into the bond to figure out just that.

~~*~*

Peln shoved through the entrance of his tent. He couldn't believe the audacity of the dragona!

No, of Caffers. If Nadie had wanted his bondmate to cooperate with us, then she would have.

If Nadie refused to even speak for ladrones he obviously knew, then he must have been lying when he spoke of wanting paz. Why else would he remain silent but that he condoned such violence?

And to offer condolences for my grief on top of that . . .

He snarled wordlessly and slammed his fist down on the makeshift desk he'd had set up in the tent. *It is beyond unforgivable!*

"Peln!"

The shout was accompanied by a hard grip on Peln's

upper arm. The duque spun around and glared at his Capitán de Caballeros. "¿Cómo?"

Gervasio eyed him narrowly. "You need to calm down. Pacing and hitting things will not help nada."

Peln ripped his arm from his amigo's grip and turned away. "You do not understand!"

"I do," the caballero murmured. "You're upset that Nadie won't help us."

"¡No!" Peln spun back around. "I am upset because Nadie is taunting me!" He lifted a clenched fist. "He pretends to be saddened at the death of my hijo but then refuses his assistance when it would be most useful."

"Perhaps there is a razón—"

"No razón could be good enough!"

Gervasio sighed. "Peln . . ."

"Enough!" Peln snapped. "Leave me alone, Gervasio."

"But—"

"Leave!"

Gervasio's mouth tightened, and he glared at Peln. For a moment, Peln wondered if his amigo would refuse and continue to insist that Peln needed to calm down. The duque smiled grimly. *Let him try.*

However, Gervasio only offered Peln a terse bow. "With your leave, Milord," he muttered before disappearing back through the tent's entrance.

Peln stared at the quivering cloth for a long time after Gervasio left. He wondered if his anger had just damaged his relationship with his best amigo, but the worry didn't linger. Certainly, Gervasio was hardly ever formal with Peln, and never in private, but Peln couldn't let that stand in the way of what was important. The ladrones had killed his hijo, and he would have his venganza.

If only someone else could understand this need.

None of his hombres seemed to agree that the ladrones had to pay in full. One of the reasons they were still bottled up in the paso after three días was that his hombres had stalled enough to keep their attacks to a minimum. And the two attacks they had managed had been driven back by a rain of arrows and impenetrable walls.

Now that they had Nadie's dragona, though, perhaps he would be able to convince his hombres that the ladrones deserved the fate he had in mind for them. Until then . . .

I need to speak with someone who understands, or I might go mad.

Turning back to his desk, Peln pulled a fresh piece of parchment from a small pile and grabbed a quill from the bottle of ink in which it stood. Pausing with the quill hovering over the parchment, he closed his eyes and took a deep breath.

I can't believe I'm going to turn to Seyan for understanding.

Unfortunately, if Peln wanted someone to understand, there was nadie more likely to than Seyan Lefas, duque of Baylin. He had lost his own hija several años ago. Although nadie knew exactly what had happened—the chica had simply disappeared—Seyan had always blamed the rebels and the mysterious Ghost for her death.

And now it seems he was right all along. We should have listened to him instead of being fooled by Nadie's pretty words.

Certain he was doing the right thing, Peln opened his eyes, replaced the now ink-splattered parchment with a new one, and began to write.

Eleven

Nothing.

There was nothing. No light, no sound, no sense of anything except the cold emptiness that surrounded and bore down upon him, pressing without pressure, silencing him and everything else.

Why? he tried to whisper, but, as before, he heard nothing.

Yet, despite the isolation, despite the suppression, there was . . . something—or someone—that prevented the panic he could feel bubbling within him. A presence that at once calmed him and incited within him a desire to comfort.

He wasn't sure when he'd become aware of the presence outside his isolated prison—or whatever else this place might be—but his sense of it had, at first, been nearly eclipsed by a disturbing darkness. A darkness he somehow knew did not belong around the calming presence.

It was the darkness that had drawn him to reach for the presence, hoping to comfort it and ease its pain. Though he couldn't move, he was certain he had felt the presence respond—he had felt the darkness softening, easing, changing form.

Now there was no darkness, only an aching loneliness that urged him reach harder. But no matter how many times he tried to say he was *here, that the presence wasn't alone, he could never hear his own words, and the loneliness persisted.*

I don't know why this is happening, *he pressed toward the presence, still straining against sensationless bonds,* **but I won't give up. I will reach you! You are not alone!**

~*~*~

Frenz drifted. At times, he floated through darkness and loneliness. At others, he was achingly aware of the freezing pressure at his front and the soft weight at his back. At one point, he wondered if he had fallen asleep in the fields again—*Is it winter?*—only to remember sharply that he had left Kensy for some reason he could not recall.

Not that the reason matters anymore. What matters is James's safety.

James. A name that meant so much, yet so little. A young boy, younger than Frenz. A mere child, but one whom so many looked to as a symbol.

More than a symbol, though. He has family, people who love him.

An overwhelming ache followed those thoughts, filling his belly and chest and rising into his throat.

I'm one of them. I know it, feel it. If only I could remember why.

Drifting memories of pain and panic echoed through him when he considered this. Isa and Wolfrik had tried to find his memories, but there was a part of him—*it's not mind magic, no matter what excuse they gave me*—that insisted the memories would separate him from James, not bring him closer.

The thoughts—*memories?*—faded as quickly as they came, and he continued to drift, his mind flowing from dream to memory to thought with little discrimination.

Now he was remembering the heat of the desert sun.

Next, the chill of the small, dark mountain tunnel to which Shadow had led them. There was a brief curiosity over the odd softness of James's chest against his back, but the thought had seemed so crass when the boy was unconscious that Frenz shook it off as soon as he considered it.

Frenz was slowly drawn from his drifting by fevered whispers. With them came a realization that the pressure on his back had disappeared.

What was it? James? But he's unconscious. He couldn't have moved himself.

"What of the estranger?"

Stranger?

"I'll come back wit' mis hombres for him and the caballos."

Hombres? Caballos? Where . . . ?

The thought drifted, unfinished, as Frenz drifted back into floating darkness and anxious loneliness. That loneliness faded, but it left behind an emptiness that reached into him with cold fingers and only increased his own unease.

He was on the edge of this increasing tension when voices teased his senses once more.

"Su Majestad will no be happy when he hears you changed the plans."

A snort sounded, quickly followed by an oddly familiar voice. "*Su Majestad* knew perfectly well that this might happen. Why else do you think he sent you wit' the pociones?"

"Still do no seem correcto," murmured another voice. "We came for the chico, no . . ."

No what? Frenz wondered idly when the man trailed off.

Another snort. "If Su Majestad questions it, remind him that one of the caballos es Nadie's estallion"—*Shadow?*—"and by the look of it, the otro es a Gris de Pecali."

Frenz frowned, confused. *Grease? Do they mean Last Chance?*

"And the hombre?" another voice asked, even as soft whistles pierced the air and someone muttered about the value of "a Gris en Evon." "What interés could Su Majestad have en a nómada?"

"He es a compañero of Nadie," the voice answered, turning cold. "He will have información, if nada else."

Frenz tensed, suddenly feeling more awake. *What are they talking about?*

"Now if you are done dawdling, you'll need to use the pociones soon. Even wit' the power of mi magia, I will no be able to keep the caballos unconscious for much longer."

Frenz shifted, certain now that these men weren't friends. Seconds later, hands pulled at his shoulders, tugging him onto his back. He tried to fight them off, but his limbs were heavy and they shook as he struggled. It wasn't long before his wrists were caught together in a firm grip.

"Seems the nómada's awake. No much fight to him, though."

"No matter. Just give him the poción."

Hands gripped Frenz's head, squeezing his jaw as something cold and hard pressed against his lips. He tried to keep his lips sealed tight, certain he didn't want whatever potion they were trying to force into him. Unfortunately, pressure around his nose stopped his breathing, and he opened his mouth with a gasp. Bitter liquid quickly spilled across his tongue.

As oblivion pressed in on his mind once more, Frenz heard the more familiar voice speak again. "And do no forget Graucen's droga for Nadie's estallion. Would no want him to warn the dragona, now would we?"

The words followed him into nothingness.

~~*~*

Fear grimaced as the thieves drugged the king into unconsciousness. *Why is it that when I'm the one who's feeling hopeful, what I hope for doesn't come to pass?*

He and Hope had followed Peace and her companions into the secret passages behind the Hidden City. When the horses and the king passed out only minutes from reaching the city, Fear had prayed to the Fates that Peace's thieves would be the ones to find them.

Instead, they'd been found by a man living in the Hidden City like a wolf among the unsuspecting sheep. Peace had been separated from the others, and now this man, a powerful Animal Mage, was directing Peace's enemies to steal away with her companions.

Silver fingers suddenly dug into the yellow demigod's arm, and Fear winced. His twin, Hope, leaned against him and glared fiercely at the thieves.

"How dare they!" she hissed. "Don't they remember what happened the last time they attempted this?"

Fear pursed his lips to restrain his immediate retort. He didn't think his sister would appreciate a reminder that the last attempt to separate Peace and her bondmates had been successful for several sevendays before she'd reclaimed them.

And only then because she'd had help.

"Do remember, sister mine," he murmured instead, "that most of these men weren't involved in the last scheme."

Hope turned her glare on Fear, and he grimaced. The last time they had seen Hate and Love, his red brother had complained to Fear about the scariness of Love's chaotic polarity.

I think that might be preferable to the constant negativity Hope has been displaying.

Hope hadn't experienced a single positive emotion since she had come to Fear the night after Mid-Season with a dazed, lost look filling her eyes. He had been in Celania at the time, overseeing a panic. The small country, a trail of islands south of the Tarsurian mountain range, had been experiencing its first, if not very severe, volcanic eruption in several decades. It seemed the people had grown lax and forgotten how to handle such situations.

Hope's arrival had transformed Fear's controlled panic into a full-blown riot. The people, who had been running for the harbors and the ships that could carry them away from the slowly flowing lava, had begun to turn on each other. Utter hopelessness had filled their hearts and desperation had driven them to madness.

Fear hadn't taken the time then to figure out what was happening before he dropped his influence, grabbed his twin, and Transported them to a more neutral setting. Only when they were safely away from mortals had Fear begun to sense the Chaos in his own being.

Since then, they'd been forced by the Fates to sit idly by while Peace and her companions were separated bit by bit. First the dragon was captured by the vengeful Tarsurian duke. Then Peace was secreted away by a hidden enemy.

And now enemy thieves were drugging Peace's stallion and the king's mare with a potion created by a master of potion making and infused with the magic of a powerful Animal Mage. Fear knew it would allow the thieves—none of them mages themselves—to direct the movements of the two horses, even if the animals weren't conscious.

And even Last Chance won't be able to resist such directives.

"Oy! They're cheating!"

The sudden declaration was so similar to Hope's complaint from the beginning of the season that Fear stared at his silver twin. As he did, Hope's expression turned from mutinous to pouty.

"Don't look at me like that," she muttered, dropping her gaze. "They're the ones using magic they shouldn't be able to."

Fear frowned, uncertain what his twin meant. Turning back to the thieves, he watched them lead their prizes through tunnels that were conveniently wider than the tunnels the horses had traveled earlier; both horses had scrapes on their shoulders and rumps attesting to the tunnels' narrowness.

"What do you mean, Hope? You know the magic controlling the horses is in the potions."

"Not that, Fear!" Hope slapped a hand against his chest. He winced. "I mean the tunnel that shouldn't be there." The same hand flew out toward the tunnel down which the thieves now traveled.

Fear eyed the tunnel. "What are you—"

He abruptly stopped and gaped as he finally noticed the dark shimmer filling the entire tunnel. The humans wouldn't be able to see it since it was restricted to the Spiritual Realm, but Fear recognized it well enough. It was the spiritual remains of earth that had been displaced by magic from a place in which it had stood for a long time.

They have mage stones?

Pulling Hope closer to the thieves, Fear eyed the hands of each man. Certainly enough, one of the men in front clutched his fingers around a glowing stone that didn't even fill his palm. The light spilling between his fingers was a warm, earthy orange, the spiritual color of Earth Magic in physical form.

Fear shivered and clutched Hope more tightly against his chest as the thieves continued down their created tunnel. He wasn't really shocked that the thieves had a mage stone. The thieves of the Hidden City had been using mage stones for centuries; it was the very reason the city had been fought over for so long. That a thief anywhere in the city's vicinity had a mage stone was almost more of an expectation than a surprise.

What struck Fear was that the thief in front was the only one using a mage stone. The others carried only throwing knives, the horses' leads, or the unconscious king.

Yet I've never seen remains this large caused by the Hidden City's mage stones. This looks almost like the work of a natural-born Earth Mage, imbued in stone. Fear swallowed and shook his head. *Which isn't possible. We haven't seen an Earth Mage among the humans since Father threw Mother into the Cycle of Incarnation and humans lost access to half the magics of the land.*

Fear shuddered. That disaster had caused all kinds of trouble, not least of which was the humans' loss of magic. Even a thousand years later, none of them knew what had become of their mother, now known as the Lost Goddess. Their father, Carith, had locked himself away in his workshop, creating souls and refusing to see anyone other than the Royal Eagle, Aquila.

Fear yelped. A sharp pain had bloomed in his arm, and he clapped a hand to the spot, turning wide eyes on Hope. "What—"

"Stop thinking about that!" Hope glanced warily around the tunnels. "Isn't it bad enough that we're facing as much Chaos as we are? Do you want to invite more?"

Fear turned and gripped Hope's face between his hands, forcing her to meet his eyes. "Hope, listen to me." Hope sniffled and pouted. "We may be facing Chaos, but we'll rise above it. All of us will, even Peace."

Hope twitched her head, but she didn't break free of Fear's grip. "How can you be so certain?"

Fear smiled. "Because that's what we were born to do, and we've never yet succumbed to Chaos. There's no reason we should now."

Hope pulled away and wrapped her arms around herself. Fear quickly laid one hand on her shoulder. He wasn't about to give Chaos a chance to affect either of them more than it already was, especially when they had no one to influence right now.

"But we've never faced this kind of Chaos spread by one of our own." Hope hesitated and glanced back at Fear. "I mean . . ."

Fear shook his head and squeezed her shoulder. He knew what she meant.

We've never had to deal with Chaos from a demigod's soul. We weren't meant to bear it—only protect against it. We're not like . . .

Fear shivered and snapped his head from side to side. He wouldn't think it. He refused to. Remembering the fight between their parents might be unlikely to invite more Chaos, but thinking the name of the one deity who spread it would do more than invite it: it would ensure the path of Chaos the Fates had predicted.

"I can't stand this, Fear." Hope turned into Fear's arms and buried her head against his neck. "I want my hope back."

Fear wrapped his arms tightly around her back. "And you'll get it, Hope. We just have to wait for Peace to wake up."

Hope leaned back in his arms and stared up at him. "What if she doesn't? What if she's trapped in unconsciousness? Then the path of Chaos—"

"Is still not certain," Fear said firmly. "Peace may sleep

now, but I have faith that she is yet equal to the task of balancing War."

Tarnished silver eyes stared up at him searchingly. "How?" she whispered. "How can you be so sure?"

Fear's lips twitched. "Because I remember how stubborn Peace was before she entered the Cycle, and she's only become more so since her birth as a human. Now that her soul is cleared of Chaos—no matter how it might have happened—there's nothing to keep her from returning to those she loves most. You'll see."

Hope closed her eyes. Her entire face relaxed, and a ghost of a smile appeared on her lips.

"If you can believe that, maybe I can, too."

~~*~*

She didn't know how long she had lain there, curled in on herself. She couldn't be sure how long the voices had tormented her, first striking at her with harsh tones and cruel words, then enticing her with tempting comfort and soothing pleas. She had no way to track the *hours/days/months* she had been alone, closing herself off from them, kindly and cutting alike.

Throughout it all, constant as the mountaintop on which she lay, a stern voice insisted it was safer to hide here like this than to give in to the other voices' torments.

They only bring pain.

She'd stopped questioning the stern voice's advice. Every time she did, pain had welled within her, chasing her back down to the mountaintop to cringe away from the other voices and curl into herself more tightly. Now she listened to that voice alone, ignoring her tormentors and everything else outside the small patch of mountaintop she occupied.

When she jerked her head up and stared around, she didn't know why.

There is nothing there.

But something is different.

A trick of the voices.

But that didn't seem right. The tormenting voices, though softer, still offered their coaxing pleas. They were the only sounds to echo around her since the dark creatures and their tearing cries disappeared altogether.

Best to leave it be, then.

She dropped her head and hunched her shoulders. She knew she should listen to the stern voice. She already knew it only wanted what was best for her. She should listen to it and go back to hiding.

But the sensation of change was no longer just a simple piece of knowledge. It was quickly becoming a *distraction/irritant/annoyance* and she found that, no matter how she tried to leave it be, it wouldn't leave *her* be.

Finally, she lifted her head again and scanned her surroundings.

Leave it be!

She shook her head. Whatever had changed was important: more important than the opinion of the stern voice and more important than the crooning pleas for her to wake. It was a change she couldn't stomach, especially here in hiding atop her lonely mountain peak.

I cannot protect myself if I go searching for this.

She gritted her teeth and clenched her hands. The stern voice had been protecting her from a pain she couldn't remember, a pain that threatened to return every time she tried to think of what had led to her isolation.

I don't care! The pain doesn't matter against this change/disappearance/loss.

Because that's what it was. Something was missing, something that had made the *cold/dark/loneliness* bearable enough for her to submit to the stern voice's protection. Without it . . .

It's not worth it.

And just what is it I'm missing?

She hesitated. She didn't have an answer for that, but she thought it was only because she couldn't remember enough to recognize what had been there before the change.

So I'm willing to risk pain to find something of which I can't be certain?

She bit her lip. Could she face the pain? She would have to if she wanted to remember what she was missing. And surely there was a difference between knowing the pain was worth it and facing it.

Swallowing, she bowed her head and worked her hands open and closed. The glimpses she had received of the pain had been nearly unbearable. Would the sudden, sharp desire to seek what she'd lost be enough to bear her through such oppressive torment?

It has to be!

Lifting her head, she glared out across the sharp peaks that surrounded her lonely mountaintop. She couldn't remain here indefinitely, lost to time and herself, not when something had *left / disappeared / been stolen* from her life.

Can I call it life when all it holds is pain?

If all it holds is pain, then why do I still live?

The stern voice didn't respond, and she jerked her chin toward her chest. There had to be something beyond the pain, but she had forgotten what in running from the pain.

No more running/hiding/shutting down, *then. I must stand against it.*

The stern voice merely sighed in response.

Closing her eyes, she focused on the sensation of loss that now throbbed like a beacon in her *mind/heart/soul.* As she did, it leaped! It bounded through her like an animal and dragged her away from her lonely mountaintop toward the haunting abyss below.

She screamed as she plummeted through air littered with shards of *grief/hurt/guilt.* The shards tore at her, dug into her, and dragged gleaming, fluttering trails of *thoughts/memories/visions* through her mind.

Heaviness, dense enough to rival the mountain on which she'd lain, grew in her chest and mind. It spread quickly, filling her throat and lungs and threatening to drown her if she continued on.

Turn back, then. I can still protect myself. I don't have to—

Nay!

Silence answered her. Even the *thoughts/memories/visions* that tore through her hesitated. When they resumed, she took them in, embraced them, forced them into herself.

They are mine! They are me!

She had finally seen past the pain to the actual images that caused it. Aye, they hurt, but pieces of them were rooted in emotions more complicated than pain. And the desire to learn what they were and where they came from had joined the desire to seek what she had lost, and both were sharpening their claws in her mind.

The desires dragged her deeper into the abyss, with no bottom in sight, but that mattered little against the images flashing through her.

She quickly discarded the images of a man in pale clothing and a cloth belt dyed black on one end. He had spoken as if he knew her, but he had been a stranger to her, so he mattered little to the desires preying on her mind.

Instead, they latched onto the images connected with the man. Guilt threatened to swallow her as they rifled through scene after scene: a mourning group of people in similar pale clothing and purple-dyed belts, a man with curly black hair and red-rimmed green eyes, a young woman with fiery-red hair and dim green eyes, a crying woman surrounded by children, a—

She sobbed as one image came sharply into focus: A woman with long black hair and worn brown eyes sat slumped in an armchair placed behind a desk. Behind the chair, a man stood tall, his firm hands supporting the woman's shoulders gently.

Despite the focus the two held for each other, their eyes were turned away from the other, turned toward *her*, and they were filled with a heavy disappointment that called forth other images.

Roiling smoke, smoldering ruins, a single stone wall burned with a damning message.

Please.

An introduction, a flee into the forest, a finely dressed *man/spy/thief* taunting her for her inability to save the ones she loved.

I didn't know.

The guilt didn't lessen. And there was blood. So much blood. How many had died by her blade? Five? Fifty? Five hundred?

Perhaps I can never have peace. Perhaps hiding is the closest I'll ever have to it.

Oddly, the stern voice's words brought forth an image that wasn't connected to the *grief/hurt/guilt* that had driven her so far.

She sat in an orchard. Sunlight filtered through the tree

branches, and the sweet scent of ripe fruit filled her lungs. Beside her sat the tall man with the firm hands who had stared at her in disappointment.

Here, though, he offered her a warm smile and tugged on her horsetail. When he spoke, answering a question she must have asked, his voice matched the smile and gesture in affection.

"It's not so simple, Gemi. Peace won't just happen. We must fight for it, as contrary as it seems. If we gave up fighting today, Fayral would simply overrun us. They would take our freedom, our land, our livelihood. The rule they would set up over us would be oppressive. That is not peace."

Father.

The image changed. This time, she could feel the desires directing her *thoughts/memories/visions* to find what she *wanted/needed/craved* to see.

The new image bore a small forest camp. Tents were torn down and trampled, the ground littered with slaughtered bodies. Strong arms held her as she and the man with black curly hair and green eyes wept for the *men/comrades/friends* they had lost.

"We can't give up," he'd whispered. *"Not after this, not when we know what Gaffen'll do to Kensy if he gets the chance. I may be a highwayman, but I won't stand by while Gaffen terrorizes the people. That may give me peace from Gaffen, but I would never have peace in my heart."*

She still couldn't believe it had taken her and Kephin less than two months to unite the kinder highwaymen against Gaffen.

Again the image changed, and again she listened as someone she knew spoke of peace.

"We'll never have peace among the clans or with the städte if we

don't try. They might attack us when we reach out to them, but we risk worse every täg without peace. The near loss of my son has shown me that."

Only days later, her vater, Hausef, had sent messages to each of the clans. And they had survived the Schlange and Skorpion Clans turning against them.

"Funny. Never would have claimed ladrones could be peaceful, but compared to Deligero's rule, mi padre's was definitely one of paz. If I can claim the throne, I swear I'll extend the paz to the pueblos. Nadie should feel what we've felt under Deligero."

Naldo had been true to his word. He'd ended Deligero's cruel rule and extended the protection of his thieves, whom he named the Ocultados, farther than his father could have ever dreamed to.

"Some people jus' don't understand peace. Take away one war, an' dey'll find someone else to fight. But dat don' mean I won' try for peace. Dat's what we rebels are all about, after all: seekin' peace for the people. I jus' think some of us need remindin' o' that."

She snorted. Rosie had always been the oddest combination of cynical and optimistic. It was what had drawn her to the young woman.

I can't lie to myself. That's not the reason the Rose Thorn caught my interest.

She blinked.

All of this, and I'm quibbling over that?

If I'm going to remember, I'd best remember it correctly.

All right.

It was true that Rosie's personality wasn't the main reason she had been drawn to her. It was, more than anything, the woman's tendency to wear men's clothing and fight with blades that had made her look up to Rosie as a role model. After all, it was exactly what she did, even if she hid the rebellion behind a male persona.

As if the stern voice had been a distraction her desires resented, she felt them *tug/jerk/claw* at her until the pain seemed newly formed. She was gasping from it by the time another image formed in front of her

"Just because there is something threatening the peace we want for Evon, it doesn't mean we can't face it and still succeed."

She gasped and slammed her eyes shut. The image felt as though it had been dragged from the depths of her soul. Yet there was no mistaking the voice that had spoken those words nor the silver and blue eyes that had met hers.

Ferez.

How could she have forgotten the *king/friend/courter* who had been her constant companion this past half season? Even Flame and Shadow—*friends/family/bondmates*—had been on the edge of each of the previous images, their crooning voices echoing alongside the stern one as she recognized they truly had come back for her.

But she couldn't feel Ferez the way she could her bondmates, and the desires had become all the more frantic now that she knew whom she was missing.

"Yeh know yeh're not alone, right? Yeh have so many people willin' to help yeh, it's amazin'. Yeh don' have to depend solely on yerself."

She sobbed. She wasn't alone. She had Flame and Shadow, who hadn't left her, even when she thought they had.

"I won't hurt you. I promise."

She threw open her eyes and glared through the darkness of the abyss surrounding her. Those words had been Ferez's. It was a promise he wouldn't have made lightly.

Yet the sensation of loss she'd felt concerned him. How, she didn't know. But since he wouldn't have left willingly, not when it would have hurt her, something must have been wrong, something she couldn't let stand.

I will not hide anymore. I will face the pain. I will face the guilt. I will face whatever I must. But I will not let anything take my soul from me.

Twelve

Gemi awoke, gasping, and broke into a coughing fit.

The coughing made her throat ache and her lungs burn, something she hadn't felt since she was six, the only time in her life she could remember ever falling ill. During her treatment, her father had cursed the healers so virulently that Gemi had managed to add five new curses to her vocabulary the following week.

Not that they lasted long. Sir Paeter, Sir Leal, and Father made sure of that.

Wrinkling her nose, Gemi finally managed to get her breathing under control, only to grimace for a different reason altogether. Her mouth was dry, her tongue felt thick, and there was a taste of rot lingering there that made her shudder in disgust.

What in Maurus's Fire . . . ?

"Gem—James?"

Gemi jerked her head up and her eyes open but quickly reversed the movements and groaned as pain stabbed through her head. A familiar warmth wrapped around her mind, crooning soothingly.

"Easy, James. You have slept for a long time."

"Is that why it feels like a rodent decided to use my mouth for a burrow and died?"

Surprised hesitation echoed through the bond. *"I suppose so,"* Flame muttered slowly. *"How do you feel? Other than the horrible taste in your mouth."*

Gemi's lips twitched. Lifting a hand, she tried to rub at her aching head . . . only to find herself dropping it back to the bed as violent tremors traveled from hand to shoulder.

Wha . . . ?

"As I said, you have been asleep for a long time."

Gemi frowned and shook her head. She stopped when the muscles in her neck quivered. *"I thought you meant a day or two, at most."*

A dark wave of sadness washed over her. *"It is the night of the twenty-seventh of Mid Autumn, James. It has been ten days since you fell to the Schlange."*

Gemi swallowed. *Ten days? How . . . ?*

Flame huffed. *"That does not matter. What does is that you finally came back to us."* More softly, Gemi heard, *Now that we have reached Tarsur.*

"Tarsur?" Gemi blinked open her eyes and peered through the surrounding dimness. Sure enough, rock walls, and not the shimmering silk of nomad tents, surrounded her. *"I know I'm usually strict about our schedule, but you didn't have to cart me out here just to stick to it."*

"I would not have if I had had the choice. Unfortunately, there were circumstances beyond our control."

An image pressed through the bond of nomads throwing stones at Flame and yelling for her to leave and take her nightmares with her.

"*Nightmares? Why would they want you to leave if you were having nightmares?*"

"*I was not the one having the nightmares,*" Flame growled. "*The nomads were, and they accused me of causing them.*"

Gemi blinked. "*All the nomads were having nightmares?*" An image of an exhausted Last Chance passed through the bond, and Gemi frowned. "*And the animals?*"

The warmth in her mind squirmed. "*The only ones unaffected were Shadow, Frenz, and myself.*"

Gemi stiffened and then bit her lip as tremors shook her body. Flame hadn't mentioned Gemi in her list of those unaffected, but those she had were all connected by one thing.

"*Me?*" The word was barely a gasp in her mind, but Flame immediately wrapped around her. "*I caused them? But how? I'm no mage.*"

Flame growled. "*Isa and Wolfrik claimed it had nothing to do with magic. They said it was the effect of a . . . darkness leaking from your soul.*"

Gemi recoiled. "*Leaking?*"

Flame rumbled mutinously.

A sudden creak pulled Gemi's attention away from the bond. Grateful for the distraction—she didn't want to think about the implications of anything leaking from her soul— she twisted her head toward the sound.

For the first time, she spotted a door in one wall of the room. Light spilled through the opening, and she squinted against the brightness.

Someone grunted. "You're awake."

Gemi blinked. The voice sounded vaguely familiar, but it didn't belong to anyone she would have expected to care for her here in Tarsur.

"Who—"

Gemi broke into another coughing fit. A large hand slipped under her neck and lifted her head up. Gemi shook it slightly when cold stone pressed against her lips, but whoever held her was persistent. Thick, bittersweet liquid slipped across her tongue, and she choked as it hit the back of her throat midcough.

"Relax, Nadie, I will no let it hurt you."

A sharp hiss filled Gemi's mind as her throat suddenly relaxed and she stopped coughing and choking. As the thick liquid slid down her throat, the warmth in her mind settled more heavily, distracting Gemi from what was being done to her body.

"Flame? What's wrong?"

"That taste," the dragon growled. *"I recognize that taste!"* She snarled and pressed further into Gemi's mind. *"I will not lose you again!"*

"How—"

Flame's heavy warmth suddenly flickered. Grunting, Gemi summoned all her remaining strength, ripped her head from the man's hand, and rolled away. She tried to gag and spit up the potion he'd poured down her throat, but her body refused to cooperate and simply finished swallowing what was left.

Gemi wavered and collapsed on her side, her vision blurring and her mind becoming hazy. She thought she heard Flame shouting her name, but the words were soft, and her awareness of the dragon faded in and out.

"Wha' did you give me?" she gasped past the thickness in her throat.

Her caretaker hummed. "Just a little something to help wit' the deshidratación and hunger cramps. Works faster than agua and food would."

Gemi swallowed, but the thickness in her throat wouldn't ease. "Why's it interfering wi' the dragonbond?"

He hummed again. "Es it?"

A soft snarl wavered through Gemi's mind. *"He knows . . . with the bond . . . have to run . . ."*

Gemi shook her head weakly. *"I can't move, Flame. How can I run if I can't even stand?"*

Those large hands gripped her shoulder and hip and rolled her over onto her back. "Now, you need to relax, Nadie. The more you move, the longer it'll take the poción to heal you."

Gemi blinked, trying to clear her vision. The moment she realized just who was leaning over her—and what that meant—a sudden, burning snarl ripped through her.

How dare he! her thoughts snapped. *Graucen's banned from making potions! And to use the separation poison again, of all things . . .*

He's a dead man!

The rage that burned through her was hotter than anything she had ever felt before, even the dragonfire building in Flame's throat. It ignited within her in a way she had never felt, but she didn't care. All that mattered was that this man was threatening her bond, and the burning could help her stop him.

Burying herself in the inferno, she pushed the heat from her chest into her limbs. She didn't know how, but she was certain it could burn away her weakness. As it curled through her muscles and licked at her bones, she turned to the bond and threw her rage through it, hoping to burn away the haze of the poison.

"There now, Nadie." Graucen loosened his grip on her arms. If not for the rage consuming her, Gemi might have been amused by Graucen's apparent decision that her sudden stillness was a sign of acquiescence. "Fighting will only—"

Gemi snarled and lunged.

Graucen cried out and fell back, but Gemi hooked her hand in the neck of his tunic. He tumbled to the floor, dragging her with him.

Snarling again, Gemi clambered over his body until she was straddling his chest and wrapped her hands around his throat. She leaned onto them, ignoring the hands Graucen raised to pull at her arms.

"What right do you have to interfere with my bond?" She snarled at the gaping Healer. "What right do you have to take away my family?"

From the choked sounds he was making, Gemi thought Graucen might actually be trying to answer her. *Doesn't matter,* she growled silently as she lifted her body up to put more weight on her hands. *After last time, he should've known we wouldn't stand to be separated again.*

"James!"

Heaviness slammed into her thoughts as Flame's presence abruptly filled her mind. Snapping her head to the side, Gemi shook off the sudden disorientation. She couldn't let Graucen get away with threatening the bond a second time.

"James, stop! You are killing him!"

Good!

"James, please! This is not like you! Not since—"

An image of a forest path littered with broken and bloodied bodies abruptly filled Gemi's mind. She gasped and sat back on her heels, squeezing her eyes shut.

"Nay," she whispered, but the image wouldn't go away. She could see the expressions of disbelief and pain twisting the dead faces. More than the sight though, the knowledge that those men had died by her hand, by her blade . . .

Gemi twisted to the side and vomited.

"I am sorry, James," Flame breathed mournfully. *"It was the only thing I could think to do to make you stop."*

Gemi only nodded. She wasn't sure she could do much else in the face of such a reminder. It wasn't that she hadn't killed her fair share of men. She had fought in the Fayralese War for too long not to have stained her hands with the blood of her enemies.

The image now blazing in her mind wasn't just any memory, though. It was the aftermath of her first kill, her revenge on Kale Caphrin and his men for the destruction of her childhood. She hadn't been able to curb her hatred then, and somehow she hadn't been able to do so now, either.

What's wrong with me?

I will face the guilt.

Gemi jerked her head up, her eyes flying open. That thought had been hers, she was certain. After years in a dragonbond and the more recent invasion by the Schlange Mindspeaker, Gemi was confident she would recognize thoughts that weren't her own.

However, the thought was so different and echoed so deeply within her that she stared sightlessly for a long time before she realized she was staring at Graucen's slack face.

When she finally *saw* him, she flinched. His head had lolled to one side, and his blue-tinged lips were parted widely in search of the breath she had denied him.

I will face the guilt.

Gemi swallowed. She didn't understand why the thought struck so deeply or rang so familiarly true, but it did. Ignoring the worried questions that reached through the bond, Gemi took a deep breath and dropped her gaze to Graucen's neck, where the purple and black of a ringing bruise was beginning to bloom.

I did this, she forced herself to acknowledge. *My anger caused this.*

In the next moment, she realized that same anger still simmered within her, pushed back only by the harsh reminder of where it could lead.

Gemi frowned. She was accustomed to only feeling that kind of anger in spurts, like in the midst of battle or when she was exhausted or injured and became snappish.

Now, though, she felt surprisingly clear-headed and much stronger than she should have after ten days of unconsciousness. Yet the anger didn't fade with the appearance of her guilt as it usually did. Instead, the two emotions simply tempered each other and forced her to acknowledge they were both hers.

"James? Are you all right?"

"I don't know," Gemi breathed. "I feel so . . . angry . . . but I don't know why."

"Perhaps . . ."

Gemi blinked as she registered Flame's distracted tone and turned her attention to the dragon. "Flame?"

Thoughts bubbled under the surface of Flame's mind for a long moment before she hissed softly. *"I cannot sense Shadow. I thought it was because he was unconscious, but . . ."*

The simmering heat of Gemi's anger began to rise again. "But I might not be the first one Graucen used the separation poison on."

Flame growled agreement even as Gemi threw herself into the bond in search of Shadow. Where she would normally find a sense of wild earth and wind, there was now nothing but an all-encompassing haze that threatened her senses as she brushed against it.

Gemi pulled back from the clinging haze. She knew from previous experience that delving into the haze wouldn't help her reach Shadow; it would only hinder her own mind.

"Where did you last feel Shadow?"

Flame didn't bother with words. Instead, images flooded the bond. Images of nights and days in the desert were followed by the constant trudge of the horses as they traveled along unknown mountain paths. Building hunger and thirst were compounded by growing despair as Flame searched for familiar terrain to no avail.

The sudden shift to a tent-filled pass and the pain of restricted limbs startled Gemi, but she didn't interrupt the flow with questions. Instead, she watched the argument between Flame and Lord Sageo and blinked as darkness abruptly filled her mind. The darkness was soon accompanied by the knowledge of closely pressing rock and the presence of Ferez, carrying Gemi, and Last Chance behind Shadow.

"And that was it," Flame muttered. *"Shadow was exhausted and eventually fell unconscious, but at some point, I lost awareness of even his unconscious mind. I just do not know when!"*

Gemi nodded, her lips pressing together tightly. "But I was with them when Shadow fell unconscious, aye?" Flame growled an affirmative. "Then, whoever found me will know where Shadow and . . ."

Gemi closed her eyes and breathed through the sudden heat in her throat. *Ferez.* He was missing, lost, and that knowledge threatened to overwhelm her with fear and anger.

But I can't let it. I have to find him.

I will not let anything take my soul from me.

Gemi shook her head and shoved the thought away. It

wasn't one she understood, despite being her own, and she didn't have time to contemplate it.

"Just be careful in your search, James. With everything that has happened with the duke, I do not think we can know for certain who currently reigns in the Hidden City."

Gemi nodded grimly.

A sudden knocking pulled her back to the physical, and she grimaced. She still sat astride Graucen's unconscious form. Climbing to her feet, she ignored the slight quiver in her legs—*"I was wondering if that odd strength was permanent,"* Flame muttered—and turned toward the open door.

Someone called Graucen's name before the knocking became a pounding. "Answer the door, Graucen. I know you're en there."

Gemi frowned and crept to the edge of the doorway, peering through. The room on the other side looked like many of the living quarters in the Hidden City. Only the table cluttered with various ingredients and the sickly smelling pot bubbling over the fire showed that this was not the room of an ordinary Ocultado.

I still can't believe he dared to brew the separation poison again.

A soft click announced that Graucen's visitor was unwilling to wait for the Mage Healer's answer, and Gemi ducked back around the doorframe with a soft curse. She reached for her belt and cursed again, even more softly, as Flame informed her that she wouldn't find any weapons on her person.

Why must rogue thieves be so thorough?

"Where are you, Graucen?" the unknown visitor called again. The impatience in his voice was belied by a soft rustling sound that Gemi imagined came from one of the dried plants she'd seen on the table. "You no gonna make me regret bringing Nadie to you, are you?"

Gemi bared her teeth and crouched low. *So this is the man who brought me here, who found me. He'll know where Shadow and Ferez are.*

A huff touched her ears, and footsteps came closer to where she stood. "Graucen, I do no have time for this. I have duties and—Graucen!"

The man ran through the doorway, intent on the Mage Healer unconscious on the floor. As soon as he knelt beside him, Gemi stepped up behind him and wrapped an arm around his neck.

The man reacted immediately, reaching up and grabbing her arm and shoulder. Gemi was quicker, though, and she reached down with her free hand for the leather band that encircled his thigh. Slipping a puñal from the sheath, she pressed it to the back of his neck, stilling him instantly.

"Good," she bit out. "You're not stupid, then."

The man stiffened further. "Nadie?"

Gemi growled. "Who else?"

There was a beat of silence. "You attacked Graucen?"

The words sounded so lost that Gemi finally became aware that the man she held was younger than she'd thought. In fact, if the thinness of his frame and the pitch of his voice were any indication, he was quite possibly younger than she was.

A second later, her hesitation disappeared beneath a renewed bout of anger. *It doesn't mean anything, not when thieves start as young as they do.*

Snarling, Gemi pressed the puñul harder against his skin, pulling a hiss from him. "When his goal was to separate me from my bondmates? Of course I did!"

The boy jerked in her grasp and tried to turn his head despite the puñal she held against him. "He did what?"

"Don't act like you didn't know!" she snapped. "You already admitted to being the one who brought me to him."

"Sí, because you needed a Curandero and . . ."

"And what?" Gemi demanded. She felt him swallow beneath her arm before he shook his head slightly.

"Fine," she spat. "Then tell me who you are."

"I'm just a mensajero."

"Tell me your name." She jerked her arm tighter. "Your full name."

He scrabbled at her arm and choked out, "Miguel. Me llamo Miguel de Aqui."

Gemi relaxed, surprised. There was something about that name. "De A—"

A sudden bark from the other room caught Gemi off guard. Releasing de Aqui with a curse, she spun around and stepped back so she could keep both the doorway and the boy in her sight. When the dog bounded through the doorway and slid to a stop, whining, Gemi stared.

"Fiela?"

The sheep hound's shaggy, spotted gray hair was blackened in several places and even missing in a couple others. However, despite the evidence of burns, her blue eyes were lively, and her tail began to wag as Gemi stared.

"James?"

Gemi tore her gaze from the hound's, suddenly aware that, in her shock, enemies could have poured into the room and she wouldn't have noticed. When she spotted the man just behind Fiela, though, relief abruptly washed through her, and she collapsed.

~~*~*

Naldo ran through the corridors of Ciudad Ocultada, his eyes locked on Fiela bounding ahead. He refused to glance away from the perra he was following for fear he would strike out at those who accompanied him.

No, for fear of striking out at Pablo, he corrected himself. *He's the one who let Gemi out of his sight.*

But he couldn't blame the hombre for that, no matter how much he might have liked to. How was Pablo, or any of them, to know they couldn't trust the mensajero he'd sent to take Gemi from the pasajes secretos, where he'd found her, to Corteza? How could he have known that leaving Shadow and Gemi's two unknown compañeros, a strange hombre and caballo, long enough to gather the hombres and supplies necessary to move them would result in their disappearance?

If Pablo had just sent the mensajero to me while he stayed in the pasajes secretos . . .

Naldo shook his head. He couldn't think like that. No matter how much Pablo might exasperate Naldo at times, Pablo was still a trusted member of his pandilla. He had done what he thought was the best thing to do: get an unconscious Gemi to Corteza as quickly as possible.

If only we knew where the mensajero took Gemi instead?

That was why he, Pablo, Cabro, and Corteza were following Fiela through the corridors of the ciudad. The perra's nose was their only chance of finding Gemi.

When the spotted gray perra disappeared through a door to a set of private rooms Naldo didn't recognize, he nearly followed until a curse from behind him made him pause. He glanced over his shoulder.

"Those're Graucen's rooms," Corteza hissed. "If he es brewing again—"

"I'm more worried about what he's done to James." Naldo spun around and darted after Fiela.

He found the perra in the bedchamber, wriggling in

place and wagging her tail. Before her stood Gemi, one hand raised in front of her, her fingers curled tightly around the handle of a puñal. Her face was pale, her eyes wide, and her chest heaved as she gasped for air.

"James?" Naldo whispered.

Gemi's gaze darted up from Fiela to him. Recognition widened those familiar amethyst eyes before her entire body relaxed and she crumpled toward the floor.

Naldo cursed and leaped forward, but Fiela was between him and Gemi. The perra yelped as his foot met her paw instead of the floor. Before Naldo could do anything else, a thump and a grunt reached his ears. He turned back to Gemi: Gemi, who now lay on top of an hombre Naldo hadn't noticed before. An hombre who, Naldo realized, had been kneeling to Gemi's left only moments ago. An hombre—*no, a chico*—whose tunic bore a small eagle on the left shoulder and whom Naldo recognized from the noche del fuego.

"You?" Naldo snapped. "You're the one who brought James to Graucen?"

Gemi began to struggle weakly. Naldo strode forward, pulling her up into his arms, his eyes never leaving the mensajero. Cabro and Pablo brushed past Naldo and pulled the chico to his feet, holding him between them so he couldn't escape.

"Who are you?" Naldo demanded.

The chico shook his head. "Just a mensajero."

"His name's Miguel de Aqui," Gemi answered when he refused to say anymore.

Naldo frowned. The nombre seemed oddly familiar, but he couldn't think why until Pablo scowled and snapped, "You're Aqui's hijo?"

The blood froze in Naldo's veins. *Aqui? As in the Mago Animal Aquilina?* He gritted his teeth and closed his eyes. *As in Deligero's mujer de vida?*

"He has to be," Gemi whispered, and the sudden weakness in her voz snapped Naldo from his shock. "Why else would he bring me to Graucen except to retrace what his *father* did?"

Anger seemed to strengthen the last few words. Before Naldo could muse on that, de Aqui snarled. Cabro jerked away from him and stared, but Pablo slapped the chico, dropping the snarl into a groan.

"Give up, chico! You canno' run, and you will tell us the verdad of what you have done."

"And while you're doing that, I will see to James."

Naldo started. Corteza already stood beside him, reaching for Gemi's face. She clucked her tongue and jerked her head toward the door.

"Carry him to the healing rooms, Majestad. I will need pociones to deal wit' this."

Naldo nodded. To many weak protests on Gemi's part, he pulled his hermana into his arms and carried her out of Graucen's rooms.

Thirteen

Several hours later, Gemi sat in a chair in Naldo's throne room. Her body was bundled up in so many woolen blankets that she would surely die from suffocation or heat exhaustion before she succumbed to the hunger, thirst, and muscle strain for which Corteza was treating her.

"Do not joke about such things, James," Flame muttered. *"Not when you only woke a few hours ago."*

Gemi huffed and scowled out the nearby window. In the predawn darkness, all she could see of the pass at the other end of the valley was the campfires of the duke's men, but that couldn't prevent her from looking for Flame anyway.

"I hate this, Flame. I feel useless just sitting here. I want to help Pablo and Pedro question de Aqui or follow Raeka and Cabro into the secret passages to look for a trail our enemies might have left behind."

Gemi shook her head and wriggled in the wool blankets, glowering as the scratchy fabric clung to her. *"Instead, I'm stuck here, trying to regain my strength."* She rolled her eyes. *"Corteza didn't even let me ask Cabro what de Aqui said."*

The snarl the boy had given after she'd mention his

father had to have been words in the animal tongue. After all, if he was Aquilina and Deligero's son, he had to be an Animal Mage like Aquilina. Magic always begot like magic, and Deligero hadn't been a mage.

"And to think I believed we were done with Deligero when he died."

Flame sighed and curled her mind around Gemi's. *"You should calm down, James. Your anger is unsettling."*

Gemi ground her teeth before forcing herself to relax into the blankets. The anger that had fueled her body when she fended off Graucen hadn't disappeared. It had only grown quieter when she realized that Naldo was still king and she and Flame were not alone in this fight. The burning emotion had increased again as her feelings of uselessness did: feelings that had grown as Flame informed her of everything that had happened while she slept.

Adalwolf's attempt to seal away Flame and Shadow's memories, the battle of Trostlosoase, fleeing Zhulan, multiple thief attacks, Flame's capture by Lord Sageo . . .

And now Shadow, Ferez, and Last Chance are missing, and I'm just as useless now as I have been for the last ten days.

"None of that is your fault, James," Flame hissed. *"You cannot take that blame onto yourself."*

"And why not?" Gemi hissed back. *"I'm the one who lost faith. I'm the one who gave up. None of this would have happened if I hadn't given into—"*

"Do not say such things!"

Gemi cringed back into the blankets. The startled silence that trailed the demand echoed between them as loudly as Flame's roar had, but Flame's silent regret couldn't stem the guilt that welled up within Gemi to bubble alongside her anger.

"I'm sorry," Gemi whispered. *"I don't . . ."*

Comforting warmth engulfed Gemi. She closed her eyes against the burn that threatened to spill out into tears.

"I can't stand this, Flame. It was hard enough being separated from you and Shadow all those years ago, but for it to happen again . . ."

And to lose Ferez at the same time . . .

She swallowed and shook her head sharply. She couldn't think about that. Only despair lay with such thoughts.

"We will find them, James," Flame soothed.

"How can you be so certain?"

To her surprise, amusement abruptly filled the bond. *"Because it is not in either of our natures to give up on those we love."*

Gemi shook her head again. *"But I did give up."*

"Yet you are awake now, are you not?"

Gemi bit her lip and said nothing.

Soon silence engulfed them. Only Corteza's nearby footsteps and distracted mutters broke into Gemi's thoughts as the Healer alternated between applying her magic to Gemi's body and stirring a small pot hanging over a fire on the other side of the chamber. Gemi sat like that for some minutes, contemplating Flame's words, before voices from outside the throne room pulled her attention away from her mental anguish.

". . . should've woke me as soon as you found him."

Gemi couldn't stop a grin from pulling at her lips. That sharp, overprotective voice could only belong to her madre, Pastora Ovillano.

"No es like I kept the información from you on purpose, Madre." Naldo huffed as he followed the older woman into the chamber. "We've been un poco ocupados trying to find Shadow and James's newest compañeros."

Pastora stopped and spun toward Naldo, fists landing on

her hips. "And have you?" Naldo grimaced and shook his head. "Then you'd've lost nada in telling me James was here."

She turned and bustled over to Gemi before Naldo could answer.

"Oh, James." She pulled Gemi into her arms, nearly unseating the girl. "I'm so glad you're awake." She murmured the words against Gemi's temple before pressing a kiss to her hair.

Gemi swallowed and buried her face in the crook of Pastora's shoulder, breathing heavily. The pressure rising in her throat might have been a sob or a snarl, and she was unwilling to release it for fear of scaring her madre. Instead, she clung to Pastora's tunic and pressed her face harder into her shoulder.

"There, there." Pastora smoothed her hands over Gemi's hair and back. "Madre's here. Let it out, chiquito. Let it out."

Gemi wanted to protest that she was neither little nor hardly child, but she couldn't. Out of all the people who had taken her in over the years and called her family, Pastora was the one who had seen her at her worst. Even Kephin, who had found Gemi just after she killed Kale Caphrin and his men, hadn't seen how deep into despair she could fall.

Only Pastora and Naldo had seen the nearly unresponsive state Gemi had fallen into when she had been separated from both Flame and Shadow five years ago.

"I hate this," she gasped, suddenly thankful to the anger beating in her breast. At the very least, it kept the despair at bay. "I need to find Shadow, Frenz, and Last Chance, and all I can do is sit here!"

Flame stirred against her mind. *There is yet something you might be able to do.* A soft rumble permeated the bond before Flame growled softly. *Unfortunately, I do not wish to wake the entire camp just to call for Turi, so it will have to wait some time yet.*

Curiosity stirred within Gemi. Before she could form a question or Flame could answer it, a sharp *tsk* brought her back to her physical surroundings.

"Your body es healing, Nadie." Corteza huffed. "You have slept for muchos días. Doing as much as you did when you first woke did almost as much damage as the inactividad did."

"What do you mean, Corteza?" Pastora snapped. "What did James do?"

Corteza only shook her head and lifted a small flask toward Gemi. Gemi glowered.

Normally she didn't mind the potions healers gave her; all too often, she needed them. But tonight's encounter with Graucen had apparently increased her body's wariness of anything similar to the bittersweet separation poison. This would be the fourth potion Corteza attempted to give her to help her heal. The remains of the first three had already been cleaned away or carted off in buckets after Gemi's body rejected them.

"If this one does no take," Corteza admonished with a glare of her own, "then you'll be espending the remainder of the estación wit' me, strengthening your muscles the long way."

Gemi grimaced. *Which would mean cutting my time with Ferez short . . . whenever we find him.* She leaned more heavily on Pastora and closed her eyes, breathing deeply as the pressure in her throat grew.

Don't think about it, Gemi. One thing at a time.

Churning thoughts and emotions brushed against Gemi's mind, but Flame remained quiet, silently lending Gemi her support.

"James?"

Gemi lifted her head and offered Pastora a tight smile. It was the best she could offer with the pressure in her throat and the heat in her chest and the tumult of thoughts and emotions vying for her focus.

"I'm ready," she choked out.

Corteza didn't look convinced, but she took Pastora's place in front of Gemi. Wrapped her hand around the back of Gemi's neck, she pressed the flask to Gemi's lips.

Before the liquid had even passed her lips, Gemi gagged. Even the soothing magic Corteza concentrated on her mouth and throat couldn't make her relax. Corteza huffed and pulled the flask away before Gemi had felt more than a small splash of the liquid on her tongue.

The single taste was enough for Gemi's body. She twisted to the side, barely getting her mouth over the basin someone held for her before her stomach revolted for the fifth time that night.

"Can he keep food and agua down?"

Gemi glanced up through bleary eyes. Naldo stood beside her, his hands wrapped around the basin over which she was leaning, concern wavering in his dark eyes.

"Sí, sí," Corteza answered shortly. "Food and agua are no the problemas. Es only pociones his body rejects."

"Not my fault," Gemi muttered. She accepted a towel from an anxious Pastora and pressed it to her lips. She didn't sit up though. Her stomach still stirred restlessly.

Corteza corked the flask. "No, no es your culpa. Es Graucen's for force-feeding you that poison after you'd been unconscious for so long." She shook her head. "I still do no understand how you managed to rid it from your system. Even if you vomited it up, there should've been traces in the rest of your body."

Gemi shook her head. She'd tried to explain the anger that had fueled her when she realized who Graucen was and what he must be doing. Corteza didn't seem to believe her.

"I do not think it is disbelief as much as a lack of understanding, as she has already stated," Flame murmured. *"Just as I do not fully understand how an emotion, even one as strong as the anger you felt, could translate into power hot enough to completely burn away the poison when you are not a mage."*

Gemi sighed and leaned back in her chair, finally certain her stomach wouldn't revolt again. *"I don't understand it, either,"* she answered Flame silently. *"I just* knew *that I could turn that anger against the poison, and it would keep it from separating us again."*

Flame crooned wordlessly.

"What poison?" Pastora demanded. "What happened to James last noche?"

Corteza huffed and began explaining the night's events to Pastora. She was just finishing up when Pedro entered the chamber, strode up to Naldo, and whispered something into his ear.

~~*~*

"I do not like how this interrogation is being handled, Majestad."

Naldo blinked and shifted enough to get a good look at Pedro's face. The hombre didn't speak often, and the clarity with which he spoke always startled Naldo.

"How so?" Naldo murmured once he realized what Pedro had said. "Pablo has always been our best interragator, and whatever he canno' learn, you always do."

Pedro shook his head, his expresión serious. *Then again,* Naldo mused, *Pedro always looks serious.*

"Pablo has used silencio more than words these last few hours, and it is a tactic I have never seen him use."

Naldo frowned. It did seem strange that Pablo had changed his methods so thoroughly.

"Perhaps," he murmured slowly, "he has seen something en de Aqui that makes him tread more carefully than he usually does?"

Pedro shook his head, but his expression and next words proved it was only out of confusion, not a denial.

"I do not know, Majestad. While Pablo and de Aqui may not speak, complete silencio is not what I hear."

Naldo jerked back and stared at Pedro. "What do you hear?" he hissed, very much aware that Gemi, Pastora, and Corteza were listening.

Pedro glanced at the mujeres but otherwise ignored them. "You know even the quietest of Magos Animales or Magos Botánicos cannot remain completely silent when communicating."

"Unless they're communicating with their Power Animal or Plant," muttered Gemi.

Pedro nodded but kept his eyes on Naldo. "We already know de Aqui must be a Mago Animal if he really is Aqui's hijo. Yet Pablo uses silencio and offers de Aqui the chance to call for animals."

Naldo nodded. "Did you mention this to Pablo?"

Pedro shook his head. "I did not wish to warn de Aqui of my observations. I was hoping to return with Cabro, but I cannot find him."

Naldo grimaced. "He and Raeka are still en the pasajes secretos. I could send a mensajero en after them, but there es no telling how long it will take for them to return."

Gemi sat up straighter. "Didn't Cabro take Fiela with him?"

Naldo frowned at his hermana. He'd been worried about her emotional state since she had awoken, but he couldn't understand what had suddenly put that attentive look on her face.

"Sí," he answered slowly. "Guido's still confined to his bed wit' healing injuries, but he wanted to help when he learned what had happened. He offered to send Fiela wit' Cabro."

Naldo winced then as Pastora crossed her arms and glared at him. "Guido knew James was—"

Gemi patted her arm, soothing her. "It's all right, Mamá. Corteza took me to the healing rooms before I insisted on being able to look out on the valley. Guido couldn't sleep, I think."

Pastora huffed but wrapped her arms around Gemi and shook her head. "I just wish Naldo had woke me earlier."

Gemi nodded. "I know, Mamá. But it's a good thing Guido was awake to send Fiela with Cabro."

"How so?"

Gemi offered her a small smile. "Naldo doesn't need to send a messenger after Cabro when Guido can simply—"

She cut off with a hiss and bowed her head. "Gemi?" Pastora gasped, but the chica was shaking her head a moment later.

"Madre, can you go with Corteza and ask Guido to call Fiela and Cabro back? There's something I need to talk about with Naldo."

Pastora frowned and glanced sharply at Naldo. He only shrugged. He didn't know what Gemi was talking about any more than she did.

"Please," Gemi insisted. Pastora stared at Gemi for a moment longer before she sighed, nodded, and headed toward the door. Corteza followed with a quick "I'll return shortly."

Once the two mujeres had left, Naldo eyed his hermana curiously. She grimaced and tilted her head toward the window, where the sky had begun to color with the promise of sunrise.

"The duke has ordered another attack within the hour."

Naldo sighed and turned to Pedro. "Find Mateo and Teodoro and have them spread the word. I want everyone away from the front of the ciudad during the ataque."

"It won't do any good," Gemi groused before Pedro could move toward the door. To Naldo's annoyance, Pedro didn't even appear surprised and simply nodded.

"What do you mean?" Naldo demanded.

Gemi's eyes burned briefly before she turned to look out the window. "Lord Sageo," she bit out, "has called for the use of battlefires."

Naldo cursed. "Arrows and swords are one thing, but the ciudad was no built to withstand fuegos de guerra." He groaned and rubbed his temple. "Which means hiding away 'til the duque gives up is no longer an opción."

"It never was to begin with!" Gemi snapped. She paused, and Naldo suspected she was trying to calm down. When she spoke again, the spite in her voice had lessened to a light simmer.

"As long as he believes the Ocultados are responsible for the death of his son, Lord Sageo will not stop seeking revenge."

"Death?" Naldo muttered. It was the first he had heard of this. Then again, none of them had known why the duque was suddenly attacking them.

Gemi nodded and growled softly. "For some reason I

don't know, Lord Sageo's convinced his son is dead by your hands. No one's bothered to explain the situation to Flame, and the duke even demanded—"

Gemi's expression cleared, and she glanced out the window again.

"What es it?" Naldo asked warily.

Gemi turned back and smiled darkly. "I might have an idea of how to stop the attack and learn what's happening, but . . ."

She glanced back out the window. "You're not going to like it."

~~*~*

Sir Gervasio winced as a roar reverberated through the camp. It wasn't the first, and by the sound of it, they were getting louder.

The dragona, whose nombre Turi had eventually learned was Flame Tongue, had been fairly calm after Peln had ordered her bound. Both Turi and Zábido, their Curandero Mágico, had insisted the rope and cloth with which they'd bound her could not withstand a blast of her fire, so Gervasio had taken her calmness and continued presence in their camp as a sign of good will on her part.

Good will that will soon disappear completely if Peln continues to insist on the use of fuegos de guerra.

Gervasio grimaced. The dragona was not the only one upset with Peln's orders. He himself hated the thought of attacking with fuegos de guerra when they couldn't be certain of just whom they were attacking.

Despite Peln's insistence that the valle was home to vicious ladrones, they had all seen the burned remains of vast crop fields; grazing fields littered with the bodies of sheep, goats, and perros; and the recently abandoned pueblo that sat at the base of the stone ciudad at the other end of the valle.

But no matter what misgivings my hombres and I might have, Peln is still our duque. Refusing his orders is not an option.

"Es there nada we can say to change his mente?" Arlo muttered. He stood with Gervasio and Turi near the front of the camp, his eyes on Peln, who barked out orders to the soldados.

Gervasio shook his head. "He turned me away after the debacle with the dragona, and I didn't see him again until this mañana when he ordered the attack. I fear he'll take nadie's advice now."

"I saw him yesterday," Turi grumbled, his gaze turned back toward the camp's rear, where Flame Tongue was snapping and snarling. "He demanded I send a letter to Lord Lefas in the evening."

Gervasio glanced sharply at the Mago Animal. "Lord Lefas?"

Turi glanced at Gervasio and nodded. "Canno' say why he wants to bring Baylin into this, though. If anything, I'd 've thought he'd turn to Caypan for help."

Gervasio pressed his lips together grimly. *Except Su Majestad hasn't lost an hijo to the rebellious groups.* And Gervasio doubted Peln was turning to Seyan Lefas for help in the attacks. He wouldn't think it necessary because he wouldn't be able to wait that long for his venganza.

"We'll worry about Baylin if and when we need to. For now, is there anything you can do to keep my hombres from tasting fuego del dragón?"

Turi offered him a flat look. "Short of no using fuegos de guerra on the ladrones?"

Gervasio huffed. "I thought not."

"Sir Gervasio!" Peln called out. All three hombres grimaced.

"He really will no listen to you now, will he?" Arlo muttered.

Gervasio shook his head and strode toward the duque. Peln was staring out at the open valle, but many soldados had turned to stare when Peln had called for the Capitán de Caballeros.

Even they recognize that something is wrong.

"Sí, Milord," Gervasio acknowledged as he stopped near Peln and offered a small bow. He doubted Peln saw it, but Gervasio refused to deny Peln the respeto his title deserved. He wouldn't give his amigo the chance to question his loyalty, not when he'd be looking for any reason to turn Gervasio away again.

"Order the caballeros to mount up," Peln commanded. His eyes never left the open valle. "We leave in ten minutes."

"Sí, Milord."

Less than ten minutes later, Gervasio's caballeros were mounted up behind the front lines of the soldados. All of them wore grim expressions. The uneasy glances they traded proved they all held doubts similar to Gervasio's.

"This is madness," muttered Sir Quinton, Gervasio's Segundo. "Isn't it enough that we burned their fields with lit arrows? To use fuegos de guerra so close to a pueblo . . ."

"I know," Gervasio muttered back. "But Peln refuses—"

The sudden blast of the horns of guerra drowned out the rest of his thoughts.

Gervasio took one last glance back toward the paso, where it sounded like the roars of the dragona had risen in pitch. Grimly, Gervasio waved the caballeros forward and urged his stallion, Pedróscur, into an easy walk.

The trek into the valle passed slowly and silently. Even the soldados, most of whom were accustomed to conversing among themselves while traveling at a quick, steady pace, remained quiet and refused to move faster than absolutely necessary.

Gervasio was beginning to wonder if the entire army would simply refuse to attack, when shouts rose up from the front lines. Pedróscur halted as the soldados in front of them simply stopped moving.

"What in the Fuego de—"

Gervasio flung out his arm, silencing Quinton with a touch to his shoulder. Thankfully, his Segundo remembered himself quickly and motioned for the other caballeros to remain silent as Gervasio peered across the front lines.

It didn't take him long to realize the soldados were echoing the same words again and again. "¡Paz de Carito!" they called out. "¡Paz de Carito!"

"Is that . . . ?" Quinton pointed over the heads of the soldados toward the open valle.

Gervasio cursed softly when he spotted what Quinton had seen. Halfway across the valle and quickly approaching their army galloped four caballos, a white cloth fluttering desperately above them.

It was the white flag of paz: Paz de Carito.

Gervasio groaned. "Now Nadie wants to talk?" He turned to search the front lines for Peln. When he found the duque, still mounted and forcing his way through the lines of soldados, Gervasio cursed again and spun back toward Quinton.

"Send someone to fetch Turi, Arlo, and Zábido immediately. Then follow me. We have to stop Peln."

Quinton stiffened. "Surely he'll honor Paz de Carito."

Gervasio met Quinton's eyes. "When all he wants is venganza?"

Gervasio only caught a glimpse of the horror filling Quinton's gaze before he turned away. He urged Pedróscur forward, calling down to the soldados to move out of his way.

Fourteen

Red. Everything was red. It burned and boiled within him, making his skin too tight, his fingers curl with the urge to tear, and his throat choke around the need to scream.

How dare they try to make a tonto of me?

They had killed his hijo and taunted him with the knowledge. They hid away within their ciudad of stone, where only fuegos de guerra would be able to reach them. They turned his own hombres against him by pretending to be simple farmers and shepherds rather than the ladrones, the monstruos, he knew them to be.

Even Nadie taunted him with his lies, pretending to seek paz even as he supported the monstruos who ravaged their country. And now—now, when Peln would have his venganza against the monstruos who had killed his hijo— Nadie turned on him the one thing that would make him a tonto more than anything else.

¡No! Paz means nada to him! Paz de Carito can mean nada to him!

Through the haze of red filling him, he saw the caballos speed toward him. He saw their riders, saw them watching him, staring at him. Fear filled their eyes, and he grinned as he reached for the only one among them whom he recognized.

He grabbed Nadie's tunic and ripped him from his caballo. He didn't care that he tumbled from his own in the process—didn't care that the fall jarred his arms and knees.

All he cared about was wrapping his fingers around Nadie's throat and doing to him what the monstruos he supported had done to Alano.

~~*~*

"James!"

Gemi barely heard Naldo's shout as she was ripped from the circle of his arms. His fingers brushed the back of her tunic, but the ground was already rushing up to meet her and the horses were moving too quickly for anyone to catch her.

Her arms hit the ground first, but as weak as she was, they quickly crumpled beneath her. She opened her mouth to cry out in pain, but grass and dirt filled her mouth as the air was driven from her lungs.

Dazed, she struggled to breathe. She could barely get her lungs to work before hands tore her onto her back and locked around her throat.

A roar echoed through and around her. In the distance, people shouted her name. All she could focus on, though, were the dark, bloodshot eyes staring down at her wildly and the snarling rictus of hate the man's mouth had pulled into.

Lord Sageo . . .

The thought was hazy. Icy fingers of fear lanced through her and settled around her chest as strongly as the duke's fingers had settled around her throat. *Why is he . . . ?*

"You will pay for what you have done to me and my familia, Nadie!"

What I have . . . ?

I have done nothing to him!

The thought echoed through Gemi more deeply than the roar she had attributed to Flame. At the same time, a raging inferno exploded through her being, evaporating the fear that had squeezed her chest and flooding her limbs with strength.

Snarling breathlessly, she jerked her knee up, reveling in the cry that spilled from the duke's lips when it met soft flesh. As his fingers loosened their grip on her throat, she threw a fist into his ribs.

Abruptly, the duke was no longer above her. Scrambling, she tried to follow him, but arms wrapped around her waist and hands gripped her arms. Crying out at the sudden restraint, she twisted her body to escape.

"James, stop!"

Horror powered the words, and Gemi froze. The fire in her limbs died as quickly as it had when she'd seen Naldo in Graucen's rooms.

"Naldo?" she gasped and then winced. She was suddenly very aware of the burning in her throat and the screaming of her lungs. "Wha—"

"Cállate, chiquito." Corteza knelt in front of Gemi and brushed her fingertips gently against Gemi's throat. Gemi winced again, certain that bruises were already forming.

A soft whistle pierced the air. Lifting her gaze over Corteza's shoulder, Gemi blinked. She wasn't the only one who had been restrained.

Behind Corteza, Lord Sageo was laid out, facedown on the ground, one arm twisted up behind his back at an awkward angle. Above him knelt an old knight, whom Flame identified as Sir Gervasio, the duke's Knight Captain. Despite his Knight Master's weak struggles and demands to be released, Sir Gervasio remained still, his eyes on Gemi.

"Fierce little thing, aren't you?"

Mortified, Gemi dropped her gaze. The memory of the burning rage behind her attacks brought a heat of a different kind to her cheeks.

"I'm sorry," she gasped. "I don'—"

"Cállate!" Corteza demanded, more strongly this time. "You'll only do more damage if you talk now." She dropped into a hissing whisper. "And we'll discuss that anger later."

Gemi grimaced. She had wanted Corteza to understand the strange rage that had overtaken her, but not like this.

"I believe it is we who should be apologizing to you, Nadie," Sir Gervasio replied.

Gemi blinked and glanced back up at the old knight. He appeared to have little trouble keeping a steady grip on the struggling duke, and his eyes shone with concern.

"Peln had no right to attack you when you approached us under Paz de Carito. Especially," he added, darting a glare down at Lord Sageo's back, "when the piratas proved that the rebellious groups honor Paz de Carito as faithfully as any nobleman should."

Lord Sageo snarled and began to struggle more wildly. "These monstruos refused to honor it when mijo came to them under it! Why should I honor it when they carry it?"

Gemi opened her mouth. She paused as fingers brushed her throat once more. Glancing at the stern expression on Corteza's face, she grimaced. Corteza could enforce her demand for Gemi to remain silent if she felt the need to.

Best not to give her a reason.

Gemi glanced up at Naldo, who sighed and shook his head.

"We have had no recent newcomers here en the valle, wit' o' wit'out Paz de Carito. Even if we had, violencia would no have been our first response."

"Lies!" snarled the duke. "Your rey himself sent me a letter with Alano's bloody ring, claiming his death."

Gemi gaped. Above her, Naldo choked and spluttered. "I never—"

"Sir Gervasio! Lord Peln!"

A few more knights joined them then, stopping several feet from their group. They glanced uncertainly between Gemi's group and their own men.

"Well, don't just stand there!" Lord Sageo snarled, twisting to glare at the men. "Capture them! And get Gervasio off me! He's a traitor, siding with these monstruos!"

For a long moment, the new arrivals simply traded glances. Gemi was suddenly reminded of the battle in Port Calay at the beginning of the season and the blatant disobedience that had begun it.

I would never have imagined you wishing for someone to disobey direct orders, Flame murmured as she heard Gemi's thoughts.

Gemi clenched her teeth. *Neither would I,* she snapped back, her gaze intent on the wavering knights, *but I've never been in a situation where such disobedience might actually save my life.*

Flame didn't reply as they waited for the knights to decide.

~~*~*

Gervasio knew his caballeros' decision even before Quinton stepped closer. He could see it in the squaring of his jaw and the small nod he gave before he moved.

"How can we help, Gervasio?" Quinton asked, his eyes meeting Gervasio's firmly.

Gervasio ignored Peln's sudden, wordless scream and nodded grimly.

"Did you send for the others?"

Quinton nodded. "I sent Fausto. He has the fastest caballo of all of us. He should be here shortly with Turi, Arlo, and Zábido."

"Good." Flicking his gaze to the others, Gervasio jerked his head back toward the stone ciudad. "Gil, would you go fetch Peln's mount? I think the stallion is trying to take advantage of what little is still available in the grazing fields."

The young knight he'd addressed snorted. "Of course he is," Gil muttered and turned back to his own caballo. The Knight Captain waited until Gil had mounted up and urged his own caballo toward the grazing fields before turning back to the three remaining caballeros.

"Quinton, bring Pedróscur over here. You two, help me get Peln up on his back."

Peln suddenly went still beneath him. "What are you doing, Gervasio?" he bit out, his words cold. "I am your duque."

"And I'm your amigo," Gervasio answered without hesitation. "I can't let you threaten possible inocentes in your search for venganza."

"They are not inocentes!" Peln snarled.

Gervasio suddenly felt weary. The longer they sat here, the more certain he became that Peln had lost all sense of reason in the face of his grief. It would be up to Gervasio to learn the verdad of their situation.

And quickly, too, before our hombres forget the doubts they showed today.

As Peln began to struggle fruitlessly again, Gervasio turned his gaze toward the ladrones—*for lack of a better word to call them.* Nadie was still being cradled against the chest of the hombre who had denied Peln's accusations.

However, it was the mujer, crouched in front of them and tending to Nadie's injury, who interested him most.

"Perdone. ¿Señora?"

The mujer stiffened, her fingers stilling on Nadie's bruised neck. Glancing warily over her shoulder, she eyed him briefly before responding tersely.

"¿Sí?"

Gervasio refused to let the sharp retort deter him. "You're a powerful Curandera Mágica, sí?"

Confusion marred her expression. She glanced back at the hombre who held Nadie, but he only shrugged. Standing on either side of him, two hombres, similar enough in features to be hermanos, traded a curious look.

"I am," the mujer finally answered, uncertainty softening her tone.

Gervasio nodded down toward Peln. "Any chance you'd be able to drop him into sleep?"

Peln squawked indignantly, while everyone else gaped at Gervasio in surprise.

"Sir Gervasio?" one of the younger caballeros asked, but Quinton silenced him quickly. The Capitán de Caballeros shook his head slightly and kept his eyes on the Curandera.

"Well?"

"You would trust me wit' such a task?" she asked mildly, her gaze now curious.

Gervasio shrugged. "I would ask my own Curandero to do so, but Zábido hasn't arrived yet."

And he should be able to reverse any damage you might cause.

He didn't speak the words aloud, though. He thought the ladrones would take such words as a test rather than the justification of trust he would have meant them as.

When she only continued to eye him narrowly, he added, "Think of it as my way of honoring Paz de Carito since Peln refused to."

The Curandera's lips twitched, though Gervasio didn't know if that was in response to his words or Peln's increased anger. Either way, she agreed with a sharp bob of her head and climbed to her feet.

"Stay away from me!" Peln snarled as she knelt beside him. Thankfully, she offered little more than an annoyed huff in response before placing her hands on either side of Peln's head.

Less than a minute later, Peln's body went limp beneath Gervasio and soft snores met the caballero's ears.

"There." The Curandera pulled her hands away and tucked them into her lap. "As exhausted as his body es, he'll sleep for several horas if left undisturbed."

"Gracias," Gervasio muttered as he sat back and stretched. He would have been able to hold Peln for much longer, but the knight wasn't young anymore; his body complained more easily than it used to.

"Let's get him up on Pedróscur, then, and—"

"Sir Gervasio!"

The caballero turned back toward the line of soldados who still awaited orders. Galloping toward him and his hombres were two caballos, Sir Fausto and Arlo riding one, Turi and Zábido the other. Turi was waving one arm above his head.

"There you are," Gervasio called, waving back. "We—"

"Sir Gervasio!" Turi yelled, as if he hadn't heard him. "The ciudad!" He stopped waving and pointed toward them.

No, he realized as gasps and cries sounded around him, *not toward us. Beyond us.*

Gervasio turned to look at the stone ciudad at the far end of the valle. What he saw made him curse.

~~*~*

As soon as Lord Peln called for Sir Gervasio to prepare for battle, Turi had disappeared back into camp, Arlo in tow. He hadn't thought he'd be able to subdue the dragona—he'd already discovered that Flame Tongue bore Magia Animal at least as powerful as his own—but he and the Mago Botánico had little else to distract them from the coming violence.

And we can do nada to stop it if Lord Peln refuses to listen to those of us he usually considers advisors.

And so, Turi soon found himself in front an argumentative dragona, trying to soothe her. Not an easy task when she was bellowing loudly enough to shake the ground beneath his feet. He tried using only his magia at first, but her insistent complaints kept distracting him. When he tried to soothe her with words, she stilled and eyed him so disdainfully that he wondered if he had misjudged her.

"*You,*" she crooned softly, dislodging the thought, "*are not the one with whom I am upset, Turi.*"

Before Turi could reply, the horns of guerra sounded. Flame Tongue wailed her outrage, making both Turi and Arlo cringe away from her in pain.

After that, Turi stopped trying to soothe her. Despite Sir Gervasio's fears, she seemed content to remain bound. In fact, as he listened to the actual meaning behind her cries, he realized she was alternating between cursing Lord Peln—as well as someone she called de Aqui—and arguing with someone Turi couldn't see.

It was several minutes before Turi realized the unseen

persona must be Nadie and that Flame Tongue was trying to convince him not to get in the way of Lord Peln's fury.

Sound advice, Turi thought wryly.

Unfortunately, Nadie didn't seem to be listening.

The roar that broke from Flame Tongue's throat when Lord Peln attacked Nadie was so loud that Turi felt his ears pop.

The world spun and went black.

When Turi came back to himself, he lay on his back. Hands tugged frantically at his arms and patted his face quickly. Turi opened his eyes.

"What happ—"

Silence.

A face came into his line of sight, peering down at him with concerned eyes. He vaguely recognized the young hombre as one of Sir Gervasio's caballeros, though he couldn't remember his nombre. When the caballero began moving his mouth without making a sound, Turi's breath became harsh.

"I canno' hear you. Why—"

Suddenly, another hombre leaned over Turi, a small, serene smile pulling at his lips. Unlike the caballero, he didn't attempt to speak. Instead, he stroked Turi's cheek, and the Mago Animal closed his eyes again as his breathing eased.

Zábido, Turi thought gratefully.

The Curandero Mágico was the calmest hombre Turi had ever met. He had a talent for spreading that calm to everyone around him, both through his magia and his words.

If only his calming influence worked on Lord Peln still.

Unfortunately, from the moment the eagle had dropped Don Alano's bloody ring in front of Lord Peln, Zábido had been unable to affect him.

As Zábido's calm radiated through him, Turi relaxed into the darkness behind his closed lids. With no sight and no hearing, all he could sense was the hard ground beneath his back and the press of hands against his arms and around his head.

And the buzzing of the magia around him.

Turi stirred and frowned. He had already been aware of the large, fiery presence that was Flame Tongue and the angry churning of her own Magia Animal. And of course, Turi was always aware of the caballos that were still corralled closer to the center of the camp.

But this magia was lighter, subtler, yet so much more invasive than anything else Turi had ever felt before. It buzzed lightly against his back, spreading through the ground farther than Turi could sense. It radiated from a short distance away, surrounding them in what Turi knew must be the rock walls of the paso.

Focusing on that faint buzzing, Turi traced it with his magia, curious about its source. It was definitely Magia Animal—he wouldn't have been able to sense it otherwise— but he had never heard of someone infusing an inanimate object with their magia.

No, not verdad, he chastised himself a second later. He had heard of magos enchanting saddles and whips and bridles, but never the entire ground.

Or valle! He started as he followed the magia and found that the very air within the valle seemed to buzz softly. *How?*

Just then, the buzzing intensified and pulled taut. Turi grit his teeth as the vibrations—faint enough he wouldn't have noticed them if he hadn't already been aware of them— sped through him. The magia left him almost as quickly as it had entered him, as if it had sought something within him and hadn't found it.

Of course it didn't! Turi snapped at himself and threw open his eyes. *I'm not an animal for it to call!*

Zábido still leaned over him. Beside him, Arlo had replaced the young caballero who had first woken him. The Mago Botánico looked worried, and his silently moving lips proved that Turi's ears were still damaged, but Zábido appeared unconcerned, as usual.

Refusing to worry about the possibility of permanent damage, Turi snapped his gaze past the two hombres and scanned what he could see of the paso's walls. At first, he didn't know what he was looking for.

Then a long, thin beak appeared out of a crevice in the wall to his right.

Narrowing his eyes, Turi watched the small brown-and-black bird slide from the small opening. It was followed by another and another, and soon a small flock of birds, all of which Turi recognized as rock ravens, clung to the rock, hanging sideways or upside down as they ruffled their feathers and no doubt cawed to each other.

When it seemed like no more would pour from the rock wall, the flock took off, winging their way up and toward the valle. Nadie but Turi noticed their flight.

At least, nadie that Turi could see.

Instead of returning to the faint buzz it had been, the magia Turi had been tracing tightened further. Above the paso, he could see larger birds flying toward the valle, a couple at first, then more as the magia's call increased.

Turi's stomach churned for one horrible moment as he realized what he might be watching.

Pushing off Zábido and Arlo's hands, Turi scrambled to his feet. He ignored the way the world threatened to tilt and the soft bursts in his ears that might have been shouted protests. He didn't care, not if what he thought was happening was verdad.

Reaching with his magia in the hopes of finding a caballo that could freely answer his call, Turi ran for the curve in the paso that prevented him from seeing the valle. They had kept the dragona at the very back of the camp, behind that curve, to prevent their enemigos from seeing her and vice versa. Now Turi wished they hadn't, just so he could see the valle himself to confirm or deny his suspicions.

He was nearly to the curve when a caballo trotted up beside him. It bore no saddle, but Turi reach for its mane, uncaring. There was no time to spare, and Turi could ride bareback just as easily as not.

He was just about to pull himself up when a hand grabbed his arm. He spun, snarling. He stilled quickly when he found Zábido at his side. Behind him, the young caballero sat astride his own caballo, Arlo sitting behind him.

Zábido tapped Turi's ear once, quickly bringing his attention back to the Curandero. Then, Zábido clasped his hands together and offered them like a foothold. Despite his small, ever-present smile, his eyes were intent as they met Turi's.

Turi nodded, understanding the message as easily as if he'd heard the hombre speak it. *Your ears still need healing, so I'm coming with you.*

The two hombres mounted the caballo quickly, and both caballos were soon cantering around the curve in the paso.

If Turi had still been on his own feet, he would have faltered as soon as he spotted the valle. As he'd feared, birds had amassed from throughout the valle, pouring together into a curtain.

A curtain that rippled violently against the cliff face of the stone ciudad.

Turi winced as the hands around his ears tightened convulsively. Leaning over the neck of his caballo, he urged it into a gallop, screaming with his magia that they needed to move as quickly as possible.

How they made it through the lines of soldados when they reached them, Turi wasn't certain. He didn't even quite understand what he was seeing when he spotted the caballeros and the personas with whom they stood. All he understood was the need to warn Sir Gervasio of the strange, overwhelming attack.

~~*~*

"What en el Fuego de Mauro es that?" Naldo demanded, unable to comprehend just what he was seeing.

"Birds," Gemi rasped grimly.

Naldo stared dumbly at the dark cloud that churned against the upper levels of the ciudad. "Those are birds? How—"

"No es the question you should be asking, Naldo!" Corteza snapped. "Focus on what they might be doing to our gente!"

Naldo cursed and jerked his head back toward the others, seeking out the caballero who had seemed only helpful so far. Sir Gervasio was questioning the group that had just arrived, but most of them were shaking their heads. The one who had called to them was scowling at the ciudad and the inconceivable cloud that shrouded its upper half.

"He cannot hear you, Gervasio," drifted the voz of one newcomer. "He had an unfortunate encounter with the dragona's voz."

"She broke . . . ?" the caballero began disbelievingly.

"Not permanently," the newcomer interrupted softly. "But, for now—"

"What are you waiting for?" the scowling hombre suddenly snarled. His eyes, to Naldo's surprise, were on him. "Those birds're being called by a powerful Mago Animal to attack your ciudad!"

Naldo inhaled sharply. "¡De Aqui!"

"Cabro must not have reached him in time," Pedro muttered.

Naldo nodded. "Sir Gervasio—"

"Go!" the caballero interrupted. "We'll speak once you've dealt with this . . . crisis." He appeared to be just as bewildered as Naldo by all of this.

"Gracias." Naldo tightened his arms around Gemi in preparation to stand, but his hermana was already shaking her head and pushing at his hands.

"Just leave me here, Naldo," she insisted hoarsely. "You need to move quickly, and I'll only slow you down."

"But—"

"Go!" Sir Gervasio ordered. Naldo snapped his gaze up, ready to retort, but the caballero's gaze was not unkind as he offered Naldo his hand. "Nadie will be safe with us. We will honor Paz de Carito; you have my word."

Naldo swallowed. He hated the idea of leaving Gemi with possible enemigos in such a vulnerable state, but he knew she was right. He couldn't worry about her when his gente were in trouble.

Grabbing Sir Gervasio's hand, he climbed to his feet. "¡Gracias!" he whispered fervently, hoping the caballero understood just how grateful he was.

Then he turned toward Pedro, who had gathered the caballos, and mounted up. The others followed suit, Pedro pulling Corteza up in front of him, and they took off across the valle.

248

Fifteen

The sight of the dark cloud inundating against the ciudad's upper levels didn't become any more comprehensible as they crossed the valle. In fact, as they came closer, it became more apparent that the birds' numbers were larger than anything Naldo had ever imagined.

"How es that even possible?" Mateo demanded. "I've never seen so many birds in one place afore."

"Nor have I ever felt so much magia," Corteza returned, startling Naldo.

"You can feel it?" He glanced back at her, wide-eyed. "I thought magos could only sense magia similar to their own."

Corteza pursed her lips grimly. "That es verdad, but these birds' bodies must be drenched wit' Magia Animal." She huffed and shook her head. "Even if Cabro had managed to reach de Aqui, there's no way he'd have been able to stop this. De Aqui has too much control."

Naldo cursed. If that were verdad, then there would be nada they could do to prevent de Aqui from destroying their gente if he so wished. *Still,* he thought, squaring his jaw, *I can't leave my gente to suffer without trying to stop it somehow.*

"Let's wait 'til we get inside afore deciding what can o' canno' be done!" He leaned farther over his mount's neck and urged it faster.

They were just passing through the ciudad's outer gate into the open-aired Plaza Central when Teodoro cried out.

"Are they dispersing?"

Naldo flicked his gaze upward and pulled his caballo to a halt with a sharp hiss. The cloud of birds had thinned and billowed out from the rock wall like a curtain blown by the wind. As he stared, it hovered there, the birds darting in among each other, seemingly uncertain of their next move.

Suddenly, Corteza gasped. "Move!"

The cloud of birds dropped.

Naldo yelped as his mount leaped forward, and he scrambled for a hold as he was nearly jerked from the saddle. He risked a single glance back as their caballos carried them swiftly toward the inner gates that led into the cliff face.

He had thought seeing the large cloud attack the ciudad had been bad.

The sight of hundreds of birds diving straight for them was absolutely terrifying.

"Por los dioses," Naldo breathed. Turning back around, he leaned closer to his caballo's neck. "Faster!" he shouted. "We will no outrun them at—"

A sharp cry interrupted him, then another. He turned his head and cursed. The birds had reached the twins, who rode at the back, and blood bloomed beneath the onslaught of talons and beaks.

"Protect yourself!" shouted Pedro, unsheathing a puñal.

"Easier said than done!" snapped Mateo, but he and his

hermano unsheathed a puñal each and struck out at their attackers.

Unfortunately, Mateo was right. There were simply too many birds. For every one they struck, more took its place. The whinnies of the caballos proved that the birds weren't restricting themselves to human targets.

"Majestad!"

Naldo snapped back around. The inner gates—two large doors set into the rock face—were just ahead, and several hombres stood just beyond them, gaping.

"Close the gates!" he shouted, even as his caballo passed through them. Cursing reached his ears as the hombres scrambled to comply, followed by the echoes of screeches and caws as the birds began pouring into the ciudad's interior.

For a long, horrifying moment, Naldo feared they wouldn't be able to close the doors before there were as many birds within la ciudad as there were without. But no matter how large the doors might be, Naldo had insisted on keeping them well maintained, and they closed quickly and with no more than a soft *boom* as they settled into place.

The small flock that had made it into the ciudad cried out and spiraled upward . . .

And dropped to the ground an instant later.

Silencio echoed through the ciudad's front hall as everyone stared at the fallen criaturas. It was nearly a full minute before Naldo could find his voz to ask Corteza if they were dead.

"Hardly," she huffed, dropping down from Pedro's mount. "I simply tweaked their hormones, like I did for Lord Sageo."

Crouching, she examined the closest bird, a medium-sized brown-and-black criatura that Naldo recognized as a rock raven. "Unfortunately," she muttered, "I could only affect a certain numero at a time."

Naldo nodded slowly, still perturbed about being ambushed by birds. "Any idea how long they'll be out?"

Corteza frowned. "Long enough to contain them, but it will no do no good if others find their way into the ciudad elsewhere."

Naldo hissed softly and turned to the hombres who had closed the gates. All of them looked pale, their eyes fixed on the unconscious birds.

"Have you received any news from the upper levels?"

One, an older hombre whom Naldo recognized as one of his padre's contemporaries, grunted and shook his head.

"Nada. The bells have no even rung yet."

Naldo cursed, realizing he was right. Naldo hadn't heard the alarm bells even once, despite the tradition of the ciudad to sound the alarm at the first sign of trouble.

"¡Mateo! Sound the bells!"

"¡Sí, Majestad!" he answered, already running for the nearest bell room.

"You five," Naldo continued, indicating several Ocultados who had joined them while they spoke. "Find everything you can to contain these birds. Nets, crates, it does no matter, but I do no want them following us if they wake up afore we're ready."

"Sí, Majestad," they chorused and dispersed.

"The rest of you, come wit' me. We canno' let a bird ataque be the downfall of the Ocultados."

~~*~*

Piegro squawked and landed on the sheer cliff face of the

ciudad. He'd lost contact with dozens of his kin. No matter how hard he tugged at the *magia* within them, they remained lost to him.

Easy, Piegro.

The rock raven settled his wings against his back and dipped his head. His maestro's presence always soothed him, but the sudden disappearance of so many was still unsettling.

I know, querido, but they won't remain lost.

Besides, his maestro's presence added with a sense of amusement, *the distraction served its purpose. I have my captive, and we have escaped the ciudad without discovery. You know what to do now.*

Piegro relaxed and chirruped. Sí, he knew what to do.

Dropping his hold on the rest of his brethren, Piegro flew from the cliff face. Darting quickly among the suddenly confused birds, he landed on the ledge of the tunnel that led to his maestro's hidden place. There he knew he would find a letter waiting for him to carry to the only persona his maestro could trust.

And then the traitors can finally be punished.

~~*~*

Gemi watched the horses carry her brother and the others away quickly. Fear tightened her chest. Mama Caler had promised chaos as one of the two possible outcomes of this season.

First Shadow, Ferez, and Last Chance, and now Ciudad Ocultada? Will we lose everything before the season ends?

"You cannot think like that, James," Flame crooned. *"Naldo will take care of his people, and we will find Shadow and the others."*

"Will we?" Gemi demanded, the now-familiar heat

threatening to burn through her chest once more. *"I can't move, and you can't safely leave the duke's camp without someone's permission!"*

Flame growled softly, but a light pressure on Gemi's shoulder distracted her from the bond. Jerking away from the touch, she twisted her body and balled her hands into fists before she even realized the man leaning over her was Sir Gervasio.

The old knight studied her with worried eyes. "How are you feeling, Nadie?"

Gemi opened her mouth to snap at him about the idiocy of that question when Flame leaned heavily against her mind.

"Careful, James. I believe Sir Gervasio's only desire is to help." After a short pause, the dragon added, *"And you really should not be speaking with the current state of your throat."*

Gemi gingerly touched her still-bruised throat with shaking fingers and winced. *"Right,"* she muttered sullenly. *"I can't talk. Just another in a long list of things to go wrong recently."*

Flame crooned and flooded her mind with warmth. Before Gemi could get lost in the comfort, though, movement in front of her caught her attention. Sir Gervasio was nodding seriously.

"Claro. Your throat is still healing. That'll make discussions more difficult, won't it?" He glanced toward the others thoughtfully, and Gemi followed his gaze.

Most of the other knights had already remounted their steeds. Gemi noticed that the one Sir Gervasio had called Quinton had Lord Sageo slung across his lap instead of Sir Gervasio's mount as Gemi had assumed the Knight Captain had ordered. Around the horses stood three of the four newcomers. One young man had his hands wrapped around the ears of an older man, who scowled darkly at Ciudad Ocultada.

"Zábido and Turi, Lord Sageo's Mage Healer and Animal Mage," Flame identified. *"The third is Arlo, the duke's Plant Mage."*

"Zábido," Sir Gervasio called. Turi barely twitched, but the young man turned to watch them curiously. "How are his ears?"

Zábido offered them a soft smile. "Healing well, though I don't expect him to regain his full range of hearing until mañana at the earliest."

Sir Gervasio grunted. "Any chance he'd be able to translate for the dragona when we return to camp?"

Gemi turned and stared up at the old knight, while Flame crooned with interest. Zábido hummed softly.

"Perhaps," he murmured. "I don't know how much of his magia depends on his hearing."

Sir Gervasio nodded sharply. "Then we can only try and hope it works." He crouched back down in front of Gemi. "Does that sound sufficient, Nadie?"

Gemi stared at the knight dumbly, only nodding when Flame nudged her lightly. Thankfully, he didn't appear to need any other answer as he muttered "Good" before standing and offering Gemi his hand.

Gemi grimaced and glanced away. She couldn't take his hand. She wouldn't be able to stand, not in her current state, not without the rage filling her limbs with strength. Bitterness filled her throat, and she couldn't have said whether it was bile or just the emotions that had been playing through her since she woke.

"You'll have to pick him up, Gervasio." Zábido murmured the words gently enough that even Gemi's odd anger couldn't find offense with them. "Lord Peln's attack is not the only one from which he is healing."

Dorothy Tinker

To Gemi's surprise, Sir Gervasio didn't question the
Healer. Instead, he picked her up with an ease that belied his
obvious age and carried her to his own mount.

~~*~*

By the time Naldo reached the upper levels of Ciudad
Ocultada, he was leading over a hundred hombres, all of
whom were intent on protecting their casa.

Unfortunately, by the time they reached the upper levels,
the corridors were almost completely empty of birds.

There were obvious signs of their passage, of course.
Feathers dusted the floors, and occasionally Naldo passed a
dead bird on the ground.

However, it was the humanos scattered throughout the
hallways that displayed the birds' passage best. Each persona
bore some form of claw- or beak-induced injury, some minor,
many worrying. Corteza had already broken away from the
group to take care of the worst.

More and more, Naldo met the gazes of his gente and
found only confusion. They hadn't been the ones to stop the
attack. The realization settled within his stomach like a rock,
but it also sparked a small coal of anger that settled within his
chest.

Does he think us tontos, to play with us like this?

As the anger surged within his chest, Naldo stalked
toward the room Pablo had been using to interrogate de
Aqui. If de Aqui had done this to prove he was just as
dangerous within a cage as he was without, Naldo would
punish him for such arrogance.

The feathers on the corridor floors grew thicker as
Naldo approached the interrogation room. Dread began to
dim the anger in his chest, but he refused to accept the

thought that was attempting to form, even as he turned a corner and the room's open door came into view.

He couldn't have escaped, he assured himself. *Pablo, Raeka, and Cabro wouldn't have let him.*

The thought only lasted long enough for him to reach the open door.

Feathers filled the room. There were so many, covering every available surface and floating gently through the air, that Naldo could see little else at first. Then, shapes began to make themselves known.

Table. Chairs.

Two bodies on the ground.

Naldo cursed and bounded toward the closest body. Brushing away feathers, Naldo found it was Cabro. His face was pale, his jaw slackened. If the sharp tang in Naldo's nose was any indication, Cabro had lost a lot of blood.

Naldo cursed again and lunged back toward the open door, shouting for help as he did. A moment later, someone appeared down the corridor, and he ordered the hombre to bring him a curandero and more help.

As the other persona disappeared, Naldo turned back to the other body. Dispersing the feathers, he quickly revealed Raeka, who appeared to be in a condition little better than Cabro.

"No . . ." Naldo moaned. He began to chase away the feathers, searching for the cause of his oldest hermana's deathly pallor.

"Get him off her!" a sharp voz snapped. Strong hands clamped around Naldo's upper arms. "Some of those feathers are clotting the blood!"

"No . . ." Naldo moaned again, struggling against the hands. Tears blurred his vision, but he'd already recognized the deep hole he'd uncovered in Raeka's left side.

"He stabbed her," he groaned as the hands pulled him to his feet and away from Raeka. "The canalla stabbed her!"

"Get him out of here!" the voz spoke again. This time, Naldo recognized Corteza's sharp tones. "I canno' work wit' him lamenting and cursing en mi ear."

"Ven, Majestad," Pedro's smooth voz murmured, and he steered Naldo toward the door.

As they left the room, Naldo glanced back over his shoulder. Corteza was leaning over Raeka's still form. She had one hand clutched around the wound he'd found, and she was waving the other toward Cabro, directing a mujer he hadn't noticed before to begin working on the Mago Animal.

Por favor, let us have reached them in time.

Naldo had never been much for prayers to the dioses, but he was willing to make an exception for Raeka.

They were nearing the throne room when a desperately shouted "¡Naldo!" reached their ears. Pastora ran toward them. Blood trailed from several cuts on her face and neck, but it was her wide, haunted eyes that made Naldo tense.

"What's wrong?"

"¡Guido!" Pastora gasped before she'd even reached Naldo. "¡Fabio! I left them en the healing rooms, and now they're gone!"

Naldo cursed. "The birds?"

She shook her head. "Guido and Fiela scared them off pretty well. That was why I left them en the first place. I wanted to make sure Nita and Mora were safe."

Anguish twisted her features, and for a split second, Naldo feared something had happened to his other hermanas.

However, all she said was, "And now I canno' find Guido o' Fabio!"

"I think I can answer that, Señora."

Turning, Naldo saw Teodoro striding toward them from beyond the throne room, his expression grim. "What do you mean?"

Teodoro glanced toward Pastora as he stopped in front of them before meeting Naldo's gaze.

"I found bloody paw prints near the entrance to the pasajes secretos." Pastora gasped, but Teodoro showed no sign of hearing it. "I also found five of Pablo's hombres dead at their posts in the same area, wit' several sets of humano prints leading into the pasajes. Two of them looked small enough to be made by chicos."

"¡Naldo!" Pastora cried out, horrified. He wrapped an arm around her. Before he could say anything to reassure her, Pedro laid a hand on his shoulder.

"Any sign of Pablo?"

Naldo cursed softly. He had been so upset over Raeka's injuries, he hadn't even considered that Pablo hadn't been in the interrogation room.

Teodoro shook his head. "Pablo was no among the dead I found. There were two o' three sets of prints that looked like they could've been made by adults, so there es a chance he followed de Aqui out of the ciudad."

Pedro nodded. "He probably didn't want to lose de Aqui after the debacle with Nadie's missing compañeros. What of the chicos?"

Teodoro offered a grim smile. "Thing is, it looks more like the chicos followed everyone else out into the pasajes."

Pastora slumped into Naldo's embrace. "Those tontos. Why must they insist on playing héroe at a time like this?"

Naldo patted her lightly on the shoulder and met Teodoro's gaze. "What makes you think they were no kidnapped?"

"The smaller tracks covered parts of the otros. That es why I canno' tell if the larger prints were made by two o' three personas."

"Perhaps we should assume three."

Naldo frowned at Pedro. "Why?"

The older hombre shook his head. "No matter how powerful de Aqui's magia might be, there is no way he could have overcome both Raeka and Cabro and escaped Pablo without help. I think we have to consider that Graucen wasn't the only remnant from Deligero's reign willing to assist de Aqui."

Naldo groaned but nodded. "Very well. Send a mensajero for Abeto. I wanna let James and the duque's hombres know what es happening. Wit' Guido missing and Cabro unconscious, we're gonna have to depend on the plantas."

Teodoro nodded and left to find a mensajero. Pastora straightened out of Naldo's embrace and excused herself to rejoin Nita and Mora. "But keep me updated," she demanded before she left, and Naldo nodded idly in agreement.

When he and Pedro were alone, the older hombre steered him into the throne room. "Naldo, perhaps there is something else we should consider."

Naldo, who'd been distracted with composing the mensaje to send through the plants, blinked up at his padre's oldest amigo. "What es that?"

"That perhaps Pablo isn't as loyal as we thought."

Naldo stared at Pedro. "How could you say such a thing? He supported mi stand against Deligero just as strongly as you did."

"Sí, but—"

"But nada," Naldo interrupted. "Pablo and I may not always agree, but he has never given me any razón to doubt his fidelidad. You and he were mi padre's best amigos. Why would he go against that after all these años?"

For a long moment, Pedro remained silent, and Naldo thought he would drop the discussions. Naldo was just turning away to find some parchment and ink when Pedro finally responded.

"Have you forgotten that Deligero once numbered among our amigos, as well?"

Naldo glanced back at Pedro. "No, I have no forgotten. But Pablo has never shown any interés en seeking venganza for Deligero's death. Why would he help Deligero's hijo seek it now?"

This time, when Naldo turned to find writing materials, Pedro didn't answer. When Abeto arrived, Pedro offered Naldo a small bow and left without a word.

~~*~*

Back in the duke's camp, the discussion between Gemi, Flame, and the duke's men flowed easier than any of them had expected.

Apparently, Turi's magic didn't depend on his ears at all, though his own speech was often overly loud and sometimes slurred. That improved as they continued since Zábido refused to leave the Animal Mage's side except to dismount and make sure Gemi was settled comfortably against Flame's chest.

That had been a comfort Gemi hadn't foreseen. Sure, she had recognized the kindness of the Knight Captain and the mages. However, she never would have expected Sir Gervasio to carry her straight to Flame and deposit her carefully between the dragon's bound and waiting arms.

The knight had met her questioning gaze as he stood and

shrugged. "Many of us nobles were raised with an understanding of the old ways from before the *criaturas mágicas* were exiled, even if some refuse to remember them."

Gemi had blinked, Flame had crooned, and Turi had snorted. When Sir Gervasio had turned to him questioningly, the Animal Mage began his translations by informing the others of Flame's comment that Lord Peln had said the same thing when they'd met in Kensy.

Since then, Turi had explained everything Flame and Gemi could think to tell them: from Naldo's utter lack of knowledge related to anything to do with Lord Sageo and his son to the hardship of their travels from Zhulan to Ciudad Ocultada to the incident that had led to Gemi's inability to move.

Gemi had questioned the wisdom of sharing that last bit of information, but Flame had insisted. *"You have spent many years insisting communication is just as necessary as proper obedience for peace and order to prosper. I refuse to let you go against that now."*

After that, Gemi had buried her head against Flame's chest and let the dragon continue with the conversation. All she really wanted to do was soak in the dragon's warmth. Flame would be able to remember anything that still needed to be discussed.

Gemi didn't know how long she'd lounged against Flame's chest, floating amid the comfort of the bond. She jerked around suddenly, though, when she heard Turi ask a question that was not one of Flame's.

"What did he ask?" she questioned Flame.

"You keep calling them Ocultados." By Turi's tone, Gemi knew he was repeating himself. "Never ladrones."

Gemi nodded and glanced up at Flame. She crooned, and Turi's expression turned thoughtful.

"They have no called themselves ladrones for five años?"

It was the first time he'd sounded uncertain in his translation, and Gemi nodded.

"So your rey wouldn't refer to himself as the Rey of Ladrones, would he?" Sir Gervasio spoke up then.

Gemi shook her head, and Turi groaned.

"The letter Lord Peln received wit' Don Alano's ring was signed 'El Rey de Ladrones.'" He glanced around at the others. "It was a trick. All of it. Even—"

He hesitated as his eyes suddenly widened. "Wait! You said your rey had no idea about any of the correspondencia wit' Lord Peln, correcto?"

Gemi frowned. *There was more than just what was sent with the ring?* Flame asked for her.

Sir Gervasio nodded slowly. "Sí. Peln sent a letter to Ciudad Ocultada not long after he returned home from Caypan. He had expected that the ladrones you had united lived there, although how that first mensaje was intercepted . . ."

"A spy en la ciudad," Turi answered, startling Gemi.

"What?" she rasped. Wincing, she touched her throat, but she didn't remove her incredulous gaze from the Animal Mage.

Turi nodded. "The magia that controlled the bird ataque was no new. It soaks the entire valle and most likely has for años. Es also subtle enough that I think it could have been the controlling magia behind most of Lord Peln's correspondencia." He frowned. "No the one wit' the ring, though. That was an eagle and controlled by two magias, similar enough to be familia."

Gemi closed her eyes and cursed silently. *Three Animal Magics?* The two similar ones would be Aquilina and de Aqui, though why two of them were controlling one eagle, she didn't understand.

But the third?

"Ciudad Ocultada doesn't have an Animal Mage of its own, though," she rasped, ignoring Flame's insistence that she should remain quiet. "And Cabro . . ."

Surely not?

"Remember, I know Cabro's magic," Flame crooned. *"Goats simply do not do subtle."*

Turi chuckled. "No, goats are no subtle, are they?"

"Er . . . Sir Gervasio," Arlo suddenly muttered. Everyone glanced toward the Plant Mage, who had wandered closer to a nearby bush.

"What is it?" the Knight Captain asked.

Arlo's expression was a mixture of hesitancy and confusion. "Er . . . I think this mensaje was meant for Flame Tongue, but it sounds like it's pertinente to this conversación."

"What message?" Gemi asked.

Arlo turned back toward the bush, frowning slightly. "The birds have dispersed, but de Aqui escaped into the pasajes secretos. Cabro and Raeka are injured, and it looks like Pablo, Fabio, Guido, and Fiela followed de Aqui. We also suspect someone helped de Aqui escape and left wit' him, but we have no discovered who yet."

Gemi closed her eyes and leaned heavily against Flame's chest. "Oh, gods."

"Nadie, are you all right?" Sir Gervasio whispered.

Gemi didn't answer. The fire in her chest had risen into her throat. If she opened her mouth, all that would escape would be a wordless snarl.

"De Aqui's father was the last man to claim the title of Rey of Ladrones." Flame tightened her arms around Gemi. *"If someone was writing to Lord Peln under that title, he was most likely the one."*

"And now he's gone!" Gemi snarled as soon as Turi had finished translating. Flame crooned, but Gemi shook her head and struggled to sit up straighter. "Nay, Flame! I won't calm down! He and his allies took Shadow, Frenz, and Last Chance. Now he's injured Cabro and Raeka, leaving the ciudad vulnerable to animal attacks, and two of my brothers are chasing after him on some reckless quest of heroism."

Gemi ground her teeth as she considered the fact, too, that Guido was still recovering from the wounds he'd received that first night the duke's men had attacked, but she still had enough sense not to mention that out loud. They seemed willing enough to listen without her attacking them verbally for their mistakes.

Instead, she snapped, "If I have to travel to Wild Eagle Pass myself to confront him, I will."

"Wild Eagle Pass?"

Gemi jerked her gaze up to glare at Sir Gervasio. She blinked, startled, when she realized all four men were watching her with curious and intent gazes.

"Aye," she whispered, her anger easing a little. "Turi mentioned that the bloody ring was delivered by an eagle controlled by two similar magics, aye?" The Animal Mage nodded. "That means both de Aqui and his mother, Aquilina, influenced the bird. If that's true, then de Aqui must be based in the same pass that Aquilina calls home: Paso del Águila Salvaje."

Sixteen

So dark. So cold.
     So alone . . .

Yet the darkness, the cold, and the utter loneliness were so much a part of him that he could imagine nothing else. If they disappeared . . .

Would I disappear as well?

Terror tore through his silent chest then and clawed up his frozen throat.

I don't want to disappear, *he gasped silently.*

Helplessness followed the thought and settled around him, suffocating him as thoroughly as the darkness and cold. Even if he could speak the words aloud, there was no one around to hear his plea.

Please, *he sobbed anyway. Ice crawled across his cheeks, and pain wracked his unmoving body.* **I don't want to disappear. I don't—**

Frenz jerked awake to a soft voice in his ears and a warm hand on his cheek. Cold and fear still clung to his mind, and he ripped away from the hand. When his shoulder slammed hard into something solid, he grunted and threw open his eyes. They only widened when he spotted the dark form looming over him.

Dark skin! Dark fur!

Wings!

A magical creature?

Suddenly, he couldn't breathe. He clawed at the rock beneath and behind him, but the rock formed an alcove around him, and the only exit was blocked by the looming figure.

"Cálmate," murmured the figure as Frenz bared his teeth and hunched his shoulders. "Estás salvo, señor."

Frenz curled into himself further and skimmed his hands along the rock beneath him, hoping to find something he could use as a weapon. The figure's voice sounded feminine, and the words familiar, but the urge to fight sang through his blood. He saw no reason to ignore it.

His hand had just wrapped around a large, loose stone when a loud screech had him jerking his head back . . . right into the rock wall.

"Cállate, Valto," the figure huffed as Frenz groaned and gripped the back of his head. He didn't drop his eyes, though, so he saw the figure wave a hand dismissively at a pair of wings hanging above one shoulder. "No le asuste nuestra visita."

Frenz nearly forgot his pain as the wings flapped and *took off from* the figure's shoulder. As he watched, the wings—which belonged to a large bird—sailed farther into the room beyond the dark figure. It was filled with a multitude of birds—eagles, by the looks of them—and their nests. Every surface not occupied by either was covered in a loose layer of feathers.

"Wha . . . ?"

Words failed him as he stared around the feather-filled room.

Nay, not a room, he suddenly realized as he caught sight of the large hole in the uneven stone ceiling, through which shone dim sunlight. *We're in a cave.*

"¿Señor?"

The questioning tone, more than the vaguely familiar term, pulled Frenz's gaze back to the looming figure.

Now that his panic was ebbing, he realized the figure was actually a human woman. Her dark hair was matted with mud and feathers, her clothes appeared to be patched together from various animal furs, and—

Frenz frowned and leaned closer. *Is that dried mud covering her face?*

"Who—"

He coughed as his throat suddenly reminded him he hadn't had water in far too long. He swallowed, hoping to find moisture, but the movement only irritated his throat and he began coughing again.

Soothing words touched his ears before a hand wrapped around the back of his neck and something round and cold pressed to his lips. Groaning, Frenz wrapped his hands around the stone bowl and sipped gratefully at the cool liquid within.

"Thank you," he murmured once he'd finished the bowl's contents. The woman, who had begun to turn away with the bowl, paused and tilted her head to one side.

"¿No hablas Pecalini?"

Oh!

Recognition rang through Frenz. That was a phrase he had heard again and again during the war from the Tarsurian soldiers.

No wonder her strange words seemed familiar.

"Nay." He shook his head. "I don' speak Pecalini."

The woman seemed to deflate with those words. She bit her lip and glanced over her shoulder before sighing softly and shaking her head.

"Yo . . ." She paused and touched a hand to her chest. "Aquilina." After another moment's hesitation, she added, "Mago Animal."

Frenz bit his lip to restrain the laughter abruptly bubbling up his throat. *If she weren't an Animal Mage, I'd worry for her sanity, living with so many birds.*

Sudden screeching filled the cave, and Frenz glanced past the woman to see two of the large eagles attacking each other with open beaks and heavily beating wings.

Aquilina turned and screeched at the two birds, but Frenz was already turning his gaze to the rest of the room. He'd already noticed the eagles and the nests, but now he noticed what wasn't there.

James. Last Chance. Shadow. Where are they?

"Tonto Valto."

Frenz glanced back at the woman, startled by the exasperated affection in her voice. To his surprise, an eagle was once again perched on her shoulder, her fingers smoothing gently over a white streak that decorated its head. It warbled lowly and bobbed its head anxiously beneath her fingers.

"Wha's wrong wit' it?"

"Él."

Frenz blinked and met Aquilina's steady gaze. "What?"

"Él," she repeated. "Valto es macho," she added when Frenz only continued staring at her. "Masculino."

Oh.

"Y Valto solamente está nervioso."

Nervous? Why would—?

Before Frenz could ask, Aquilina reached forward and laid her hand flat against his chest. "¿Y tu nombre?"

Frenz smiled despite his confusion. "Frenz. My name is Frenz."

Aquilina repeated his name softly before chuckling. "Como—"

Footsteps interrupted her words, and she jerked around, dislodging the eagle from her shoulder. Valto squawked and landed awkwardly beside Frenz, hopping around to stare past Aquilina. Surprisingly, the eagle kept its wings half spread and its head lowered, and Frenz had the strange impression that it was attempting to protect him.

From what?

A moment later, two men shuffled into the chamber, a third hung between them, unconscious. They half carried, half dragged him toward another alcove in the cave wall and deposited him there with little consideration for his comfort.

"¡Cuidado!" Aquilina bustled over to the unconscious man and began straightening his limbs.

"Do no understand why you care, Aqui," sneered one of the men. "He es just a noble. His tipo never did anything for personas like us."

Frenz frowned curiously. *He's a noble?* The man's skin was covered in a mixture of cuts, bruises, swelling, and mud. His clothes, too, were torn and muddy, so even if they were of good quality, there was no way of recognizing it now.

"His nobility has nada to do wit' why Aqui dotes on him."

Frenz started and glanced back toward the chamber's entrance. Just inside stood a large man with arms folded across his chest and a sneer pulling at his lips. The sneer accentuated a grooved scar that carved its way from the top of his forehead, across one brow, and down one cheek to the corner of his jaw.

The scar gave the man a feral look, but it was the confidence in his stance and the almost violent energy radiating from him, even as he stood still, that warned Frenz this man was dangerous. If he had been a gambler, Frenz would have wagered his farm that this man was the leader.

"Es that no correcto, Aqui?" the scarred man growled. "You're drawn to him because he es someone's hijo, sí?"

Frenz glanced back at Aquilina. She hunched her shoulders, but she didn't look up as she brushed her fingers over the unconscious man's injuries.

A snarl had Frenz jerking around in time to see the scarred man stride over to Aquilina, dig his fingers into her matted hair, and snap her head backward. Frenz bit his lip to keep from protesting on her behalf.

"Answer me!"

Aquilina swallowed but firmed her jaw. "Quiero saber que mi Gallito esté a salvo."

The scarred man snorted. "Your Gallito abandoned you, Aqui." He lowered his face toward hers. "Betrayed us and abandoned you."

Aquilina shook her head slightly within his grasp. "No. Nunca."

Her denial only appeared to amuse the scarred man. He relaxed his grip on her hair and stroked a hand down one of her cheeks. "And yet he sent your own bird to warn our enemigos. How es that no a betrayal?"

Aquilina only bit her lip in answer. The scarred man nodded and released her.

"Do what you can for him, Aqui," he growled softly, indicating the unconscious man once more. "I want him conscious by mañana. He still holds too many secretos for mi liking."

The Animal Mage bowed her head. "Sí, Ésteban."

The scarred man patted her cheek and turned his hard gaze on Frenz. The urge to fight rose up within Frenz once more, buzzing across his back and neck, but he kept himself still. This man was dangerous and not alone, and a quick check had reminded Frenz that he himself was unarmed.

"And you, nómada," the scarred man growled, stepping toward Frenz. "Now that you're awake, I have a few questions for you."

"An' wha' makes yeh think I'll answer them?"

Frenz silently cursed himself in the next moment. The scarred man stilled, and his eyes narrowed dangerously. Frenz had known better than to make such a retort, but the war instincts sang through his veins worse than they had the morning he attacked Wolfrik.

"You think," the scarred man hissed and slowly stepped closer, "you have the right to talk to me like that, nómada?"

Before Frenz could respond, Valto screeched. Frenz winced away from the bird and watched as it puffed up its feathers and flapped its wings slightly.

"¡Aqui!" The scarred man whirled on the mage, but Aquilina was staring at Valto with confusion-softened eyes.

"No sé—"

A scream ripped through the cave system. Frenz jerked forward, nearly upsetting the eagle in front of him. The bird squawked in complaint, but Frenz barely heard it over the blood rushing in his ears and the fear beating up his throat.

James?

A second later, he knew it couldn't be. He'd heard enough screams during the war to know the difference

between a human scream and an animal's. This scream
sounded more like a horse's.

Last Chance! Shadow!

"What are yeh doin' to my friends?"

The scarred man snorted, and a smirk pulled at his lips.
"Nada at the momento. But I think Shadow Racer must have
just discovered the obstrucción of the bond."

Frenz stilled, cold spreading through his chest.
Obstruction? It had only been about ten days since Flame and
Shadow had reformed the dragonbond with James. If these
people had done something to interrupt it again . . .

Another scream echoed through the caves, and Aquilina
turned toward the scarred man hesitantly.

"Él te llama, Ésteban."

The scarred man raised an eyebrow. "He es calling me?
By nombre?"

Aquilina hesitated and shook her head.

His smirk grew. "Claro que no. No since five años ago."
He chuckled. "Very well. I'll go speak wit' them. Shadow and
I have some catching up to do, anyway."

Snapping a sharp "¡Vámonos!" at the other men, he led
them out of the chamber. Frenz soon found himself alone
with Aquilina, her eagles, and the injured noble.

~~*~*

Of course, there were beings in the chamber of which the
amnesiac king was unaware. Death stood near the chamber's
entrance, glaring after the scarred man as he disappeared
down the tunnel.

"You are lucky, human," Death growled softly, "but not
forever. One of these days, you will do something Balance

cannot forgive. When that day comes, I will gladly call down the Hunt upon your soul."

A soft admonition brushed Death's ears, and he glanced behind him. Across the chamber, Life sat with the injured noble and the wild Animal Mage. Death clenched his jaw when he caught sight of her.

Despite the days they had spent resting together, Life's soul was already darkening. It was subtle, hardly a change in shade, but to Death it was a warning that Chaos only grew stronger.

Life whispered again, asking if the Hunt would truly be necessary, and Death felt as if a vice was tightening around his soul. Life's words were in Pecalini only, and while the Animal Mage refused to speak Fayralese, the young noble under Life's care normally spoke a mixture of both languages.

Just another sign that Chaos is growing beyond our control.

"If that human even touches the king," Death answered, ignoring the fear that churned his soul, "then I will call the Hunt upon him. He has caused too much damage, brought too much Chaos, for Balance to refuse the call to the Hunt."

Turning back to the tunnel, he glared down it. "He is only lucky the eagle responded to me as it did."

If the eagle had not answered Death's urgings, had not called to the horses when it had . . .

Balance would have sought its revenge. One way or another.

~~*~*

Last Chance woke to a screech that echoed around her oddly. However, neither the distortion nor the fact that the language was more Pecalini than Fayralese interfered with her understanding of the message.

Ferez is in trouble!

A sense of déjà vu rushed over her. She tried to get her hooves beneath her, but something long and thin dug into her throat and pulled at her ears. She fell still with a snort. Glancing around, all she could see was close, bare stone, Shadow lying to her left, and the ropes that tied them both to metal hoops embedded in the rock floor.

The strange metal hoops distracted her momentarily as she realized the rock surrounding them wasn't cracked. Peering at them more closely, she realized there was no sign at all of how they might have come to be where they were.

They look like they grew there. How—?

Shadow screamed.

Last Chance jerked her head away from Shadow. The rope once again tightened around her throat, and she stilled with a soft whinny. The next moment, she eyed Shadow worriedly. He was cursing worse than a drunken soldier, and the accusations he was making . . .

How can he be separated from the bond again?

When Shadow screamed a second time, it was a pure expression of his desire for revenge.

"*Shadow?*"

He twisted his head to stare at her. His eyes were so wide and wild that she couldn't resist nudging him softly with her muzzle.

"*They stole them, Last Chance. Dosed me with separation poison and hid me away from them and . . .*"

He jerked his head against the restraining rope and screamed again. "*I don't know where Gem—James is!*"

The slip, more than Shadow's wild jerking and heavy breaths, was a sure sign of the stallion's desperation. Not since their first meeting in Puretha had Last Chance heard him even come close to giving away the true identity of either of their masters. The knowledge quickened her own breaths, but Last Chance refused to panic.

Then three men stepped into the small, stone room that held them.

Shadow froze.

"You."

The sound was barely a strained huff. Last Chance pressed her head as close to Shadow's neck as she could with the rope restraining her, but Shadow didn't even seem to notice.

"You should be dead."

A soft chuckle answered him, but the sound quickly became a full-blown laugh.

"You should see your face, Shadow Racer," sneered the man in front. A scar carved its way from his forehead down around the right side of his face, giving him a predatory quality that made Last Chance flatten her ears in both hatred and fear.

"Why aren't you dead?" Shadow demanded, his voice rising.

"Amazing, es it no, how one hombre being alive can change everything?"

Last Chance lowered her head. *"He's not an Animal Mage."* She knew it was true, could feel that it was, yet the man spoke as though he understood Shadow and was responding to his words.

"How?" Shadow snapped. Last Chance was beginning to wonder if he could even hear her with how focused he had become on this dangerous-looking man.

"Your dragona should've checked the cave afore she declared me dead. O' perhaps it was the tonto, Naldo, who decided I must be dead. Mm?"

"James saw you fall beneath the rock. He saw the rock strike you

before Flame pulled him out of there. You shouldn't have been able to survive a cave-in like that."

"Then again, it does no matter who decided I was dead. All the better for me to hide away and heal here under Aqui's care."

"But how?" The question was nearly a scream.

The scarred man smirked and pulled a dark gray chip of stone from his pocket. It looked innocuous enough, yet it reminded Last Chance of the jagged rock that Ferez had pulled from Gemi's belt.

Shadow stiffened. *"Is that . . . ?"*

"Oh, no es a mage stone from Ciudad Ocultada. No, Naldo had already stolen that from me afore I fled."

His smirk grew as he tossed the stone up and caught it neatly in the palm of his hand. As it settled and stilled, it glowed a soft, warm orange before fading back to its original dull gray.

"No, this beauty es much more especial than the ones from the ciudad's vein. En fact, that cave you left me en contained a vein of Magia Terrena more powerful than anything I'd ever seen afore."

A vein of Earth Magic? Last Chance had seen Gemi's mage stone—she and Ferez had used it less than a month ago to visit the Zhulanese duke. But then, Last Chance had only understood its purpose. Its source, she had never thought to ask.

The scarred man leaned toward Shadow. "Magia strong enough to respond to mi desire to live when Nadie and Naldo left me to die."

Shadow screamed and lunged toward the scarred man, but the rope around his neck held him tight. He tumbled to his side, his eyes glaring up at the man with more hatred than Last Chance had ever seen from him.

The scarred man straightened slowly and laughed. "Still impulsive, eh, Shadow Racer? Es a good thing I had mis hombres make the ropes so short. Whatever you manage to do to me, I can easily have done to Nadie and his nómada amigo. You would no want that, now would you?"

Last Chance tensed. *"If you harm them . . ."*

The scarred man turned to her and raised an eyebrow. "So the Gris de Pecali does have an interés en all this. I was beginning to think you'd just sit there prettily."

Last Chance bared her teeth. *"I don't know who you are, but if you harm either of our masters, you will die."*

The scarred man laughed again. "I almost wish I had Aqui here to translate. I'd like to hear what a Gris as bella as you would say to me."

A sudden squawk made Last Chance twitch, and a black and brown bird winged into the room and landed on the scarred man's shoulder.

"Ah, Piegro. A mensaje?"

The bird squawked and dropped a scroll into the man's waiting hand. The man began opening it but paused and glanced at Last Chance and Shadow.

"Perdone," he said with a short bow, "but I have to take care of this. I'll visit again soon, Shadow Racer. Until then . . ."

He spun away and strode out of the room, the bird still clinging to his shoulder.

Unfortunately, his departure didn't help ease Last Chance's tension any. The dangerous man might have left, but the subtle yet powerful magic radiating from the bird had chilled her to the core.

Why does this man have access to an Animal Mage's Channel?

Seventeen

"*S*hadow?"

Last Chance was worried. She'd waited until she was certain the thieves—for what else could these men be?—were no longer nearby before addressing the stallion, but he hadn't moved from the place where he'd fallen after attempting to attack the scarred man.

"*Shadow? Who was that man?*"

The stallion twitched. When he finally answered, his whicker was so soft that Last Chance nearly didn't hear him.

"*The most vicious . . . the most bloodthirsty man we've ever known.*" He gave a distressed nicker and tried to curl his head toward his body, but the rope kept him still. "*He was supposed to be dead. And now . . .*"

A shudder shook his body. "*Oh, gods. This was never supposed to happen again. We were never . . .*"

Shudders continued to rack his body as he fell silent. Last Chance was at a loss. She wanted to comfort the stallion, but she didn't know if she could. Despite their growing closeness over the last few sevendays, she didn't know enough about his history to help him.

There is one thing I can do, though.

It took several minutes of jerky movements and pushing with her legs, but Last Chance finally managed to shift her body far enough over that she could press her nose to Shadow's.

"Roll up, Shadow. You need to loosen the rope. Come on."

The stallion didn't respond. The shivers were beginning to calm, but that did little to reassure Last Chance.

"Come on, Shadow. You can't give up. Not now, not after everything we've been through. What would your bondmates say?"

Shadow gave a soft snort. *"Flame's been captured by the duke, and Gemi already gave up. They can't say anything about it, can they?"*

When he didn't even try to catch his slip, Last Chance knew it was worse than she'd realized. She glanced sharply at the small room's entrance, but she could tell there were no Animal Mages nearby.

Not even that damn bird that feels like an Animal Mage's Channel.

She wanted to ask Shadow about the bird, but she doubted he'd understand, not in his current state. *I have to break him out of this.*

"Well, neither of your bondmates might be able to say anything to you right now, but I can, and I'm not giving up. Do you hear me, Shadow?"

Shadow's ears twitched. Last Chance watched as his eye rolled down to meet her gaze. After a moment, he nickered softly.

"You don't know what it was like last time. To be separated from them for sevendays on end, lost in the haze of the separation poison, isolated from everything else . . ."

He closed his eye. *"I can't take it again."*

Last Chance snorted and shoved him hard with her nose. His eye flew back open.

"You may be separated from them now, but I won't let you be isolated or lost in the haze of whatever this separation poison is. I'm not about to let them separate us, but I can't do that if you give up and let yourself become lost.

"Do you understand me?"

For a long moment, Shadow simply stared at her. Last Chance stared right back. She couldn't let Shadow fall into the apathetic state threatening to overtake him, not when it could mean their or their masters' lives.

Finally, Shadow lifted his head slightly and tilted his ears forward. *"Have I ever told you how much your resilience amazes me?"*

Last Chance snorted in relief and nudged him affectionately. *"I believe Flame mentioned something about it when we officially met."*

Shadow huffed. *"But I didn't."* Curling his legs closer to his body, Shadow rolled up onto his knees and shifted until his body was pressed fully against hers, neck to rump.

"You really are the most amazing mare I've ever met, you know."

Last Chance rubbed her head against his. *"Be that as it may,"* she muttered, *"you still haven't told me exactly who that man is."*

Shadow shifted against her. *"Didn't I?"*

"Nay. You only said he was the most vicious and most bloodthirsty—"

Oh.

"His name's Deligero," Shadow answered, even as Last Chance remembered his words from the minutes before Flame was captured. *"Ésteban Deligero, the previous king of thieves."*

~~*~*

As the thief king left the horses' chamber, Hate lingered for a moment. He had been drawn to the cave system by his brother's hatred. He had arrived minutes before the rock raven though, just in time to feel the spike of hatred fill Peace's stallion.

The level of hatred had astounded Hate. He'd checked himself, but his influence had been under control.

Then why is the stallion feeling such hatred?

Not that it was unusual for a mortal to feel such hatred without Hate's influence, but it had only been two sevendays since Hate and his twin had discussed the tendency of Peace and her bondmates to lean toward positive emotions.

Then again, everything has changed since Mid-Season.

Shaking his head, Hate left the horses' chamber, knowing he was probably doing them more damage than good. Besides, he wanted to keep an eye on Deligero, who seemed to have the unenviable ability to anger Death.

I just hope Death doesn't feel the need to do to him what Life has been doing with the king. If Death takes it upon himself to pry a mortal soul from its body . . .

Hate shuddered.

A moment later, he came upon Deligero in his sleeping chamber. He had dismissed the other men and was opening the note the rock raven had brought him. Said bird was still perched on his shoulder, and it tilted its head to eye the entrance as Hate stepped through.

Hate eyed the bird in return. "If only I could influence you against him." He snorted. "If only I could influence you against your master, but you're far too loyal for that."

Hate frowned then and eyed the bird more closely. There was something odd about it that he'd never noticed before.

After a moment, he realized the bird wasn't simply soaked in Animal Magic, as he'd originally thought.

The bird was radiating it.

It's a Channel?

Channels were rare. Most Animal Mages had a Power Animal, a specific species that responded most strongly to their magic. Many of these Animal Mages even had a single animal that acted as their constant companion.

But it was the rare Animal Mage who had the ability to channel their magic through that particular animal, imbuing it with the ability to use Animal Magic itself.

Hate shivered and glanced over his shoulder. He'd seen perhaps twenty-five Channels in all the millennia he'd influenced human mages; that's how rare they were.

Yet this is the second I've seen in this generation.

The problem with Channels wasn't the power of their masters. The problem was that most Animal Mages with Channels took them for granted and let the connection and control corrupt them.

Out of all the Channels Hate had seen, fewer than five of them had been used by their masters for good.

Abruptly, Hate shook himself. "Stop thinking like that," he snapped. "It's just a coincidence we have two Channels so close to each other. And it's not like the other one will cause us problems."

No matter his words, though, Hate couldn't shake his unease. After all, the gods knew the Fates would orchestrate certain things if they thought it necessary.

~~*~*

Piegro squawked and ruffled his feathers. There

was . . . something . . . at the entrance of the chamber, but he couldn't see it.

"Cálmate, Piegro." Deligero smoothed his fingers down the rock raven's back. "You can find your brethren en a momento."

Piegro chirruped and turned to eye the humano his maestro trusted above all others. Deligero thought he was eager to find the wild mago's eagles and settle among them as his maestro had ordered. While this was verdad—Piegro was always eager to follow his maestro's orders—that strange presence made his feathers itch.

Deligero murmured soothingly before turning back to the note Piegro had carried from his maestro. Trying to ignore the itch, Piegro dipped his head and read the note as well.

Ésteban,

I have the traitor, and I am bringing him to you. I have set the birds of Valle Ocultado on the ciudad and left the Ocultados with the impression that the traitor is responsible for both this attack and the ones rumors connect to you. That should keep them ocupados for some time, no matter how the situation with the duque turns out.

Make sure Aqui gives Piegro a place to settle among her eagles. I've already given him orders to keep them in line, as well as to keep an eye on anyone else you might need him to.

—Your oldest amigo

Deligero chuckled. "Ah, old amigo. You always were slyer than you let on." Glancing at Piegro, he smoothed a finger along the rock raven's neck and jerked his head toward the entrance.

"Go on, then. There are two prisioneros wit' the eagles that you might wanna keep an eye on, but they should no be much trouble. I need to make preparaciones for your maestro's arrival."

Piegro chirruped and took off, winging through the tunnels until he reached the wild mago's eyrie. He circled the chamber twice, observing the wild mago, her eagles, and the two prisoners, before aiming for the largest nest.

By the time he'd settled on the rock wall, the wild mago was glaring at him and most of the eagles had puffed up their feathers and were edging away from him.

Piegro shook himself and settled his wings. It mattered little to him. These birds were not his brethren. All that mattered was his maestro's requests and the power that flowed between them.

Ignoring the complaints, both animal and mágico, Piegro ducked his head beneath one wing and reached out with the magia his maestro gave him.

By the time Maestro arrives, the eagles won't be able to cause any problemas.

~~*~*

Frenz didn't know how long he sat in his alcove, idly watching Aquilina and the birds or eating from the platter of food he was given. At one point, when the thieves had left them alone for a while, he'd tried to get up and wander the chamber, but a sharp look from Valto, who refused to leave his side, told him that wasn't going to happen.

So he sat and stared. His mind spun in circles as he tried—and failed—to avoid the worry and fear gnawing at his chest and gut.

James. Last Chance. Shadow. Flame.

The names circled through his mind again and again until they became a litany to the gods. *Let them be safe. Please let them be safe . . .*

Even a vague memory of soft, concerned voices

accompanying the realization that James was gone couldn't ease Frenz's worry. He distinctly remembered recognizing one of the voices from the group that captured him, and since the only voices he'd heard since entering Taursur were either attacking thieves or . . .

Or the people who took James were the same ones who grabbed me. And if that's true . . . if these thieves have James here somewhere, unconscious and unable to defend against whatever torture their violent leader decides to put him through . . .

Memories of James bloodied, bruised, and tied to a post threatened to overwhelm him then. He shoved them away, only to fall into worry for Flame and the horses.

"¡No! ¡No! Get off me!"

The endless circle of Frenz's thoughts came to an abrupt halt. He snapped his head around, blinking as he tried to figure out where the cry had come from.

What he didn't expect to find was Aquilina's patient awake and struggling away from her. She murmured soothingly, but Frenz remembered his own sudden awakening and the need to fight. The tortured man would not be so easily calmed.

Slipping past his feathered guard, Frenz hurried over to Aquilina in time to catch the man's fist before it struck her cheek. The Animal Mage turned to him, startled, but Frenz kept his attention on the wild-eyed man, who pulled at his grip and gasped out a denial.

"Easy, friend." Frenz loosened his grip on the other man's wrist. Frenz was still weak from the earlier lack of food and water, but this man's struggles were pitiful. Aquilina probably wouldn't have been in much pain if the man had managed to hit her.

Stillness answered Frenz's words. Reddened eyes stared up at him as the man's brow knitted together in confusion.

"You're not one of them."

Frenz raised his eyebrows, impressed. He wouldn't have been able to make such a distinction if he had been as panicked and hurting as he was sure this man was.

"Nay," he answered softly, "but I'm no' really in a position to help yeh either, I'm 'fraid."

The man shook his head. Frenz could read exhaustion in the way he sank back against the rock.

"At least you can still stand." He gave a small huff. "Enjoy it while you can, amigo."

"Wha' do yeh mean?"

The injured man didn't say anything and simply gestured weakly toward his legs. Frenz followed the motion with his gaze and hissed. He hadn't noticed before, but wood and bandages supported his lower legs.

"They broke yer legs?"

"Only the right one. Aquilina's assured me the left is just a sprain." He gave a small, humorless laugh, which quickly became a gasp and a grimace as he squeezed his eyes shut. "And they must have cracked some ribs with that last round of torture, too."

Frenz shook his head. "Why're they doin' this? Wha' do they wan' from yeh?"

Slitting his eyes open, the injured man offered Frenz a smile that was as humorless as his laugh had been. "The secretos of my familia? The weaknesses of my casa?" He leaned his head back against the rock with a soft groan. "Anything they can get out of me before they kill me.

"But that's not why I'm here. That información would just be a bonus for the rey."

"The rey? Don' tell me tha' violen' man is the king o' thieves." Frenz glanced toward the chamber's entrance and lowered his voice. "He canna be, no' when . . ."

Not when the king of thieves is supposed to be a friend of James's.

"Well, he wasn't the rey I was expecting to meet, certainly." Frenz glanced back down at the injured man curiously. "My padre set up a meeting of paz with the Rey of Ladrones. After meeting Nadie—"

"Wait, meetin' Nadie?" Frenz frowned. "Who are yeh?"

The injured man blinked. "I'm Alano Sageo, oldest hijo of the duque of Tarsur."

"Alano Sageo? As in Captain Alano Sageo, commander o' Tarsur's third division?"

Sageo blinked again. "Sí, but only in the last two años of the guerra."

Frenz snorted. "Tha's all I fought of it." He shook his head. "An' yeh shouldn' talk like that. We may ne'er have met, but I heard yeh were one o' the bes' commanders o' the war."

Sageo snorted and groaned. "You sound like a good amigo of mine, talking like that."

"Maybe yer friend has some sense, then."

Sageo groaned again. "More sense than you if you keep trying to make me laugh. I'm surprised Aquilina hasn't chastised you yet."

Frenz glanced to the side. The mage had been silent for the past few minutes. When she met his gaze, all he saw was relief before she turned back to mixing together what looked like mud and eagle feathers.

She's probably just glad to see someone raising his spirits. How close must he have been to simply giving up?

He shrugged. "She doesn' seem to mind." Then, because he thought his own curiosity might distract the other man from his pain, he added, "So who's this friend yeh say I sound like? Another noble?"

Sageo's smile faded. "Doesn't matter, really. Dioses, if he could see me now . . ."

"Now don' start that," Frenz insisted. "Yeh haven' exactly had much of a chance, it seems. Yeh've been here how long?"

Sageo shook his head. "A siétedia, maybe?"

Aquilina spoke up, and Sageo lifted his head to stare at her. "Eleven días? Really?" When she nodded, he dropped his head back and stared up at the stone above him. "My head must've been more rattled than I thought."

"Eleven days is a long time, friend. Seems to me yeh're in pretty good shape for so long. I mean, James—"

Frenz clamped his jaw shut and ground his teeth as pressure suddenly pushed up his throat and his eyes stung.

Gods, James, please be safe.

"James? You don't mean James Caffers, do you?"

Frenz blinked open his eyes. He grimaced as wetness stroked his cheek. He rubbed at his cheeks and eyes before nodding.

"Aye, James Caffers. I've been travelin' wit' him for . . ."

Frenz hesitated. His back had tightened at the thought of telling anyone about the incident with the Mindspeaker, even if the thieves could already tell James wasn't waking up.

"For a few sevendays now."

"Did something happen to him?" Sageo pushed himself up on his elbows, ignoring Aquilina's complaints. "I mean, obviously, if you're here—"

Aquilina snapped something that had them both turning to her, though Frenz couldn't understand her words.

"Wha'd she say?"

Sageo frowned. "Nadie isn't here."

Frenz swayed where he stood, suddenly light-headed. "He isn't?"

Aquilina spoke again, and Sageo blinked. "No. She says only two caballos were brought to the paso with you. No other humanos and . . . nada else?"

Meaning Flame, Frenz realized. So only Shadow and Last Chance were somewhere in the system of caves.

Which means I need to find a way for us to escape so we can find James and Flame.

~~*~*

Death stared at the amnesiac king. The man's thoughts had whirled darkly with uncertainty and dread for so long that Death had worried he would become as lost in his mind as Peace had.

As soon as the man learned that Peace had not been captured by these thieves, though, the fear and worry were replaced by a determination so thick that even the birds seemed to notice. The rock raven especially, who had pretended to sleep since its arrival, twitched its head out from under its wing and eyed the chamber warily.

The sudden determination drove the king to lean closer to the duke's son and whisper fiercely that he would find a way to get them out of there—all of them. Pained hope lit the injured man's eyes.

Death huffed. If the situation had not been so dire, he might have found it amusing. Here were two men who, despite the nine years Sageo had on Katani, had been raised together, trained together, and had fought in the war together. Yet neither recognized the other: one because he did not remember that life, the other because this was the last place he would have expected to find his king and friend.

Death's potential amusement was quickly doused, though. The wild mage grabbed the king's arm and hissed for him to be quiet. Although she spoke in Pecalini, he fell silent immediately and turned to her with a question in his eyes.

Death nodded approvingly. Even without his real memories, the king was an instinctive tactician.

The wild mage jerked her head toward the rock raven and hissed softly. Sageo grimaced.

"She says the rock raven isn't hers."

"Tha's a bit obvious, isn' it?" the king muttered. "The eagles—"

"I don't think that's exactly what she means, amigo."

The king stilled. He eyed the rock raven more warily. "Have yeh seen it afore?"

That startled the duke's son, and he stared at the bird with wide eyes. "Maybe . . . I don't know . . . I mean—"

He shook his head. "I've spent much of the last few días either unconscious or being tortured; you can hardly expect me to remember something like that."

"Bu' think," the king whispered insistently, his eyes never leaving the bird. "It could be important. Have yeh seen tha' bird afore?"

Sageo frowned at the rock raven for a long moment before nodding slowly. "Sí, I . . . I think so. Once or twice, maybe? Usually with the rey."

"But he's not an Animal Mage." The words weren't a question, but both Sageo and the wild mage shook their heads.

"No," Sageo agreed, "and the bird's never stayed, either."

The king nodded. "Which means our enemies aren' all here, bu' the raven's master is mos' likely on his way."

"Impressive."

Death started and turned to find Hate leaning against the semi-solid spiritual essence of the rock wall near the entrance.

When he realized his brother was alone, Death took a step back toward Life.

"Hate? Where is Love?"

Hate hummed, distracted, as he studied the amnesiac king. When he finally turned and focused on Death, he murmured a soft "Ah" and waved one hand dismissively.

"She's looking after Peace and her allies. It's all right," he added reassuringly, though the words did nothing to ease Death's apprehension. "Now that Peace's soul has been purged of Chaos—"

"What? How?" Behind him, Death could hear Life give her own startled gasp. "I thought a dragonbond was not strong enough to purge Chaos, only protect against it."

Hate eyed them, bemused. "I forget you two have been holed up here for over a sevenday." He shook his head. "She's been clear of Chaos for several days now. She even woke up not long after she was separated from this lot."

Behind Death, Life sighed. "Ella está despierta."

Death closed his eyes, suddenly weary. This was good news, most definitely, but could they truly rejoice when he and Life had to be here? What good were Hate's words when Death could not steal his twin away to their pocket realm for fear of the negative consequences of War's struggle to reclaim his own?

"Peace may have been cleansed," he whispered, "but that does not mean the rest of us are safe from the Chaos. Does not War still rampage under its influence?"

"He does . . ."

Hate's words were so slow and solemn that Death opened his eyes to stare at the red demigod. To his surprise, his brother was eyeing the humans, of all things, nervously.

"Hate?"

The red demigod shrugged, but the casualness of the gesture was belied by the flinch that had preceded it.

"I've spent years ignoring him," he whispered. "Generations, even. I've even gone so far as to refuse to influence him because . . ."

He waved a hand toward the humans, and Death turned to them, confused. The wild mage, Aquilina, was crying softly while Sageo whispered quietly with the king about what the mage kept repeating: "mi Gallito" literally meant "my little rooster," a term that could be applied to a male eagle as easily as other male fowl.

"Her son, then?" Katani muttered thoughtfully. Sageo hesitated, but the king was already continuing.

"The thief king accused Aquilina o' bein' worried about yeh because yeh were someone's son. An' then she started talkin' about 'mi Gallito,' which is why the words sounded familiar."

"That's probably verdadero," Sageo answered slowly. Katani hummed curiously, and the duke's son muttered, "Aquilina was kind the first día I was captured, but she became even more solicitous after the chico disappeared."

"A boy?"

Sageo nodded slightly. "He looked to be fifteen, maybe sixteen at the most. He mostly stayed out of the way when I was captured, but I watched him argue with Aquilina on that first noche. They were just screeching at each other, but he looked angry and Aquilina looked terrified."

He glanced at the wild mage, but the woman was lost in her own thoughts of her son. "The next mañana, he had disappeared, and she began snapping at anyone who hurt me. Well," he qualified, "anyone but the rey."

Death shook his head. He was surprised the duke's son

remembered that argument, though he obviously did not understand its full significance. The wild mage had been preparing her main eagle, Valto, to travel to Hacienda Sageo with young Sageo's blood-encrusted ring. Before the eagle could leave, her son had demanded they send a warning to the Ocultados.

The ensuing argument had involved so much Animal Magic that Valto, who responded to the son as easily as the mother, had left the pass with two missions: give the duke his son's ring and warn the Ocultados. The boy had fled the pass as soon as they'd realized what had happened.

"And the eagle was intercepted by the wolf of Ciudad Ocultada before it could find anyone who would warn Peace's king of thieves."

Death turned back to Hate curiously. His red brother was more distracted than he had ever seen him if he was responding idly to Death's thoughts as if they were part of the conversation.

"Who did you mean, Hate?" he whispered. "Whom were you referring to when you said you had refused to influence him?"

Hate's eyes, when they met Death's, were dulled by an exhaustion that was surely older than this current bout of Chaos.

"What other soul could be important enough to warrant such an extreme?"

Death inhaled sharply and glanced back at the three humans. Only one among them stood out—had ever stood out, really—but he could not fathom why Hate would fret so much over a single mortal soul, even one as unique as the king's.

"Have you truly never considered the implications of his

soul's appearance?" Hate whispered. "Its two-toned nature has never worried you?"

Death frowned curiously and eyed the king's soul. The distinct blue and silver had always made the soul easy to spot. Death could well remember the first time he'd seen it: a toddling babe who had nearly drowned in the waters of a Zhulanese oasis perhaps two millennia before. Even then, as Life won that round of The Game, Death had merely been startled by the soul's appearance, not overly concerned.

"And it doesn't bother you that it looks like it should belong to a demigod?"

Death started and stared at his brother. "That is why you are so worried?" When Hate nodded, Death peered at the blue and silver soul once more. "I admit, I have always been curious as to why Father would create such a simple mortal soul, but he has never caused us any problems.

"In fact, I would even go so far as to say he has been quite helpful in holding back the Chaos."

Hate gasped. "You've seen what he can do?"

Death frowned at his brother. "I have watched him unite entire peoples, aye, but . . ." He watched Hate close his eyes. "I suspect that is not what you are referencing."

Hate shook his head rigorously. "His soul *changed* the Chaos when he was out in the desert with Peace. Love thought it might just be how their Soul Bond worked, but—"

"Soul Bond?" Death's thoughts whirled. First Hate compared the king's soul to a demigod's, and now he was saying there was a Soul Bond involved?

"With whom?" he whispered. Surely he had misunderstood his brother's meaning.

"With Peace!" Hate hissed, confirming Death's fears. "He's the reason she gave herself over to Lupus, the reason we're facing the Chaos now! I don't care how his soul interacts with it; he's the one who caused this!"

Death shook his head. "You cannot say such things, Hate. I may not deal in relationships, but even I understand that Soul Bonds are not created by the souls themselves. This is not the king's fault."

"Perhaps," Hate grumbled. "But if he didn't exist—"

"If he did not exist," Death snapped impatiently, "then neither would most of the human countries that fill our land!"

Silence met these words. The two brothers stared at each for several long minutes before Death finally shook his head wearily.

"Go to Love, Hate. I do not understand what drew you here, but perhaps it is best you do not stay."

For a moment, Hate looked as though he wanted to say more, but the urge seemed to disappear quickly, soon followed by the red demigod himself. Once he was gone, Death turned to the humans. His soul sank as his eyes landed on the king once more.

"A demigod Soul Bonded to a mortal soul. Is such a thing even possible?"

Life murmured soothingly, but her words were little comfort when they only reminded him of the growing Chaos.

Eighteen

Shadow didn't know how long he and Last Chance lay together in that small, stone chamber. Other than the feed and water the thieves had provided, there was no way to tell how time passed. Neither sunlight nor moons-light could reach them; a single torch was the only source of illumination in their barren accommodations. Most sounds that reached them echoed through the cave system, only frustrating Shadow more.

And without the bond, I can't count on Flame's natural sense of time to help, either.

Shadow snorted and flattened his ears. Despite Last Chance's words and her constant presence at his side, the entire situation was too much like his imprisonment by Deligero five years ago for him to ignore the panic and fear fluttering through his chest and threatening to overwhelm his mind.

He didn't tell Last Chance. As grateful as he was for her presence and assurances, she could not have understood the pain and absolute loneliness of being so completely separated from his bondmates.

So he suffered in silence. He tried to control his breathing as the chamber—several times larger than the stall he'd been raised in—grew cramped and stifling. He tried to still himself as the haze blocking the bond reached cold tendrils through his chest and drew fine shivers from his muscles. He did everything he could to hide the pain he felt from Last Chance; he didn't want to worry her when there was nothing she could do.

"You said that Frenz told you some of my history, aye?"

With a startled whinny, Shadow jerked his head up, but the rope digging into his neck kept him from moving too far. He tilted his head to stare at Last Chance, but she simply met his gaze evenly.

"Aye," he finally answered when she refused to look away. The high pitch of his whinny made him flinch.

"Did he tell you he found me on a Pecalini merchant ship?" Shadow dipped his snout. *"Did he mention the state I was in?"*

Shadow hesitated. He knew what she was talking about. He remembered Flame's distressed question about whether Last Chance had been raised on the ship and his own horror that a mare as beautiful and strong-willed as Last Chance had been treated with such neglect.

"He said you were dirty, starved, and covered in sores."

For a long moment, Last Chance didn't reply. As the silence lengthened, Shadow wondered if there had been a reason for the question. When she did finally answer, she turned her head away from the stallion.

"What Frenz doesn't know is that that state was mostly self-inflicted."

Shadow tilted his ears forward. *"What?"*

Last Chance twisted her head farther away, but she was

held in place just as firmly as he was. *"Frenz wasn't my first master,"* she nickered softly. *"My first was a Pecalini Animal Mage. He . . . he died nearly a year before Frenz found me."*

Shadow stared. *Animal Mage? Does that mean . . . ?*

"Were you his Power Animal?"

Last Chance's ears twisted back, and she dropped her chin. *"Aye . . . he . . . I . . . "*

Shadow nickered softly and nudged her nose with his own. He had been separated from the bond several times now, so he knew how difficult such separation could be. Yet he couldn't imagine the pain he would feel if he ever lost Gemi or Flame permanently, the way Last Chance had lost her first master.

"I'm sorry."

Last Chance snorted softly and shook her head the little she could. Throwing her ears forward, she met Shadow's gaze once more.

"Frenz took me off that ship. I was stubborn in my grief and gui—my desire for solitude"—Shadow tilted his head curiously but didn't ask about the correction—*"but he was just as stubborn in caring for me. It was his constancy that reminded me I could live beyond the pain.*

"And I refuse to let you give into yours."

Shadow snorted and glanced away. *"I'm not—"*

"You're hurting, Shadow." The nicker was so soft, Shadow could have ignored it, but doing so would have only been an insult to Last Chance. Instead, he leaned his head against hers and huffed.

"It's all too similar."

"Will you tell me about it?"

Shadow jerked away from her, more startled than he'd been when she'd first interrupted his thoughts. *"Isn't it bad enough I'm reliving it in my mind? Telling you—reliving it that way—"*

He shuddered.

"It might help," she offered. *"Lay it out in words, and you might understand the pain better; you might be able to step back from it."*

Oddly, the words were familiar. Shadow searched his memory, trying to figure out why. When he found the memory, he nearly laughed.

"You're quoting Master Ekin now?"

"Perhaps. Although I thought you were still pretending not to be formally trained as a warhorse."

Shadow snorted. The conversation she was referencing—the first time they'd spoken truthfully to each other—felt like it had happened years ago instead of less than a month.

"With you? Never." He pressed his cheek to hers. *"I don't want to hide anything from you."*

"Good," she answered. *"Then you'll stop trying to hide your pain, as well?"*

Shadow huffed but didn't protest. *I really have to start thinking before I speak.* Settling himself more firmly against her side, he began to tell her about the first time Deligero had captured him and Flame.

~~*~*

Last Chance listened to Shadow's story with one ear. It wasn't that she wasn't interested in his past—she'd never been more interested in a stallion than she was in Shadow. As he began to talk though, she felt a spike in the Animal Magic surrounding them. She refused to ignore such a thing when an Animal Mage's Channel had already shown itself familiar with this place.

The increase in power didn't dissipate as she had half

hoped it would, either. In fact, there was such a conflict among the magic that Last Chance knew the sudden increase accompanied the arrival of multiple mages.

And it's probably too much to hope that any of them are here to help us.

Last Chance stretched her senses, something she hadn't done in years, and felt out the Animal Magic. There were four sources she could feel. Two were similar enough to be parent and child—first-born Animal Mages always inherited the Power Animal of their Animal Mage parent. But it was the two other sources that held her attention. They radiated magics that were more than similar; they were exactly the same.

The Channel's master just arrived.

"Last Chance?"

The mare started and met Shadow's gaze. He was eyeing her curiously. Chagrined, she suddenly realized she had stopped listening to Shadow's tale.

"*I'm sorry,*" she nickered. "*I didn't mean to ignore you.*"

To her surprise, Shadow only flicked an ear before nudging her nose. "*What's happening? You seem worried.*"

Last Chance glanced at the small chamber's entrance. "*Have you ever heard of an Animal Mage's Channel?*"

Shadow tilted his head curiously. "*Nay. What is it?*"

"*Dangerous,*" Last Chance muttered before flicking her ears and meeting Shadow's gaze again. "*It's rare, but some Animal Mages have the ability to give a single animal their magic to influence animals at a distance. That animal becomes their Channel and can use Animal Magic just as easily as their mage can.*"

Shadow flattened his ears. "*And there's one here?*"

Last Chance paused, considering the irony of Shadow's wording. There were secrets in her past she had refused to share with anyone, even Shadow. She had the unpleasant feeling they weren't going to stay in the past for much longer.

"Aye, there is. You remember the black and brown bird that arrived before Deligero left?"

Shadow grunted. *"That little thing is an Animal Mage's Channel?"*

Last Chance snorted. *"The smaller the Channel, the less likely it is to be noticed."*

Shadow flicked his ears and eyed the entrance. *"Is there anything we can do about it? We're not exactly free to move around."*

"Unless we can grab the bird—"

Last Chance stilled. Magic flared at the edge of her senses. As she reached for it, a howl echoed through the cave system. Shadow lifted his head.

"Is that . . . ?"

"A wolf," Last Chance nickered, confused. The howl had definitely belonged to an animal, but she could feel magic flaring outside the cave. *"I think there's a mage with it, but—"*

Last Chance cut off with a sharp whinny as magic flared from farther inside the cave system. Moments later, screams echoed through the tunnels, and Last Chance choked.

~~*~*

Once Frenz had deciphered Aquilina's belief that the enemy mage was bringing her son to the caves, he had grown optimistic despite the woman's tears. Frenz thought it was safe to assume the boy would be an ally of theirs instead of another enemy, and his Animal Magic, combined with his mother's, had to be strong enough to stand against whatever mage controlled the rock raven.

That assumption steadied him as they awaited news and drove him to return quietly to his alcove when men came with food and water for Sageo. It kept him from snapping when Deligero returned with a hard smile for Aquilina and sharp assurances that she would soon see her "Gallito," sending Aquilina into tears once more.

Frenz even managed to hold his tongue when Deligero grabbed Aquilina by the arm and dragged her from the room.

"I hate that hombre," Sageo muttered. "And the way he treats his own mujer de vida . . ."

Frenz glanced at him, surprised. "Aquilina's his lifemate?"

Sageo nodded. "From what I've gathered. I don't understand how she can stand him, but from what I've seen, he's the only one she won't stand against."

Frenz grimaced, realizing the flaw in his earlier thoughts. "She wouldn' turn her magic against him."

"Why would she? She hasn't before now."

Frenz eyed the entrance. "Not e'en for her son?"

Sageo sighed. "Who knows, amigo."

A sudden screech from in front of Frenz had him jerking backward, away from Valto. He glanced down at the eagle, surprised. The bird faced the chamber's entrance, wings half spread and head bobbing low.

"Valto?"

"Do no think your eagles can help you here, Miguel," snapped a low voice, and Frenz's eyes darted to the entrance. "No when Piegro has spent the last few horas making sure your influencia is the last they'll accept."

I know that voice.

In the next moment, someone stumbled through the entrance and sprawled to the ground. A man strode in afterward, a sneer firmly twisting his lips.

"Such a disgrace. No es a wonder why your padre has always been disappointed en you."

"No es mi padre!"

Frenz glanced at the figure on the floor and nearly grimaced. Despite his fiery denial, the boy—for he looked even younger than James—sat hunched, his head bowed and his hands curled into loose fists.

His words may be fierce, but his posture says he's already given up.

The enemy mage seemed to think so too because he gave a sharp, barking laugh. "No your padre? He es your sire, no matter how you might detest him." He leaned closer and snarled. "Show a little respeto!"

The boy hunched his shoulders further and dropped his head to one side, exposing the side of his neck. Frenz closed his eyes, unable to watch. It was like seeing a young hound being chastised by its master.

"Ah, old amigo. Starting his punishment wit'out me?"

Frenz opened his eyes to see the thief king stride through the doorway. The enemy mage turned. With a sharp smile that still managed to look softer than his earlier sneer, he grabbed the thief king into a strong hug.

"Es bueno to see you again, Ésteban." As he pulled back, his smile morphed into a smirk. "Have to admit, I was quite disappointed when Naldo announced you had died in a cave-in, of all things. It was quite the relief when I learned you were still alive."

The thief king chuckled. "And I was glad to hear you were no as loyal to the brat as I had feared."

The mage snorted. "Loyal? To Naldo? Only ensofar as I refused to leave mi casa. He may have been raised as a ladrón, but he dreams too much of paz for the comfort of our tipo. Honestamente, I blame Renaldo for that; he may have been our amigo, but he was as soft on his hijo as he was on his trono."

"Which es why he had to die." The words were spoken so flippantly that Frenz couldn't hold his tongue any longer.

"How can yeh speak so lightly o' killin' a friend, if that was what he was to yeh?"

Both men turned toward Frenz, startled. Even the boy glanced up at him with horror in his eyes. The enemy mage recovered first and stepped closer to peer at Frenz from the other side of Valto.

"So the nómada has some fire yet. I'm surprised, Ésteban. You were always fairly quick to tame prisioneros, even if you could no break them."

The thief king harrumphed. "Have no had the chance. Piegro arrived no long after he woke, and I've been busy since."

The mage chuckled. "Then perhaps you'll give me an oportunidad wit' him, mm? After all, you have your own traitorous offspring to deal wit'." He jerked his head back toward the boy without removing his gaze from Frenz's.

Frenz glared at the mage, refusing to let his words intimidate him. This was the man who had separated him from James; he was certain of it. It was his voice that had commanded the thieves to capture and drug him, the same voice that had spoken of returning with his men when James was removed from Frenz's back.

"Yeh don' scare me."

The mage smirked. "Good. That'll make your taming all the more satisfactorio."

~~*~*

Death snarled as the wolf of Ciudad Oculatada reached for the amnesiac king. "You cannot have him!"

Ignoring Life's murmurs, Death reached for the eagle standing protectively in front of Katani. Any other bird, and Death's influence would not have been able to override the power of the wolf. As he focused on the bird, Death could feel the delicate Balance that threatened to break if he commanded the eagle to protect the king as he had earlier.

"It does not matter!" He shoved at the eagle's soul. "Protect him! Give yourself to the Cycle if need be, but you cannot let them touch the king!"

Not when there is a Soul Bond involved! Not when my very soul refuses his pain and death! Death bared his teeth. *Not when he may be the very key to the end of this Chaos!*

~~*~*

Valto leaped at Piegro's maestro. He didn't know what drove him to it. One moment, he was being subdued by magia that belonged to neither of his maestros. The next, he was filled with a sudden need to protect the humano behind him.

The mago cried out. He brought his arms up to fend off Valto's talons, but Valto's claws had already caught at his cheeks and lips. Valto's wings beat heavily at the sides of his head.

Then pain stabbed through Valto's back, and he screeched as he was driven off the mago. Screams echoed around him, and he could feel the fear and hatred of his maestros swirling through his mente. He couldn't let it stop him though, not when the humano, the one they called nómada, was still in danger.

Valto tried to attack the mago again, but Piegro was there, catching at Valto's chest and belly with his talons and snapping at his eyes and beak with his own. Valto tried to pull back, but the smaller bird had latched onto him. His wings

beat in time with Valto's—or Valto's beat in time with his—
and they simply flew around the chamber together, neither
breaking free of the other.

"Get it off him!" Valto heard distantly as he tried to
angle his beak for Piegro's neck. "It's gonna kill him!"

I have to if I'm going to protect the nómada.

Then Valto realized the nómada had been the one
speaking. The humano was currently struggling with the
mago, reaching for Valto with one hand even as he attacked
the mago with the other.

He thinks—

Pain exploded through Valto's neck, shooting through
his head and chest and blinding his eyes. Screams, louder than
before, overwhelmed him until he was hearing pain as much
as he was feeling it.

A smaller, barely noticeable pain briefly pierced his chest
and belly before hands, gentler even than those of his
maestros, caressed his front and wings and cradled his head.
Valto briefly wondered at the stickiness of the fingers, but
then the nómada leaned over him. Dew hung in his silvery
eyes, and Valto gave a soft, oddly gurgling warble and nudged
the thumb that sat near his beak.

"Don'. . . . sad . . . nómada." The sounds were difficult to
get out with the pain in his throat, but Valto thought he
managed to get them out well enough. The nómada even
gave a weak smile.

"I'm so sorry, Valto," the nómada whispered, which
made no sense, really, since the humano hadn't done anything
to Valto. "I canna—maybe if—"

A scream, filled more with anger than fear or pain,
pressed on Valto then. He closed his eyes and leaned his beak
into the gentleness of the nómada's sticky fingers. That

gentleness eased the pain until all that was left was black and silent.

~~*~*

Miguel screamed and launched himself at Deligero. He may not have been the one whose bird had just killed Valto, but none of this would have happened if Deligero hadn't survived that cave-in five años ago. None of it would have happened if he hadn't come to Paso del Águila Salvaje demanding that Miguel's madre take him in and care for him.

All he's done since Madre took him in is hurt us again and again.

Unfortunately, Miguel had never been much of a fighter. Deligero grabbed up his hands in one of his own and slapped him hard enough that Miguel staggered back a step, his head spinning slightly.

"¡Tonto!" Deligero snarled. "¡Chico estúpido! If you had no commanded the bird to attack—"

"I did no!" Miguel cringed as he realized how breathy his voice sounded. "I did no tell him to do nada!"

Miguel didn't want to think about why Valto had attacked. He had thought Valto was quelled by the other mago, just as the rest of the eagles had been. Then he'd launched himself at the other mago with no encouragement from Miguel. And he knew his madre hadn't done it either, not when she refused to go against her beloved Ésteban.

Miguel yelped as Deligero suddenly grabbed him by the back of his neck. "Liar! Even now you refuse to obey! I was going to make your punishment swift and privado for Aqui's sake, but es clear you will no respond to nada short of a público punishment."

Miguel blanched. "No . . ." Public punishment might not have meant much if this had been the Ocultados, but

308

Deligero's ladrones were vicious and ruthless. They would cheer Deligero on and then follow the punishment with their own beatings. Miguel had seen hombres die in such displays.

Deligero shoved him toward the chamber's entrance and called for other hombres to grab the two prisoners. "I want them to see what happens to those who stand against the Rey of Ladrones."

Deligero drove Miguel through tunnels so familiar, the chico could have walked them in his sleep. Unfortunately, the caves that had once meant love and safety for him might now become his grave.

Deligero didn't stop moving until they stood in the center of the cave system's largest cavern, and already ladrones were gathering eagerly. They eyed Miguel hungrily, and his throat went dry as he noticed several of them fingering their puñales.

"You all know mi hijo, Miguel." Deligero addressed the crowd once everyone had gathered and the ladrones had begun shifting anxiously. Murmurs ran through the crowd, even some chuckles, and Miguel ducked his head, trying to make himself smaller. It was the way he had survived since Deligero made the paso the center of his reign. It wouldn't help now though, not when all eyes were on him.

"Miguel"—the way Deligero sneered his name made the chico wince—"refuses to obey. He thinks he es better than us and that the way we make our livelihood es malo."

That gained laughter and sneers from the crowd.

"He tried to betray us to our enemigos. He tried to warn them of our plans by bird and then en person." Deligero turned to Miguel with a harsh, falsely sympathetic smile. "How did that work out for you, Miguel?"

Miguel hunched his shoulders, unwilling to answer. He'd been confused when he arrived at Ciudad Ocultada about ten días ago, only to find that there was no talk of either the duque or Deligero and his ladrones. After stealing the tunic of a mensajero—one of the few things Miguel was good at was blending in—it hadn't taken him long to figure out that Deligero had a spy in the ciudad.

Miguel glared over his shoulder at the other mago. *Too bad I didn't figure out who it was until it was too late.*

Fingers dug into his chin. He gasped as Deligero jerked him back around to face him. "Even when you are already facing punishment, you canna be bothered to listen, can you?"

Miguel swallowed but met Deligero's eyes. If he was going to die now—and the likelihood of that was growing with Deligero's rage—he might as well earn the death. Gathering all the hatred he had ever felt for this hombre who had sired him, Miguel did the one thing he'd wanted to do ever since his madre had taken Deligero in.

He spat in his face.

Silencio echoed through the cavern, thick and heavy as a wolf's pelt. Miguel didn't drop his gaze, no matter how much he might want to at the sight of the fury burning in Deligero's eyes. The hombre didn't even bother to wipe his cheek before he leaned forward and growled low enough to make a wolf proud.

"I should kill you myself."

The words barely registered to Miguel. The silencio had become a heavy humming in his ears, and his veins buzzed with magia that wrapped around him like a pair of eagle wings. The feeling was familiar. It gave him a sense of warmth and safety that reminded him of the earlier años of his life.

"Madre." His eyes closed as he fell into memories.

Suddenly, something large hit him in the chest. Miguel grunted as he automatically wrapped his arms around it. Blinking open heavy-lidded eyes, Miguel stared into a familiar gaze, one that held a tender look he hadn't seen since the años before Deligero took over their lives.

"Madre?"

"Mi . . . Gallito . . ."

Abruptly, the magia fell away from Miguel. He gasped as his madre slumped in his arms. "Madre? Wha—"

He couldn't finish the question. Behind his madre stood Deligero, his eyes wide and his fingers still trailing along the hilt of the blade he'd buried in her back.

"¡No!" Miguel screamed as soon as he found the air. "¡No, no, no, no, no! ¡Madre! ¡Mamá!"

But her eyes had already closed, and he staggered to the ground as he tried to support her. "Por favor, no." He gasped a sob as he realized her chest was no longer moving. "No . . . no . . . oh, dioses, no . . ."

"Tonta mujer."

Miguel jerked his head up and stared at Deligero. The hombre watched them with eyes as cold as a snake's and a sneer as harsh as any Miguel had ever seen him wear.

"She just had to go and find the will to stand up to me now, of all times. Maldita perrita."

"How . . . ?" Miguel could hardly breathe. "How can you say such things? She's mi madre—your mujer de vida!"

"And a tool whose sentimentalismo was often more trouble than her magia was worth."

Miguel gaped up at Deligero, unable to find the breath or the words to respond. All these años—all the times Miguel had remained quiet despite his hatred—he'd only done so because he thought that, somehow, in some way, Deligero made his madre happy. Yet now Deligero was telling him he hadn't even cared for her except as a powerful mago whose devotion he commanded.

How . . . ? Why . . . ?

A howl broke through his shock. Reaching for the sound, Miguel gaped for an entirely different reason. The entire cave system abounded with animals, and the howl was followed by whinnies, snarls, and screams. Miguel had barely a moment to realize there must be *yet another* Mago Animal present before the first of the strange group bounded into the cavern.

Nineteen

ven as he followed the flow of wolves, horses, and goats into what must have been the cave system's largest chamber, Shadow still had trouble believing he and Last Chance were free. He was more inclined to believe the separation from his bondmates had finally driven him mad.

Especially considering Gemi's younger brothers are responsible for our freedom. He tossed his head to catch a glimpse of Guido clinging to the back of a large, gray wolf. *And all done with Guido still recovering from both burns and a leg injury.*

Only Shadow's certainty that Last Chance wouldn't let him go mad reassured him that this was really happening . . . and that Guido's assurance that Gemi was both safe and awake was not a desperate creation of his panicked mind.

A lancing pain across his shoulder reminded Shadow they were surrounded by enemies. Turning, he threw his head into the chest of the thief who had cut him.

Shadow had taken down four men when he heard a familiar squawk. Throwing up his head, he sought the small rock raven Last Chance had claimed was an Animal Mage's Channel. When he found it winging toward the center of the cavern, he trampled one more thief and trotted after it.

Last Chance said we need to grab that bird. If I can catch it . . .

Shadow pushed past animals and thieves alike as he followed the bird. When it dipped down out of sight on the other side of a thief half fighting, half talking down a horse that must have belonged to the thieves, Shadow shoved past them, intent on finding the rock raven. He broke past them into an open space and stumbled to a halt. He stared. He shook his head and stared some more, but what he saw refused to change.

How . . . ?

The drab-colored bird had landed on the shoulder of a small, wiry man. As the bird rubbed its beak lovingly against the man's jaw, the man raised a hand and cupped it over the rock raven's back. Not to hinder the bird, as Shadow might have hoped, but to welcome it, as though it were a long-lost friend.

The action itself was familiar to Shadow (how many times had Gemi greeted him so?), but he couldn't reconcile it with the man before him. He couldn't reconcile the familiarity between bird and man with the familiarity to Shadow of the man's sharp features

Shadow snorted and pawed the ground with one hoof. *It can't be him, right? It can't be Pablo.*

And then the small, wiry man turned to Shadow and his sharp features folded into a familiar sharp smile, and Shadow knew there could only be one conclusion.

He's a traitor! Pablo's an Animal Mage and a traitor! We thought him a friend! How—

"Ah, Shadow Racer."

A thrill of cold shot through Shadow, and he jerked his head back. He tried to step away, tried to run, but his hooves were sluggish.

"Nay," he whinnied. *"You can't—you won't . . ."*

Except Shadow wasn't connected to Flame now, not with the separation poison throwing the bond into a haze. He could already feel his will slipping, tangled and burdened by the barely tangible magic seeping from Pablo and his damned rock raven.

"So weak." Pablo stepped closer and ran a hand up Shadow's nose. Shadow snorted, but didn't break away from the touch. Perhaps he should have; after all, he didn't let just anyone touch him with such familiarity.

But Pablo is familiar. He's been our friend for years.

A light weight on Shadow's back had him turning to curiously eye the small rock raven that had landed there. It watched him as well with a calm that Shadow thought he should emulate.

Calm. That's what I need. I haven't felt calm in ages.

"Just a couple of tasks, Shadow Racer," Pablo crooned, and Shadow turned back to meet the man's warm gaze. *"Just a couple of annoyances to remove, and then we can find the calm you seek."*

Shadow dipped his head. He could remove annoyances. He had done it before, he was sure. *"Whatever you need."*

Pablo's sharp grin filled Shadow with a contentment he thought he must've been lacking. When Pablo indicated the pale mare who fought with the ferocity of a desert cat, Shadow agreed.

A shame to remove such a beauty, he thought idly as he moved toward her, *but annoyances are unacceptable.*

~~*~*

Last Chance had just knocked out two thieves when a flash of hooves to her right forced her to twist out of the way.

"*Shadow!*" The stallion was so close to her that neither of them would have been able to fight their enemies without hurting the other. "*Watch where you're kicking!*"

To her surprise, Shadow blinked slowly and flicked his ears forward. "*But I am watching where I'm kicking.*"

The shock of those words nearly prevented Last Chance from avoiding the next kick. She only just managed to dance clear at the last moment.

What is he doing? Why is he—

A small bird circled several feet above him.

Nay!

Silent shock—icy fear—fiery rage. The emotions slid through her so quickly she could do nothing more than stare blankly at Shadow and the Channel wielding him like a puppet. Still worse, memories from her foalhood—images she had been doing her best to avoid since she'd first sensed the rock raven—unfolded mercilessly within her mind.

"*You are my world, and I am yours.*"

The cut of Shadow's teeth against her neck broke her from the trance. She whinnied but couldn't avoid him as he threw his body against hers, shoving her into the cavern wall.

"Last Chance! Shadow!"

Last Chance wished she could explain to Ferez. What their struggle must look like to him, who couldn't feel the pull of the Animal Magic guiding Shadow's movements! He couldn't know that the magic had invaded Shadow's mind as easily as it had his body.

And Shadow has no way to resist it. Not like I do. He's as susceptible as any other animal. I never considered it. Not when he seemed so confident. Not when I've only ever seen him controlled by the Pferdetanz. And he went into that so willingly—

A squawk silenced Last Chance's thoughts. Her gaze darted to Shadow's back, where the rock raven was landing with an imperious flick of its wings. It watched her with small, black eyes for nearly a full minute before it shook its head and squawked again.

"Do you yield, mare?"

For a confusing moment, Last Chance thought the raven had spoken in a human tongue. Then, with a deep hatred she had only ever learned to feel for her first master, she realized the rock raven's Animal Mage had approached them and laid a hand on Shadow's flank.

Snorting, Last Chance lowered her head and flicked her gaze around the cavern. What she found nearly made her give in.

At the entrance, the thieves had managed to corral the wolves, horses, and goats that had accompanied her and Shadow. Their placid demeanors, as much as the soft buzz of the magic filling them, proved the raven's influence of them.

Even the wolf the young Animal Mage had ridden in on lay still, seemingly unconcerned that its former rider and his brother were struggling fruitlessly in the grasps of several thieves. Only a single sheephound, shaggy and spotted gray, growled softly, but even she knew better than to attack at this point.

Closer to the center of the chamber, Ferez was down on his knees, his arms gripped tightly behind his back and a puñal pressed tightly against his throat. Behind him slumped a man Last Chance recognized with a ringing shock.

Peln's oldest son is alive!

She couldn't remain focused on him, though. Not with the threat that stood before her. Not with so many gazes hanging upon her.

Not when . . .

She wanted to ignore the thought, to shove it away and forget it existed. She averted her gaze from Ferez and Alano, but it only landed on a boy near them who clutched a dead woman to his chest. His wide eyes shone with wonder and recognition, and Last Chance knew she couldn't ignore it. If he could recognize what lay within her, as surely as she recognized the same within him . . .

I've spent years ignoring it—hiding it—calling it something it's not, but now—

"Well, mare? Do you yield?"

"If we let others separate us, what will we be left with?"

Last Chance huffed and tossed her head. She refused to give in, either to her memories or to this mage who called them forth. She hadn't given in to an Animal Mage since she'd broken away from her first master, and she refused to give in to one now.

Especially not to one with a Channel.

"Interesante," murmured the mage. "I've never encountered a beast as resistente as you. However, I fear resistencia is no appreciated here. I will only ask one more time: do you yield?"

Last Chance lifted her head, flipped her ears forward, and glared at the mage. *"And leave Shadow in the clutch of your magic?"* A shiver rippled through her body as she considered leaving the stallion she had come to care for so greatly at the mercy of an Animal Mage.

"Never!"

The raven squawked and ruffled its feathers. The mage simply ran a soothing hand over its wings as he considered her with raised brows.

"Wit'out the dragona, Shadow Racer es as vulnerable to Magia Animal as any animal. He es under mi control now. There es nada you can do for him." He shook his head.

"Your only choice es to yield o' to die. If you choose death, so be it."

Last Chance closed her eyes and breathed deeply, filling her lungs with the scent of the animals around her. The mage was right, in a way. Most animals in her position would only have the two choices, assuming they'd been able to resist his magic for as long as she had.

But most animals weren't once an Animal Mage's Channel, either.

"Shadow Racer," the mage directed, switching to the tongue of the animals, *"see to it that . . ."*

Last Chance released the breath. With it, she released the block she'd formed years ago around a piece of herself that was more a part of her than she'd ever wanted to acknowledge. She had hidden it away and tried to forget about it and the master she had hated and betrayed, but she couldn't continue to do so when using it could save her friends.

When it can save Shadow.

"Last Chance!"

Ferez's shout was followed by a cry of pain, but Last Chance refused to let it distract her. Opening her eyes, she watched Shadow step closer and shift his weight toward his hind legs.

"Forgive me, Shadow."

She shoved the magic residing within her into the stallion.

The next moment, Last Chance wondered if it would even work. It had been years since she had influenced another animal, and Shadow was already rearing, his front hooves kicking out toward her. She pressed her head and body closer to the wall, closing her eyes in expectation of the coming blows.

A second later, she threw her eyes open. Shadow was

twisting and snapping his head around. He struck at the raven, who squawked and tried to escape, but Shadow was already locking his teeth into one of its wings and pulling it from his back. Landing back on all fours, he tossed it to the ground at Last Chance's hooves.

The mare didn't hesitate. She raised her hoof and slammed it down hard on the bird before it had a chance to do more than flutter its wings. The human scream that joined the bird's wasn't enough to prevent her from lifting her hoof and slamming it down again and again until she could feel the mage's power ebbing away from the wolves, horses, goats, and distantly, the eagles that called this cave system home.

She might have continued stomping on the bird's corpse if a nudge to her neck hadn't pulled her from the haze of rage. Lifting her head, she met Shadow's worried gaze.

"Are you all right?"

Last Chance lowered her head and glanced behind Shadow. The raven's mage knelt there, sobbing, with one hand clutched to his head, the other to his chest. A heavy satisfaction settled in Last Chance's belly at the sight.

"Aye," she nickered in answer. *"I am."*

"I *like* James's new amigos!"

The cheer from the youngest Animal Mage broke the stunned silence that had filled the cavern. Howls, whinnies, and screeches soon followed.

~~*~*

Frenz didn't know what to make of anything that had just happened. He knew Last Chance had stood up to the enemy Animal Mage—not unusual when Last Chance had been able to resist Animal Magic since before Frenz's father had given her to him. He even realized that Shadow had fallen to the mage's magic—a bit more unusual since the dragonbond should have protected him.

Yet if he fell to it, how did he ultimately break free?

And why does it seem like Last Chance had something to do with it?

He didn't have time to consider it, though. Already, wolves and eagles were attacking the men who held him. Frenz ducked and twisted, grabbing one thief's boot knives before the man was hauled away by a pair of wolves.

So armed, Frenz leaped into the fight. He stepped around wolves and goats. He ducked under eagles' wings. He even scurried away from rearing horses. All these animals, it seemed, could handle the men they faced. With tearing precision and deadly weight, they brought down every thief Frenz passed, so he continued his search for an opponent they couldn't defeat.

When he stepped around one horse and spotted Miguel tumbling to the ground, Frenz knew his search had been more specific than he'd thought. He hadn't just been looking for a worthy opponent.

He'd been looking for the thief king.

The king stood over Miguel, a long knife clutched in his left hand while he flexed the right open and closed. "How many times have I told you that you are no even a rival for me, Miguel? Yet you persist en attacking me still. Are you that impaciente for me to finish what Aqui interrupted?"

Miguel snarled and tried to roll to his feet, but the thief king kicked him in the chest. Miguel collapsed back to the ground with a groan.

"You're pathetic!" the thief king growled. "Just like the perrita who—"

He choked and staggered as Frenz buried a stolen blade

in the back of his right shoulder. Frenz twisted it into the flesh for good measure.

"*That*," Frenz snapped as he jumped back to avoid a wild swing, "is for Aquilina."

The thief king grunted and turned, raising the blade he held in his left hand. "¡Tonto! You did no even know her!"

"I know she treated me kindly despite our differences in language." Frenz adjusted his grip on his remaining blade. "I know she stood up for those she cared for, even to protec' them from others she loved."

He darted a glance to the center of the cavern where Aquilina's body still lay. Anger stiffened his jaw.

"An' I know yeh killed her an' don' e'en mourn the loss."

The thief king barked out a laugh. "She was a pathetic tonto who let herself be ruled by love." He snorted. "She was weak."

"Mi madre was no weak!"

Frenz glanced at Miguel. The young man was on his feet, but he held one arm to his chest and the other shook as he brandished his knife at his father.

He's not a fighter. He may hate his father more than anything else, but he wouldn't survive a fight against him. Frenz tightened his grip on his remaining knife. *That means—*

Frenz sneezed as something light touched his nose. Wiping his face, he stared uncertainly at his hand when it came away gritty.

"Fabio!" shouted one of the boys who had come in with the animals. "What're you doing?"

"No es me!" the other boy answered. "Plantas do no even grow that deep en this rock."

"Tontos," growled the thief king. Frenz swung back around to find him backing away, one hand digging into a pouch at his belt. Before Frenz could wonder what he was reaching for, the floor shook, nearly pulling his feet out from under him.

"You canno' run from this, Deligero!" Miguel stepped after the retreating thief, but he stumbled to one knee as another tremor shook the rock.

"Earthquake!" someone shouted.

"Who es using their mage stone?" someone else cried.

"Es too powerful for a mage stone!" yelled another thief. "We gotta get out of here afore the ceiling collapses."

Frenz cursed. He didn't know if this was a trick of the thieves or not—he didn't know what a mage stone was—but he knew earthquakes weren't unheard of in Tarsur. Calling out to Last Chance and Shadow, he stumbled toward Miguel, grabbing the boy's shoulders and steadying himself against him as the rock shook again.

"We have to get out o' here!" He tugged the boy toward the wall where Captain Sageo lay. Already, the cavern was half empty as animals and men alike fled for safety. "We canna risk gettin' caught in a cave-in."

"¡No!" Miguel surged against Frenz's hold. "He'll get away!"

Frenz glanced over Miguel's shoulder even as he stumbled and tightened his grip on the boy's arms. The thief king had turned around and was stumbling unsteadily toward the wall opposite the cavern's entrance, a wall that appeared to be made of unbroken rock.

"Is there an exit from the caves in tha' direction?" Frenz asked. Miguel shook his head but continued to press against Frenz's hold. "Then he's only riskin' death by goin' that way. Come on!"

Miguel tossed his head from side to side. "But he has a

mage stone! He can just make his own exit and survive that way." He moaned. "He's done it afore, and he es sure to do it again."

Frenz shook his head and hauled Miguel toward Captain Sageo. He didn't have time to contemplate the power the boy was attributing to a single stone. Shadow and Last Chance were already shifting impatiently as the two boys who had accompanied the animals—both too small to do much good—attempted to help the nearly lame noble onto one of the horses. A large wolf and a shaggy hound waited near them anxiously.

"Come on!" Frenz snapped when Miguel continued to strain against his hold. "We have to leave!"

"¡Madre!"

Startled, Frenz loosened his grip. Miguel slipped free and fell to his knees beside the body they'd nearly stumbled over. He pulled her up against his chest, but the boy was neither fully grown nor trained in strength, and he couldn't find his feet no matter how he tried.

"We canna take her wit' us." Frenz muttered, even as he dropped to one knee beside the boy. "We—"

"Let the chico take his madre, nómada."

Frenz whirled to his feet to face the enemy Animal Mage but hesitated when he saw the dead bird in the man's arms. He cradled it as though it were a child. Frenz suddenly remembered the screams that had echoed through the cavern as Last Chance killed it.

"We've lost too many today, nómada. The least we can do is bury them properly, sí?"

Another tremor shook the rock, and Frenz cursed. Spinning back toward Miguel and Aquilina's body, he took Miguel's place and lifted Aquilina into his arms. He'd staggered two steps before Last Chance reached him. With the help of both Animal Mages, he settled her over the mare's back.

Three tremors later, they had Captain Sageo across Shadow's back, the youngest Animal Mage astride his wolf, and all of them were running for their lives.

With the tremors shaking the rock, the tunnels seemed impossibly long and convoluted. Frenz whooped when he finally turned a corner and saw light only body lengths ahead of them.

"Almos' there!" he shouted. "We're almos'—"

The ground gave a shudder that rumbled more than it shook. A series of deep *cracks* resounded in Frenz's ears before darkness overtook the light.

~~*~*

Aquila the Royal Eagle clacked her beak as she settled herself within the cave system just off Wild Eagle Pass. The quake that shook the rock meant little to her spiritual form, and she hardly noticed the shivers in the rock that scared away the mortals.

The quake's implications, however, were worrisome.

Since Mid-Season and the trouble that had followed, five quakes had struck different points of this mountain range alone. To the south, the Celanian volcanoes had broken a decades-long silence by erupting twice in the span of two sevendays, nearly burying the entire island country in smoldering rock.

To the northeast, the Northern Tar mountain range, which formed the northern border of the neighboring country of Pecali, had experienced several quakes itself. What was worse, the mountain range, which had never once shown signs of a volcano, had sprouted a molten eruption violent enough to threaten the northern portion of the Pecalini rainforest.

The Chaos is spreading.

It was the only explanation Aquila could find for the sudden upheaval of the elementals who formed and tended the mountains and other features of the land. That one mountain elemental had gone so far as to grow an unprecedented volcano . . .

I hope the Ladies are correct that this can be resolved by season's end.

Aquila tried not to think about the Ladies' assertion that the season might end in broken Balance as easily as not.

All these thoughts churned within her mind as she swept her multi-colored wings through the cave system, collecting within her feathers the souls that had already left their mortal shells.

Once the loose souls were collected, she peered at the mortal forms that littered the floors of the trembling caves, peering through broken and falling rock when necessary. This set of caves, she knew, had survived several quakes intact, but the recent Chaos must have aggravated the elemental of this particular mountain enough for it to center so violently on this cave system.

Then again, she thought as a sharp, shivering chill pierced her being, *perhaps the Immortal Hunt has as much to do with it.*

Aquila had paid little attention to the demigods when she first arrived in the caves—she tended to ignore them unless she had a message for them or unless Life and Death were fighting over a soul. However, she was suddenly very aware of the increasingly dense emotional cloud now swirling around Death.

And Hate and Fear, she realized with a start as both the

red and the yellow demigods appeared—sans Love and Hope—and stalked closer to their brother.

"Who's the prey?" Fear muttered. His voice was cold and whisper-soft. Aquila blinked. It had been so long since she had last witnessed a Hunt that she had forgotten he could sound that way.

Despite having arrived with Fear, Hate jabbed his finger sharply toward the entrance of a small tunnel that had appeared in what should have been an unbroken wall of stone. The color of his body throbbed, and he glowered at the small entrance.

It was Death, however, who replied to Fear's question in a low growl. His words were less an answer, though, than a call to the Hunt.

"Run, run, little thief, but you cannot hide, for none escape the shade of Death."

Aquila ruffled her feathers, unsettled. With the words, Death's features had sharpened and grown shadowy at the same time. It was as though she could see beneath his black form's outer layer to a sharper, more skeletal layer that should not have existed.

Has Death always looked this way on the Hunt?

She did not think so. She had always thought he took on more feline attributes, like a large cat stalking its prey. It had been over two centuries, though, since the brothers last converged for a Hunt, perhaps even longer.

Maybe Peace's absence and the Chaos have changed the siblings more than we thought they could.

Such thoughts did not calm the Eagle.

"He's the one who held Peace's dragon and stallion away from her, aye?" Fear breathed. "The one who ruled the Hidden City with fear?"

"So much death," the black brother answered.

"So much hatred," answered the red.

"A warmongering fool!"

Death, Hate, and Fear all jumped at the violent words, and even Aquila was ashamed to admit they had startled her. They also frightened her because all the gods knew their owner had become overrun by Chaos.

Despite their startled reactions, though, none of the older demigods appeared worried by War's appearance. In fact, they greeted him with nods and turned their attention back to the tunnel, accepting his presence as though it were necessary and welcome.

Which it very well might be.

Aquila had never seen a Hunt that had not involved all the brothers who lived at the time. And while she did not understand how the Hunts first began, she knew the brothers were not driven to them by choice. Instead, they were spiritually incited to cleanse the realm of a soul that had crossed into each of their influences too often for Balance to reassert itself any other way.

Aquila glanced toward the center of the large cavern from which the mortals had originally fled. Although the shell had been removed by kinder mortals, the very stone was tainted by the death of a mortal who had been named after Aquila herself—a death that had occurred mere minutes before the earthquake began.

Perhaps . . .

"Run, run, little thief," Death repeated, "but you cannot hide . . ."

The gods' revenge will not abide.

The line leaped to the forefront of Aquila's mind. Memory stirred within her, recalling a poem she had once overheard an elven mage use to describe the Immortal Hunt.

It had been a surprisingly accurate description, and it filled her mind as she watched the brothers engage their prey.

> *Run, run, little thief, but you cannot hide;*
> *the gods' revenge will not abide.*

The four brothers stalked into the wall. Their spirits were mostly obscured by the essence of the rock, but Aquila could still sense them and their actions easily enough.

> *A beast who steals, who kills, depraved,*
> *who preys on souls and can't be saved.*

The man they stalked crouched at the end of a small tunnel. He had one hand clenched in a tight fist, the warm glow breaking through between his fingers a testament to the stone he held within it. His other hand was pressed awkwardly against the deep wound in the back of his shoulder. Despite the wound though, his concentration was fully focused on holding the Earth Magic of the mage stone steady.

> *You cannot still the burning Hate,*
> *which beats within the souls you take.*

Hate came upon the man first, and he tugged on the swirling cloud of emotions that had followed them. Aquila felt an answering tug on her wings, like a plucking of feathers. The sensation turned from a sharp plucking to a taut strum, and the Eagle knew Hate was collecting the hatred those souls she had collected had felt toward their prey.

The red demigod wove the hatred together, funneling it into their prey's soul and turning it on his own self.

Burning hatred eased into the man's mind. At first, he began to question small things he had done, ways he had led his men or left them. Doubt became distaste, then disgust, until an inferno of hate raged within him. Soon he had no choice but to release his shoulder and punch the walls with his bare fist and claw at his own face to relieve it.

Nor burn away the sickly Fear,
which chills your bones and draws your tears.

Even as rage filled their prey's mind, Fear weaved together the terror the man had instilled in this place. While Hate had funneled his emotion into the man's soul and turned it on himself, Fear wrapped the terror around their prey's neck, tying it like a noose and folding it around his head and shoulders like a shawl.

Shadows appeared in the corners of the man's eyes, and the hairs on the nape of his neck stood upright as cold seeped down into his bones. Light, barely-there touches eased down his face, then neck and arms, until his entire body felt like it was crawling with tiny creatures unknown. Only then did the shadows take more shape, still not defined, but visible enough to let any man's imagination increase his terror to panic.

And panic he did. Even as he struck out in rage, he cowered and screamed. The screams tore at his throat and burned his ears, burrowing into them and morphing into the voices of his greatest fears. As those voices grew louder, his own grew softer, until he was gasping and sobbing and tears drenched his cheeks.

You cannot fight the raging War,
which churns and burns within your core.

When War took his turn, he did not use the emotions that others had felt toward their prey. Instead, he plucked at a part of the man's soul that was nearly unused, calling forth his conscience to wage war upon the man's antipathy and greed.

The man doubled over, gasping and groaning against the emotions. Tears stained the stone beneath his feet, and he clutched at his head with both hands. As he did, the mage stone dropped from his hand, forgotten. The small stone bounced and rolled as it struck the ground and was soon clattering out into the main cavern.

And none escape the shade of Death,
which stops all hearts and steals all breath.

Death stepped forward as soon as the magic of the stone had dissipated and rock had begun to grow slowly over the tunnel's entrance.

"Keep him distracted," he growled to his brothers. "Do not let him escape."

As he spoke, Death stroked shadowy fingers through the rock essence that filled the tunnel, urging it to regrow faster than the rock over the entrance.

"Why not just let the tunnel entrance close first?" Hate hissed spitefully. "It would increase his fear, wouldn't it?"

"And hasten his death," the black brother added with a shake of his head. "I do not wish him to die because he cannot breathe. I *want* him to feel the crush of the rock against his skin and bones and lungs. I want him to *die* by it, the way he should have five years ago."

All four brothers bared their teeth, vicious grins that sent a shiver rustling through Aquila's feathers. They were united in the Hunt, and they would revel in this man's pain and agonizing death and draw both out until the man's soul was little more than tattered material.

The shiver struck deeper into Aquila's being as she remembered the final line of the old elf's poem.

When gods join force against your crime,
you'll pray your death takes little time.

Twenty

Back in Valle Ocultado, Sir Gervasio was still debating whether to send a small group to Paso del Águila Salvaje when the earthquake occurred.

The tremors were small; they did little more than startle the animals and send a scattering of pebbles tumbling down the sides of the paso. The Capitán de Caballeros didn't even think much of the quake except to send soldados to check for damage and send a mensaje to the ciudad to make sure the Ocultados were all right.

It wasn't until the screaming horde of birds attacked the camp about an hour later that Gervasio thought anything new might be amiss. Cursing, Gervasio drew his sword and shouted to the soldados to protect themselves, but the birds swept up and out of reach before anyone could lay blade to bird.

"Do no attack!"

It took a moment for Gervasio to realize that Turi's words were for the soldados rather than the birds. Lowering his sword, Gervasio strode toward Turi. "Why not?"

"The eagles are mensajeros, no enemigos."

Gervasio began to demand why someone would send an entire horde of eagles when a deep, mourning low broke through his thoughts. He snapped his gaze back toward the rear of the camp. Many of the birds had landed on or around Flame Tongue while the remainder circled her head.

"What mensaje do they bring?" he demanded. Nadie was snapping his head from side to side and had begun scrabbling at Flame Tongue's arms and chest as though he thought he could find his feet that way.

When Turi answered, his words were so soft that Gervasio didn't recognize their significance at first.

"There's been a cave-in at Paso del Águila Salvaje. Those who were being held captive were still inside."

~~*~*

Nay, nay, nay! Oh, gods, nay! Shadow! Last Chance!

Gemi gritted her teeth and squeezed her eyes shut. *Oh, gods! Ferez!*

The next moment, the simmering fire in her chest exploded. She shook her head hard, throwing off the aching fear that tried to cling to her.

Nay! I will not let anything take my soul from me!

Gemini didn't question the source of the thought as she reached for Flame Tongue's arms and chest in order to drag herself to her feet. She was vaguely aware of Flame Tongue crooning softly, but she wasn't interested in whatever comfort the dragon might try to offer. She had to find Ferez, and she couldn't do that if she couldn't even stand.

She'd just gained her feet when pressure on her shoulders had her spinning around and reaching for her weapons. She hissed when her hands met only cloth and dropped into a crouch.

"Nadie?"

Gemini snarled wordlessly. She knew the man standing before her had helped her and returned her to her dragon bondmate. However, she also knew he was still Knight Captain to a man who hated her, and she couldn't trust that he wouldn't stand in her way.

I will not let anything take my soul from me!

Someone else spoke up, and Gemini turned a snarl on him, too. This man's gaze remained calm, his smile gentle. He murmured something else, something Gemini didn't care to listen to as she turned back to the Knight Captain, dismissing the Healer as nonthreatening.

The Knight Captain watched her with a wary gaze that made Gemini twitch, and the urge to snarl increased. Before she could make another sound, though, he pulled his knife and stepped to her left.

Gemini hissed and nearly attacked him. A hand on her arm and a twitch of magic beneath her skin interrupted her, and she snapped back around to the Healer.

How dare he try to affect me with his Body Magic!

"Easy, Nadie. He's only trying to help."

A knife will help nothing!

Gemini bared her teeth. Before she could decide whether she should attack the Healer or the Knight Captain, Flame Tongue gave a long, low croon and shifted behind her.

Spinning back toward the dragon, Gemini watched as she climbed to her feet and unfurled her wings, stretching them high above her back. As they dropped, half furled, to her sides, Gemini nodded and stepped forward, already reaching for the dragon's neck.

Pressure fell on her shoulder once more. Gemini turned

and snapped her teeth at the man. Surprisingly, he didn't even flinch; he simply watched her with eyes that were both wary and worried, which made no sense to her.

They stared at each other until Flame Tongue crooned and the Animal Mage murmured softly. Only then did the Knight Captain release her shoulder, heavy resignation joining the wariness and worry in his eyes.

Gemini bared her teeth one last time before scrambling up onto Flame Tongue's back. The dragon launched herself into the air and toward their missing pieces.

~~*~*

Flame felt like she was swimming through hate and fear as she flew for Wild Eagle Pass, a convocation of eagles surrounding her in escort and Gemi clinging to her back and horns with a stiffness Flame had never felt before.

The hate overflowed through the bond from Gemi, but the fear was purely Flame's. She had never seen Gemi in such a state. Not even when the hatred had ruled her in the Hidden City and she tried to kill Graucen had she seemed so . . . *feral.*

Flame beat her wings harder to prevent a shudder from shaking her form. Worse yet was Gemi's thoughts. Flame knew they belonged to Gemi, but she had never heard them sound so . . . resonant. They seemed to come directly from the center of her being rather than her conscious mind.

I do not know how to help her with this.

It was not the first time Flame had felt so helpless when it came to assisting her human bondmate with certain emotions, but she usually knew why, at least. But this? In this, she could not even tell what was causing the problem, let alone find a way to ease Gemi's pain.

Or hatred.

The only solution Flame had been able to consider—mainly because it had become the only solution in Gemi's mind—was to fly to Wild Eagle Pass to verify the eagles' message. Now that they were in flight, Gemi's thoughts had become a litany of their companions' names and a phrase Flame recognized from the first time the hatred had filled Gemi.

I will not let anything take my soul from me!

Flame growled lowly as she navigated the mountain peaks. She did not understand what Gemi meant by "my soul," but Flame thought it must refer to Ferez. In less than two months, Gemi had become closer to the young king than she had to any other creature they had ever met. Even, in a way, Flame and Shadow. It had been Flame's fault alone that Gemi had not shared her true identity with Ferez on the night of the Mid-Season Festival.

And my fault Ferez might have died without Gemi even knowing he could not remember himself or that night.

But Flame refused to regret the decision not to share that piece of information with Gemi. Gemi's emotions had been in such a delicate state since she woke—and so much had happened—that Flame had feared the knowledge would only send Gemi back into the depths of her mind. Despite the odd hatred filling Gemi now, she was at least conscious and able to acknowledge that Flame and Shadow had not abandoned her.

"How much longer, Flame Tongue?"

Flame could not prevent the shudder Gemi's words provoked in her. Even her mindspeech resonated in a way it should not have, and the raw hatred within them burned Flame in a way fire never could.

"Not much," Flame hissed softly and threw herself harder into the flight.

She had left her eagle escort behind by the time she reached Wild Eagle Pass. The walls of the pass were too close together for her to navigate by wing, so she circled once and dropped to the ground at its entrance. She pulled her wings in toward her sides, but she was too tense and shaking to furl them completely.

Sudden movement upon her back had Flame snapping her head around to find Gemi scrambling down her side. *"James!"* The girl ignored her, dropping to the ground and running into the pass without even a glance back at Flame.

The dragon hissed and bounded after her. If the eagles had been mistaken or lying, there could be unknown numbers of enemies waiting for them within the pass. Despite Gemi's hatred, she was still unarmed.

A scream from ahead made Flame curse. Even as she sped up though, she knew from Gemi's thoughts that it came from emotional pain, not physical.

Nay! It can't be!

Flame gave her own mourning cry as she reached Gemi. Rubble filled what must have been the entrance of the cave system the Animal Mages had used here. Gemi was already reaching for the nearest rocks, prying them from the pile, but an ominous rumble had Flame snatching her away before the pile could shift and bury her beneath it, too.

"Nay! Let me go! I have to—"

Flame winced but kept her hold on Gemi tight. *"There is nothing we can do, James. The rock is too unstable. Even a mage stone would not be powerful enough to move it safely."*

Gemi snarled wordlessly and beat against Flame's arm with her fists, but Flame did not budge. She could not allow

Gemi to risk her own life when there could be no doubt the ones she sought were dead.

"Flame? James?"

Gemi froze in Flame's arms. For a long moment, Flame could not move either. When she did, she slowly swung her head to the right, unable to believe that her mind was not playing tricks on her.

There, stepping slowly from a small niche in the rock, was a man enveloped in dust. If Flame had not been able to see the bright silver-blue of his eyes, she would not have recognized him.

"Ferez?"

Flame cursed as Gemi collapsed in her arms. A moment later, she whined. Gemi had not just lost her odd strength. She had completely lost consciousness.

"Flame? Is James all right?"

Heat burst through Flame's chest as she jerked her head back around. *Shadow!* The stallion's black coat was barely recognizable beneath the thick layer of dust, but she would have known that gentle nicker anywhere.

Then Flame noticed who else stood, dust covered, with Ferez and Shadow, and she released a joyous croon. Last Chance, Fabio, Guido, Fiela, Pablo. Even de Aqui stood among them, but Flame could not find the will to care when so many she had feared were dead now stood before her.

"You are alive!"

Shadow snorted softly. His words, when he answered, were not as happy as Flame had expected. *"Mostly."*

Flame gripped Gemi more tightly to her chest. *"What do you mean?"*

"Mi madre es dead," de Aqui muttered. "And Valto."

"And Piegro," Pablo muttered in turn.

Flame stared at the group as the others murmured

comforting words. She was missing something, she was certain she was, but she could not understand what it might be. *Why do they act more awkward with Pablo than with de Aqui?*

"An' Captain Sageo needs a Mage Healer as quickly as possible."

Flame snorted and stared at Ferez. *"Sageo? As in . . . ?"*

Shadow nickered, sounding happier than he had earlier. *"Aye. Alano Sageo is alive, but he's been through enough torture to need a Mage Healer quickly."*

Flame ambled forward, using one arm to hold Gemi to her chest. Ferez immediately moved forward to take the girl into his arms. He stroked short, black strands out of her face. "Is he all right? Fabio, Guido, an' Pablo all said he was awake but . . ."

Flame crooned and nudged her snout gently against Ferez's back. *"He will be all right. He was just a little overwhelmed to find you alive and well when the eagles had claimed you were dead."*

Guido translated even as de Aqui murmured an apology. "I was reaching for them when the rock caved in. I was distracted enough to drop the conexión, so they must have panicked and fled."

Flame cocked her head curiously. *"Straight to me?"*

De Aqui shrugged. "Who else would they have gone to? Mi madre and I were fairly isolated, and after mi last attempt to warn Ciudad Ocultada of danger—"

Flame snorted. *"What?"*

"Perhaps we should leave explicaciones for later?" Pablo muttered. "The nobleman does need a Curandero Mágico."

Flame peered at the small, wiry Ocultado but nodded and moved closer. Alano Sageo was propped up against the edge of a small ragged tunnel at the back of the crevice they had been hiding in. He offered Flame a wan smile, distracting her from thoughts of the curious tunnel.

"So Nadie really does have a dragón."

Flame snorted. *"And you really are alive. Unfortunately for my friends, your father does not know this."*

Guido giggled. "Are you going to fly him back to the duque's camp, Flame?"

Flame dipped her chin even as she reached into the crevice to gather up the injured nobleman. He tried to shift closer, but the movement did little more than cause him to grimace. Flame huffed and pulled him securely into her arms.

"The sooner the duke learns his son is alive, the better, I think." She pulled Alano Sageo close to her chest and turned back toward the end of the pass she had come from. *"I will leave James here with you and have Sir Gervasio send men to retrieve the rest of you."*

Tired murmurs of thanks followed her out of the pass. Once free of the restricting rock, she stretched out her wings, steadied her grip on the young Sageo, and launched herself into the air.

~~*~*

Death watched the dragon disappear with the injured noblemen. In front of him, Life leaned against his chest, her head tucked beneath his chin.

"Should we follow them?" she whispered.

Death shook his head slowly, though his lips quirked up into a tired smile. If nothing else, he was glad his twin was speaking Fayralese once more.

"Nay. The nobleman's condition is not dire. The dragon will find him a Mage Healer soon enough."

Life sighed and settled herself more firmly against Death's chest. "Then what shall we do now? Find the others?

I think Hate said Love was at the Hidden Valley. Perhaps we could join them and watch the duke reunite with his son."

Death snorted. As amusing as it would be to watch the duke realize just how senseless his attempted vengeance had been, Death did not think he was in the mood to see the mortals rejoice in a continued life. He may be willing to give up a few deaths to regain Balance, but he refused to revel in life.

"Very well," Life murmured, understanding his thoughts well enough. "Then perhaps we can locate Hope and Fear?"

Death shook his head. "I doubt they would be far from the Hidden Valley either, sister mine. Besides," he added, sinking one hand into the white locks at the back of Life's neck, "I have a much more relaxing idea of what we might do."

Life giggled softly and pulled away from Death's chest just far enough to meet his eyes. "You do realize the Ladies will likely call us again soon, do you not? They will not be happy if we do not respond promptly."

Death let the corner of his mouth twitch up into a small smirk. "But they have not called us yet. And they can hardly complain about us finding rest when we have completed the tasks they assigned to us."

Life sighed and leaned against Death's chest once more. She remained there for several minutes without speaking, and Death let her. Why should he not when he felt lighter than he had in sevendays—perhaps longer?

"The Hunt really does make a difference," Life whispered finally, startling Death. "Not just for you and our brothers. It—" She paused, considering. "It clears the air of Chaos, helps restore the Balance. I never really considered it with previous Hunts, but I have not felt this clear since Peace led the king into Zhulan."

Or since the Ladies called on us to mitigate the damage War has been causing.

But Death saw no reason to speak the words aloud, not when Life would insist they could not defy the Ladies, that they could not turn their backs on their siblings. And Death did not truly want to do either of those things himself; he simply wished the threat of Chaos were not quite so overwhelming.

"As do I, brother," Life whispered. "As do I."

Death buried his nose in Life's tresses, no longer feeling as light as he had. Refusing to delay any longer, he tightened his grip on Life and Transported them both to their personal pocket realm. There, the eternal struggle against Chaos that suffused the Mortal Realm could not reach them.

He prayed the Fates would not think to call on them for the rest of the season.

Such prayers, though, were no doubt fated to remain unanswered.

~~*~*

Aquila huffed as she landed in her nest next to the Cycle of Incarnation and shook out her wings. Small, colorful beads of light fell from her feathers, shimmering softly in the soul-light that shone from the Cycle.

"Another batch already, sister?"

Aquila ignored the voice and gave herself a final shake. To her dismay, even that violent a motion was not enough to dislodge the tattered smudge of a soul that clung to her breast feathers. Squawking softly, she plucked it away with her beak and dropped it among the others.

"What is that?"

Aquila twisted her head around to watch her lupine

brother sniff cautiously at the dull-colored soul. It looked more like torn cloth than the crystal beads dormant souls usually took the appearance of when her feathers touched them.

"That *is a soul.*" She turned her beak back to her breast feathers. Mortal souls did not usually leave any essence behind on her feathers, but the feathers the tattered soul had clung to felt unclean.

Lupus lifted cold, yellow eyes to glare at her. *"I can see it is a soul, sister. What I want to know is why it looks like you had to hunt it down to collect it."*

Aquila huffed. *"I am not the one who decided a Hunt was necessary."*

The Hungry Wolf stilled. *"Carith's sons?"*

Aquila crooned her agreement, her beak never leaving her breast feathers. *"It has been centuries since I last witnessed a Hunt. I would be happy indeed if many more passed before I witness the next."*

Lupus nodded slowly, his eyes dropping warily to the tattered soul. *"What did the mortal do, exactly?"*

Aquila twitched her beak away from her cleaning. The Wolf's tone held an odd note she did not recognize.

"Besides entering each of the demigods' influences too often? He attempted to murder his own child and remorselessly took the life of his lifemate."

A shudder rippled through the Wolf, causing his multi-colored fur to shimmer in the Cycle's soul-light. *"And you carried it here?"*

Aquila screeched and unfurled her wings. *"I have little choice in these matters, Lupus. We cannot leave such souls to languish in the Mortal Realm. Chaos threatens enough as it is."*

Lupus bared silver teeth. *"Yet such souls taint the Cycle."* He turned his nose to one side. *"And they taste horrible."*

Those words surprised a squawking laugh out of Aquila, and she dropped her wings. *"Chaos threatens, and you worry about how a soul will taste?"*

Despite her words, Aquila understood her brother's reluctance. She had only had to carry the soul and touch it with her beak once, but she already felt like the grime from the soul was spreading among her feathers and there was an odd taste on the edge of her beak she would rather not think about. Her poor brother had to eat the dormant souls she carried to remove their memories before they were thrown into the Cycle.

The Wolf's cold, yellow glare was not as strong as it had been before, and it quickly returned to the ragged, dull soul.

"You know, there was a time when such a soul would have been given to the Destroyer instead of being thrown back into the Cycle."

For a long silent moment, Aquila simply stared at Lupus. When he finally lifted his yellow gaze to her deep purple one, he dropped his head to his paws and flattened his ears.

"There was also a time," Aquila replied once her brother appeared properly remorseful for his comment, *"when Chaos did not threaten our Domain, mortals and gods alike."* She shook her head. *"Carith's twin has not been able to play the part of Destroyer since the First Chaos spurred Carith and his lifemate to first have children."* The Eagle cocked her head to one side. *"Why would you address such a subject now?"*

"Lupus? Aquila? What are you two doing?"

Both Wolf and Eagle shifted and watched as a large reptilian head lifted out of the swirling "waters" of the Cycle. *"I can sense the new batch of souls from here,"* Serpens hissed, *"yet you two speak idly. What is wrong?"*

Aquila ruffled her feathers. Out of all the gods, Serpens probably had the least understanding of what happened outside his own influence; he never left the Cycle of

Incarnation—only swam through it, tending to the souls it held. Only Carith, locked away in his Workshop, probably rivaled the Great Serpent for ignorance.

"Lupus is reluctant to eat a soul that has been Hunted by Carith's sons."

For a moment, Serpens did not answer. Aquila watched as his long, forked tongue slipped from his mouth and tasted the air. When he did speak, his tone was thoughtful.

"I see. Such taint is distasteful. However, as long as Chaos threatens . . ." Serpens tilted his head noncommittally. *"Might I suggest you eat that one first and hope the taste of the other souls can overwhelm the unpleasantness of the Hunted one's darkness?"*

Lupus obviously did not like the idea, but Serpens remained unaffected by the bared silver teeth and the cold, yellow glare the Wolf offered him. The Serpent simply watched him with his own bland, yellow stare until Lupus sniffed and bent toward the ragged soul.

"I do not know why I attempt to find sympathy from either of you." Snagging the tattered soul between silver teeth, he bit into it.

Aquila winced as the action produced little more than a sickening *squelch* instead of the soft *crack* she was accustomed to hearing from the Wolf's "meals." At the same time, the Wolf choked and gagged, though he did not release the soul.

Closing his eyes and grinding his teeth, Lupus growled, *"I have never tasted a soul so . . . despicable. Not only did he kill the woman he took as his lifemate and attempt to kill his own child, but he felt less for either of them than he did for his friends. And he killed one of those friends."*

"Such a grievous life for the species into which he was born," hissed Serpens. *"Hopefully Phoenicia will find him a better fit for his next life . . . like a nice fat rat, perhaps?"*

Aquila eyed the Serpent, amused. *"So one of our mortal formsakes can have a nice meal before I retrieve the soul again?"*

Serpens offered her a slow blink. *"I am merely suggesting that the soul be allowed to live a life or two in which he can learn what it means to be preyed upon as he seems to have done upon others."*

"I could not care less what Phoenicia places him as next!" Lupus spat.

Aquila twisted her head around to find him working his tongue around his mouth and realized, with a brief spasm of disappointment, that she had missed her chance to watch the Hunted soul's memories form upon Lupus's coat. She never grew tired of examining the rainbow-colored dewdrops that grew from his fur when he ate new memories.

Although I suppose memories like the Hunted one's would not display prettily.

"He could be a mindless mud-digger in his next life, for all I care," Lupus continued, and Aquila chirruped curiously. *"He would still be unworthy of the form, and he would still draw Chaos."*

Serpens narrowed his eyes. Before he could respond to the Wolf's words, Aquila felt her soul draw taut, and she screeched softly and ruffled her feathers.

"The Ladies call," she muttered when her brothers turned to her. *"No doubt they can See better now that Carith's sons have Hunted for Balance. Perhaps they will be willing to give me an update on the season's outcome."*

"Bring us news," Lupus demanded even as Serpens disappeared back into the Cycle. *"You cannot allow the Ladies to hold out on us."*

Aquila flipped her wings noncommittally and took off from her nest. She knew Lupus would take care of the rest of the souls she had brought from Wild Eagle Pass, and she was curious as to why the Ladies were calling her now, when the Mortal Realm seemed to be calming down.

Twenty-One

Gemi woke to soft murmurs and a gentle rocking motion so reminiscent of the sea rocking the *Pretty Pauper* that she wondered if she was waking from the strangest dream she'd ever had.

Or maybe a nightmare. There was too much pain for a simple dream.

"James?"

Flame's mindspeech and presence were so filled with worry that Gemi sat bolt upright and snapped her head around in search of enemies. She gasped when she found herself surrounded by oddly pale and flickering faces, and she cringed away from them as they all turned toward her.

"Easy," murmured a soft, familiar voice as hands gently wrapped around her shoulders. "Yeh're safe, James."

Wrong name! Gemi's thoughts protested, even as she twisted around in search of the voice's owner. Her eyes met silver-blue orbs, and she leaned heavily against the body that had apparently held her as she slept. All thoughts of dreams and nightmares fled as she stared up into those beautiful eyes.

"Ferez."

Flame hissed, but Gemi ignored her as Ferez offered her a crooked smile. "How're yeh feelin', James? Yeh worried us earlier, collapsin' like yeh did."

Gemi frowned. *Collapsing? I haven't seen Ferez since I woke up in Ciudad Ocultada. How could he have seen me collapse?*

Flame's complaints about Gemi's lack of discretion suddenly stilled. *"Do you not remember your last bout of anger?"*

Gemi blinked, confused. *"What are you talking about, Flame? What—"*

A hand sliding up Gemi's cheek and a worried "James?" had Gemi blinking for a different reason altogether. Ferez, she realized, was peering down at her worriedly. She smiled and rubbed her cheek against his hand.

"I'm all right."

A familiar snort met her ears and was soon followed by a giggle. "Shadow es right, James," a young voice spoke up brightly. "I do no think we've *ever* seen you this relaxed afore."

Shadow?

Pain lanced through Gemi's chest, and she gasped, squeezing her eyes shut. The hand on her cheek and the one still on her shoulder tightened, but Gemi couldn't reassure Ferez, not when memories and emotions were rushing through her like water through a broken dam.

The burning anger. The haze that kept her from Shadow, which had threatened to separate her from Flame. The nearly overwhelming despair that had threatened to drown her from the moment she realized Ferez was missing.

She didn't know she was speaking a litany of "Oh, gods" until she was pulled up against a solid chest and a hand was plunged into her hair, the other smoothing up and down her back.

"It's all right," Ferez whispered soothingly. "I've got yeh. Yeh're safe. I've got yeh."

The words wrapped around Gemi's mind as firmly as Ferez's arms wrapped around her body. As he continued speaking, offering her a soft stream of comforting words, Gemi fell quiet. The sudden tension that had coiled in her chest slowly unwound.

Gemi didn't move for long minutes as she struggled to find a balance between the hate, fear, and pain she'd felt since she'd awakened in Ciudad Ocultada and the sudden joy and relaxation she'd fallen into upon seeing Ferez. Through it all, Ferez's hands kept her grounded, rubbing along her back and pressing lightly along the base of her scalp.

"You know," someone muttered after a long silence, "for someone who does no remember his time wit' Nadie, the two of you look awfully close, nómada."

Gemi jerked in shock, and Ferez's arms tightened around her. "Why'd you have to go and say something like that, Pablo," complained the young voice from earlier. Gemi realized abruptly that it belonged to her brother Guido. "Shadow says James might no have been aware of that."

"James?" Ferez whispered.

Gemi shook her head and pressed her face more tightly against Ferez's shoulder. She didn't know if the gesture was supposed to be an answer to Ferez's implied question or a denial of the others' words, but she couldn't meet anyone's eyes, not when her mind was reeling from this latest information.

"Flame didn' tell yeh."

Both the words and the hand on her cheek were gentle. It was only that gentleness that coaxed Gemi to raise her face from Ferez's tunic. When she finally met his gaze, the tenderness she found there made her breath catch.

"I won' leave yeh, James," he murmured. "I may no' remember the sevendays I spent wit' yeh afore Mid-Season, bu' tha' doesn' mean I don' care about yeh."

Gemi closed her eyes and swallowed. *He doesn't remember me. He doesn't—*

"It does not seem to have affected his emotions any," Flame murmured.

Gemi stiffened. She knew Flame's words were supposed to be a comfort, but they reminded her there was no way Flame could not have known about Ferez's missing memories.

"But you didn't tell me. Why?"

"I did not want you to be worrying about his memories when everything else was in chaos."

Gemi frowned. She thought she could understand the reason, no matter how upsetting she found it, but there was a wariness in the dragon's tone that didn't match her words.

"There's something you're not telling me."

Silence met her query. *"Flame?"*

"James?" Gemi blinked open her eyes. Ferez watched her worriedly. "Are yeh talkin' to Flame?"

"Course he es talking to Flame Tongue," snapped Pablo. "Anyone who's met Nadie would know that."

Ferez's hand twitched on Gemi's cheek, but she wrapped her own hand around his wrist and squeezed comfortingly. For the first time since she woke up, Gemi glanced around and realized she and Ferez were nestled within a horse-drawn cart. Scattered lanterns revealed horses escorting the cart. Most bore uniformed men, but Shadow and Last Chance were there as well, keeping pace on either side of the cart.

"What's going on?" Turning to the others who filled the cart, she stiffened when she saw that Pablo and her two younger brothers were not their only companions. "What's he doing here?" She jerked a finger at de Aqui.

Guido, who had been chastising Pablo for his previous remark (which surprised Gemi as much as de Aqui's presence did), turned to Gemi and shook his head.

"Miguel es no the enemigo, James." Guido glared at the wiry Ocultado. "Pablo and Deligero were."

Cold rushed through Gemi, and she shook her head vigorously. "Deligero's dead. He died five years ago."

"Well, he's dead now," Pablo muttered. Gemi stared, wide eyed, at the thief, who shrugged. "He survived the cave-in five años ago because the cave held a vein of Magia Terrena. Unfortunately for him, the mage stone he had now failed to keep him alive en this cave-in."

Gemi shook her head, not wanting to believe that Deligero had survived all those years ago. "If you betrayed the Ocultados, Pablo," she whispered, "why should I believe you now?"

"'Cause he's no' the one who sensed Deligero's death."

Gemi jerked around and stared up at Ferez, who watched her with solemn eyes. "What do you mean?"

"Frenz es the one who got us out after the cave-in," Guido chimed in.

Frenz glanced away, his cheeks reddening beneath the pale tint. "I only helped Pablo wit' the magic."

Gemi blinked. "You did?" It wouldn't have been the first time Ferez had used a mage stone—she'd taught him to use one when they'd snuck into Parshen Gut in Zhulan to speak with the duke. But if he didn't remember his time with her . . .

"I might've been able to keep the cave-in from killing us," Pablo muttered, "but even one of Deligero's mage stones was no powerful enough to both keep the rock from crushing us and form us a way out."

"An' when I saw the orange glow o' Pablo's mage stone," Ferez added, "I remembered this." He pulled a chip of stone from a pouch at his belt, and Gemi stared. The jagged piece of rock was dark gray and appeared completely mundane, but she recognized it immediately. She had spent months getting to know its contours when she was younger. While she didn't pull it out nearly as often anymore, she'd never forgotten those jagged lines.

"You still have my mage stone." Gemi lifted her gaze to Ferez's and blinked up at him. "It wasn't stolen with everything else?"

Ferez shrugged. "One o' the las' groups to attack us on our way into Tarsur might've tried, but it go' caught in yer belt." He dropped his gaze to the stone, and his cheeks darkened beneath the paleness tinging his skin. "I nearly threw it away, actually. If Flame hadn' picked it up an' made me keep it . . ." He shrugged again.

"And then he just went and used it!" Fabio proclaimed, awe shading his words enough that Gemi glanced at him with raised brows. Fabio grinned. "He swore he did no know how to use it—even though Shadow later said he had afore—but he just made it glow, easy as you please, and—"

Fabio fell silent with a grunt and a glare at Guido, who only met his glare with a smile. "And Frenz built the tunnel to get us out," Guido finished.

"Not immediately, though," Ferez insisted.

Gemi frowned. "Did the magic give you trouble?" Mage stones always took getting used to, she knew. It was impossible to use one the first time the connection was made, which would have meant that Guido and Fabio, at the very least, wouldn't have been able to use the mage stone to get them out.

But Ferez shook his head and smiled widely, making Gemi blink. There was an awed joy in that smile, so reminiscent of the childlike joy he'd shown during the Mid-Season Festival that her chest ached.

"No trouble. None at all, actually. I was jus' too caught up in experiencin' the magic, at first. It fel' like I could sense the entire mountain peak an' deep into the earth."

Gemi chuckled. She knew he had to be exaggerating. Mage stones from Ciudad Ocultada simply weren't that powerful, no matter how skilled the user. Gemi herself had a certain talent for the stones due to her bond with Flame, but even she could not sense so much with her stone.

However, she could appreciate the awe of feeling like that she could.

"An' I could sense the entire cave system," he continued. "Excep' for us, it was empty. Well . . ."

His smile faltered, and his blue-and-silver gaze solemnly met Gemi's once more. "I could feel Deligero. It must've been the Earth Magic. I could feel two other flares o' magic like the kind I was usin', an' Pablo's was righ' nex' to me.

"An' I could feel the rock tha' Deligero had displaced. It felt . . . angry. Like it wanted to be where he was. I . . ."

Ferez ducked his head, hiding his eyes from the surrounding lamplight. Gemi slid a hand up alongside his neck. "You what?" she whispered.

Ferez shook his head. "It fel' like I took on the rock's anger. Or maybe it was my own. After what he did to Aquilina . . ." He took in a deep breath and met Gemi's gaze once more. "I had to make sure he couldn' hurt anyone else like that again, James. I'm no' sure how I knew to, but I used yer mage stone to call on his. I pulled it away from him. An' when I knew he couldn' use it anymore . . ."

He ducked his head again and wrapped his arms around Gemi. "I urged the stone to close around him quickly," he whispered against her ear. "I le' the rock give in to its anger an' listened to it complain 'cause it couldn' return to its original position."

Gemi winced. Somehow, being encased in and crushed by the rock in such a way seemed worse than simply being caught in a natural cave-in.

"Deligero deserved it," Flame growled. *"After everything he put us through, only a slow roasting would have been more appropriate."*

Gemi frowned but didn't respond. As much as she disliked violence, Deligero had caused Gemi and her bondmates enough pain and grief for her to agree with the dragon's assessment.

"So . . ." Gemi pulled back enough from Ferez's embrace to meet his eyes. When he nodded, she smiled and then glanced around at the others. "Deligero *is* dead, but he was the one behind the recent troubles." She sighed and shook her head for a different reason. "Lord Sageo is going to find that explanation far too convenient, especially since we thought Deligero died five years ago."

Ferez made a soft sound of surprise. "Flame didn' tell you?" he asked when Gemi met his gaze curiously.

She mentally prodded the dragon. "Tell me what?"

"Alano Sageo es alive!" Fabio proclaimed excitedly before either Ferez or Flame could answer. "Flame flew him back to the duque's camp to find him a Curandero."

"Although Lord Sageo has not awakened yet, so we do not know if this will change his disposition toward us."

When Gemi repeated Flame's words aloud, the others stared at her. "How could it not?" Ferez asked.

Gemi stared up at him, surprised. The question was so innocent, as if he'd never met the duke before and didn't know his temperament, that her mind went blank momentarily.

"Surely knowing his *hijo es* alive and returned to him would gain the Ocultados some goodwill," Pablo muttered.

Gemi tore her gaze away from Ferez's to frown at the older thief, though worry still churned in her mind.

"You didn't see him, Pablo. We approached his camp under Care's Peace, and he rode out and attacked us anyway." Lifting her chin, she gently tapped at her still-sore neck. "He tried to choke me to death and might have succeeded if his Knight Captain hadn't restrained him and had a Mage Healer force him into unconsciousness."

She didn't mention the odd anger that had driven her to attack the duke back. Only Ferez and her bondmates had any right to that knowledge, and that was a conversation she would prefer to put off for as long as possible.

Gentle fingers traced along her throat beside her own, and she met Ferez's gaze once more. "The duke did this to you? Under Care's Peace?"

Gemi nodded slowly, blinking. Anger burned beneath the king's words. Despite her own anger toward the duke, she would have expected Ferez's to be tempered by his relationship with a man he considered one of his advisors.

'Flame? What am I missing? Frenz acts as though—"

She stiffened as she realized what she'd been about to say. *'Flame?"* she pressed, desperately hoping her sudden thought wasn't true. *'How much does Frenz remember?"*

Once again, silence answered her query, but Gemi refused to let the issue lie. Leaning more heavily against the dragon's mind, she narrowed her mental presence until she could slide through Flame's barrier of silence and into her mind.

Flame whined, startled, but Gemi ignored it. She could feel that the dragon wasn't in any pain. Instead, she sought the memories that would answer her question.

When she found memories of a confused Frenz Kanti—not King Ferez Katani—being shoved into the nomad camp by Last Chance on the day after Mid-Season, Gemi bit her lip and tried to steady her now-quickening breath.

Why? Why would the Mindspeaker have done such a thing?

But Gemi knew they were lucky that suppressing Ferez's memories was all their enemy had done. If he had truly wanted to throw Evon into Chaos, he could just as easily have killed the king as left him alive and thinking himself a farmer.

"Isa and Wolfrik tried to recover his memories." Flame's tone was so complex that Gemi wouldn't have recognized the mixture of obstinacy, wounded pride, and curiosity if she hadn't been inside the dragon's mind. *"They said his mind rebelled against it, and Wolfrik thought a part of him must still remember courting you despite . . . certain circumstances."*

Certain circumstances. Gemi's cheeks burned as she considered those circumstances. Ferez had, in his mind, turned his back on his throne by not only kissing a supposed peasant-born boy but also promising not to hurt "him."

Not to leave me.

Gemi squeezed her eyes shut and pressed her forehead back into Ferez's chest. His arms wrapped around her, but she couldn't take comfort in them anymore.

He doesn't know who he is. He doesn't—doesn't know he's king. How can I take comfort from him when he doesn't remember the throne he's supposed to return to?

But when Gemi considered sending him away, perhaps handing him over to Lord Sageo, her mind rebelled.

I can't. I can't send him away. I know Evon needs him, but . . .

I will not let anything take my soul from me!

"Then we will find a way to retrieve his memories ourselves," Flame crooned. *"He refused to leave you when you were unconscious. We can do nothing less than the same when he needs us."*

Gemi nodded against Ferez's chest. Flame was right. They would find a way to get Ferez his memories back.

I'll tell him the truth of who I am. If it eases his mind enough for him to regain his memories, I'll do anything.

Now she just had to wait for a chance to be alone with him so she could tell him.

~~*~*

As Gemi made the conviction to tell Ferez the truth, Flame pondered something else that worried her just as much as the situation with Ferez's missing memories did.

Flame had learned everything she knew about dragonbonds from Mama Dragon years ago. According to her, unless a dragon bonded with a creature of similar abilities, only the dragon had the ability to take control of the bond and the magics contained within it. She had never had a reason to doubt Mama Dragon's teachings, not after the years she had spent controlling the bond with Gemi and Shadow.

Except now Flame was not so certain. When Gemi had pressed her for an answer about Ferez, the girl had not simply asked and waited for Flame to be ready to answer as she usually needed to. Instead, she had pressed forward, *into the bond*, in a presentation of magical control that Gemi had only ever shown with mage stones.

Or the anger that now strengthens her muscles when she truly needs it.

Flame's mind reeled. *That cannot be a side effect of the bond . . . can it?* She did not think so—Mama Dragon had never mentioned anything similar—but she could not explain it otherwise.

"Stand down, soldados!"

Flame lifted her head with a snort, all worries concerning Ferez and Gemi pushed aside. Lord Sageo was shoving past the men who stood guard at his tent's entrance. From here, she could see the uncertainty on the men's faces as they struggled between obeying their duke and following the orders they had been given by their Knight Captain.

"Sir Gervasio!" Lord Sageo shouted once he was clear of the soldiers. "Where are you? You will answer for—"

"Milord!" Turi called out, scrambling to his feet from where he had been sitting near Flame. "Milord, wait! Afore you—"

"¡No!" the duke snapped. "I will not wait. Gervasio must be punished for—"

Just then, the Knight Captain stepped out of the healing tent. Even in the lantern light, it took Lord Sageo a mere moment to spot him. "¡Gervasio!" he snarled and strode toward the oblivious man. Startled, the knight spun toward the duke, and his eyes widened just before Lord Sageo's fist landed on his jaw.

Flame lowed as cries echoed throughout the camp, but Sir Gervasio looked more surprised than in pain. "Peln," he gasped before Lord Sageo snatched him by the collar and punched him again.

This time, the cries were accompanied by men leaping forward. Soldiers and knights alike scrambled to pull the duke off his Knight Captain. Flame considered wading into the crowd herself, but she knew she would be more of a hindrance than a help.

Still, it took several minutes of struggle for the men to pull the duke away from Sir Gervasio and secure him enough that he would not break away from them. Throughout the struggle, Lord Sageo cursed them all rigorously. Flame snorted. The enforced sleep had apparently done more for the man's strength than it had for his disposition.

"¡Cálmate, Peln!" Sir Gervasio finally snapped, dabbing at his bloody nose. "You are acting like a loco!"

"I am not loco!" the duke snapped back. "You have betrayed me, turned against your country, and joined the monstruos who killed my hijo. Why can't any of you see that?"

The last words were aimed at the men holding him. Fortunately, the men did little more than shift uncomfortably. Their hold on the duke remained strong, their gazes more on the Knight Captain than the noble.

"¡Se maldice!" Lord Sageo snapped. "All of you! My hijo is dead, and you—"

"I'm not dead, Padre."

Silence echoed through the camp. Not even the animals seemed willing to speak up as Lord Sageo snapped his head around to stare at the entrance of the healing tent. There stood Alano Sageo, one arm pulled over Zábido's shoulders as he leaned heavily against the Mage Healer's smaller frame.

For a long moment, the duke simply stared. Flame wondered if he was so far gone in his convictions that he would deny his son's return. With everything that had happened this season, it certainly would not have surprised the dragon.

"Alano?" Even as a dragon, Flame had a hard time hearing the word. "You're alive? You're . . ."

The duke fell silent, apparently too shocked to say anything else as he continued to stare at his son. Alano, for his part, limped forward with Zábido's help until he stood directly in front of his father.

"I'm alive, Padre. And the Ocultados aren't the ones who captured me and sent you my ring. They're inocentes in all of this, as much victims of the hombre who hurt me as we are."

Lord Sageo shook his head slowly. Flame gathered her feet beneath herself, uncertain how she would react if he denied his son's claims, but certain she would not let it stand.

A sharp sob broke through the air. The duke reached shakily for his son's face. "Mijo," he whispered. "Mi Alano. I—I—"

Alano wrapped his free hand around the back of his father's neck and pressed their foreheads together. "I know, Padre. I'm alive, but I need you to acknowledge that none of this was the culpa of the Ocultados. They weren't the ones who killed my hombres and captured me."

Lord Sageo sobbed. "Lo siento, Alano. I thought you were dead. I took the ladrones at their word and sought revenge instead of seeking you out. I should never—I should—"

Whatever else the duke might have been trying to say was lost in sobs. Alano wrapped his arm more firmly around his father even as one of the knights took Zábido's place as his crutch.

"Well," muttered Turi, who still stood near Flame, "I guess that es the best we can hope for right now. At least he's no longer violente."

Flame crooned her agreement and turned her attention back to the bond to pass on the news. They could not be certain the duke would accept his son's claims without argument, but Flame doubted he would cause as much trouble as she had feared.

Now if only he were our greatest obstacle.

Twenty-Two

Gemi spent the rest of the journey back to Valle Ocultado worrying over Ferez's memories and soaking in the warmth of his embrace. She accepted Flame's updates with little thought, too caught up in considering how they might help Ferez remember the truth to be concerned over the activity in the duke's camp.

Which is why she was startled when their party was first greeted by a familiar female voice. "Bring them closer to Flame! I need Shadow near his bondmates for the poción to work."

Gemi lifted her head and tried to peer beyond the mounted knights and soldiers who had escorted them from Wild Eagle Pass. She couldn't raise herself high enough to see—more because Ferez refused to release her than because of her weak muscles. Thankfully, Guido and Fabio were already scrambling to their feet and calling out the names of several Ocultados who must have been waiting for them.

"Sit down, Guido!" snapped the sharp female voice once more. As the cart rolled to a halt, Corteza appeared at the end, arms akimbo. "You should no be putting such pressure on that leg when it es still healing!"

Guido lowered himself back to the cart's floor, but the grin never left his face. "Lo siento, Corteza. I only wanted to greet everyone."

"You can just as easily wait for us to come greet you," answered another familiar female voice. By the time Pastora came into view, even Gemi was grinning widely. "Corteza, why no take care of Shadow first? I can keep an eye en mi rebaño well enough, I think."

Corteza huffed and waved to someone Gemi couldn't see. "The older your rebaño gets, the more preocupada I become, Pastora. I fear your youngest might be taking after their more adventurous hermanos."

"Now do no start blaming Gemi and me for that, Corteza." Naldo appeared beside her, grinning as widely as Guido was. Mateo and Teodoro were right behind him, their faces just as bright. "They do no see us enough to take after us."

Pastora huffed. "Which is exactly the problema."

"Problema o' no," Corteza interrupted, "I need both James and Shadow close to Flame for the poción to work." When nobody moved immediately, she waved insistently at Naldo and the twins. "Up! I'm sure Shadow would like to return to the bond sometime soon."

Naldo laughed but climbed into the cart and crouched down in front of Gemi, where she was still nestled against Ferez's chest. Behind him, the twins and other men began to help Guido, Fabio, Pablo, and de Aqui out of the cart.

"How're you feeling, James?" Naldo asked, his smile softening. He glanced at Ferez. "I suppose this is the new amigo you were talking about, sí?"

Gemi nodded, relaxing despite the worry that had

troubled her mind for the last few hours. "Frenz, this is my hermano, Naldo Ramírez, king of the Ocultados. Naldo, this is Frenz Kanti. He's been traveling with me since Kensy."

"And courting you for how long, exactly?"

Gemi jerked in Ferez's embrace, but his arms tightened around her, keeping her close. Gemi barely registered that as she stared at her hermano, shocked. "What?"

Naldo rolled his eyes. "I've known you for five años, James. You do no travel wit' humanos, and you do no get this . . ." He waved a hand between Gemi and Ferez. "Close to someone unless they're familia. And the last time I checked, Frenz Kanti was no familia."

Gemi's cheeks burned. For a brief, silly moment, she wished she could turn around and bury her face against Ferez's chest. It wouldn't keep her hermano's questions at bay, but she wouldn't have to meet the knowing grin that grew wider the longer she remained silent.

"Since Mid-Season."

Gemi jumped and glanced over her shoulder at Ferez. His words had been soft, and he watched Naldo solemnly. When Gemi turned back to Naldo, his grin had disappeared, and his cheeks were pale. He swallowed.

"I—er . . . lo siento," he finally muttered. "I did no realize."

"¡Naldo!" Corteza snapped, reappearing at the end of the cart. "What es taking so long?"

Naldo shook his head. "Nada, Corteza." He stood and offered Ferez his hand. "Just making a tonto of meself," he muttered.

Minutes later, both Gemi and Ferez were seated between Flame's arms. To Gemi's surprise, the dragon greeted Ferez with just as much warmth as she did Gemi. In return, Ferez smiled warmly and smoothed his hand up over her snout, glided it gently beneath one eye—which Gemi was surprised the dragon allowed—and curled his fingers into the base of the horns crowning her head.

"I really was asleep for far too long," she muttered.

Ferez glanced down at her, surprised. "James?"

Gemi shook her head, but the smile she offered him was strained. "I'm just not accustomed to Flame . . ."

She bit her lip, uncertain how to explain. Flame was close enough to other people, certainly. Gemi couldn't deny that Flame saw Maxwell, Hausef, and Isa as family. But the dragon had always held part of herself aloof, even with them, though only someone in the bond would have been able to recognize it.

But with Ferez, Flame was engaging fully in a way Gemi had only ever felt her connect with her or Shadow.

Flame's mind churned against her own before she crooned softly. *"When you awake missing memories and feel that the only creatures you can trust are others who are missing memories or the mare one of them woke next to, it is difficult not to fully engage."*

Gemi's breath caught. It wasn't the words that shook her, but rather the sensations and images accompanying them. The joy of a flight shared, despite the unusual weight and form straddling her back. Respect and trust born of soothing logic, gentle compassion, and a depth of caring that could surpass the suppression of memories. A desire to protect and comfort and *possess* that was all too common within the bond, yet directed toward creatures outside of it.

"You want . . ."

But Gemi couldn't even find words to express the desires she could feel churning within the dragon's mind. It wasn't as simple as the desire to grow the bond. There were others' emotions and desires to take into account. Gemi felt pressure grow behind her eyes and within her throat as she realized how strongly Flame had worried over her. It hadn't just been a worry for her physical and emotional health. She had worried over how Gemi might react if she ever learned Flame trusted and cared for someone powerfully enough to consider bonding with him as well.

"Considering my replacements so soon?"

Gemi's head shot up, all thoughts of Flame and Ferez washed away as joy sang through her. "Shadow?" she whispered when she found herself face-to-snout with the stallion.

Wild earth and wind stormed through her mind, and Gemi closed her eyes and nearly sobbed as Shadow pressed his cheek to hers. Flying fire soon followed, wrapping their minds so tightly with Flame's presence that Gemi almost missed the joyous croon beating against her ears.

"Oh, gods." Gemi wrapped shaking hands around Shadow's muzzle. "You're back. You're truly back."

Relief flowed through her from all sides, filling her up with not only her own emotions but also both her bondmates'. It wasn't long before she did start sobbing and tears spilled down her cheeks, and she couldn't even care enough to try to stop them.

All the while, fingers smoothed through her shortened hair and over her cheeks and shoulders, and a third muzzle joined Flame and Shadow's, snuffling at her hair. Gemi gasped out a laugh when she realized Last Chance was making sure she was safe, and she reached for the mare's chin in greeting and thanks.

Shadow must have sensed Gemi's thoughts because he pressed even deeper into the bond and opened his memories of the last few days for Gemi to see. Worry over Gemi, over Last Chance during the nightmares. Caring and respect for the mare that only increased as she showed him her strength and stubbornness. Fear and hatred toward a man considered long-dead.

Gemi gasped and groaned as she realized what Shadow had been through under Deligero's care.

"But he's dead now," Shadow reminded her. *"And Last Chance helped me keep my sanity when I would have fallen into despair. And . . ."*

Gemi blinked when Shadow's mind went quiet. She sat up against Ferez and Flame's chests, worry thrumming through her. *"And what?"*

"And she saved me when Pablo took me over with his magic and convinced me I needed to kill her."

"What?" Gemi pulled herself from the embrace of the bond. Anger pulsed through her chest and up her throat. "Pablo did what?"

Flame rumbled lowly and lifted her head to scan the camp. *"I understood he was an Animal Mage and an ally of Deligero's . . ."*

"But no one mentioned that!" Gemi snapped.

Last Chance nickered softly and snorted before nudging Shadow and jerking her muzzle toward Gemi. Flame crooned curiously as Shadow translated.

"Pablo won't be a problem anymore. Last Chance says rare Animal Mages like him store most of their magic within a single animal, who acts as their Channel. And she killed the rock raven who was his Channel, so he's lost most of his magic. He might gain it back over time—"

Last Chance snorted and tossed her head.

"But she doesn't think he will."

Gemi stared at the mare. Now that she was looking at her, Gemi thought there was something different about her. She had always been proud—she was a warhorse with the ability to resist Animal Magic, after all. But she seemed . . . bigger, somehow. Perhaps stronger? It was as though she'd grown, but in a way Gemi couldn't define.

"What you are sensing is magic," Flame crooned, awed. She rubbed her nose against the mare's neck, and Last Chance returned the gesture. Gemi wasn't the only one who gasped as something pressed back against Flame's magic. *"She is radiating Animal Magic—magic she can actually control."*

Shadow rubbed his own muzzle against Last Chance's neck. *"Will you tell us now?"* he asked. *"I know you didn't want to share your history earlier, especially with Pablo so close—"*

Last Chance snorted, her shoulders tightening, and her ears twitched. The pale mare suddenly looked like she wanted to pull back, but with Shadow on one side and Flame on the other, there wasn't much room for her to move away. Gemi blinked. Shadow retorted something about there always being people around, but Gemi was more intent on Last Chance's increased breathing and wide eyes.

Without thinking about it, Gemi reached for Last Chance's chin again. The mare huffed as Gemi cupped her hand behind her soft, stubbly chin, but Last Chance didn't resist when Gemi urged her head down. Once the mare's head was low enough, Gemi laid her forehead against the mare's nose.

"You don't have tell us if you don't want to," she whispered. Behind her, Ferez stiffened, and Gemi laid her free hand against his thigh. "I—I understand how hard it can be to share your history." Her lips twisted wryly, and she closed her eyes, suddenly glad she didn't have to look at anyone for this. "But I'm sure you were already aware of that."

The tightening of Ferez's arms around Gemi's chest suddenly made her aware of the growing lump in her throat, and she squeezed her eyes closed more tightly. She couldn't prevent fresh tears from spilling down her already wet cheeks, but she didn't think she could face meeting Ferez's gaze right now.

I want to tell him the truth about who I am. I should have told him on Mid-Season. But now—

A warm, heavy breath against her chest and a gentle nicker startled her out of the thought. She pulled back to look up at Last Chance, but the mare pressed her head forward, keeping Gemi in place. Gemi half-sobbed and half-chuckled as she firmed her grip around the mare's chin. The gentle nickers continued, and through the bond, from both Shadow and Flame, spilled Last Chance's words, in fits and starts. Gemi did her best to speak the words for Ferez in turn, but the lump in her throat only grew and Ferez's grip on her tightened as the words came forth.

"I . . . already told Shadow, but . . . Frenz wasn't my first master. My first was . . . was a Pecalini Animal Mage." She snorted heavily. *"I didn't even know his name. I only knew him as Maestro.*

"But Maestro was everything to me back then. And I to him . . . or so I believed. He'd named me Mundomía. My World." Another snort. *"I was so naïve back then."*

She paused. Gemi massaged her chin, earning a soft huff and a gentle nudge of the mare's snout before she continued.

"I wasn't just a Power Animal to Maestro, though. He gave me his magic, channeled it through me. Had me . . . had me . . ."

Last Chance's jaw worked under Gemi's hand, but Gemi didn't say anything, only waited. Behind Gemi, Ferez kept silent, patient, and his hand stroked up and down under Last Chance's jaw.

"He would send me into villages," Last Chance finally continued. *"He would have me work his magic throughout the village . . . into all the village's animals . . . and then . . . and then . . ."*

She was silent for a little while, and the sounds of the

people and animals around them threatened to break through their communion. But Last Chance must have been determined to get her story out by then, because she suddenly surged forward in the telling.

"Maestro would enter the villages the day after I did and demand things of the locals. Common goods, village secrets, prized treasures. It didn't matter. I don't think he cared so much what he got from the villages as much as the control he could exercise over them.

"And for most of my time with him, I didn't care. I didn't understand that what we were doing was wrong. It took . . . it took . . ."

Last Chance shuddered. Gemi tightened her grip on the mare's chin and pressed her forehead more firmly to her nose.

"I killed a young Animal Mage, maybe ten years old, whose family stood against Maestro. The rest of his family were killed by other animals, but I . . . I'm the one who trampled him. I didn't mean to, but I did, and I still don't know for certain if it was a misjudgment on my part or a direction on Maestro's."

The words ended on a sobbing whinny, and Last Chance fell silent. By the time she continued though, her nickers had grown stronger.

"But after that, I learned to listen to his demands and the reactions of the villagers. I came to understand just what Maestro was and that I had no control. I couldn't keep myself from doing what I had begun to think of as evil, and I didn't like it.

"And so I taught myself to pull away from him. I trained myself to resist his demands, his pulls on the magic. And more importantly, to do so without his knowledge." She snorted. *"I trained myself so well that six months after I killed the boy, I preceded Maestro into a well-guarded town, took control of the animals, and then held them still when he needed their protection against the guards."*

Last Chance's sides heaved by the time she fell silent,

and Flame rubbed her head against the mare's neck. *"You watched him die?"* Flame murmured.

Last Chance snorted. *"I watched him die and listened as he cried out for me. But I couldn't let him continue using me to harass and kill. I refused."*

Flame crooned. *"And the magic?"*

Last Chance shuddered. *"The moment he died, it snapped fully into me. I could feel every animal within the town. I could sense their health, their relations to each other . . ."* She shuddered again. *"I wasn't prepared. The only reason it didn't drive me mad then was because a Mindspeaker took pity on me and helped me control it. Helped me lock it away."*

"But that didn't stop the guilt or the grief," Shadow added. When Gemi touched his mind curiously with her own, he told her what Last Chance had shared with him in caves. *"The state Frenz found her in on the Pecalini merchant ship—it was mostly self-inflicted."*

Ferez shuddered against her back as she shared the words—sans the Pecalini merchant ship that Gemi even wondered if he would recall. *"'M so sorry, Last Chance. I didn'—"*

Last Chance snorted, interrupting Ferez, and pulled her head away from Gemi's. She didn't pull back far, though, just enough to tilt her head and stare at Ferez.

"You have nothing to be sorry for, Ferez. If not for you, I'd still be punishing myself for what I had done instead of reveling in what I can do."

She twisted her head and nudged Shadow then. *"And if not for you, I'd . . . well, I never would have acknowledged the magic again."*

Shadow huffed. *"Why do I get the feeling you'd have been just as glad not to?"* Last Chance shoved her head against his neck, but her nickers were more amusement than indignation. When Gemi shared the stallion's words with Ferez, they both fell into watery snickers.

With the amusement came a relaxation that finally allowed the world around them to break through their communion. A young voice cried out in frustration, and Gemi peered around the horses to find the source.

"I tried to stop the bleedin' wit' the feathers, but Pablo was escapin' and—"

"Cálmate, Guido," Pastora soothed. Gemi finally spied Guido and Fabio seated not too far away, Fiela curled comfortingly around them. Pastora and Corteza knelt in front of them, fussing over the squirming brothers.

"But, Madre," Fabio complained, as though Pastora were dancing around a question they'd asked several times already. "How are they?"

"Raeka and Cabro are fine, chicos," Corteza assured them with a huff. "Thanks to your quick thinking, the feathers clotted the blood long enough for us to find them. They'd have been here to thank you themselves, but I insisted they stay en the healing rooms and rest." She frowned at Guido. "Just like you should've done."

Ignoring the Healer's reprimand, Fabio nudged his younger brother. "See? I told you, you did the right thing." Guido grinned and nodded and then buried his face in Fiela's fur as Corteza ran her hands over his still-injured leg.

"Nadie?"

The word was spoken so softly that Gemi didn't recognize the voice. Glancing toward the sound, she stiffened. Lord Sageo stood nearby, Sir Gervasio just behind him.

"James?" Ferez's mouth was so close to Gemi's ear, she

doubted any but Flame and the horses heard him speak. "Is that . . . ?"

"Lord Sa—geo."

Gemi winced as her voice broke. Anger may have driven her when the duke attacked her, but she couldn't forget the feel of his fingers digging into her throat. Her fingers twitched with the urge to reach up and touch her throat, but she refused to do so with the duke watching her.

"I had . . . hoped to speak with you . . . Nadie."

Gemi blinked. The duke's eyes were downcast, his face worn. She had never seen him so hesitant. She'd seen him angry, intent, and possibly even curious, but never once had his shoulders slumped or his head hung or his fingers rubbed at each other idly.

Could he—

"An' why should he let yeh?"

Gemi glanced back at Ferez, surprised. He was glaring at the Pecalini duke. "Frenz . . ."

Ferez shifted his gaze to her, and his eyes hardly softened. "He tried to kill yeh, James. Under Care's Peace, no less. Yeh canna seriously consider forgivin' him."

A sharp grunt came from the duke's direction. Gemi winced and closed her eyes. This was not how she had wanted Lord Sageo to learn of Ferez's missing memories. Ferez's current attitude, though, was a sharp reminder that Lord Sageo was not the only one who had failings to atone for.

"I don't know about forgiveness." Gemi opened her eyes again to peer up at Ferez. "But I think he's right that we need to talk." She glanced at the duke, who was now eyeing them both with open curiosity and worry. "There are some things I need to discuss with him in private." Turning back to Ferez, she offered a weak smile. "Just between him and me."

Ferez frowned, his gaze moving between Gemi and the duke. "Yeh wanna be alone wit' him? After what he did to yeh? To the Ocultados?"

Gemi lifted a hand to Ferez's face. "It was not all his fault, Frenz. He'd had his son stolen from him—"

"Aye, an' he immediately turned on the Ocultados in search o' revenge instead of investigatin' what really happened."

"I am quite aware," Lord Sageo suddenly said, the words stronger and colder than his earlier plea, "of the wrongs I have committed against Nadie and the Ocultados, señor. I have every intention of making amends for them in whatever manner necessary. I had simply hoped to apologize to Nadie first since my crímenes against him were the most personal."

Ferez looked ready to argue, but Gemi squeezed his arm. She shook her head when he met her gaze. "I do need to speak with him alone, Frenz."

Ferez flushed but turned his gaze back to Lord Sageo and glowered. "If yeh harm him . . ."

Lord Sageo's gaze was definitely curious as he observed Ferez silently. Finally, he dipped his head in a brief bow. "I wouldn't dare. Besides, we will not be completely alone. Assuming you're amenable, Nadie," he added with a nod to Gemi, "I would like Gervasio to be present for this conversation."

Gemi hesitated for only a moment before nodding. She was certain the duke must realize she wished to discuss Ferez. If he was comfortable sharing such information with his Knight Captain, she wouldn't object. The knight had already proven himself to be fair, after all.

Despite Ferez's misgivings, Gemi was soon ensconced in the duke's tent with Lord Sageo, Sir Gervasio, and to her surprise, Lord Sageo's son. The latter had been sprawled across a cot in one corner of the tent when they'd arrived, but he quickly sat upright and watched the two men settle Gemi into a chair.

"Nadie," Lord Sageo murmured once she was comfortable, "this is my hijo, Alano." She nodded to the bedridden man, who appeared to be in his late twenties. Alano nodded back, his eyebrows raised in surprise. "I believe I am indebted to you and the Ocultados for his safe return."

Gemi nodded. "Maybe not to me, but to the Ocultados, certainly. And Frenz. As I understand it, none of them would have survived if he and Last Chance hadn't been there."

"Frenz." The duke shook his head. "He seems to have become rather taken with that role, doesn't he?"

"Frenz? A role?" Alano glanced between Gemi and his father. "What are you talking about?"

Frowning, Lord Sageo turned to his son. "You told me you spent several hours imprisoned with him. Surely you recognized the rey you once helped train."

"Rey? What—"

Suddenly, Alano cursed and closed his eyes. "Frenz Kanti. Of course. That was the nombre Ferez always claimed when he and—when he would disappear from the palace."

Gemi eyed the noble, curious about what he'd been about to say. Lord Sageo was already turning back to her though, so she sighed and shook her head.

"I'm not surprised you didn't recognize him. He didn't recognize you, did he?"

Alano frowned. "Maybe not on sight, but I wouldn't have expected anyone to recognize me in that state. He recognized me once I told him my nombre, though. He said . . ." He flushed. "I even remember thinking it was something Ferez would say." He glanced aside. "I can't believe I didn't recognize him."

Gemi frowned. "What did he say?"

Alano glanced up, startled. "What?"

Gemi made a beckoning motion with one hand. "What did he say that made you think of him?"

"Something about me being one of the better commanders during the guerra. Why?"

Gemi nodded firmly. "So not something personal."

Alano frowned. "Sí. So what?"

"So . . ."

Gemi hesitated. She didn't want to tell them like this. She didn't want potential allies—no matter how much damage Lord Sageo had already caused—to turn on her. Worse was the fear that they would look at her with hatred and blame, only confirming the guilt she already felt.

"What Adalwolf did to Frenz is not your fault," Flame hissed. *"You cannot blame yourself for his missing memories."*

Gemi smiled bitterly. *"I've learned the hard way that guilt doesn't need a reason, Flame."*

"Nadie?"

That was the duke, and Gemi nodded to the man. "Things have happened this season that I would gladly change if I could."

"Does this have anything to do with the Mago Mental that attacked you after Mid-Season?"

Gemi's breath caught, and she turned to stare at the Knight Captain. "How?"

"Gervasio?" Lord Sageo questioned.

The knight glanced at his Knight Master and shrugged. "We discussed a few things while you were asleep, Peln." The duke flushed, but Sir Gervasio didn't seem to notice. "One thing mentioned was the attack that left Nadie with the weakness that currently prevents him from standing."

Gemi felt her own cheeks burn, but she didn't protest. She would have been even more uncomfortable if she had had to explain it herself.

"A Mago Mental suppressed the dragona's and the stallion's memories of Nadie, blocked their bond, and kidnapped Nadie and tortured him into unconsciousness. The mago was killed afterward, but Nadie didn't wake until after we'd capture the dragona."

Lord Sageo stiffened and glanced sharply at Gemi. "When I asked your dragona for an explanation . . . ?"

Gemi shook her head. "I was unconscious. And the others were lost, starving, and frustrated. I'm sure you can imagine why Flame might have been rather furious with your demands."

Lord Sageo stared thoughtfully past Gemi. After a long moment, he shook his head and waved a hand at Sir Gervasio. "So what exactly does this Mago Mental have to do with Ferez?"

The Knight Captain glanced at Gemi, but she refused to meet his gaze. She had little doubt he had guessed the truth about what had happened. She didn't want to see whatever accusations might hang in his eyes.

"The mago didn't restrict himself to invading the mentes of you and your bondmates, did he?"

Startled by the gentle tone—a tone that reminded Gemi too much of Ferez—she glanced up to find the knight watching her with eyes full of compassion and sympathy. She quickly glanced away again, not certain she could handle seeing that, either.

"Nay," she breathed, focusing on the words the knight had spoken. "Ferez was with me when the Mindspeaker attacked. I just learned . . ."

Gemi swallowed. The sudden knot in her throat felt immoveable, and she had to breathe deliberately for a full minute before she could speak again.

"Like Flame and Shadow after the Mindspeaker's attack, Ferez doesn't remember his time with me, but . . . more than that . . . he doesn't remember being king. He . . . he thinks he was born Frenz Kanti, a farmer from Cosley Ruins who fought in the war and who is now taking a request to Caypan to set before the king."

Gemi laughed bitterly.

"And the worst thing is, his mind rebels when someone tries to retrieve the memories because he began courting me the night before the attack."

Twenty-Three

When Peln had asked about Su Majestad, he'd expected . . . well, he hadn't known what to expect. But missing memories? The rey actually believing he was a farmer?

No, that wasn't what he'd been expecting at all.

Yet he couldn't find it within himself to blame Nadie. Perhaps he'd learned his lesson about jumping to conclusions and allowing his emotions to cloud his judgment. However, this particular reluctance probably had more to do with the pain Nadie obviously felt concerning the rey's situation.

And if they were courting . . .

Peln closed his eyes wearily. Memories of his younger días rushed through him, and he grimaced. Su Majestad wasn't the first noble to find love outside the noble class, or even with someone unable to bear chicos. Those who did, though, usually left it behind in the face of their peers' expectations.

Not really surprising he would give up the verdad of his self to keep what love he could find.

Despite the grimness of the situation though, Peln didn't think it was futile. After all, Su Majestad was still alive. Unless that changed, there was still hope.

He opened his eyes and peered down at Nadie. "You said his mente rebels. What do you mean?"

The chico—*only a chico, after all of this*—appeared startled by Peln's words. "My tante—my aunt—is one of the most powerful Mindspeakers among the nomads. She and another Mindspeaker tried to retrieve the lost memories, but . . . but Flame says Ferez panicked and attacked them. After that, they decided not to try again."

Peln frowned. "Perhaps if a Mago Mental with more intimate knowledge of Ferez's mente—"

Nadie shook his head. "I don't think anyone could have more intimate knowledge of Ferez's mind than Wolfrik does."

Peln blinked but didn't question that. The estación hadn't been easy or simple for any of them. He was beginning to wonder if he would have known the rey even if he hadn't had his memories suppressed.

"Perhaps intimate knowledge of his mente isn't the only thing that's necessary."

Peln glanced over his shoulder. Alano was watching Nadie thoughtfully. "What do you mean?"

Alano nodded to Nadie. "I think Nadie was the one Ferez was most worried about while we were imprisoned. When I first met him, he was tense and distracted. Then Aquilina assured us that only two caballos were brought with him. After that, he was focused solely on trying to find a way for us to escape."

He shrugged. "Maybe all he needs to allow his memories to be retrieved is to trust that Nadie is safe and well and to focus on the need to regain them. If Nadie insists he needs to have them . . ."

"Then perhaps a Mindspeaker would be able to retrieve them safely," Nadie finished, relief palpable in his words.

Peln turned back to the chico. To his surprise, Nadie was sitting up straighter. His hands, which had quivered occasionally before, were now clenched in his tunic, and his expression was firm.

"Milord," he added, meeting Peln's gaze steadily, "you mentioned Mindspeakers with intimate knowledge of Ferez's mind. Do you know where we can find some?"

"Caypan, of course," Peln answered. "Five Magos Mentales make the palace their casa. Two of them, Comyn and Earnan, have known Ferez since his birth. If anyone should be able to find the missing memories, those two should."

Nadie nodded firmly. "Then as soon as I'm strong enough to move on my own, we'll head for Caypan. We'll fix this."

Peln's lips twitched. The determination in the chico's voz was so strong, Peln could feel his own spirits lifting. No, the situation was not hopeless. And Peln could trust Nadie. He had done so before he'd received his hijo's bloody ring, and the disappearance of that trust had only proven that Nadie and his allies were not his enemigos.

"Now, then," Nadie continued strongly, lifting his chin. "While I take care of Ferez, how do you plan to atone for the wrongs you've committed against the Ocultados?"

Peln pursed his lips to prevent the smile playing at his lips. This was serious, and he didn't want Nadie thinking he felt otherwise. However, Peln thought he could now understand why Tern had thought this chico was interesting and how Su Majestad managed to fall for him.

Dorothy Tinker

~~*~*

Hours later, Gemi was back in Ferez and Flame's arms, though they'd managed to move to the front hall of Ciudad Ocultada. The negotiations with the duke had taken longer than she'd expected. Despite the light now creeping into the sky above the walls of the valley, she was so close to simply dropping into sleep.

Gemi smiled slightly as she considered the negotiations. They had eventually been forced to leave the duke's tent to consult with Naldo and the other Ocultados who had come to the duke's camp, but Gemi thought that had only increased the goodwill forming between Lord Peln and Gemi's Tarsurian family. Certainly, by the end of the discussion, everyone had seemed pleased with the results.

Lord Peln had agreed to pay a wergild to each family that had lost someone to the recent attacks. In addition, he had promised to replenish Ladrasid and Ciudad Ocultada's winter stores, which would have been severely depleted due to the burned fields. He had also offered to pay a wergild to each injured survivor (including Guido, much to Gemi's amusement), but Naldo had rejected the offer as outrageous.

"Es no like our gente must pay for a curandero's servicios," Naldo had explained. "A wergild to each survivor would be redundante when Corteza and the otros have already healed most of the grave injuries."

When Lord Peln had tried to argue that the curanderos should be compensated for their skills instead, the offended look Corteza offered him from her place beside Guido had silenced him pretty quickly.

Gemi giggled. Flame crooned warmly, amused by her thoughts, while Ferez's arms tightened gently around her middle.

382

"Yeh're in a fairly good mood," he murmured against her hair.

Gemi shrugged, a grin tugging lazily at her lips. "Why shouldn't I be? Despite all the attempts of our enemies, I'm reunited with you, Last Chance, Shadow, and Flame, there's a chance for peace between the Ocultados and Lord Peln, and our enemies are all either dead or incapacitated."

Even Pablo, Gemi added silently. After being allowed to bury his rock raven, the traitor had been simultaneously banished from Ciudad Ocultada and arrested by the duke's men for his part in the deception that had led to Alano's capture, the death of his men, and the duke's attack on Ciudad Ocultada.

The worst thing is he doesn't even seem to feel guilty about intercepting Lord Peln's letters and pretending to be the king of thieves they were addressed to.

The stroke of a hand through her shortened hair startled Gemi back into the present. She twisted in Ferez's arms enough to meet his solemn gaze. "What's wrong?" she murmured when he didn't return the smile she offered him.

Ferez's jaw tightened, but he held her gaze and slid a hand across one of her cheeks. Warmth—a different kind from the subdued anger that still twisted in her chest despite everything—flushed through Gemi. She smiled shyly, leaning her cheek into the caress.

"Yeh talk abou' peace between the duke an' the Ocultados." Ferez's voice was low and unexpectedly charged. "Bu' there was ne'er once any talk o' compensation to yeh for his attempt to kill yeh."

Gemi blinked. "Compensation? He apologized and is making amends to the Ocultados. That's more than I thought I could expect."

Ferez shook his head. "Bu' tha's to the Ocultados. Tha's not atonement for his attack on yeh."

Gemi frowned. Ferez's continued anger toward the duke surprised her. He was usually easygoing, seeking peace whenever possible. For him to hold a grudge against the duke after the night's negotiations . . .

"I believe he cares for you too much to forgive Lord Peln so easily," Flame crooned softly. *"Just as you were unwilling to forgive Wolfrik at first for the damage he had caused to Frenz's mind."*

Gemi flushed but nodded. She remembered the rage she had felt both the first time she faced Wolfrik and the night they had returned to Helloase and learned that Wolfrik's magic had done more damage than even he had realized. Ferez had willingly forgiven the Skorpion Mindspeaker, but Gemi hadn't subsided until Flame pointed out that Ferez wouldn't sleep until she did.

Lifting a hand to Ferez's face—and noting idly that her limbs were already stronger than they had been—Gemi held his gaze insistently. "Lord Peln apologized, Frenz. His regret and the amends he has promised to make are the most important compensations he could give me. I don't want his gold or his suffering or whatever other payments you might be considering, not when his worth as an ally far outweighs any of that."

Ferez searched her eyes for a long time. Gemi could feel the moment he decided to accept her forgiveness of the duke. His body relaxed beneath hers, and he leaned heavily against Flame's chest and arm.

"'M sorry." He pulled her against his chest and pressed his lips to her hair. "All I've wanted to do since I learned about yeh is to protect yeh, bu' then I wasn' here to protect yeh from him, an'—"

Gemi pulled away from his chest, and he fell silent. His

blue-and-silver eyes were still solemn as Gemi met them, but she couldn't prevent a soft smile from stretching her lips.

"Frenz, I understand. I felt the same way when . . ."

She trailed off. Ferez wouldn't remember the incident Flame had referenced. The angry heat in her chest flared, but she shoved it aside and focused on the decision she'd made in Lord Peln's tent.

"You can protect me now, Frenz," she whispered. "And once I've regained my strength, I'll protect you, too."

And I'll help you reclaim your memories, no matter what it takes.

~~*~*

Aquila flipped her wings back and dropped into the Tapestry Room of the Fates. Despite her curiosity over the Ladies' previous call, she had been forced to make another trip into the Mortal Realm to collect souls from victims of a volcanic eruption that had burned through several villages in the northeastern section of the Pecalini rainforest.

Running her beak through her feathers to make sure the souls were secure, the Eagle waited for the Ladies to greet her as they usually did. When only silence met her ears, she squawked softly and lifted her head to scan the cavernous realm.

She squawked again as she realized the Ladies were nowhere in sight. Instead, she was surrounded by towering pillars hung with multicolored tapestries that felt centuries old.

Odd. I have not misjudged my Transportation so badly in centuries. Not since the last reign of Chaos have I—

Aquila hissed sharply, suddenly certain she knew where in the Tapestry Room she had landed. Eyeing the nearest pillar, she nodded grimly. There, scattered frequently among the multicolored threads that represented the lives of mortals, were a multitude of tears. From their length, Aquila could recognize that they had lasted for an entire two and a half decades.

Not long when the First Chaos lasted nearly a millennium.

But twenty-five years of Chaos had been long enough to nearly destroy entire species of mortals. Whole kingdoms of bipedal mortals, including elves, dwarves, and goblins, had fallen to ruin as anarchy, disloyalty, and mistrust had turned the creatures against each other.

And even after Peace and War balanced the Chaos, it was mainly the humans who flourished, not their more magical counterparts.

That, she knew, had as much to do with one particular soul as it did with the destruction the Chaos had wreaked. Eyeing the tears, it did not take her long to find the silver-blue thread that danced among them, never once interrupted by the chaotic gashes. In fact, it looked almost as though the thread closed up the ends of certain breaks before dancing farther down the tapestry.

He helped ease the Chaos at that time. Aquila gently traced the silver-blue thread with her beak until it surpassed the tears altogether. *Perhaps he could—*

A familiar thrum echoed through Aquila's soul, and she uttered a soft squawk as she pulled away from the Tapestry. The Ladies must be impatient if they felt the need to call her to them when she was so close.

Glancing around to orient herself, Aquila launched herself into the air and soared between the pillars, which were spaced widely enough to accommodate her wingspan. She aimed for the newer section of the Tapestry Room, and she could feel the Tapestry becoming younger as she passed its many folds.

When she was in sight of the loom, she squawked in relief and settled to the ground behind the Fates.

"By the Cycle, I have not made such an error in centuries."

"Since Chaos last reigned, correct?" breathed Neris the Maid.

Aquila screeched and ruffled her feathers. *"And?"*

"And that should give you an idea of why we sent for you, Eagle!" snapped Findi in her gravelly tones.

Aquila tilted her head. *"I do not see how—"*

That's when she caught sight of the Tapestry beneath Tapeta's fingers. A single gaping tear, large enough to rival the ones Aquila had been inspecting only moments ago, had opened across the weave, threatening to unravel it faster than Tapeta could put it together.

"I thought the Hunt was supposed to ease the Chaos. I mean—" She clacked her beak and shook her head. *"Life seemed more clear-headed the last time I saw her. Surely . . ."*

"The Hunt might have smoothed the surface of the Chaos," Findi growled. "However, it was induced not by Balance but by Carith's sons themselves. The Hunt itself was corrupted by Chaos."

Aquila hissed. *"Then Chaos . . . ?"*

"Has only grown worse," Neris answered with a sigh. "You felt it, did you not, when you collected this last batch of souls? The elementals are only growing more frantic in their outcries."

Aquila ducked her head and buried her beak in her breast feathers. The Maid was correct. She had noticed the riled elementals, but she had thought it was the tail end of the Chaos, not its heart.

"Is there anything we can do?" she crooned. *"I assume War is worse than ever and only Peace can fight him still?"*

"That is true," Tapeta answered, her usually vibrant voice subdued. "However, there is one being who may be able to interfere in a way we and the children cannot."

Aquila raised her head and eyed the Ladies warily. They held themselves taut in a way Aquila had never seen, and dread pooled heavily within her chest.

"Which being?"

"Carith's lifemate."

Aquila screeched and beat her wings. *"She has been lost to the Mortal Realm for centuries. Why would you turn to her now?"*

"We have little choice in this!" snapped Findi. "Carith's lifemate bears both a physical form and her immortal memories. If any god has a chance of subduing the Chaos, it is she."

"And how do you expect to find her? The few who still remember her call her the Lost Goddess for a reason."

Findi turned and glared, but Aquila only lifted her beak and met her gaze. The Ladies might be able to intimidate the children, but Aquila had never been so weak.

"You forget, Eagle," Findi finally ground out. "We weave the lives of every being in mortal form. The mortals may call her the Lost Goddess, but she has never been lost from our Sight.

"Besides," she added with a knowing glance, "you cannot tell us you do not know her mortal form when your sister was the one to place her soul within it."

Aquila shook herself. *"Perhaps. But how do you plan to request her assistance? I cannot imagine she will appreciate being acknowledged after hiding for so long."*

Findi snorted but fell silent at the quelling glance Tapeta offered her.

"She will not scorn your approach, Aquila," Tapeta answered.

Aquila screeched. *"My approach? But she is in mortal form."*

"With access to Sight and Mindspeech powerful enough to interact with the nonphysical," Neris breathed before Findi could reply. "Unfortunately, we fear she will not understand our request if we offer it only through Sights."

"Or that she will ignore it altogether, which is more likely," Findi growled.

Aquila tilted her head. *"Why would she ignore it? Lack of care for her children was never one of her faults."*

"We fear . . ." Tapeta paused in her weaving just long enough to settle a hand lightly on Findi's. "Carith's lifemate may not realize that her soul is not restricted in the same way a mortal's is. She is already eager to interfere, but she has retained a respect for mortal magics that might do more damage to the current situation than good."

"But if she ignores mortal restrictions," Aquila squawked, *"then would that not simply increase Chaos's hold?"*

"We would rather deal with the consequences of that," Neris murmured, "than risk what might come if her children destroy the Mortal Realm with their quarrels."

Aquila shivered. The urge to return to the Cycle and hide herself away in her nest suddenly burned through her. *"And you want me to try to convince her that this would be the best course."*

All three sisters nodded. "If she does refuse," Findi rasped, suddenly subdued, "then pray to Magmater that Chaos does not overtake us all."

~~*~*

War snarled and clutched at his head. *She* and her allies had been reunited, and *his* soul was left reeling as it sought some way to bring her down again.

She's further from the pain I feel than she was even days ago! How is this possible?

He didn't even have the threat of Deligero's return to hang over her thoughts. He had hoped the thief might prove useful, even in death.

But then the damned king had to prove himself talented with a mage stone!

He snarled again and uselessly swiped one hand out from his body. *And I can't even hate Death for instigating the Hunt or even the elementals for stirring in outrage. If Deligero hadn't been stupid enough to attempt killing his own offspring, let alone to kill his lifemate without a hint of remorse, neither would have happened.*

He hadn't been nearby to see it, but he knew those were the two things that had initiated the thief's demise. He had been all too willing to follow the drive of the Hunt. To kill family in war was one thing—War had driven many a man to kill his kin under its influence. But to take a blade to one's own blood with such chilling intent was unacceptable.

And Aquilina was beloved to the local elementals. It's no wonder they shook the mountain in rage at her death.

Shaking his head, War gnashed his teeth and squeezed his eyes shut. All these rambling thoughts were little more than an insignificant attempt to shield himself from the pain that throbbed and burned and beat within his soul. Screaming out in frustration and pain and everything else that filled his mind, he beat and clawed his hands on his chest and arms and legs, the way Deligero had in response to Hate's influence. But War was not mortal. He couldn't damage his soul the way a physical being could destroy its own body, no matter how desperate he was to relieve the Chaos and hate and . . .

War gasped and threw open his eyes. "War!" he hissed. "Uncontrolled war. That's what—"

He snarled suddenly and tossed his head from side to side. "Doesn't matter! I need a way to break P—"

The scream that tore through him then was pure pain. It tore at his throat and mouth and burned at his eyes. When he could finally fall silent, he was on his hands and knees, gasping and panting like an animal.

"This can't go on," he half moaned, half growled. "I need—"

A sudden twitch and tug at his soul had him on his feet before he could think. Blinking, he focused on his surroundings for the first time since he had arrived. As soon as the Hunt had ended, just before the clarity accompanying it had abandoned him, he had thrown himself into a Transportation that would carry him away from his brothers. He hadn't aimed for a specific destination, though.

Now, he found himself in a dim study, only a low-burning fire and several candles lighting the room's desk and its only occupant. War's entire being loosened and relaxed as he realized just whom he'd sought out.

"Seyan Lefas," he growled and stalked closer to the Baylinese duke.

The man was hunched over his desk, scribbling furiously, and parchments littered the desk's surface haphazardly. Once War was close enough to read them, he realized most of them contained the same message.

A savage grin pulled at War's lips. *So my time in Tarsur was not a waste.* He scanned the parchments and chuckled when he found the letter he had prodded the Tarsurian duke into writing.

"Sageo might have been amenable to me only in his grief, but you have always sought the battle, haven't you, Lefas?"

The Baylinese duke snarled suddenly as the nub of his

quill snapped. Tossing it to the floor and tearing up the parchment he'd been using, he scooped up a new quill, grabbed a fresh sheet of parchment, and began again. War smirked and watched as the man kept his handwriting neat, despite his obvious anger.

"Good," War praised. "The nobles must know you're serious. They must understand there can be nothing more pressing than this summons."

The duke simply kept writing, unaware of his immortal guest, and War nodded, settling in to keep the man company. Once Lefas finished the letters, he would send them off and summon all of Evon's nobles to Caypan.

Summon them to Caypan—summon them to Council—and by season's end, Evon will have a new king.

War crowed triumphantly.

A new king! And a new war!

To be
continued

in

**Forgotten
Goddess**

Language Glossary

Pecalini Glossary

advertir – warn

agua – water

amigo – friend

Animal Poder – Power Animal

año – year

asustar – to frighten; *no le asuste* – don't frighten him

ataque – attack

banda – groups of men under someone's command; generally
used by thieves and Ocultados

bella – beautiful

bueno – good

caballero – knight

caballo – horse

¡cállate! – Be quiet!

¡cálmate! – Calm down!

Capitán de Caballeros – Knight Captain

Carito – Carith

casa – house, home

chico/a – boy/girl; *chiquito/a* – little one

ciudad – city

Ciudad Ocultada – Hidden City; home of the hidden ones

claro – of course

claro que sí – of course

claro que no – of course not

como – like

compañero – companion

conexión – connection

conversación – conversation

correcto – correct

correspondencia – correspondence

criatura – creature

criatura mágica – magical creature

crímenes – crimes

¡cuidado! – be careful!

culpa – fault

curandero – healer

Curandero Mágico – Mage Healer

deshidratación – dehydration

día – day

dioses – gods; *por los dioses* – by the gods

dragón/dragona – dragon

droga – drug

duque – duke

él – he, him

enemigo – enemy

especial – special

estación – season

estar – to be (impermanent state); *estás* – you are; *está* – he/she is

excusa – excuse

explicaciones – explanations

familia – family

fidelidad – loyalty

fuego – fire; *noche del fuego* – night of fire

Fuego de Mauro – Maurus's Fire

fuegos de guerra – battlefires

gallito – little rooster; little male eagle

gente – people

Gris de Pecali – Pecalini Gray; breed of horse specific to the eastern rainforests of Pecali, Grays are born with a dark coat that fades to pure white as they mature; Last Chance is of this breed

guerra – war

hablar – to speak; *no hablas* – you don't speak

Hacienda Sageo – Sageo Estate; where Lord Peln Sageo and his family live

hermano/a – brother/sister

héroe – hero

hijo/a – son/daughter

hombre – man

honestamente – honestly

hora – hour

humano – human

impaciente – impatient

inactividad – inactivity

indicación – indication

información – information

informativo – informative

inocente – innocent

instinto – instinct

interés – interest

interesante – interesting

inventario – inventory

ladrón (ladrones) – thief

loco – crazy

lo siento – I am sorry

luz – light

llamar – to call; *me llamo* – I call myself, my name is; *te llama* – he/she is calling you

macho – male

madre – mother

maestro/a – master

magia – magic

Magia Animal – Animal Magic

Magia Terrena – Earth Magic

mágico – magical
mago – mage
Mago Animal – Animal Mage
Mago Botánico – Plant Mage
Mago Mental – Mindspeaker
Majestad – Your Majesty; *Su Majestad* – His Majesty
maldecir – to damn; *se maldice* – damn you
maldita – damn
malo – evil
Mamá – another name for mother
mañana – morning
masculino – male, masculine
Mauro – Maurus
mensaje – message
mensajero – messenger
mente – mind
mi – my
mijo – short for "mi hijo"; my son
momento – moment
monstruo – monster
montaña – mountain
mujer – woman
mujer de vida – female lifemate
nada – nothing
nadie – no one; *Nadie* – James Caffers' title in Tarsur
necesitar – to need; *necesito* – I need
nervioso – nervous
no – nay
noche – night; *noche del fuego* – night of fire
No le asuste nuestra visita – don't frighten our visitor
nómada – nomad
nombre – name
no sé – I don't know

nuestra – our

numero – number

nunca – never

obstrucción – obstruction

Ocultado – Hidden One; preferred name for the unified
thieves in Tarsur

ocupado – busy

opción – option

oportunidad – opportunity

otro – other

padre – father; *padres* – parents

pandilla – group of friends; term used by king of thieves to
refer to closest friends and advisors

pasajes secretos – secret passages; hidden tunnels running
through the mountain that la Ciudad Ocultada is built
into, used as secret entrances/exits

paso – pass (as in a mountain)

Paso del Águila Salvaje – Wild Eagle Pass

paz – peace

perdone – excuse me

perro/a – dog; *perrita* – derogatory word for a female

persona – person

pirata – pirate

planta – plant

Plaza Central – Central Plaza; plaza that is the center of the
outdoor portion of la Ciudad Ocultada

pobre – the poor one

poción [pociones] – potion

un poco – a bit, a little

por favor – please

preocupada – worried

preparaciones – preparations

prisioneros – prisoners

problema – trouble, problem
protección – protection
pueblo – village
puñal [-es] – throwing knife
que – that
querido – dear one
Quiero saber que mi Gallito esté a salvo – I want to know
that my Gallito is safe.
quietud – calm
razón – reason
rebaño – flock (of sheep); Pastora uses the term to refer to
the children she's taken in
resistencia – resistance
resistente – resistant
respeto – respect
rey – king
saber – to know; *sé* – I know
salvo – safe
satisfactorio – satisfactory
siétedia – sevenday
Señor – mister
Señora – madam
sentimentalismo – sentimentality
sí – aye
silencio – silence
sol – sun
solamente – only
soldado – soldier
tarde – late
tío – uncle
tipo – type
tonto – stupid, foolish
trono – throne

tu – your
valle – valley
Valle Ocultado – Hidden Valley
vámonos – let's go
venganza – revenge
verdad – truth
verdadero/a – true
¡Ven! – Come!
vínculo de dragón – dragonbond
violencia – violence
violente – violent
visita – visitor
voz – voice
y – and
yo – I

Zhulanese Glossary

aber (*ah-behr*) – but

abschaum (*ahb-showm*) – scum

Adlerfest (*ahd-lehr-fehst*) – Mid-Autumn Festival; literally, "Eagle Festival"; represents the Royal Eagle, first guardian of the Cycle of Incarnation

adliger (*ahd-lee-ghehr*) – nobleman, lord; old term; generally used more for nomad ruling families, while Mylord is used for nobles recognized by the Evonese monarchy

ausländer (*ouse-land-uh*) – foreigner

bitte (*biht-uh*) – please

bruder (*broo-dehr*) – brother

clansmann (*klahns-mahn*) [-männer (*klahns-may-nehr*)] – clansman

dame (*dah-muh*) – madam

danke (*dahn-kuh*) – thank you

dankpflicht (*dahnk-flickt*) – formal thanks; obligation born of gratitude; held in high regard by the nomads

dieb (*deeb*) [-e (*dee-buh*)] – thief

drache (*drah-kuh*) – dragon

Drache Krieger (*drah-kuh kree-ghehr*) – James Caffers' title in Zhulan; literally means "dragon warrior"; title originally belonged to first Erstehäuptling of the Clans

dracheband (*drah-kuh-bahnd*) – dragonbond

Einäscherung (*eye-nay-shehr-oong*) – nomad ceremony of burning the dead

erstehäuptling (*ehr-stuh-hoypt-ling*) – leader of unified clans

es tut mir leid (*ehs toot meer lyde*) – I'm sorry; literally "it gives me sorrow"

falke (*fahl-kuh*) [-n (*fahl-kin*)] – falcon

familie (*fah-mih-lee*) [-n (*fah-mih-leen*)] – family

feind (*find*) – enemy

feuerdrache (*fewr-drah-kuh*) – fire dragon

Flammezunge (*flah-muh-zoon-guh*) – Flame Tongue's Zhulanese
name

frau (*frow*) [-en (*frow-in*)] – woman

fräulein (*froy-line*) – young woman; Miss

freund (*froynd*) [-e (*froyn-duh*)] – friend

Frieda (*free-dah*) – the demigoddess Peace

geist (*ghyste*) [-er (*guy-stehr*)] – nonphysical part of a creature:
mind, spirit, soul, ghost

geisternetz (*guy-stehr-nehtz*) [-e (*guy-stehr-neht-zuh*)] – mental net;
web of Mindspeakers

Geistmagie (*ghyste-mah-ghee*) – mental magic

Geistmagier (*ghyste-mah-gheer*) – Mindspeaker

Gift Clans (*ghift klahns*) – Poison Clans

Gleichrat (*glyke-raht*) – formal meeting held between the
erstehäuptling, the Drache Krieger, and the häuptlinge of
all the Unified Clans; literally "equal council"

guten täg (*goo-tehn taygh*) – good day

halbgott (*hahlb-ghoht*) [-götter (*hahlb-ghehr-tehr*)] – demigod

häuptling (*hoypt-ling*) [-e (*hoypt-lin-guh*)] – clan leader

Heilemagie (*high-luh-mah-ghee*) – Healing Magic

Heilemagier (*high-luh-mah-gheer*) – Mage Healer

Heilig (*high-lihgh*) – Holy Man

Heiligesicht (*high-lihgh-uh-sihkt*) – Sight; literally means "Holy
Sight"

herr (*hehr*) – Sir, Mister

hexe (*hehk-suh*) – derogatory word for a female

Hoffnung (*hohf-noong*) – the demigoddess, Hope

ich will keinen tod (*ihk vihl kine-ehn tohd*) – I want no death

ja (*yah*) – aye

jahr (*yahr*) [-e (*yahr-uh*)] – year

komm (*kohm*) [-e (*koh-muh*)] [-t (*kohmt*)] – come!

krieg (*kreegh*) – war; *Krieg* – the demigod War

kriegrat (*kreegh-raht*) – war council

Leben (*leh-bin*) – the demigoddess, Life

lebenfrau (*leh-bin-frow*) – female lifemate

Letztechance (*lets-tuh-chahn-tsuh*) – Last Chance's Zhulanese
    name

Liebe (*lee-buh*) – the demigoddess, Love

magie (*mah-ghee*) – magic

magier (*mah-gheer*) – mage

mann (*mahn*) [männer (*may-nehr*)] – man

Maurus's Feuer – Maurus's Fire

mein (*mine*) – my

Mitte Jahreszeit (*miht-tuh yahr-eh-zite*) – Mid-Season

Mitternacht (*miht-tehr-nahkt*) – midnight

morgen (*mohr-ghehn*) – morning

mütter (*mew-tehr*) – mother

nacht (*nahkt*) – night

nein (*nine*) – nay

nomade (*noh-mah-duh*) [-n (*noh-mah-dehn*)] – nomad

oase (*oh-ah-suh*) [-n (*oh-ah-sehn*)] – oasis

pferd (*ferd*) [-e (*fer-duh*)] – horse

Pferdetanz (*fer-duh-tahnz*) – the *Horse Dance*; a song created by
    Animal Mages that bears magic powerful enough to
    make a horse dance

recht (*rehkt*) – right

scharfmond (*sharf-mohnd*) [-e (*sharf-mohn-duh*)] – Twin Moon
    Blade; literally means "sharp moon"

Schicksale (*shihk-sahl-luh*) – the Fates

schlampe (*shlahm-puh*) – immoral woman

schlange (*shlahng-uh*) [-n (*shlahng-ehn*)] – snake

Schutzmagie (*shoots-mah-ghee*) – Protection Magic

Schutzmagier (*shoots-mah-gheer*) – Protection Mage

schwester (*shwehs-tehr*) [-n (*shwehs-tehrn*)] – sister

siebentäg (*zee-behn-taygh*) [-e (*zee-behn-tay-ghuh*)] – sevenday

skorpion (*skohr-pee-ohn*) [-e (*skohr-pee-oh-nuh*)] – scorpion

spinne (*shpin-nuh*) [-n (*shpin-nehn*)] – spider

stadt (*shtahdt*) [städte (*shtayd-tuh*)] – city

statusgürtel (*shtah-toos-gewr-tehl*) – status belt; thick spider silk
    belt dyed at one or both ends; it declares a nomad's clan
    and status

täg (*taygh*) [-e (*tay-ghuh*)] – day

tante (*tahn-tuh*) – aunt

Tieremagie (*teer-ah-mah-ghee*) – Animal Magic

Tieremagier (*teer-ah-mah-gheer*) – Animal Mage

Tod (*tohd*) – the demigod, Death

vater (*fah-tehr*) – father

verdammt (*fehr-dahmt*) – damn

Vereinte Clans (*fehr-ine-tuh klahns*) – Unified Clans

Zhulan (*jhoo-lahn*) – middle province of Evon

Zhulanbürger (*jhoo-lahn-bewr-gehr*) – citizen of Zhulan

Dorothy Tinker grew up dreaming of fantastical worlds and creatures, of plots in space, and of strange new cultures. Certain she needed something else to support her through life, she spent her time at the University of Texas at Dallas focusing on math and computer science. Two years after graduating with a BS in applied math, she rediscovered her true passion and rededicated herself to her literary dreams.

Since then, Dorothy has published an ongoing series of young adult fantasy novels, including *Peace of Evon*, *Gift of War*, and *Lost King*. Her short stories have appeared in HWG Press's *Riding the Waves* and *Out of Many, One*, Inklings Publishing's *Eclectically Cosmic* and *Eclectically Heroic*, and Writespace's *In Medias Res*.

Dorothy is also the owner of D Tinker Editing and works as copy editor and formatter for Inklings Publishing.

Excerpt from
Forgotten Goddess

*F*og rolled over the banks of the River San, between trees both old and ancient. It was not a natural fog, which might form on the water's surface and reach idly for the banks with drifting tendrils. Instead, it curled up from the banks themselves, drifting around the humans who lined one side of the river and the magical beasts who occupied the other, and reached purposefully across the river to intertwine above the churning surface.

As the fog obscured the sight of each bank from the other, it magnified the sounds that rose from them. Human voices swelled from the western bank and mingled with the Fae tongue and animalistic sounds that flowed from the river's eastern edge. They flowed over each other and into each other until no single sound was decipherable from the multitude.

With the fog and the voices rose the magics of the land, called upon by human mages and magical creatures alike so that all twelve might come together to form and strengthen the barrier they wished to create. It was a barrier that had been agreed upon by all parties at one time, though there were now those who might wish to renege on such agreements.

One such man stood on the western bank, pale eyes peering fruitlessly into the growing fog. Unlike the other humans, he was no mage, but he was no less important to the unfolding magic than any others present. In fact, many would say that he was the most important, for it was he who would bear the magics back to his throne and keep the barrier in place with his presence there.

As the voices finally began to fade, a young woman with bitter eyes turned from the fog and frowned thoughtfully at the pale-eyed man. She offered him a murmur, too soft for anyone else to hear, and he shook his head.

"I know my duty," he answered with a strength that belied the yearning in his gaze. "My people require security from magic, and my throne demands I do no less." He turned to her then, his gaze suddenly steely. "But what do I tell my children and their children and the generations to follow when we must keep our reasoning from them even as we keep them from breaking our promise?"

The bitter-eyed woman bared her teeth. "Tell them the truth, as told by your Seer. Offer them a prophecy they dare not question, words to be shared with few outside your line for fear of panic."

The pale-eyed man raised one brow. "What prophecy? You and Mama Dragon have only ever spoken of avoiding increased bloodshed when speaking of this barrier. What other consequences could its breaking possibly hold?"

The bitter-eyed woman smiled sharply before closing her eyes and humming softly.

"When three months empty stands the throne," she answered, her words ringing with otherworldly knowledge, **"the reign of Chaos is all you'll know."**